6-2015

Have a great Summer;
guy's.

Steve Wallace

VALLEY
FORGE

ALSO BY DAVID GARLAND

Saratoga

VALLEY
FORGE

DAVID GARLAND

St. Martin's Press ❧ New York

This is a work of fiction. All of the characters, organizations, and events portrayed in this novel are either products of the author's imagination or are used fictitiously.

www.stmartins.com

Library of Congress Cataloging-in-Publication Data

Garland, David, 1940–
    Valley Forge / David Garland.—1st St. Martin's Press ed.
       p. cm.
    ISBN-13: 978-0-312-32722-4
    ISBN-10: 0-312-32722-6
    1. United States—History—Revolution, 1775–1783—British forces—Fiction.
    2. United States—History—Revolution, 1775–1783—Fiction.   3. Washington, George,
    1732–1799—Headquarters—Pennsylvania—Valley Forge—Fiction.   4. British—United
    States—Fiction.   5. Valley Forge (Pa.)—Fiction.   6. Agents provocateurs—Fiction.
    7. Soldiers—Fiction.   I. Title.

    PR6063.I3175V35 2006
    813'.6—dc22

                                                                                    2006045059

First Edition: December 2006

10   9   8   7   6   5   4   3   2   1

VALLEY FORGE

CHAPTER ONE

Cambridge, Massachussetts, November 1777

Skoyles was angry. Within days of arrival, he had reached his decision. He simply refused to remain a prisoner of war. When he first confided in his friend, however, all that he got in response was wide-eyed disbelief.

"Escape?" cried Caffrey.

"Yes, Tom."

"Why?"

"Because it's our duty as British soldiers."

"Our duty is to abide by the terms of the convention negotiated by General Burgoyne, and I'm happy to do that. We may have been defeated but we weren't humiliated by an unconditional surrender."

"All surrenders are humiliating," said Skoyles.

"Think of the concessions."

"They're meaningless."

"Not to me," said Tom Caffrey firmly. "As soon as transports arrive, we can wave goodbye to America and sail home to the safety of our own country. I call that good fortune."

"I call it shameful."

"Don't you *want* to go back to England?"

"No, Tom," Skoyles asserted. "This is my home now."

They were standing outside one of the barracks on Prospect Hill where the British soldiers were quartered. Captain Jamie Skoyles and Sergeant Tom Caffrey of the 24th Foot were part of the bedraggled and dispirited army that had trudged two hundred miles from Saratoga to Cambridge with their tails between their legs. As they struggled through the Green Mountains, enduring biting winds and frequent rain, they had had ample time to reflect on the dis-

1

grace of being part of an elite force that had invaded from Canada, only to be humbled on the battlefield by a makeshift army of American rebels. Skoyles felt that disgrace more keenly than most. It rankled.

"I joined the army to fight," he insisted.

"There'll be other battles, Jamie."

"Not if we get shipped back to England. Under the terms of the convention, we're forbidden to take part in this conflict anymore."

"I can live with that."

"Well, I'll not do so."

Caffrey gave a shrug. "You have no choice."

"Yes, I do. I can get out of here."

"Easier said than done."

"I'll manage. The question is, will you come with me?"

Tom Caffrey heaved a sigh. A sturdy man in his forties, he had a broken nose, set in a craggy face, that gave him a kind of raffish charm. Caffrey was the son of a Devon butcher, but he had somehow ended up as a surgeon's mate in the British army. The hideous sights and nameless tragedies that he encountered had, miraculously, not deprived him of his natural affability. He and Skoyles had been friends for several years, but that friendship had never been put under threat before. It was different now. Loyalty was at stake.

Caffrey licked his lips before speaking.

"I'm not sure that I can, Jamie," he said at length.

"Why not?"

"We've been through hell in this campaign. We need a rest."

"How can you rest when you're being held prisoner?"

"We're not exactly under lock and key."

"That's beside the point, Tom."

"No, it isn't," Caffrey argued. "Instead of rotting in chains, we have some freedom of movement. As an officer, you could have even more license. You could have had parole and found accommodations in the town. Officers are even allowed to wear sidearms. Why on earth did you volunteer to stay with us?"

"I prefer it here," said Skoyles bluntly.

"Well, we're very pleased to have you."

Caffrey was speaking on behalf of the rank and file. Three officers per regiment were assigned to stay in the barracks with the men, and Jamie Skoyles was the only one who did so willingly. Having risen from the ranks himself, he never felt entirely comfortable among his fellow officers, some of whom still treated him as a plebeian who had wandered mistakenly among patricians. Skoyles was ready to share the privations of his men and they appreciated him for that. They knew that the tall, lean, rock-hard, fearless soldier, now in his thirties, had earned his promotion on merit. Most officers bought their commissions. Skoyles had won his by conspicuous gallantry in the field.

"Will you turn your back on us now?" asked Caffrey.

"I hate being held against my will."

"Jamie—"

"And don't tell me that it could be worse," said Skoyles vehemently. "Look at the barracks they've given us—they're nothing but henhouses. They're cold, dirty, and they stink to high heaven. Most of the officers fare no better. Seven or eight of them are crammed into tiny rooms. General Burgoyne himself is stuck in a filthy tavern and forced to share a bed with General Phillips."

Caffrey laughed. "Gentleman Johnny won't like that. General Phillips is a poor substitute for Mrs. Mallard. What man would want to sleep with an artillery officer instead of a mistress?"

"Forget her. Lucinda Mallard belongs in the past. The point is that conditions here are unbearable. Everyone is suffering. What happened to the promise to treat us with honor?"

"Take that up with our captors."

"General Burgoyne has already done so—to no avail. When they can't even find decent accommodations for our commander, what hope is there for the rest of us? Remember where we are, Tom," said Skoyles with a sweeping gesture of his arm. "This is the very heart of the rebellion. The people here detest us, and with good cause. They know how much damage British soldiers did here. They'll never forget that the Charleston peninsula was set ablaze. No wonder they're not rushing forward to offer us hospitality."

"Count your blessings, Jamie."

"I didn't know that I had any."

"Well, I do," said Caffrey soulfully, "and I'm grateful for them. We're still alive, whereas several hundred of those who marched with us are not. We came through with only a few scratches—I lost count of the number of arms and legs

3

that I had to amputate after a battle. We've soldiers who were blinded, crippled, or disfigured, young men hideously changed from the way God made them. You and I escaped any real injury, Jamie. If that's not a blessing, then what is?"

"Peace of mind."

"You won't find that in the army."

"I would if we'd been on the winning side."

"But we're not. We lost."

"That's why I have to escape from here, Tom. Come with me."

Caffrey fell silent. Torn between competing demands, he did not know which one to choose. After all that they had been through together, parting from Skoyles seemed like an act of betrayal, and that preyed on the sergeant's conscience. At the same time, he was weary of battle, and the prospect of returning home was a very seductive one, especially as another person was involved. Caffrey agonized for some time before committing himself.

"It's Polly," he admitted.

"What about her?"

"I promised to marry her when we got back to England."

"You could still do that," Skoyles reasoned. "The wedding will just have to come later rather than sooner."

"Polly is expecting to sail home when the transports arrive."

Polly Bragg was the wife of a British corporal who had died in action the previous year. She had become not merely Caffrey's lover; she was his nurse, his cook, his washerwoman, and his trusted friend. Adversity had brought them even closer together. He could not imagine a life without her. After staying at his side through the horrors of war, Polly deserved to be taken far away from danger.

"I'm sorry, Jamie," said Caffrey, biting his lip. "I stay here."

"Trapped in these foul barracks, eating dreadful food?"

"It's only a for a limited time."

"Escape with me," Skoyles urged.

Caffrey shook his head. "I'd have to leave Polly here," he said, "and I could never do that. It would be so unfair."

"Then bring her."

"What?"

"Bring her," Skoyles repeated. "I intend to bring Elizabeth."

Elizabeth Rainham pulled her shawl around her to keep out the cold. Glad to escape the discomfort of the house where they were staying, she was enjoying a morning stroll through the woods with Friederike von Riedesel. During her time in America, all of Elizabeth's expectations had been dashed to pieces. She had braved the voyage in order to be with the man to whom she was betrothed, Major Harry Featherstone of the 24th Foot. However, his behavior toward her had been so intolerable that she had broken off the engagement, provoking him into an assault on her. But for the timely intervention of Jamie Skoyles, someone she had once loved would have raped her. The memory of the incident could still make her blood run cold.

"Let's turn back," Friederike suggested.

"As you wish."

"I miss the children."

"Where did your maids take them?"

"To feed the ducks at the farm."

"At least, they get some amusement here," said Elizabeth, turning around. "I do admire your daughters. All three of them look so small and fragile, yet they seem full of life. You must be very proud of them."

Friederike smiled sweetly. "We are, Miss Rainham. We are."

Elizabeth was deeply grateful to her. In the wake of the shocking and unanticipated defeat of the British army, Friederike had taken the attractive young Englishwoman under her wing. On the journey to Cambridge, she had allowed Elizabeth to travel in her little carriage, and when she was billeted in a house in the country, Friederike even invited her to share their mean lodging. Cooped up in a noisome attic, they slept on beds of straw while the servants made do with the floor.

It was a far cry from the privileged life to which Friederike, a German baroness, was accustomed. Her husband was Major General Frederick von Riedesel, commander of the regiments from Hesse-Hanau and Brunswick that were part of the British force. Unlike him—another reason for Elizabeth's gratitude—the delicate baroness with a porcelain beauty spoke good English.

"I forgot to ask after General Burgoyne," said Friederike.

"He is not well, I fear."

"Is he sick?"

"It's not a physical illness," Elizabeth explained. "When I saw him yesterday, he was morose and distracted—so different from the General Burgoyne I know. Our defeat has played on his mind."

"It is the same with my husband. His pride was wounded."

"It's more than a case of wounded pride with our commander. He was always so forceful and decisive before. Now, his spirits are very low. His attention wanders. I don't think that he heard half of what I said."

"Did you complain about the way we are being kept?"

"I did," said Elizabeth, "and he was very sympathetic. The general is disgusted with the accommodations we've all been given, and by the terrible shortage of food and firewood. He's written a strong letter of protest to General Gates, and is even prepared to advance money of his own so that the army is properly housed and fed."

"General Burgoyne is a kind man."

"And generous to a fault. Because my father served with him, he's been a friend of our family for years. Wherever he's held command, the troops revere him. It pains me to see him so hurt and dejected."

"Have you told him about Major Featherstone?" Friederike inquired.

A long pause. "No, I haven't."

"Perhaps the major has confessed to General Burgoyne."

"He'd be too ashamed to do that," said Elizabeth briskly. "Harry would never admit that he's lost me."

"But he has."

"Oh, yes—for good!"

"You sound very certain about that."

"I am, believe me."

Getting to know Friederike von Riedesel had given her a female friend in whom she could confide, and Elizabeth had told her much of what had happened to her since joining the British force in Montreal. Her maid, Nan, was also aware of the various setbacks, and her support could be taken for granted. What the diminutive baroness could offer was the compassion and understanding of a married woman. As an outsider, Friederike's sympathy carried more weight. Elizabeth was very fond of her but she also envied her. Though she had entered into an arranged marriage with a man who was years

6

older, the baroness was patently happy. When she and her husband were together, they were so delighted in each other's company that it was clearly a love match. Elizabeth's own love match with Major Featherstone had proved to be a mirage.

"Are you looking forward to going home?" asked Friederike.

"If we ever get there."

"There is no doubt about it, surely?"

"General Burgoyne thinks that there may be," said Elizabeth, face puckered with anxiety. "Since the Americans have already broken some terms of the convention, he's afraid that they will renege on the commitment to send us back to England. If they repatriate us, all that would happen is that one army will be dispatched to replace another."

Friederike was worried. "They will keep us here?"

"It's a possibility. General Burgoyne obtained some important concessions for us, and that will not please Congress. They may feel that the terms of the convention were too benevolent, and will look for an excuse to disregard it completely."

"That's dreadful! Have they no decency?"

"They want to win this war."

Friederike was alarmed. When she brought her family to America, she was convinced that she would be accompanying a victorious army that swept all before it. Instead, she had watched a large force of professional soldiers being cruelly whittled down by death, disease, and desertion until it was a shadow of its former glory. At Bennington, over nine hundred German troops had been lost in a single engagement. In the two battles near Saratoga, some British regiments had been more or less wiped out. Friederike had been confronted by the ugly realities of warfare. They had nauseated her. All that she could think about was taking her husband and children back home.

"This is terrible news, Miss Rainham," she said.

"Let us pray that it never happens."

"They do not show us any respect. It is the same with the people at the house where we stay. They treat us as interlopers, not as guests. The wife is the worst. Whenever we sit down to eat, she combs her children's hair all over our food. It is a revolting habit."

"I told her so," said Elizabeth. "She replied that it was her home and that we were there on sufferance."

Friederike bridled. "That woman is an ogre."

"Her husband is not as bad as her."

"They are poor hosts, Miss Rainham. I cannot wait to leave them."

"We are bound to be allowed home eventually."

"But when will that be?"

Elizabeth was about to reply when she caught sight of a uniform among the trees ahead. Her heart lifted at once. Only one man would come looking for her from the town, and that was Jamie Skoyles. She quickened her step instinctively. Short and dainty, Friederike von Riedesel struggled to keep up with her.

"Wait for me," she called. "What's the hurry?"

Nights were getting colder but at least they had chosen a dry one. As he slipped out of the barracks, Jamie Skoyles looked up at the sky, glad that the moon was largely obscured by cloud. Darkness would aid his escape. He was no longer wearing his uniform. It was folded up neatly in the bag that he was carrying. He had changed into the hunting shirt and breeches that he used on scouting missions. A broad-brimmed hat helped to conceal his face. His only weapon was a long hunting knife. Skoyles moved stealthily through the camp. Guards were on duty but most of them were too busy trying to keep warm to pay any attention to the dark figure that flitted past them. The fugitive was soon clear of Prospect Hill.

His only regret was that Tom Caffrey had not gone with him, but he held no grudge. His friend had his own priorities and Skoyles respected them. They would meet again one day. He felt sure of it. He might have lost the sterling qualities that Caffrey would have brought, but he had gained precious time alone with the woman he loved. Elizabeth Rainham had not hesitated for a moment. When he had asked her to flee with him, she had agreed immediately. It added spice. Flight from imprisonment now took on the aspect of a romantic adventure. Skoyles was stirred.

He made his way to the appointed place as swiftly and furtively as he could. It was a route he had been over a number of times. As soon as arrangements were made, Skoyles had been careful to familiarize himself with the geography of the town by making nocturnal sorties. Buildings looked different at night. Streets could easily deceive in the gloom. Stray dogs were an additional hazard, but, thankfully, the stiff breeze was keeping them under cover at that hour. Roads, lanes, and alleyways were deserted. Cambridge was fast asleep.

In order to effect her sudden departure, Elizabeth had decided to take a room at a small tavern in the town, and it was toward this that Skoyles hurried. When he reached the place, however, there was no sign of her, and the doors of the tavern were locked. He spent a fruitless ten minutes, pacing up and down outside the building. He could not believe that Elizabeth would let him down. Had she changed her mind? Been delayed in some way? Or had her intentions been discovered and frustrated? That was the most disturbing thought of all.

The sound of footsteps made Skoyles step into a doorway, and his hand went to his knife. Having gone to such trouble to set up the escape, he was not going to be caught now. As the footsteps got closer, he readied himself for attack. When the body was inches away from him, he reached out to pull it into the doorway. One hand was clapped over the newcomer's mouth, the other held a knife to the throat. Elizabeth's cry of fear was muffled. Overcome with relief, Skoyles released her and sheathed his weapon before enfolding her in his arms and hugging her reassuringly. Then he kissed her on her lips to seal their love. Holding her tight, he spoke in whispers.

"Where have you been?"

"I could not stay here," she told him. "The landlord began to pester me. When he tried to come into my room the third time, I went off and found another place to stay. I'm sorry if I kept you waiting, Jamie."

"You're here now. That's the main thing. How do you feel?"

"I'm shaking like a leaf."

"You've come well wrapped up, I see."

"And I've brought very little with me."

"We must travel light."

Elizabeth was wearing a dark cloak over her dress, and the hood was pulled up. As well as clothing and money, her leather satchel contained a few items of food that she had managed to save. Eager to accompany Skoyles, she had been sad to leave her maid behind.

"Nan sends her regards," she said.

"I offered to take her with us, Elizabeth."

"She's terrified of horses and even more frightened of wild animals that we might meet on the way. I hope that you've got something other than that knife to keep them at bay."

"Otis will see to that."

"Otis?"

"Otis Tapper," he explained. "The man from whom I bought the horses. For an additional sum, he agreed to provide me with a musket, a pistol, and ammunition for both." Arm around her shoulders, he eased her forward. "Let's go and find him."

Keeping to the shadows, they headed toward the outskirts of the town, conscious that this was the first time in their lives that they had been truly alone. The only intimate moments they had shared before had been in the middle of an army encampment, and those had, of necessity, been rather snatched. Now they were together, unhampered by the presence of others or by the strict social rules they were obliged to follow. It gave them both a thrill of excitement, but Skoyles made sure that it did not affect his concentration. They had some way to go yet and needed to stay alert. At the slightest sound, they took instant cover. Only when they were sure that it was safe did they move on.

"How did you find this Otis Tapper?" she asked.

"I was given his name by one of the guards."

Elizabeth was surprised. "A guard helped you to escape?"

"No," he replied, "and he'd not have spoken to me if he'd known what was on my mind. I simply asked where I could buy extra food and blankets and a new pair of boots. He said that Otis Tapper could get me anything I wanted—at a price. I went to the tavern where he drinks and sounded him out. Tapper is no loyalist, but he was more than ready to defy his countrymen and give me what I wanted. Horses and guns."

"Did you pay him?"

"Only half of what we agreed. The other half comes on delivery."

"Can you trust him, Jamie?"

"I believe so."

"Which way will we ride?"

"Southwest."

Most women would have blenched at the notion of a daring escape on horseback, but Elizabeth Rainham was not among them. An excellent rider, she had complete faith in Skoyles and was prepared to take any risk to be with him. He issued a warning.

"There'll be problems," he told her, "and not only from packs of wolves. The countryside is crawling with militia. We'll have to dodge and weave all the way. And we must keep our wits about us, Elizabeth."

"I'll not let you down."

"I know. But we can't sleep rough in this weather."

"We'll need a roof over our heads."

He turned to her. "That means we may have to pose as man and wife," he said softly. "How would you feel about that?"

Her blush went unseen. "Content."

He squeezed her shoulder and they turned down a narrow street.

Otis Tapper had agreed to meet them near a derelict house on the very edge of town. When they got within thirty yards of it, Skoyles halted and moved Elizabeth behind a tree that had shed all of its leaves and was left with a tangle of spectral branches.

"Why have we stopped? she asked.

"We have to wait for the signal."

"What is it?"

"Tapper will wave a lantern twice."

"I hope I haven't delayed you."

"Not at all," he said. "I allowed extra time in case we got held up along the way. We've a little while to wait before he shows up. Cold?" She nodded and he pulled her closer. "We have to escape now. If we held on until winter really sets in, we'd have no chance of getting away."

"The weather was so beautiful when we set out from Canada."

"Things have changed a lot since then, Elizabeth."

"I know. So much loss, so much suffering."

"It will be better when we get to New York. The British army holds sway there. You'll be given proper accommodations at last."

"What about you?"

"I'm a soldier. They'll find plenty of work for me."

Before he could tell her about his ambitions, he heard the clack of hooves in the distance. Horses were approaching, and it was not long before their shapes were conjured out of the darkness. A lantern was waved twice in their direction.

"Tapper is early," he said. "Come and meet him."

Carrying their baggage, they trotted toward the derelict house and saw that two riders awaited them. Each had another horse on a lead rein. Skoyles and Elizabeth were pleased. Their hopes rose. When they reached the waiting men, however, Skoyles did not recognize either of them. It made him wary.

"Where's Otis Tapper?" he asked.

"Waiting for you," replied one of the men. "Follow us."

Skoyles held his ground. "He promised to meet us here."

"Well, he's not able to fulfil that promise right now."

"Who are you?"

"We're the people that own these horses."

"Then hand them over."

"There's no hurry. Come and see Otis first."

The men wheeled their horses and trotted toward a copse nearby. Skoyles and Elizabeth had no option but to follow. They felt at a distinct disadvantage. Skoyles only had his knife, whereas both men were armed with muskets. When the four horses vanished into the trees, the fugitives went slowly after them. They met up again in a clearing. One of the men used his musket to point toward a hazy figure that seemed to be moving to and fro in the wind. It was only when Skoyles and Elizabeth got closer that they realized someone was dangling from the bough of a tree.

"This is Otis Tapper," the man continued with a grim chuckle. "It's where he belongs. We always hang horse thieves."

Elizabeth let out a cry of horror and turned away. Skoyles pulled her to him. There would be no escape that night. The man paid to assist their flight had been summarily killed. When the two riders leveled their muskets, it looked as if Skoyles and Elizabeth were fated to join Otis Tapper in the grave. The bigger of the two men cleared his throat and spat on the ground before speaking.

"Stealing horses is a crime," he said, "and you were party to it. So let's start by having the rest of the money you were going to pay for our animals." His voice hardened. "Hand it over." Skoyles hesitated. "Do I have to shoot you to get what's owed to us?"

"Give it to him," Elizabeth begged, clinging to Skoyles's arm.

"I will," he said.

Skoyles pretended to comply with the order. Stepping forward, he reached

12

inside his bag as if about to extract money. Without warning, he then swung the bag hard to knock the bigger man's musket from his grasp, then he reached up to haul him from the saddle. The other man fired at Skoyles but the musket ball missed him. The sudden noise made the three riderless horses bolt. Skoyles, meanwhile, grabbed the fallen weapon and used its butt to pound the man on the ground until he was senseless. Elizabeth could not bear to watch. Having disposed of one man, Skoyles turned to deal with the other and pointed his loaded weapon. It was enough to frighten him away. Pulling his mount in a half circle, the man used his heels to kick the horse into a canter. He was out of sight in seconds. Skoyles discarded the musket, picked up his bag, then glanced up sadly at the body of Otis Tapper, still swinging in the breeze. The captain had made a bargain with the wrong man.

"Run!" he said, taking Elizabeth's arm. "Run!"

CHAPTER TWO

Though they spent St. Andrew's Day in captivity, the tattered remnants of the defeated British army were determined to celebrate the occasion. A quarter of the common soldiers who bore arms for King and Country in the American war hailed from Scotland, and while many served in such quintessentially Scottish regiments as the Black Watch or Fraser's Highlanders, several were scattered throughout other regiments. The 24th Foot had its fair share of them, and they desperately needed something to relieve the boredom and discomfort of their imprisonment. When they gathered in Morland's Tavern to toast their patron saint, therefore, they were in high spirits.

Never one to miss the chance of a drink, Sergeant Tom Caffrey went with them. He sat at a crowded table beside a jocular private.

"You're no Scot," McKillop said to him.

"I am on November 30."

"What about St. David's Day?"

"Oh, I'm a leek-eating Welshmen then," replied Caffrey with a grin. "On St. Patrick's Day, of course, I'm as Irish as a sprig of shamrock, but on St. George's Day, I remember where I was really born."

"Only a true Scot can appreciate the importance of St. Andrew's Day," McKillop insisted, taking a sip of his whiskey. "It's something you feel in your bones—and it's a day when you wear a kilt with pride."

Like others in the tavern, McKillop had somehow contrived to get hold of a length of plaid to replace his breeches. It looked more like a woman's skirt than a kilt, but Caffrey did not mock his little companion. On his head, Private Andrew McKillop wore a crumpled bonnet with a piece of heather in it. He was a man of astonishing resilience. Injured in battle, he had lost a leg but

14

surrendered none of his cheery optimism. Though he was in constant pain, he never let it show and—when Caffrey was actually removing the limb—the Scotsman had been a model of bravery and resignation. Beneath the makeshift kilt was a wooden leg that McKillop now used to tap out the rhythm of the various Scots ballads that were being sung so lustily.

The place was full, the voices raucous, the mood convivial. Those who were not drunk soon would be. Those already inebriated were either aggressive or maudlin or had simply lapsed into a stupor. Loud arguments had already broken out. As McKillop raised his glass, he had to shout at the top of his voice in order to be heard.

"A health to General Burgoyne!"

"General Burgoyne!" chorused the others.

"A true gentleman and a wonderful soldier."

A great cheer went up, and Caffrey joined in willingly. In the light of their disastrous campaign, the sergeant had severe reservations about Burgoyne's tactical skills, but this was not the time to voice them. Their commander remained enduringly popular with the men, not least because he had contributed the enormous sum of £20,000 out of his own pocket to pay for the accommodations and provisioning of his army. Though their lot remained a sorry one, it was evident that General Burgoyne had done his best for them.

"When are we going home, Sergeant?" asked McKillop.

"I wish I knew," said Caffrey.

"I'd hoped we'd be on our way by now."

"So did I, Andy. We've been cooling our heels here for almost a month now. The weather's colder, the beds feel harder, and the food is worse than ever. On top of that," he went on, "the guards have got much nastier. They don't like being here any more than us."

"That's no reason to taunt us," McKillop complained. "A wee bit of respect is all we ask—that and a fleet of ships to take us away from this godforsaken place. Some of the lads are beginning to think that they'll *never* let us go home."

"Oh, I don't know about that," said Caffrey, hiding his own fears about their future. "I just wish that General Gates would remember the terms of the convention. When Gentleman Johnny proposed it, the rebels got four thousand prisoners without firing a single shot. It's high time they met their obligations."

"Yes—free whiskey for every Scotsman in the regiment."

Caffrey chuckled. "That's asking too much."

"Then it's just as well that St. Andrew is our patron saint."

"Why?"

"He was a martyr—just like us."

A big, heavy man in his thirties, with red hair and a thick beard, plopped himself down on the bench between them, forcing them apart. His eyes were rolling, his body swaying, his speech slurred. He peered uncertainly at the stripes on the arm of Caffrey's uniform.

"What are ye doing here, Sergeant?" he said belligerently.

"Talking to St. Andrew McKillop the Martyr."

"Ye don't belong here."

"Sergeant Caffrey saved my life," announced McKillop, "so he's here as my guest. Let's have no trouble from you, Duncan Rennie, or I'll do something with my wooden leg that will make your eyes water. If you want a fight, pick on someone else."

"I want to punch an Englishman."

"We're on the same side," Caffrey reminded him.

"Not on this day of the year," the other declared. "It brings back too many bad memories. The Rennies fought against their English tyrants for generations. My grandfather fell at Sheriffmuir in the first rebellion. My father was butchered, along with so many other gallant Scots, at Culloden." He spat expressively on the floor. "Ye want us to lay down our lives for ye in battle but ye'll no let us wear the kilt anymore. Even the Black Watch is forced to put on trews now."

Duncan Rennie had drunk too much whiskey to show deference to Caffrey's rank, or to his reputation as a man who could handle himself well in a brawl. All that the Scotsman could see through his bleary eyes was the sad history of his country. He wanted revenge for endless years of subjugation. At that moment, Tom Caffrey seemed to embody the cruel and oppressive English. Rennie wagged a finger at him.

"Get oot while ye can, ye lousy Sassenach!" he growled.

"Let me buy you another whiskey," said Caffrey.

"I'll no drink with the likes of ye!"

"We can raise a glass to good King George."

"Bugger the king!"

"I'll forget I heard that," said Caffrey tolerantly, "or I'd have to remind you that, from the moment you put on a red coat, your life became the property of His Majesty."

"Aye, show some loyalty, Duncan," McKillop advised.

"Keep out of this," Rennie warned. "I want to tell this English bastard why I hate his nation and want him to—"

"Save your breath to cool your porridge," said Caffrey, interrupting him. "And learn to hold your drink. We're both of us in the same boat, Rennie. We're British soldiers—we obey orders."

"And where did obeying orders get us?"

"Calm down, Duncan," said McKillop, a hand on his arm.

"Locked up in this shit hole!" roared his fellow Scot. "Now are ye going to get oot of here, Sergeant, or do I have to throw ye oot?"

Caffrey was unsure what to do. He was not afraid of Rennie and was confident of getting the better of him in a fight. But a tussle with one man could easily turn into a general free-for-all and that would serve nobody's purpose. For the sake of keeping the peace, Caffrey wondered if it might be better to finish his drink and slip quietly out of the tavern. In the event, the decision was taken for him. Armed guards burst in through the door to be met by a torrent of abuse from the revelers.

"Time's up!" bellowed one of the newcomers. "Out you go!"

Threats and curses came from every corner of the room. As prisoners of war, soldiers were only allowed out of their barracks between 8:00 A.M. and 3:00 P.M. Even on St. Andrew's Day, there were no concessions. Having their pleasure cut short enraged the Scotsmen beyond measure. The boisterous atmosphere inside Morland's Tavern suddenly turned mutinous. Duncan Rennie elected himself the leader.

"Away with ye!" he boomed, struggling to his feet. "And tek your ugly faces with ye! Nobody can tell us what to do upon St. Andy's Day!"

"You know the rules," said the guard sternly. "Get out."

Rennie folded his arms. "Supposing I don't?" he challenged.

"Supposing none of us do?" called another voice.

"Aye!" cried a dozen Scotsmen in unison.

"Now then," said Caffrey, standing up in an attempt to prevent any violence breaking out. "We don't want any trouble, do we? You've had your celebration. Sing your way back to the barracks."

17

"That's good advice," McKillop put in. "Let's go, lads."

"No," said Rennie stoutly. "I'll no' shift an inch from here." He looked around the room. "We stay put. Who's with me?" A general cry of consent went up. "There ye are, ye lily-livered Yankees. We'll not move from here even if that long streak of puke, George Washington, comes banging on the door."

"You'll move right now," said the guard, advancing on him, "or I'll shave your beard off with this bayonet."

Rennie was incensed. "Come closer and I'll kill you!"

He pushed two people off a bench and snatched it up to use as a weapon. Others urged him on and clustered around Rennie in support, waving their fists at the Americans in a show of resistance. Roused by the tumult, more guards came into the tavern, bayonets pointed at the howling Scots. Caffrey tried to plead for calm but his voice went unheard. Tension soared until it reached the point of release. Duncan Rennie hurled the bench, a guard was hit, and pandemonium broke out.

Anger and resentment that had built up during long weeks of imprisonment now found an outlet. Missiles of all kinds were thrown at the guards, then they were charged by a berserk mob. The noise was deafening. Outnumbered and fearing for their safety, the guards fell back quickly and the riot spilled out onto the street. Rennie was one of the first who stumbled after them, hungry for blood and heedless of personal danger. When additional guards came to the aid of their fellows, he was not deterred. He flung himself at the man who had first given them the order to quit the tavern.

"I'll murder ye!" yelled Rennie. "I'll tear oot your black heart!"

As he tried to grab the guard, however, the man stepped back and jabbed with his bayonet, piercing the Scotsman's thigh. Rennie let out a screech of pain and fell to the ground, clutching his wound. The sight only drove his friends to a higher pitch of fury.

"They've killed Duncan!" someone cried. "No quarter!"

Swearing volubly, they punched, kicked, bit, and grappled with the guards, forcing them back and ignoring any blows they took in return. After making futile attempts to enforce his authority, Tom Caffrey turned his attention to the injured Rennie. All around him, people were spilling or losing blood in an uncontrollable brawl. When a guard was beaten to the ground, he was mercilessly stamped on. When a Scotsman tried to relieve one of the

Americans of his musket, he was hit in the face with the stock. Turmoil had come to Cambridge, Massachusetts.

It did not last long. Another detachment of guards came running around the corner to see what was causing the uproar. The lieutenant in charge took one look at the melee, then barked an order. There was a harsh volley of musket fire. It passed harmlessly over the heads of the battling Scotsmen, but it was enough to stop them. Sobered instantly by the shots, and faced by the threat of a bayonet charge, they drew back at once and started to dust themselves off. They had made their point. There was no need to risk their lives.

The newcomers marched toward them in a menacing line.

"Who started all this?" the lieutenant demanded.

"That man on the ground," said the guard who had stabbed Rennie. "He's the ringleader, sir."

"Then he'll pay for it. So will the rest of these ruffians."

"We were trying to enjoy St. Andrew's Day," McKillop explained.

"Is this your idea of enjoyment?" said the lieutenant, gazing around at the bruised and blood-covered faces. "Round this scum up and get them back to the barracks!" he snapped. "They're going to suffer for this!"

Important anniversaries such as the king and queen's official birthdays, the coronation and accession of George III, and the restoration of the monarchy, were marked with celebrations throughout the British army. Parades, twenty-one-gun salutes, formal dinners, and—for the queen's birthday— lavish balls were arranged. The patron saints merited less formality but no less commitment. Even though money was scarce and supplies of food limited, General Burgoyne had invited many of his officers to dine with him on St. Andrew's Day.

Captain Jamie Skoyles was among them, and he found the occasion both gloomy and disturbing. There was a prevailing air of solemnity that made it impossible to relish the event, and he heard speculation about their future that was deeply troubling. It was three weeks since his failed attempt at escape and nothing had happened in the interim to reconcile him to the notion of staying in captivity with the Convention army. Still bent on flight, he was biding his time. Dinner was served in another of the town's many taverns. It was toward the end of the meal when the landlord gave him a scribbled note that had been sent to him. He recognized Tom Caffrey's handwriting at once. As soon as he read the note, he excused himself from the table and left.

Alarmed by the news, Skoyles hurried back to the barracks. He arrived as his friend had just finished binding the wound in Duncan Rennie's thigh. Oblivious to it all, the bearded Scotsman lay fast asleep, snoring away as if he did not have a care in the world.

"What happened, Tom?" asked Skoyles.

"All hell broke loose."

"We've had scuffles with the guards before."

"Not like this, Jamie. Somebody could easily have been killed."

"Who started it all?"

"This madman," said Caffrey, looking down at his patient. "Rennie lost his temper and attacked one of the guards. When he was pricked in the thigh, everyone reacted as if Scotland had just been invaded."

He went on to give as full and accurate an account of the riot as he could. Skoyles listened patiently so that he could pass on a verbal report to General Burgoyne. Since the Americans would use the incident to impose further restraints on them, it was vital that their commander spoke up for the British soldiers involved. Friction between prisoners and their guards had been there from the very start, but it had never reached this scale. There could be dire consequences.

"I'm sorry to drag you away from the dinner table," said Caffrey.

"It was something of a relief, Tom."

"Was the food that bad?"

"I've tasted worse."

"So why were you glad to leave?"

"Because of the rumors," said Skoyles, pursing his lips.

"Rumors?"

"Yes, Tom. I'm telling you this in strictest confidence, mark you. We don't want it to reach the men—they have enough to worry about as it is." He took a deep breath. "General Burgoyne fears that we won't be released at all."

"But it was in the terms of the convention."

"So were many other things and they haven't been honored either. Gentleman Johnny is very annoyed. He wrote to General Gates about it. There's been no reply."

20

"Why not?"

Skoyles shrugged. "The feeling is that Gates has been overruled by General Washington and by Congress. They won't let us sail away from here because they fear that we'll divert the convoy to New York and join our army there. It's certainly what General Howe would want. My guess is that he's written to General Burgoyne to that effect."

"Did Gentleman Johnny confirm that?"

"He gave us a vague hint—nothing more. But it's obvious that General Howe needs reinforcements in New York now that he's moved the bulk of the army to Philadelphia."

Caffrey was upset. "So there's *no* chance of us going home?"

"Only a very slim one, Tom."

"They can't keep us here forever."

"No," said Skoyles. "Including those that live here, there's seven thousand of us in a town that can barely support a third of that number. I reckon that they'll move us out before long."

"Where to?"

"Another prison camp."

"Is that what the other officers believe?"

"They talked of nothing else over dinner."

"I can see why you didn't enjoy your meal," said Caffrey.

"It stuck in my throat."

"So what are you going to do about it, Jamie?"

"The only thing I can do—escape."

"You tried that once before."

"We'll be more careful this time, Tom."

"We?"

"Elizabeth is eager to come with me."

"Is she still sharing a room with old Red Hazel's wife?"

"Baroness von Riedesel has been very kind to her," said Skoyles, "but their hosts begrudge every morsel of food they give them. It's a daily ordeal. Elizabeth is dying to leave."

"I daresay she wants to put distance between herself and Major Featherstone as well. Her betrothal to him turned sour."

"That was his doing, Tom."

"Serves him right for setting those two men on you."

21

As his dislike of Skoyles had grown, Harry Featherstone had paid two Canadian axmen to assault the captain. Fortunately, Skoyles was forewarned and was therefore able—with the help of Tom Caffrey—to turn the tables on his attackers and give them a good hiding. The incident was one more reason why Skoyles was glad to take Elizabeth Rainham away from his superior officer.

"Has he given you any more trouble?" asked Caffrey.

"The major has had the sense to keep out of my way."

"I don't blame him." He scratched his chin pensively. "This new plan of yours— Is there any hope that it could include me?"

"You insisted on staying here, Tom."

"That was before I realized what lying rogues these Yankees were. I want to sail home, not get marched off to some other camp. This war could go on for *years*, Jamie."

"I think it will," Skoyles agreed. "And I also think that General Washington will do his best to keep us all out of it. That's why I've set my heart on escape. I'm going to join General Clinton in New York."

"Take me with you."

"Are you sure that you want to come?"

"Yes," said Caffrey firmly. "Especially after what I saw today. The men are red raw with anger. They're chafing at the bit. There'll be other riots just like the one at Morland's Tavern. I don't want to spend my time bandaging the casualties."

"What about Polly?"

"Where I go, Polly goes as well."

"Then we'll be glad to have you along, Tom."

They shook hands on it. Duncan Rennie opened an eye, groaned in pain, then went off into a deep sleep again. Caffrey was sorry for him.

"There was no call to use a bayonet on him."

"General Burgoyne will make that point very strongly."

"The man responsible should face a court-martial."

"He may well have to do that."

"Then I'll be called as a witness."

"I doubt it," said Skoyles. "You won't even be here."

"Are you saying that we'll have left by then?"

"I'm certain of it."

"When do we go?"

"Soon."

George Washington read the letter with interest. As a rule, he was not given to smiling, but the edges of his mouth twitched perceptibly. Tall, thin, and muscular, the commander in chief of the Continental Army was a dignified man in a well-cut uniform. Though he was in his midforties, the cares of office and the vagaries of warfare had made him seem older. He and Ezekiel Proudfoot were at Whitemarsh, a mixed camp of tents and brushwood huts that had been hastily erected in the hills some thirteen miles north of Philadelphia. The army had a good defensive position, but there was little threat from the British soldiers who had occupied the rebel capital. Winter was at hand. It was a time to postpone hostilities until warmer weather.

"Good news, General?" asked Proudfoot.

"Very satisfying," replied the other. "You've brought us luck once again, Ezekiel. I haven't forgotten that our victories at Trenton and at Princeton were achieved when you were there."

"I can't pretend that I was responsible for either. I was only there to record the event, not to take part in it."

"Your presence always brings us good fortune."

"I wish that were true."

"It is true," said Washington half-seriously. "You were at Saratoga when we achieved that magnificent triumph over the British. And as soon as you come back to me," he went on, holding up the letter, "I receive a copy of this from Congress."

"What is it, sir?"

"A fatal mistake."

"Is that to our advantage?"

"Oh, I think so. Our hands are no longer tied."

Proudfoot would like to have read the letter, but Washington stood up behind his desk and slipped the missive into his pocket. They were in the wooden hut that was being used as a temporary headquarters. While he was no soldier, Ezekiel Proudfoot was dedicated to the rebel cause and helped it in the way he knew best. A talented silversmith, he made engravings of any military advances against the British and found a ready market for his prints. Some appeared in newspapers and gave a much-needed boost to the morale of the Continental Army and the local militias. Washington was quick to recognize the importance of the work that Proudfoot was doing.

"The drawings you made at Saratoga are excellent," he said.

"I can't vouch for their accuracy, General. So much was happening on the battlefield at the same time that it was difficult to know what to record. Freeman's Farm was confusing enough," recalled Proudfoot, "but the action at Bemis Heights was even more bewildering. I watched it from the branches of a tree."

"And you caught all the drama of the occasion."

"I'm not sure how I did it. My hand was shaking."

"Daniel Morgan was delighted with that sketch you made of him, and the sight of Benedict Arnold on his horse was inspiring. He's a real daredevil on the field of battle. What I didn't see," Washington went on with a hint of reproach, "was any drawing of General Gates."

"He remained in his tent during the action."

"So I understand."

"He felt able to control affairs more easily from there."

"The only way to control a battle is to be directly involved in it. However, his strategy clearly worked on the day and, for that, Horatio Gates deserves congratulation." His face clouded slightly. "I just wish that he'd had the grace to tell me about it."

"Did he not write to you?" asked Proudfoot.

"He sent word of his victory to Congress. They informed me."

"But you are the commander in chief."

"I'm glad that someone remembers that."

Ezekiel Proudfoot was not entirely surprised by the news. He had got sufficiently close to Horatio Gates to learn something of his character and ambition. It was clear that the victor of Saratoga thought himself a better soldier than George Washington and believed that he should replace him in overall command of the Continental Army. In his opinion, Proudfoot had no doubt that Congress had chosen the right man. They might criticize his patience and restraint, but Washington could show lightning audacity in combat when required. Proudfoot had seen firsthand evidence of it in two battles and regarded his companion as superior in every way to Gates. Soldiers merely obeyed the latter. George Washington had earned their respect.

Beside the elegant commander in chief, Ezekiel Proudfoot looked decidedly unkempt. He was a lean, lanky, bearded man in his thirties with a pockmarked face and long, straggly brown hair. Years of working as a silversmith had rounded his shoulders and given him a tendency to squint. Washington had received only a written report of the victory at Saratoga. Proudfoot's sketches had enabled him to understand more fully what had actually happened.

"Earlier on," said Proudfoot, "you mentioned a fatal mistake. May I know who made it?"

"General Burgoyne."

"Then it's not the only one."

"Quite so, Ezekiel. Errors on the battlefield cost the lives of his soldiers. This mistake may deprive the survivors of their liberty."

"I thought that they were being sent back to England."

"General Gates should never have made such a promise."

"Nevertheless, it's enshrined in the terms of the convention."

"They should have been articles of surrender," said Washington. "When a beaten army is surrounded by a force almost four times its size, it is no time to be generous. It is certainly not the moment to make the kinds of concessions that General Gates felt obliged to give."

"He showed magnanimity in victory," said Proudfoot.

"Be that as it may, Congress was very unhappy with the terms that were offered to the British. Thanks to this letter," he went on, patting his pocket, "we may not have to abide by them."

"Why not?"

"General Burgoyne has been too intemperate. Before he put pen to paper, he should have chosen his words with more care."

"Oh?"

"The letter was addressed to General Gates, who dispatched it to Congress. They, in turn, sent me this copy, and they place the same construction upon it as I do."

"In what way?"

"Imprisonment clearly irks General Burgoyne. He became so exasperated that he accused General Gates of failing to abide by the terms of the convention.

That being the case—and here I quote his exact words—'the public faith is broke.' Do you see what that means?" asked Washington, eyes glinting beneath his prominent brows. "In five words, he has repudiated the document."

"He does not intend to fulfil his commitments?"

"Apparently not, Ezekiel."

"But he is famed for being a man of honor."

"And rightly so. I have the greatest admiration for him. But he is now trying to threaten us. Read between the lines of his letter and you can see his purpose. He will use our alleged failure to comply with the terms agreed in order to rejoin the conflict. In short," said Washington, "when the transports arrive, he will order the convoy to take his army back to General Clinton in New York. We could never permit that."

"How can you avoid it?" said Proudfoot.

"By keeping the redcoats in captivity."

"In Cambridge?"

"We'll move them south in due course."

"So the convention will be torn to pieces?"

"General Burgoyne started the process," Washington argued. "As part of the agreement, all cartridge boxes were to be handed over by the British, but several went mysteriously missing. There's also the question of regimental colors. Instead of being surrendered, they've been held back somehow."

"Smuggled away, most probably."

"General Gates should have insisted on taking them."

"How will he feel if the terms that he drew up are revoked?"

"That's neither here nor there, Ezekiel."

"Oh, I fancy that he'll have a strong opinion on the matter."

"General Gates will do as Congress dictates," said Washington with a dismissive flick of his hand. "The point is that we now have grounds to act entirely as we wish. Since Burgoyne has no faith in the treaty, then we need have none. A fatal mistake on the part of the British."

"A very costly one, too," Proudfoot noted. "An army of over four thousand professional soldiers are now prisoners of war. They'll hate that. As soon as they realize the hopelessness of their position, there'll be lots of desertions."

"There will also be men who will come over to us. They will readily trade life in a prison camp for a chance to fight in the Continental Army. I am so glad that Burgoyne sent his letter—we are its beneficiaries."

"So it would seem, General."

"Heartening news before we go into winter quarters."

"No more campaigns this year?"

"Nothing beyond a few odd skirmishes."

Proudfoot gave a wry smile. "Then I'll have to go into hibernation," he said. "My skills have no employment."

"That's not true at all," said Washington earnestly. "We'll find work for you, Ezekiel, have no fear. Once we have settled into our new home, I will have an important assignment for you."

"Our new home? I thought we would stay here at Whitemarsh."

"We will be moving out very soon."

"Why?" asked Proudfoot.

"Because we have found somewhere more suitable."

"Oh? And where is that, General?"

"Valley Forge."

CHAPTER THREE

It was a blustery morning with a promise of rain in the air, but Elizabeth Rainham nevertheless went for a long walk with her maid so that the other occupants of the room they shared could have some privacy. Elizabeth was also glad to get away from the churlish woman in whose unwelcoming and drafty house they were forced to stay. The walk gave her the opportunity to talk with Nan Wyatt, a plump, rosy-cheeked, vigorous woman in her forties. As much a friend as a maid, Nan had always shown a maternal interest in her mistress. She was loyal to the core, and in spite of the many setbacks and indignities they had suffered, she had never once complained. Confronted with the prospect of parting from Elizabeth, however, she felt that she had the right to offer advice.

"I think it's far too dangerous," she cautioned.

"Not if we take care."

"You should stay here."

"No," said Elizabeth. "Living in that house is intolerable."

"Then use your influence with General Burgoyne. Ask him to find us more suitable quarters."

"He's not able to find proper accommodations for himself, Nan, let alone for anyone else. General Burgoyne is responsible for the whole army. It would be unfair to burden him with our problems."

"Have you told him that you mean to escape?"

"Of course not."

"He'll be very upset when he realizes that you are gone."

"I'm the least of his worries."

"No, you're not. He's very fond of you."

"He'll hardly notice that I've gone missing."

"I'll make sure that he does," said Nan. "General Burgoyne is very protective. If he knew what you had in mind, he'd do everything in his power to talk you out of it."

"That's why I could never confide in him," said Elizabeth. "My mind is made up. I simply can't stay here any longer, Nan. Given the chance to leave this dreadful place, I'll take it—whatever the risks. Why not reconsider and come with us?"

"I'm too old and too frightened of horses."

"So what will you do?"

"Remain here until the ships arrive," said Nan ruefully, "though I'm not looking forward to returning home alone, I can tell you. Your parents will never forgive me for letting you go off like this. It's sheer madness. Look what happened last time—you and Captain Skoyles were lucky to escape with your lives."

"We'll not put ourselves in that position again."

"How can you be so sure? It's hundreds of miles to New York. You may meet all kinds of perils along the way."

"Captain Skoyles is used to traveling through enemy territory," said Elizabeth with a note of pride. "I trust him implicitly."

"Stay here," Nan pleaded. "Where I can keep an eye on you."

"No. We simply have to leave."

Elizabeth stopped and hugged her maid. They had been through so much together over so many years that it would be a huge wrench to go their separate ways, but the urge to escape—and the need to be with Jamie Skoyles—was too powerful to resist. Nan would have to be left behind. A tear rolled down the older woman's cheek and Elizabeth was on the point of crying herself. They walked briskly on. It was minutes before conversation was resumed.

"What am I to say to your parents?" asked Nan.

"Tell them what they already know—that their daughter is a foolish, headstrong young woman who acts on impulse. Have you forgotten how horrified my mother was when I told her I wanted to come to America in the first place? Yet she couldn't hold me back. I felt that I had to be with Major Featherstone."

"That was different. You and the major were engaged to marry."

"Yes," said Elizabeth as ugly memories crowded in upon her. "I'm afraid that there have been drastic changes since then. It never occurred to me that Harry—that the major—would behave so appallingly."

"Better that you should learn the truth before you became his wife," said

Nan wisely, "or you might have let yourself in for some unpleasant surprises. It was a fortunate escape."

"That's one of the reasons I have to get away from Cambridge. As long as I'm so close to Major Featherstone, I'm caught in the shadow of my past. I simply must escape from here—and from him."

"I can understand that, ma'am."

"Then stop trying to keep me back."

"I'm bound to fret."

"We'll get through to New York somehow."

"You said that last time," Nan observed drily.

"We were badly let down. That won't happen again."

"How do you know?"

"Because I have complete faith in Captain Skoyles."

"So do I—but that doesn't stop me worrying about you."

"I worry about you as well, you know," said Elizabeth, slipping an arm around her shoulders to give her an affectionate squeeze. "You've been a rock, Nan. I'd never have come through it all without you."

"Thank you."

"I'll miss you."

Nan brushed away another tear. "Not as much as I'll miss you."

Their stroll had taken them over three miles in a wide circle and they were now within sight of their house again. Light rain began to fall. Pulling up the hoods on their cloaks, they hurried on. They had reached the front gate when one of Friederike von Riedesel's maids came tripping out to speak to Elizabeth in broken English.

"The gentleman, to see you, he is come."

Elizabeth did not wait to hear any more. Convinced that it was Jamie Skoyles who had called, she was equally convinced that he had brought details of their imminent escape. She ran up the path and in through the front door to find a trim figure in uniform awaiting her.

"Good morning, Elizabeth," he said politely.

She gasped in dismay. Her visitor was Major Harry Featherstone.

Jamie Skoyles had gone to great lengths to ensure that he had picked a more trustworthy man this time. After a first, secret, exploratory meeting with Cabal

Mears, he made discreet but exhaustive inquiries about the fellow, and heard nothing but praise of him. Common report held Mears to be honest and reliable. He also refused to take any money from Skoyles beforehand, and that was the best argument of all in his favor. Mears was a fisherman, a brawny man in his fifties with a pair of small blue eyes set in a weather-beaten face fringed with a white beard. When they met that morning at the quayside, Mears was seated on an upturned wooden pail, smoking a pipe and mending one of his nets. He gave Skoyles a nod of recognition.

"Good day to you, Captain," he said.

"And to you, my friend."

"Come in out of the rain."

"Thank you." Skoyles ducked under the roof of the little shed where Mears kept his fishing tackle. "Do you have any news for me?"

"I think so."

"Well?"

"Tomorrow."

"So soon?"

"You did tell me you were in a hurry," said Mears with a throaty chuckle, "and there's no point in waiting. Besides, tomorrow will bring fine weather."

"How do you know?"

"I'm a sailor."

"What time will you want us?"

"About an hour before dawn. That's when I usually set out in search of my catch. This time, of course, I'll have bigger fish in my nets. Two of them."

"Four," corrected Skoyles.

"Oh? Since when?"

"Since I talked to Tom Caffrey. There'll be four of us aboard—two men and two women. I'll be happy to pay an extra charge."

"I'm not doing this for the money," said Mears, "though I'm not so stupid that I'll refuse to take it. Some of us are still loyal to the Crown. We're not allowed to say so, mind you, not unless we want to be tarred and feathered—but we can show it. That's what I'm doing."

"I'm eternally grateful."

"How much baggage will you be carrying?"

"Very little."

"Good."

"And we'll take our turn at the oars."

"If there's enough wind, the sail will do most of the work." Mears removed his pipe and studied Skoyles. "Have you been out in a boat before, Captain?"

"Many times. Back in England, I was born and brought up in the Lake District. I learned to handle a boat at a young age."

"A lake is very different from the Atlantic Ocean."

"I know that," said Skoyles. "I crossed it to get here."

"Yes," the other conceded, "but you came in a three-masted frigate that was built for heavy seas. I only have a fishing boat. You'll notice the difference as soon as we hit those big waves."

"We're ready for any inconvenience."

"I was thinking of the ladies."

"Forget about them, Cabal. They know what to expect."

Mears popped the pipe back into his mouth. "I doubt that."

There was a quiet solidity about the man that Skoyles admired. The fisherman was a familiar sight at the quayside, a regular denizen who had earned his living out of the sea for years and who intended to go on doing so. He was no horse thief like the late Otis Tapper. Skoyles felt certain that Cabal Mears would not fail them.

"Where will you take us?" he said.

"That depends," replied Mears.

"On what?"

"The weather. It will be fine in the morning, but there's no telling what may happen later on. All that I can guarantee is that I'll have the four of you well clear of Boston. Where I put you ashore, I can't say."

"I accept that."

The other man studied him shrewdly for a moment. "May I ask you a question, Captain Skoyles?"

"Of course."

"Why do you choose to leave by sea?" asked Mears. "It would be a lot easier and far safer to escape by land. You could buy some horses."

"We tried that."

"What happened?"

"They hanged the man who stole the horses for us."

The fisherman grimaced. "That would make you think twice, I grant you," he said. "One thing about Cabal Mears—nobody can put a noose around his neck for stealing his own boat."

"But if you *were* caught . . ."

"Then I'll swear blind that you came to help me fish." He gave another chuckle, then rose to his feet. "I know the risk I'm taking, but I do so without any hesitation. If I'm helping two more British soldiers to rejoin the battle against the rebels, then I'm more than happy."

"Thank you, Cabal."

"An hour before dawn, mind."

"We'll be there," said Skoyles.

"Just remember one thing about the sea, Captain."

"What's that?"

"It's very wet," Mears warned. "If you carry anything of value, make sure that it's wrapped in something that won't let in water. For the rest, we'll have to take our chances."

"We're ready to do that."

After exchanging a handshake with him, Skoyles stepped out of the shed to discover that the rain had stopped. It was a good omen.

Since there was no hope of privacy inside the house, they moved to an outbuilding where they could step in out of the rain. Taken aback to see Harry Featherstone again, all that Elizabeth Rainham wanted to do was to get rid of him as quickly as possible. His manner was penitent.

"How are you?" he asked.

"As well as can be expected in the circumstances."

"This is no place for you. General von Riedesel has told us how badly you and his wife are treated here. You deserve better, Elizabeth."

"I survive."

"Do you?"

"Yes, Major," she said coldly.

It was the first time they had spoken to each other for several weeks and both of them felt slightly awkward. Featherstone was uncharacteristically nervous, and Elizabeth's heart was pounding. He was a man of medium height, upright, well built, and immaculately dressed. His neat black mustache matched his dark hair and dark eyes. Though he could never be described as truly handsome, his appearance was striking and, in spite of her hatred of him, she was reminded how impressed she had been when she first met him.

"I understand that the food is inedible," he said.

"It keeps body and soul together."

"I'll see if I can send some provisions out to you."

"There's no need to do that."

"It's a gesture of goodwill."

"I don't need your goodwill, Major."

There was a long pause. He searched her eyes for any vestigial trace of affection but found none. Elizabeth was poised and watchful. When she broke the silence, her voice was firm.

"We have nothing to say to each other."

"I believe that we do."

"Major—"

"No, let me finish," he said, taking a step closer. "You may not want to speak to me, but the very least I deserve is the chance to tender my profound apology to you. What happened back in Saratoga was unforgivable. I'm deeply ashamed of it."

"So you should be."

"I would simply ask you to remember the situation."

"Situation?"

"Yes, Elizabeth," he went on. "I'd fought in the fiercest battle I'd ever known. I'd seen some of my closest friends shot dead or hideously wounded. I'd watched our army being cut to shreds by those confounded rebels. The pain of it all was indescribable. I was tired, distracted, grieving. I simply wanted solace."

"I'd prefer to leave the incident in the past," she said crisply.

"But I need to explain."

"Your behavior was self-explanatory."

"I was pushed to the very edge. Don't you understand?"

"What I understand is that you tried to take by force what should only be yielded up out of love in the marriage bed."

"And why did I do that?" he continued, a touch of anger showing through. "It was because something that was mine—something that was very precious to me—was being offered to another man."

"You've only yourself to blame for that."

"Elizabeth, you *loved* me. You promised to marry me."

"I promised to marry the Harry Featherstone whom I had seen courting my sister, a true gentleman and a dashing soldier. Then poor Cora fell ill and knew that she was going to die. When she asked me to love you in her stead," said Elizabeth, grappling with a painful memory, "I had no difficulty in doing so. There was no sense of duty involved. I wanted you for myself."

"What changed?"

"You did."

"No, it was your feelings toward me that altered."

"Only because I saw new sides to your character."

"We all have our weaknesses, Elizabeth."

"These are far more than weaknesses," she retorted hotly. "You not only molested me, you actually tried to kill Captain Skoyles on the battlefield."

"I simply meant to give him a fright," he said with irritation.

"That's not true. It was a heinous crime, an act of attempted murder. Anybody else but Captain Skoyles would have reported it to General Burgoyne and had you called to account."

"Skoyles had more sense than to do that."

"More restraint, you mean."

"He knew that it would be his word against mine."

"And you have more influence with your fellow officers," she said bitterly. "That's another example of the sort of man you really are—hiding behind your friends. Please, Major, leave me alone."

"Not until you accept my apology."

"It's gone well beyond that stage."

"My conduct was outrageous. You are right to be annoyed."

"Annoyed?" Elizabeth echoed the word with disgust.

"To put it no higher than that. I just wanted you to know that I've been brooding on it ever since and looking for a way to make amends. I know my faults, but I can overcome them. I can reform, Elizabeth."

"Then that's something in your favor at last."

"I can be the man again that you once fell in love with."

"Never. That's a delusion."

"I can," he said, spreading his arms. "I'm not the ogre you think. I can improve. I can mend my ways. I can swear to you that I will never again descend to such a swinish level."

"It's too late, Major—much too late."

"I refuse to accept that. For the sake of what we once meant to each other, you have to give me the chance."

"Chance?"

"However long it takes, I'll keep my promise."

She was puzzled. "What chance?"

"The chance to make you mine again."

Elizabeth could not believe what she as hearing. This was a man who had lied to her, bullied her, and, when rebuffed, offered her sexual violence. The very thought of allowing him close to her again made her cringe. Nothing that Harry Featherstone could do would ever gain him the right to woo her again. It was unimaginable. Unable to put any trust in words, she stood there and bristled in silence. Minutes passed.

He looked over his shoulder. "The rain has stopped," he said.

"Goodbye."

"You haven't given me your answer yet."

"You already know it."

"Elizabeth—"

"I never want to see you again," she said, cutting him short. "If you have any affection for me at all, then you'll see that the kindest thing you can do is to stay away from me. I want to *forget* what happened. Every time I see you, I'm reminded of it. Now go away—forever!"

He nodded soulfully. "It's no more than I deserve," he confessed. "I'll just have to convince you by other means. Yes, I did some disgraceful things, I own that, but my love for you never once faltered, Elizabeth."

"Go!" she implored, hands to her face. "I don't want you here."

"As you wish." He backed away. "I did not come to upset you."

"Well, that's exactly what you did."

"Then I'll tarry no longer. Goodbye, Elizabeth."

She turned away without bidding him farewell. Harry Featherstone hovered for a few seconds, teeth clenched and eyelids narrowed, then he swung on his heel and marched off. He had gone only a few hundred yards when he saw someone coming toward him. Featherstone's ire was rekindled. The man who was striding along so purposefully was Jamie Skoyles, the obstruction that blocked his way to Elizabeth's heart. When they got close, the major was ready for a confrontation.

"Where are you going?" he demanded.

"I might ask the same question, Major."

"Damn you, Skoyles! I'm not answerable to you."

"You are where Miss Rainham is concerned."

Featherstone glowered at him, but Skoyles met his gaze without flinching. Officers who had once been friends were now implacable enemies. In every other matter, the major held the superior rank. When it came to Elizabeth Rainham, however, he had to take second place, and it made him fume.

"General Burgoyne wants a meeting this afternoon," he snapped.

"I'll be there."

"Four o'clock. Make sure that you are punctual."

"I always do, Major," said Skoyles.

"And learn to exert proper discipline. We can't have another outburst like the one we had on St. Andrew's Day. You share the barracks with the men. Keep the riffraff in order."

"Yes, sir."

Their eyes locked again, but it was Featherstone who was finally compelled to look away. He tossed a wistful glance over his shoulder.

"Don't bother Miss Rainham," he said. "She's weary."

"Yes, I know that you have that effect on her."

"Remember who you're talking to, man."

"That's exactly what I am doing, Major."

Featherstone bit back a reply. Seething with suppressed rage, he gave the captain a curt nod, then pushed past him. Skoyles watched him go before heading in the direction of the house, anxious to find out why the major had been there and eager to pass on to Elizabeth news of their approaching departure. In less than twenty-four hours, they could leave Harry Featherstone behind them. Escape could not come soon enough.

The British attack was bold and well organized. Had it been launched on an unsuspecting foe, it would certainly have succeeded, but the American force still camped at Whitemarsh had been warned of the forthcoming action. Secure behind their fortifications, a mixed army of Continentals and militia held their line. After a concerted exchange of fire, the British were compelled to withdraw, having achieved none of their objectives. Ezekiel Proudfoot not only watched the skirmish, he was in position to make sketches of some of the action. When the smoke had cleared, and the enemy had limped back to Philadelphia, he showed his work to George Washington. The general was complimentary.

"You have a rare talent, Ezekiel," he said.

"Thank you."

"It must be employed to advantage."

"That won't happen if I spend the winter with you in Valley Forge. Prints of your men building huts will hardly bring in new recruits. People want to see evidence of military victories. Soldiers want to know that they are joining the side that will win."

"We *will* win," Washington asserted. "Eventually."

"Are you certain of that?"

"Absolutely certain. The British have to fight on several fronts. That means their resources are stretched. Strike them at their weakest points—as happened at Saratoga—and we chase them from the field."

"How long will it take, sir?"

"Years—no question of that."

"And what will my role be?"

"I'm sending you to Philadelphia," Washington told him.

"Philadelphia?" the other repeated, taken aback. "It's full of Tories. Not to mention ten thousand British soldiers."

"We're not entirely without friends in the city. Our supporters were not all put to flight. How do you think we learned of that attack?"

"I assumed that one of your spies raised the alarm. Thank heaven he did or they might have caught us unawares. The man deserves our thanks and congratulations."

"It was not a man, Ezekiel."

Proudfoot was amazed. "A *female* spy?"

"An extremely good one. You may meet her."

"Is that what I am to do, sir? Gather intelligence?"

"That's only a small part of your work," said Washington seriously. "Your principal function is to help with the production of a newspaper. As you've proved in the past, a patriotic print by Ezekiel Proudfoot is worth a hundred articles in praise of our cause."

"You flatter me."

"Not at all. When the war started, we lifted the spirits of the men by reading out the words of Tom Paine. Now, I'd much rather show them the sketches you made at Saratoga. They prove what we can do."

"Only by force of arms."

"Art is a legitimate weapon of war. Dramatic pictures can have a powerful impact on the mind. We need more of them."

"Then I'm your man."

They were still at Whitemarsh, standing beside a brushwood hut so that it could shield them from the worst of a fierce wind. All around them camp was being struck. Flapping tents were being taken down. Weapons were being gathered. Powder kegs were being rolled into position. Drums and fifes were being packed away. Hatchets, kettles, canteens, axes, water buckets, forage cords, picket posts, picket ropes, wooden mallets, and all the other assorted items of camp life were being loaded into wagons, in readiness for the move to Valley Forge. Surveying the scene of activity, Ezekiel Proudfoot felt sorrowful.

"I'll miss all this," he admitted.

"All what?"

"Being with an army on the march. I never thought I'd hear myself saying this, but I feel strangely at home with soldiers."

"Our problem is that many of these men are not real soldiers," said Washington, running an eye over his Continentals. "They've not been properly trained or equipped to take part in a war. The militias are even less like a credible fighting force. Some of them wear nothing but rags," he went on, indicating four soldiers, in threadbare tunics and bare feet, who were trying to maneuver a piece of heavy artillery into place. "Dear God! Are *these* the men with whom I am to save America?"

"The selfsame fellows won at Bennington, sir."

"True."

"And they trounced the great General Burgoyne at Saratoga," Proudfoot reminded him. "Sometimes passion counts for more than good tailoring. I'll miss them."

"You'll not be stuck in Philadelphia forever, Ezekiel. We shall expect you to visit us in Valley Forge from time to time, and bring all the latest news. We'll not be much over twenty miles away from you."

"There'll be British patrols on the road."

"They seem to have eased off," said Washington. "Going in and out of the city should present no problems. Where you may have trouble is in concealing the whereabouts of the press."

"Where is it located now, General?"

"I'm not certain. It had to be moved to safety only last week."

"Then how will I find it?"

"You'll make contact with the editor, Pearsall Hughes. He's a good man. I'd trust him with my life." Washington handed him a letter. "All the details you need are in here. Commit them to memory, then destroy the paper. It must not fall into the wrong hands."

"What manner of man is this Pearsall Hughes?"

"His own."

"You mean that he calls nobody his master?"

"Wait until you meet him. You'll understand."

"And what about you, General?" asked Proudfoot.

"Oh, I'll be fully occupied at Valley Forge, trying to get the log cabins built before the snow comes. Harboring our resources and hoping to lick this motley crew into something resembling an army."

"I'll make sure that you get a copy of our newspaper."

Washington almost smiled. "I insist on seeing every issue."

"Then you can use it to kindle a fire."

"That's your task."

"Is it?"

"Yes," said Washington, looking him in the eye. "I'm counting on you to set hearts and minds ablaze with the newspaper. It has to be a clarion call for independence."

"It will be, General."

"Good. You'd best be on your way, Ezekiel."

"One moment," said Proudfoot before Washington could move off. "I was wondering if you had any news of the Convention army?"

"Why are you so obsessed with their fate?"

"It's no more than casual interest."

"Come, Ezekiel," said the other, "there's more to it than that. You've brought up the subject of the Convention army every time we've met. You care about them. What's your concern?"

"I have a friend who is involved."

"What sort of friend?"

"A close one, sir—a captain in the 24th Foot. He did me a big favor when I was captured at Hubbardton. I would just like to know what's going to happen to him."

"The decision lies with Congress."

"But your opinion will be taken into account, General."

"If only it were!" said Washington with a sigh. "I sometimes think that Congress only appointed me in order to disagree with everything I do and say. However, as it happens, with respect to the Convention army, our viewpoints do actually coincide for once."

"You want them to remain as prisoners of war."

"Frankly—yes."

"Even though that means rescinding some solemn promises?"

"General Burgoyne was the first to do so."

"I dispute that," said Proudfoot, reasonably. "Far be it from me to defend our enemy, but I've been thinking about that letter we discussed earlier. It's a commander's duty to speak up for his men, and that's all that General Burgoyne was doing when he wrote to General Gates."

"He let his frustration get the better of him."

"Possibly."

"That's a bad mistake in a leader."

"His letter contained a justified rebuke."

"Nonsense!"

"Undertakings were given at Saratoga," Proudfoot urged. "I was there at the time. I was a witness. All that I wish to suggest is that it reflects badly on the Continental Army if those undertakings are now cast rudely aside."

"Our hand was forced."

"You chose to read the letter that way."

"Burgoyne was saying, in effect, that the terms of the convention were meaningless. Congress proposes that we take him at his word."

"That's grossly unfair."

"I can see that you're not a politician, Ezekiel."

"Neither are you, sir, yet you're at the mercy of their decisions."

Washington inhaled deeply. "I can't deny that."

"I'm an artist. I think in pictures. I care about how things *look*."

"Go on."

41

"If a solemn agreement is so blatantly disregarded—if an army is kept in captivity instead of being sent back to England—it will be seen as a dark stain on our reputation."

"This is war, man. We have to seize every advantage."

"But there are more honorable ways of doing it."

"Are you doubting my honor?" Washington demanded with a flash of righteous indignation. "Do you dare to call that in question?"

"Of course not, General," said Proudfoot, holding up both palms by way of appeasement. "I support whatever you decide without criticism. I merely point out what the perception will be—in this country as well as in England. We will be seen as having betrayed a sacred trust."

"No, Ezekiel. We will be viewed as having taken a decisive step against an army that was sent here to destroy us. What would you have us do—let them sail back to King George so that he can replace them with a force of equal proportions?" He thrust out his jaw. "Congress will not permit that. I would not recommend it. Burgoyne's army will remain indefinitely as prisoners of war. That will rule out any possibility of their renouncing the convention and sailing to New York to reinforce the British army there." He shot Proudfoot a warning glance. "I suggest that you forget about this friend of yours in the 24th Foot."

"Why?"

"Because the chances are that you'll never see him again."

Captain Jamie Skoyles got them to the quayside well ahead of time. The night was cold but dry, and a cloud of stars twinkled in the sky to give them a bit of light. The women wore cloaks with the hoods up. Both men had exchanged their uniforms for hunting shirts, breeches, and capes. Wide-brimmed hats covered their heads. Each person carried a small bundle of clothing and personal items. Sergeant Tom Caffrey, surgical kit safely aboard, bore a musket stolen from one of the guards. Inside his baggage, wrapped up in sealskin to protect it from the water, Skoyles had a pistol, powder, and ammunition. A charcoal portrait of Elizabeth Rainham, drawn at his request by his friend Ezekiel Proudfoot, was also in his bag. His knife was sheathed at his side.

They moved with caution and communicated with gestures. When they reached the quay, they hid behind an upturned boat careened for repair. Even at that hour, there were people about. Cabal Mears was not the only fisherman about to sail down the Charles River. The quartet of fugitives lay low and waited for their signal. After what seemed like an age, Skoyles picked out the distinctive outline of Mears as he waddled past them toward his boat. He tapped each of his friends on the shoulder. Before they could set off, however, they heard footsteps behind them. When they swung round, they found themselves facing one of the guards from the barracks. Peering at them through the gloom, he covered them with his musket.

"What have we here, then?" he asked.

"Nothing, my friend," replied Skoyles, trying to sound at ease. "We promised to take the ladies out fishing with us today, that's all."

"No, you escaped from the barracks."

"We live in Cambridge. I own a cobbler's shop in George Street."

"All that you own is a lying tongue," said the man. "You're British soldiers. I can smell the pair of you from here. I thought I saw someone stealing away earlier on, and I was right." Caffrey took a step toward him. "Stand back or I'll shoot. And the sound will bring a dozen guards."

"Yes," Skoyles advised Caffrey, moving him back a pace. "Leave this to me. Our friend here is quick-witted, and he won't be fooled by anything we say. There's only one way to settle this."

"Back at the barracks," the guard declared.

"No. What does it matter to you if you have two fewer people to look after and feed every day? You caught us fair and square. That deserves a reward." Skoyles took out a handful of coins and let them jingle in his palm. "Here's a month's wages for you."

"Keep your money!"

"Even if I offer you six months' wages." The man's interest was now aroused. "That's the bargain, my friend. Let us vanish into the night and you go home with a full pocket. What do you say?"

The soldier pondered. "If the captain of the guard got to hear of this," he said at length, "he'd have me shot by a firing squad."

"There's no way that he'll ever learn the truth," said Skoyles. "Now help us. Let us go and you become a rich man." He jingled the coins again. "Would you like to count it out?"

The temptation was too great. After more consideration, the guard looked around to make sure that nobody was about and thrust out a hand. Skoyles offered him the money, then closed his fist as the man tried to grab the bribe.

43

"Wait," said Skoyles, clicking his tongue. "Do not be so hasty. Release the others first, and then you get your reward." There was a long pause. "Well, can they go?" The guard nodded. Skoyles turned to his companions. "I'll join you on the boat," he said. "He's just lit the lantern. Tell him I'll be there in a moment"

Elizabeth Rainham wanted to stay beside him, but Skoyles moved her firmly away. Only when she, Tom Caffrey, and Polly Bragg had been swallowed up in the darkness did Skoyles face the guard again.

"Thank you," he said, releasing the money into the other man's hand. "Now I'll keep my side of the bargain."

But the guard wanted more than his reward. He intended to have the money and capture the fugitives as well. Thrusting the coins into a pocket, he suddenly swung the butt of his musket in an attempt at clubbing his prisoner to the ground. Skoyles reacted with speed and anger. He ducked beneath the weapon and shot out a hand to grasp the man by the throat, squeezing so hard that all the latter could do was splutter in agony. With his other hand, Skoyles whipped out his knife and thrust it deep into the guard's heart. Seconds later, the man lay dying at his feet.

Skoyles did not hesitate. After reclaiming his money, he took the musket, powder, and ammunition pouch from the guard. Then he dragged the corpse unceremoniously along the ground and hid it behind one of the boathouses. By the time he reached the others, they were all aboard. Cabal Mears was ready to cast off.

"What kept you?" asked the fisherman.

"Unfinished business."

"Did you buy him off, Jamie?" said Tom Caffrey.

"Yes," replied Skoyles. "He got what he deserved."

CHAPTER FOUR

The one thing they had not anticipated was the smell. Having braced themselves against the prospect of high winds and choppy water, they now found themselves holding their noses against the pervading stink of fish. Cabal Mears had been loading his catch into the sloop for over thirty years and its wood was impregnated with a compound of pungent odors. It took some time for the passengers to get used to it. When they had cast off, Jamie Skoyles and Tom Caffrey took an oar apiece to row the boat while Mears held the tiller. Huddled together near the prow of the vessel, Elizabeth Rainham and Polly Bragg peered into the semidarkness with trepidation.

The two women had met before because Polly had befriended Nan Wyatt during the long journey south from Canada. Attractive, shapely, and with a ruddy complexion, Polly spoke with the same soft Devonian burr as Caffrey. It was one of many things that had drawn them together. Though she had done menial jobs for the army, there was no suggestion that Polly would now replace Nan as Elizabeth's maid. Adversity made the women social equals, and they traveled as friends, knowing that they would have to support each other during the testing days ahead. It was one thing to escape from Cambridge. Reaching the safety of New York was another matter altogether.

When they had rowed their way to midstream, the sail was hoisted and the combination of current and a stiff breeze carried them along at a steady speed. Skoyles and Caffrey were soon able to ship their oars. Canvas flapped noisily. The mast creaked and strained. Foam-edged water was left in its wake as the sloop moved forward. They were on their way at last. Skoyles took the opportunity to have a private word with Cabal Mears.

"We had a spot of trouble at the quay," he explained.

"So I gather."

45

"One of the guards trailed us all the way from the barracks."

"Yes," said Mears. "You bribed him to keep his mouth shut."

"The bribe wasn't enough to satisfy him. I had to shut his mouth another way. I just thought I should warn you, Cabal. By the time you get back, the body will have been found. Questions will be asked."

"I'm used to talking my way out of an awkward situation."

"There's nothing to connect him with you."

"Then I've no worries," said Mears blithely. "One less rebel in the world is a cause for celebration. In your place, I'd have done the same."

"He left me no choice."

"Forget about it."

"I will." Skoyles looked around. "This is a big boat for one person."

"I manage."

"Have you always fished alone?"

"My son used to help me."

"What happened to him?"

"He died."

"I'm sorry to hear that, Cabal."

"I wish that I'd been," said Mears coolly, "but I shed no tears over him. Peter never really took to the sea. He wanted to fight. When the war broke out, he ran off to join one of the Massachussetts regiments."

"He was a *rebel?*"

"Yes. It broke my heart. Divided loyalties in one family are a terrible thing. I tried to hold him back but Peter wouldn't listen. We never saw him again. Our son was killed at Hubbardton."

"I was there myself," said Skoyles, remembering the carnage on the battlefield. "I took part in that engagement. Your son was one of many who did not survive."

"All they told us was that he'd fought gallantly under the command of Colonel Francis." Mears chewed on the stem of his pipe. "Peter was on the wrong side. I wish I could find it in me to mourn his death."

"War is cruel. It separates father from son, and brother from brother. It can also play havoc with friendships."

"You've no need to tell me that."

"I'm sure. You must have lost many friends."

"Dozens of them," said Mears sourly. "Cambridge used to be such a happy town. We were a community. Then the trouble broke out and every-thing changed for the worst. People who had got along well with each other in the past suddenly fell out. They began denouncing their neighbors as loyalists. It was like a witch hunt."

"How did you come through it?"

"By keeping my opinions to myself."

"Your son must have known you were no rebel."

"He did, but he kept my secret. I owed him for that. Peter was ready to fight against everything I believe in, but he would not accuse his father of treachery. It's a terrible thing to say," he went on guiltily, "but there was a sense of relief when we heard that he'd been killed in action. More than that—God forgive me—I felt a peculiar satisfaction."

"I take no satisfaction in another man's death," said Skoyles, "even if he is an enemy. When I first came to America with the army as a mere lad, I was bil-leted on a farm and became close friends with one of the sons there. We kept in touch for years. I always knew that our paths would cross again somehow."

"And did they?"

"Yes, Cabal. Oddly enough, it was at Hubbardton."

"Was your friend in the rebel army as well?"

"Not as a soldier, but he was dedicated to their cause. When I met him again and saw that he was uninjured, I was glad. I wanted him to live even though I knew that he'd use his talents against us."

"His talents?"

"He was trained as a silversmith."

"Just like Paul Revere," said the fisherman with a sneer.

"Two of a kind," Skoyles continued. "Like him, Ezekiel produced prints that were aimed at stirring the emotions, and acting as recruiting officers for the patriots. We met again at Saratoga but he was on the winning side that time. Somehow," he added, "we remained friends, even though I killed his brother in battle at Bemis Heights."

Mears was astonished. "You killed his brother?"

"It was in self-defense."

"Yet this man still looks upon you as a friend?"

"I think so."

"Then he's a strange fellow indeed. What's his name?"

"Proudfoot," said Skoyles. "Ezekiel Proudfoot."

The bookshop was halfway down a lane off Front Street, close to a busy thoroughfare yet somehow quiet and secluded. Ezekiel Proudfoot soon found it. He had had little difficulty getting into the city. All that he had to do was to join the long column of people and wagons that streamed into Philadelphia at dawn for the market, and he slipped past the patrols unnoticed. He rode down Front Street, located the lane he was after, and saw the name of Pearsall Hughes swinging on the board outside the bookshop. It was early, but the shop was already open.

Proudfoot tethered his horse and went into the building. He found himself in a long, low, narrow room whose walls were covered with bookshelves. A table stood in the middle of the room with a display of new books to catch the eye. There was a faint musty smell to the place. The proprietor was seated in a chair beside a window at the far end of the room, reading a large leather-bound volume. Nobody else was in the shop. Proudfoot walked toward him.

"Mr. Hughes?" he asked.

"That is so," replied the man, looking at the visitor over the top of his spectacles. "How may I help you, sir?"

"General Washington sent me."

Hughes blinked. "That's a bizarre thing to say."

"He warned you of my arrival, surely?"

"No, sir."

"But he must have."

"I've no idea what you are talking about."

"He told me to contact you here."

"I doubt that very much," said Hughes, snapping his book shut. "I have no truck with the rebel commander, and would never make him, or any of his misguided supporters, welcome in my shop."

Proudfoot was baffled. "You are Mr. Pearsall Hughes, are you not?"

"That much I freely admit."

"Then you are the editor of a newspaper."

"I'm nothing of the kind," returned Hughes, hauling himself to his feet. "I'm a respectable bookseller, the best—though I say so myself—in the whole city. I'll thank you to make no more absurd allegations about me, sir. Newspaper!" he went on with utter distaste. "I inhabit the literary world. I would never demean myself by sinking to mere journalism."

Proudfoot was bewildered. The shop was at the address he had been given, and it was clearly owned by the man whose name he had been told. Why was he being given such a frosty reception? He looked at Pearsall Hughes more carefully. There was much to occupy his vision. The bookseller was a man of middle height but outsize proportions, fat to the point of obesity and with heavy jowls that shook as he spoke. His face was red, his nose even redder, and his wig too small for the bulbous head. Snuff had spilled down the lapel of his coat. Well into his fifties, Hughes exuded an air of erudition mixed with truculence.

"Well, sir?" he demanded. "Do you intend to buy a book?"

"No, Mr. Hughes."

"Then I'd be obliged if you quit my premises."

"But I came to see you."

"And I have been duly seen." He lowered himself into his chair and opened the book again. "Excuse me while I return to Plato."

"Something is amiss here," said Proudfoot, running a hand across his chin. "There can surely be only one bookseller in Philadelphia with your name and address."

"And with my reputation, sir. Beyond compare."

"Then why do you refuse to acknowledge me?"

"Because I have never seen you before in my life," said Hughes brusquely. "And since you make such preposterous assumptions about me, I hope never to set eyes on you again. Away with you."

"But I was told that you've heard of me."

"Indeed?"

"And that you would be glad of my assistance."

"My wife and I can run this place quite well on our own."

"I'm not talking about the bookshop," said the visitor. "I am Ezekiel Proudfoot. Does that name mean anything to you?"

"Should it?"

"I'm a silversmith and engraver."

The bookseller looked mystified. "Ezekiel Proudfoot?"

"Standing before you, Mr. Hughes."

"How do I know that?"

"Because I just told you. I am he."

"Any fool could walk in from the street and pretend that."

"I am Ezekiel Proudfoot," the other insisted, "and I can prove it." He undid the strap on the satchel that hung from his shoulder. "I have my engraving tools with me. You can examine them."

"There are lots of silversmiths in Philadelphia. Each one of them has a set of tools. I do not accept those as proof of identity."

"You must, Mr. Hughes."

"I sense that you may be an impostor."

"An impostor!" Proudfoot exclaimed with an edge of desperation in his voice. "Why should I try to deceive you? There must be some way that I can convince you who I am."

"There is, sir."

Hughes got to his feet again, crossed to the table, and opened a drawer in it. He took out a sheet of paper and handed it to Proudfoot.

"What's this for?" asked the other.

"Draw."

"Why?"

"Draw," Hughes ordered. "I know a little about this Ezekiel Proudfoot. I've seen his prints. He has a very distinctive style. Let me see if you can match his skills."

"What must I draw?"

"The first thing that comes into your mind."

Taking out a pencil, Proudfoot put his satchel on the floor, then bent over the table. His hand moved quickly and fluently over the paper. Pearsall Hughes, meanwhile, sauntered across to the door and locked it so that nobody else could disturb them. He waited until his visitor had finished, then took the drawing from him. The portrait of George Washington was remarkably life-like. After one glance at it, the bookseller's manner changed completely.

He offered a flabby hand. "Welcome to my shop, sir."

"A moment ago, you were about to throw me out."

"That was before I realized who you really were, Mr. Proudfoot. This sketch of yours has persuaded me completely. Nobody else but you could have drawn it."

"Why were you so hostile to me?"

"I'm suspicious of anyone who walks in here and makes such a bold claim as you did. The city is full of spies. You would not have been the first person who used the name of George Washington in the hope of tricking me into declaring my sympathies." He beamed at the other man and pumped his hand. "I am sorry that I was inhospitable."

Proudfoot relaxed. "I'm so grateful to learn the truth."

"Then learn something else. Be more discreet. Never use names, least of all that of our revered commander. It will give you away at once. When you are in Philadelphia, you are a Tory."

"I'll remember that."

"Befriend the British troops. It's the best way to gain intelligence."

"And the newspaper?"

"All in good time," whispered Hughes, a finger to his lips. "Let's get more closely acquainted before we touch on that. When did you last eat?"

"Yesterday."

"No breakfast?"

"Not so far."

"My wife will make you some food at once."

"I don't wish to put her to any trouble."

"Miranda will be more than happy to prepare you a meal." Hughes tugged at a bookcase and it swung forward on hinges to reveal a doorway. "Come and meet her, Ezekiel Proudfoot."

The farther they sailed down the Charles River, the more signs of life they saw. It was not just the appearance of other craft heading for the sea. There were gulls wheeling in the sky, ducks swimming in the shallows, and cows in the fields, waiting to be milked. As the fisherman had predicted, it was a clear day. He was still at the tiller, pulling on his pipe and steering his boat in midstream. Tom Caffrey sat with his arm around Polly Bragg, wondering how on earth she had managed to doze off while he was kept so wide-awake. He was more concerned about her safety than his own, and was having second thoughts about the wisdom of bringing her on what was bound to be a hazardous journey.

The other passengers were now in the stern of the boat. Elizabeth Rainham nestled against Jamie Skoyles, sad to have left so many good friends behind her but relieved that she was sailing away at last from Major Harry Featherstone.

"What will they do?" she asked.

"Who?"

"The people who discover that we've gone."

"Our disappearance will be duly reported," said Skoyles, "and our names added to the list of deserters. We're not the first to run away, by any means, and—when it becomes clear that our army will be kept here as prisoners of war in defiance of the agreed terms—there'll be a lot more people searching for a means to escape."

"Do you really think that we'll get to New York, Jamie?"

"We have to."

"It's such a long way."

"Would you rather stay in that crowded attic?"

"No!" she said with a shiver. "It was gruesome."

"There were no featherbeds in the barracks either."

"It was just as bad for the German troops on Winter Hill. According to Baroness von Riedesel, they were treated no better than animals."

"It can only get worse," said Skoyles. "Provisions are running low."

Elizabeth let out a squeal of surprise as a little water came over the gunwales and wet her feet. They had reached the mouth of the river now and had to contend with the rolling waves of the bay. The increased undulations brought Polly Bragg awake and made Elizabeth cling more tightly to Skoyles. The sun was lifting above the horizon and throwing dazzling patterns across the green sea.

As their gaze traveled over the wide expanse of Boston Harbor, they saw boats and ships of every kind and size. A harbor that had once been occupied by a menacing British navy was now filled with rebel craft. Frigates, schooners, sloops, brigantines, cutters, and galleys lay at anchor. Gondolas and pinnaces bobbed on the waves. The fleet was nowhere near as large or as imposing as its British counterpart, but it gave the rebel stronghold a feeling of reassurance.

The women were still trying to adjust to the unruly movements of the sloop, but Skoyles had noticed something. A line of vessels was blocking the entrance to Boston harbor.

"That explains it," he said.

"Explains what?" asked Caffrey.

"Why the transports failed to arrive from New York. Look at those frigates guarding the harbor, Tom. They've been put there to turn away any British ships. The likelihood is that they've already done so."

"Then there's no hope of the army being allowed back home?"

"They can't sail without ships."

Caffrey was bitter. "I wonder if they ever intended to release us?"

"I'm sure that General Gates did when he drew up the terms of the convention. His superiors obviously thought he was too lenient. They won't let us off the hook so easily." Skoyles surveyed the panorama before them. "This is where it all began," he said.

"What?"

"The war."

"Well, I wish they hadn't brought us to fight in it."

"You're a soldier, Tom. You thrive on combat."

"Only when I happen to be on the winning side."

"That time will come again."

"If we ever get off this boat alive!"

Caffrey grabbed the gunwale to steady himself. Though the fisherman was doing his best to keep the boat on an even keel, it was starting to tilt and buck. The swell combined with a gusting wind to remind the passengers that their voyage would not be an easy one. Water splashed into the boat, spray moistened their faces, and the mast creaked more noisily then ever. As the sail was buffeted by a fresh gust, Caffrey had to shout in order to be heard.

"Is it always this bad?"

Mears cackled. "Do you call this bad?"

"That's what my stomach is telling me," Caffrey complained.

"This is like a duck pond."

"Then I'd hate to be a duck!"

"You'll get used to it, Tom," said Skoyles.

"Not me. I'm a landlubber."

"This is nothing. We're still in the harbor."

"Yes," said Mears cheerily "Wait until we're clear of the Charleston Peninsula and Boston Harbor. Then you'll really get to see what the Atlantic Ocean can do."

Caffrey shuddered. "I'm not sure that I want to," he said.

"I'll make a sailor of you, Sergeant."

"As long as you keep me out of the water."

"I've never lost a passenger yet," Mears told him, then his face split into a wicked grin. "Not unless it was deliberate."

Miranda Hughes was an unexpected partner for the rotund bookseller. She was short, delicate, and soft-spoken, a gracious, middle-aged lady who gave Ezekiel Proudfoot a much warmer welcome than he had first received from her husband. Wearing a pretty blue dress with a hoop skirt, she had the kind of slender waist that needed no corset. Though they had a maid who helped with the cooking, Miranda insisted on preparing some breakfast for their visitor. It was only when he was eating it that Proudfoot realized how hungry he had been. They were in a room at the rear of the shop that served both as dining room and as a storage place for books.

"This is so kind of you, Mrs. Hughes," said Proudfoot.

"It's my pleasure," she replied. "It's such a treat for us to have the famous Ezekiel Proudfoot in our house."

"Famous or infamous?"

"A good question."

"Famous to all true Americans," said Hughes. "Infamous to the British army and the Tories. They would dearly love to catch you."

"Have my prints aroused so much enmity?" asked Proudfoot.

"Yes. That shows how effective they are."

"Good."

When Proudfoot had finished his meal, Miranda cleared the plate away, then returned almost immediately. She snapped her fingers.

"We must find a new name for you," she decided.

"Why?"

"Because your own could get you hanged."

"Am I really in such danger?" said Proudfoot.

"If your identity becomes known."

"Miranda is quite right," said Hughes peremptorily. "You must be baptized afresh, my friend. What shall we call you?"

"Choose a simple name. It's easier to remember."

"Then I have just the one," said Proudfoot. "I've a cousin in Boston named Reece, and another whose Christian name is Allen. Put the two of them together and we have Reece Allen."

"Reece Allen," she repeated. "Yes, I like that."

"From now on, that's what we shall call you," said Hughes.

"This is an extraordinary bookshop," remarked Proudfoot with amusement. "I come in hungry and walk out fed. I arrive with one name and leave with another. What other transformations will there be?"

"Only time will tell, Reece."

Proudfoot liked them. The more he heard about Pearsall and Miranda Hughes, the more unconventional they seemed as a couple. The wife was by no means confined to domestic duties. Miranda was an astute woman, who had once edited a newspaper in Baltimore and who now lent her journalistic talents to the cause of independence. It emerged that they had five children, a surprise to Proudfoot, who found it hard to imagine how two people of such dramatically contrasting sizes could produce any progeny between them. Miranda seemed too small and fragile to contemplate motherhood, and Hughes looked as if he would prefer to read a book in bed rather than sire a child.

They were enjoying a leisurely conversation when, without any warning, Hughes fired a direct question at their guest.

"What did you say your name was?" he demanded.

"Ezekiel Proudfoot." He bit his lip. "Oh, no," he said, annoyed that he had been caught out so easily. "It should be Reece Allen."

"Remember that."

"I will, Mr. Hughes."

"It could be the difference between life and death."

"Then I won't make that mistake again."

"Where will Reece stay?" asked Miranda.

"We'll find him somewhere, my dear. Meanwhile, I daresay that there are a few questions that he'd like to ask us. Is that not so, Reece?"

"It is," said Proudfoot. "I've been sent here to work on a newspaper, but I don't even know what it's called."

"*The Pennsylvania Patriot.*"

"How often is it published?"

"Once a week at least."

"At least?"

"If events justify it, we sometimes produce a special issue."

"On what day of the week does it normally come out?"

"No specific day," Miranda explained. "We change the day of publication regularly in order to confuse our enemies. If they knew that it was issued on the same day every week, they would be waiting to see how it was distributed."

"And how is that done?"

"We have a system."

"But there's no need for you to know what it is," said Hughes blandly. "The less you know about that side of it, the better. Secrecy is our watchword, Mr. Allen. Complete secrecy."

"I understand, Mr. Hughes."

"All that need concern you is the *Patriot*. It's the sole reason you're here. You supply the pictures, we write the words."

"While we're on that subject," said Proudfoot, "I have a few comments to pass on from General Washington."

"Comments?"

"Suggestions about what you might put in the newspaper."

"Keep them to yourself."

"Why?"

"Because *we* decide what goes into print, Mr. Allen."

"Naturally."

"An editor needs complete authority."

"General Washington is surely entitled to express a view."

"Of course," said Hughes, striking a combative pose, "but we are equally entitled to ignore it. Miranda and I would never dare to tell him how to fight a battle. By the same token, we do not feel that we need his advice—or anyone else's for that matter—on how to wage war in print."

"I see."

"*The Pennsylvania Patriot* is our flag. We know best how to fly it."

Proudfoot remembered what he had been told earlier about Pearsall Hughes, and he realized how accurate an assessment of him it had been. Evidently, he would brook neither criticism nor interference. The bookseller was very much his own man.

Crossing the bay was a real trial for those unaccustomed to sailing, but it was far worse when they reached the open sea. The swell increased, the wind freshened, and the temperature seemed to fall. They also had to contend with swirling undercurrents. Jamie Skoyles sat with a soothing arm around Elizabeth Rainham's shoulders and, in spite of her apparent discomfort, she smiled bravely. Polly Bragg was also troubled by the random agitation of the boat, but she made no complaint either. What irritated Tom Caffrey was the way Cabal Mears remained at the helm, calmly smoking his pipe and giving every indication that he was actually enjoying their voyage.

"I'm glad I'm not a fisherman," said Caffrey.

"But it's a perfect day for sailing," Mears responded.

"Perfect!"

"Clear sky, calm sea, strong wind."

"We're being blown all over the place."

"No, Tom," Skoyles explained, much more at ease than the others. "Cabal is tacking to make best use of the wind. Trust him."

"I have no choice," Caffrey moaned. The boat dipped, then rose as another wave hit them. "Nobody told me that it would be like this."

"Would you rather be back in those squalid barracks?"

"No, Jamie."

"Then stop protesting. It's the same for all of us."

"True."

"Be grateful to Cabal. He's helping us to escape."

Caffrey was too jangled to be able to express any gratitude, but he had the grace to apologize for his outburst. He tried to put his own anxieties aside and devote himself to cheering up Polly Bragg. Veering one way, then the other, the boat continued south. The most likely place for it to be intercepted had been in the bay. With that behind them, they felt marginally safer. Elizabeth tossed an admiring glance at the fisherman.

"It's so brave of him to do this for us, Jamie," she said. "Did you have to pay him a lot to persuade him?"

"I haven't paid him anything yet," Skoyles replied.

"Oh?"

"Cabal insisted on getting us away from Cambridge first."

"How honorable of him!"

"The same can't be said of Otis Tapper. He wanted all his money *before* he provided the horses. I only gave him half of the agreed amount in advance— or I'd never have seen him again."

"As it was," she recalled, "he was dead before we even got there. They'd hanged him on the spot. We not only lost the chance to escape but you forfeited all that money as well."

"There was plenty more where that came from."

"Was there?"

"Yes," he said with a confiding smile. "General Burgoyne has been kind enough to invite me to the card table, and I rarely lose."

"What he said to me in Montreal was true, then."

"Yes, Elizabeth."

"It was at that ball, the first time I met you. He warned me never to play cards with Captain Skoyles because he had the luck of the devil."

He squeezed her hand. "Lucky at cards, and lucky in love."

"Do you really believe that?"

"Of course. Don't you?"

"Well, yes," she said uncertainly, "though I'm not sure that being tossed around in this boat is exactly my idea of good fortune."

"We escaped, Elizabeth. Most of the others are still there."

"I know."

"They're doomed to remain in captivity until the war ends."

"And then what?"

"They'll have to be set free."

"I'm not talking about them, Jamie. I was thinking of us. When the war is finally over, what will happen?"

"We'll get married and settle down here."

"In America?"

"Where else?" he said. "I told you from the very start that this is where I intend to stay. That's why I've taken every opportunity I've had for gambling. The card table has earned me the money I'll need to buy a decent amount of land. I couldn't do that on a captain's pay." He sensed her reluctance to agree with him. "When we first discussed it, you seemed happy enough with the idea."

"I couldn't be happier with the idea of marrying you, Jamie, but I do have qualms about staying in this country. Think of all the blood that's been shed. We'd be living among enemies."

"Memories fade in time."

"They would never accept us."

"They would if we showed them that we were determined to become one of them," he maintained. "If we were ready to live as Americans."

"I'm still too British to conceive of that."

"This country will grow on you."

"Frankly," she admitted, "it's starting to repel me."

"That's because it holds too many uncomfortable memories for you at the moment. Wait until you get to know America better, Elizabeth." He gave her a teasing look. "Would you rather go back home to England to marry Major Featherstone?"

"Heaven forbid!"

"He could offer you a wedding in Canterbury Cathedral."

"That's meaningless to me."

"Is it?"

"Yes, Jamie. I never want to set eyes on him again."

"Don't be too harsh on him," he said. "But for him, we'd never have met. You didn't sail all the way to Canada in order to meet that notorious cardsharp, Captain Jamie Skoyles. We have the major to thank for making that possible."

"I never saw it that way."

"Perhaps you should, Elizabeth. I loathe the man as much as you do, but I'm not blind to his finer qualities. He's a true philanthropist."

"Philanthropist?"

"Yes," he said with a smile. "My plans for the future cost money. And the person who put most of it in my pocket was none other than that selfsame Major Harry Featherstone. Every time I won at cards, he lost—heavily, as a rule. It was he who paid for the hire of Cabal's boat," he went on. "I wonder what he'll say when he finds out that he made our escape possible."

"Gone!" Harry Featherstone was astounded. "What do you mean—gone?"

"Miss Rainham is no longer here, sir."

"Then where on earth is she?"

"I don't know."

"You must have some idea, woman."

"All that I can tell you is this," said Nan Wyatt, feigning ignorance, "when I woke up this morning, Miss Rainham was nowhere to be seen. I searched the whole house, and the fields nearby, but there was no sign of her. I'm as puzzled as you, Major Featherstone."

"Did your mistress leave no note?"

"Not a line, sir."

"Damnation!"

Harry Featherstone slapped his thigh hard out of sheer frustration. They were outside the house where Elizabeth Rainham had been staying with Friederike von Riedesel and her children. Having gone to the trouble of scavenging a supply of food, the major was mortified to hear that Elizabeth was no longer there. He had hoped to ingratiate himself with her. Instead of that, he was left in the lurch with the bag of provisions he had carried all the way there.

"Tell me the truth," he said, fixing Nan with a stare. "Miss Rainham would go nowhere without her maid."

"She did this time. It's very upsetting."

"Don't lie to me or you'll live to regret it."

"Why should I lie?" asked Nan. "I worry about her. I've looked after Miss Rainham for many years, yet she leaves me without a word of explanation. I'm fretful, Major. I want to know that she's safe."

Nan Wyatt was on the verge of tears. Though she had been warned of her mistress's departure, she was very skeptical about her chances of escape and, as a result, was patently anxious. Unsure whether or not he could trust her, Featherstone saw no point in badgering the maid. He had just remembered the other visitor whom Elizabeth had seen on the previous day, and he spat the name out.

"Captain Skoyles!"

"What about him, sir?"

"How often has he been out here?"

"Once or twice."

"What brought him here yesterday?"

"Who knows, Major? I did not speak to him."

"Skoyles is behind this," he concluded, lip curling in disgust. "That's where Miss Rainham must be—she's run away with that rogue! Captain Skoyles has led her astray." He spun on his heel and marched away. "Damn the man! I'll make him pay for this."

The first sign of trouble was when the sun disappeared. Having dazzled their eyes until midafternoon, it suddenly vanished behind a cloud. The wind picked up and had a much harsher bite to it. The sky began to darken. Cabal Mears had been hugging the shore to get a measure of protection from the elements, but he could foresee danger.

"There's a squall coming," he warned.

"How bad will it be?" asked Skoyles.

"Bad enough. We need to run for cover."

"Where can we hide out here?"

"There are some islands around the next headland," said Mears. "I've anchored there before when the weather turned against me. Been there for days on end sometimes."

Caffrey was curious. "Where did you sleep?"

"Here on the boat."

"You must have been soaked to the skin."

"I hid under the tarpaulin. The sea is a capricious master," he went on resignedly. "You have to obey its rules."

"What must we do now, Cabal?" said Skoyles.

"Sit tight and be ready to get wet. Oh, and one more thing."

"What's that?"

"Pray," Mears suggested. "Pray that we're not swept out to sea."

CHAPTER FIVE

During his childhood in England, Jamie Skoyles had run before a storm on more than one occasion, but he had been sailing on a placid lake at the time. The worst he had feared was a soaking from the rain. Far greater dangers threatened now. The wind was much louder, stronger, and more variable than anything he had experienced in his native Cumberland. It seemed to change direction every other minute, pounding their bodies with random brutality, deafening their ears and tossing the vessel hither and thither. In the space of twenty minutes, the Atlantic Ocean had become a heaving cauldron that rocked the boat violently and flung ice-cold water into their faces.

"Tie everything down!" yelled Skoyles, anxious to save their precious cargo. "Help me, Tom!"

"We need to tie ourselves down," cried Caffrey in alarm.

"Pile it all together!"

Shifting his feet to maintain his balance, Skoyles put the four bundles together with the two muskets. Caffrey passed him a rope and he lashed the items together to one of the seats. Elizabeth Rainham and Polly Bragg were clinging to the side of the boat as it rolled and pitched. They had never anticipated such upheaval. Feeling sick, both women withdrew deeper into their hoods. The sky grew blacker, the sea wilder, and the wind more punitive. The noise was earsplitting. Instead of helping them, the flapping canvas now became a liability.

"Take over here, Captain!" Cabal Mears bellowed.

"Right," said Skoyles.

"I need to lower the sail before the mast cracks."

"Leave go—I've got it."

Skoyles grasped the tiller and needed all his strength to hold it against the surging waves. To his horror, they were being carried farther away from land, helpless against the force of wind and water. Planting his feet wide apart, Mears tried to lower the sail, hardly able to control it as the boat plunged madly on. The canvas appeared to have a life of its own, billowing crazily and trying to break free of its mast. As the fisherman struggled manfully with the halyard, the rain began to fall, hard, cold, and biting, making it even trickier for him to keep his footing. Frightened that they might be knocked into the sea, Caffrey and the two women held each other more tightly. When he finally got the sail down, Mears lashed the canvas firmly before going back to the stern.

"Let me take over," he said.

"She's a real handful," Skoyles warned, releasing the tiller. "It feels as if the rudder is about to snap any moment."

"We've been through much worse than this, Captain."

"What can we do to help?"

"The ladies might feel safer if they were tied to the mast."

"And then?"

"I'll need you and the sergeant to pull on the oars again," said Mears. "Otherwise, we're completely at the mercy of the storm. It could carry us any-where, and we need to make for those islands."

"What islands?" said Skoyles, blinded by the downpour.

"They're not too far away, Captain. At least, I hope not."

As if to confound his prediction, the wind howled angrily, the rain drenched them to the bone, and the biggest wave yet lifted the boat up, then hurled it down into a long, deep, dark, seething valley of water.

"This will be your room, sir," Henry Gilby explained, opening the door for him. "If you find it agreeable, that is."

"I'm sure I will," said Proudfoot. "Your tavern was recommended."

"That's always good to hear. Go inside."

"Thank you."

He stepped into a room that was small, square, sparsely furnished, but im-peccably clean. The landlord followed him in. Since darkness was starting to fall, there was even a candle burning in its sconce to shed some additional light. The bed looked serviceable and would be very welcome after the malodorous straw mattress on which he had been sleeping at Whitemarsh. A jug of water and a basin stood ready. A cracked chamber pot poked out from beneath the bed. After appraising the room, Proudfoot put his luggage on the little table beneath the window. He looked through the glass and had a clear view of the River Delaware. He turned back to the landlord.

"This will do admirably, Mr. Gilby," he decided.

"Thank you, sir."

"You'll need some rent in advance, you said."

"If that's not too much trouble for you, Mr. Allen."

"Not at all."

"And if our charges meet with your approval."

"It's a very fair price," said Proudfoot, taking out some coins to pay him. "You know, I was much mistaken. I thought that Philadelphia was the Quaker City. I never expected to see so many taverns here."

"Oh, lots of other people have moved in since the days of William Penn, sir. We now have churches and chapels of every kind." Gilby gave a quiet smile. "Fortunately, the Society of Friends no longer rules the roost here. Unlike them, other Christians enjoy a good tipple. The same, of course, can be said of the British soldiers."

"How many of them do you have here?

"Thousands."

"That must cause a lot of problems."

"It does, Mr. Allen."

"Are any of the troops staying under your roof?"

"A few."

They were upstairs in the King George Tavern, a name that betokened loyalty and which therefore attracted regular custom from the occupying force. Henry Gilby had such an impassive face and such an expressionless voice that it was difficult to know what he felt about the British entry into the city. He was a small, thin, stooping man in his fifties with wisps of gray hair around a rapidly balding pate. Gilby had a habit of rubbing his hands together as if perpetually washing them. Ezekiel Proudfoot tried to take his measure.

"I saw plenty of redcoats downstairs."

"The King George has always been popular."

"But you would not wish to have an army of occupation here forever, surely? Do they not drive away other custom?"

"That's not for me to say, sir."

"And where are they all billeted?"

"You'll have to ask them yourself, Mr. Allen," said the landlord tactfully. "My job is to serve anyone who comes in through the door and who can afford our tariff. Damaris and I make no distinctions."

"Damaris?"

"My wife, sir. I think you'll find her cooking to your taste."

"I'm sure I shall."

"We'll look after you while you're here." Gilby lifted an eyebrow. "Do you have any idea how long that may be?"

"Not at this moment."

"This room is at your disposal for as long as you need it."

"I'm glad to hear it, Mr. Gilby. It's more than satisfactory."

"Then I'll let you settle in, sir." About to leave, the landlord paused at the door. "Do you have business in the city, Mr. Allen?"

"Yes," replied Proudfoot, careful not to disclose what that business might be. "But I also came to visit old friends nearby. In fact, it was they who suggested I might stay at the King George."

"Then I owe them my thanks. May I know their name?"

"Hughes—Mr. and Mrs. Hughes."

"Would that, by any chance, be Pearsall Hughes, the bookseller?"

"The very same."

"Then you are doubly welcome," said Gilby, face lighting up at once. He pulled the door shut. "Mr. Hughes has been kind enough to point a few people in our direction and we have always found them most serious gentlemen."

The phrase was carefully chosen. What the landlord meant was that the guests had all shared his belief in the cause of American independence, a view that he could never declare openly in a city overrun by British troops. The name of Pearsall Hughes had opened a door for Proudfoot. He was now trusted.

"Will you be visiting the bookshop soon?" asked Gilby.

"Very soon."

"Then you might care to pass on an interesting piece of information to our mutual friend. Until now, it has only been a rumor but I'm given to understand that it's become an established fact."

"And what is this established fact, Mr. Gilby?"

"General Howe has resigned."

Proudfoot was startled. "He intends to leave America altogether?"

"Apparently," said the other. "I heard two officers discussing the subject earlier. General Howe feels the task of subduing the colonies is beyond him, and he's aware that he does not enjoy the wholehearted support of his political masters back in England. In other words," he pointed out, "he's grown tired of the whole campaign."

"This is cheering news."

"Of course, there are some who will say that it was Mrs. Loring who tired the general out—his mistress is much younger and far more robust than he."

Proudfoot grinned. "I've heard the ribald stories about Mrs. Loring."

"They are about to come to an end."

"General Howe to go, eh?" said Proudfoot, savoring the intelligence. "That's tantamount to a confession of defeat. He knows that he will never bring us all to heel. When does he leave?"

"He'll first sit out the winter here."

"Ah. That news is not so welcome."

"The Continental Army is unable to displace them as yet."

"Yes, I know. Meanwhile, the city is occupied. Mr. Hughes tells me that the British soldiers are making the most of the situation. There are plays and dances, I hear."

"Plays, dances, dinners, and celebrations of all kinds. They are living off the fat of the land here, Mr. Allen. A Quaker city?" He gave a hollow laugh. "There's not much plain dress and self-denial here anymore. Taverns do a brisk trade and, in my position, I can hardly condemn that. But the streets are full of brawling drunkards at night, and the brothels are busier than ever. There is also a gambling fever. We wallow in corruption, sir. The British have dragged us down to their own level."

"For the time being."

"Quite so, Mr. Allen," said the other, a knowing glint in his eye. "For the time being." He washed his hands with invisible soap. "Enjoy your stay at the King George, sir. I'll see that your horse is fed and watered."

"Thank you, Mr. Gilby."

"And I'll make sure that nobody bothers you up here."

Proudfoot looked around once more. "Something tells me that I have chosen the right place," he said contentedly. "I think it will be ideal for my purposes."

They had no idea where they were. Blown miles off course and battered unmercifully by the elements, the sloop sailed on into the unknown. Failing light combined with the driving rain to leave them, literally, in the dark. All that Cabal Mears could rely on was instinct. While the fisherman remained at the tiller, Jamie Skoyles and Tom Caffrey heaved on the oars in a vain effort to impose some control. Both were powerful men, honed in battle and used to physical challenges, but the effort of rowing the boat was slowly sapping their energy.

"We can't do this for much longer," Caffrey shouted.

"Keep at it," Skoyles urged.

"Where are these islands we were told about?"

"Cabal will get us there."

"The water is up to my ankles."

"It's the same for all of us, Tom."

"If only this rain would ease off!"

"Pull hard on the oar."

"That's what I'm trying to do, Jamie."

"It's bound to ease off in time. We have to be patient."

Caffrey gritted his teeth and tugged on his oar. Hard though it was for him, he knew that the women would be suffering even more. He was consumed with guilt at having unwittingly put Polly Bragg's life in danger. He called out to her.

"Forgive me, Polly," he said. "I should never have brought you. I didn't expect anything as terrible as this."

"Forget about me, Tom," she said. "Just row us to safety."

"I'm doing my best."

She gave a shiver. "It's so *cold* now."

"We'll freeze to death."

"Don't even think that," she scolded, rubbing her arms to keep warm. "Have faith. We'll survive somehow."

Polly Bragg was a strong-willed, resilient woman who never let circumstances beat her down. There had been many setbacks in her life, but she made light of them. Caffrey was chastened by her steadfastness. He resolved to stop moaning. Though his hands were blistered, and his arms and shoulders aching, he put additional effort into his rowing. Polly Bragg and Elizabeth Rainham had taken the fisherman's advice and tied themselves to the mast. It made them feel less likely to be tossed overboard but it did not still their fears. Like the others, they were completely sodden, their clothing so wet that it stuck to their bodies. Salt spray filled their mouths and left a sour taste.

"How close are we to land?" Skoyles yelled.

"Not too close, I hope," Mears replied.

"Are there rocks?"

"Rocks and sandbanks along part of the coast."

"What about sharks?" said a worried Caffrey. "I think I'd prefer to drown than be eaten alive."

"We'll pull through," Mears assured him. "The storm is passing."

"It doesn't feel like it to me."

"Bear with me, Sergeant. You'll see."

The change was imperceptible at first but it was definitely there. The wind dropped a little and the rain turned to fine drizzle. The waves continued to pound them but there was no longer the same unrelenting swell. Twenty minutes later, Mears was confident that the squall had blown itself out. The boat had more stability and the tiller was easier to control. The worst was over.

"Let her drift," Mears ordered.

Caffrey was relieved. "We can stop rowing?"

"Yes, Sergeant."

"Thank heaven! Now I know why I never joined the navy."

"You're a born sailor, Tom," Skoyles teased him, lifting his oar clear of the water. "I've never rowed with a better man." He brought the dripping oar back into the boat. "Where are we, Cabal?"

"I can't tell you yet," Mears replied, "but the tide has turned. You can feel it. We'll be carried back toward the coast."

"What will you do?"

"Wait until we reach shallow water, then drop anchor."

"Aren't you going to put us ashore?"

"Not until I know it's safe, Captain. We've worked hard. We need a rest. We could also do with some food and drink to keep up our spirits."

"We've brought some supplies," said Skoyles.

"So have I, my friend. Food and rum."

"Rum!" Caffrey echoed. "That word warms my heart."

"I never sail without it," said Mears.

The wind had dropped even more now, and the waves had lost their fury. Elizabeth Rainham felt able to untie herself from the mast.

"Oh!" she cried, putting a hand to her face.

"What's the matter?" said Skoyles.

"I just felt something wet brush my cheek. There it is again."

"I can feel it myself, Elizabeth."

"Not more rain, I hope."

"No," said Mears with a cackle. "That's not rain—too cold for that."

"Then what is it?" she wondered.

"Snow."

Leaving his horse in the stable at the rear of the King George Tavern, he went on foot to the bookshop. There was not much to see in the evening shadows, but Ezekiel Proudfoot heard enough to give him some notion of what Philadelphia was like. Founded by the Plain People, the city was a haven of Quaker simplicity no more. Every tavern he passed was filled with blazing light and boisterous laughter. In every street, redcoats were abroad, exchanging loud banter or telling crude stories. When he passed a hall, Proudfoot caught the sound of lively music. Clearly, those inside were not quaking at the word of God. They were dancing a reel.

The bookshop was closed when he got there, but one pull on the doorbell brought the maid. Proudfoot was invited in and joined Pearsall and Miranda Hughes in their parlor. The three of them were soon sharing a small bottle of wine together. The visitor passed on the tidings he had gleaned at the King George Tavern.

"Excellent!" said Hughes, patting his knee. "We've put one British commander to flight and we'll do the same with his successor."

"And who will that be?"

"The obvious choice is General Clinton."

"Yes," said Proudfoot. "I suppose that it is. After his defeat at Saratoga, the much-vaunted General Burgoyne has ruled himself out. That will really disappoint him. He nursed ambitions of becoming commander in chief."

"How do you know that?" asked Miranda.

"I was told it by an officer who sat at Gentleman Johnny's table."

"A spy?"

"A friend," said Proudfoot wistfully. "A captain in the 24th Foot. Destiny has put us on opposite sides in this war but it has not dimmed our respect for each other."

"Pah!" Hughes exclaimed. "I could never bring myself to respect a British officer. They are here to enforce royal tyranny. How can you call such a man a friend?"

"We've known each other for a long time, Mr. Hughes."

"I've known colonial oppression for a long time, sir. That doesn't mean I have to like it. An enemy is an enemy."

"And a friend is a friend," Proudfoot returned with emphasis. "Nothing can change that. Besides," he went on, "Jamie is foresighted. He knows that the war will end one day and he means to settle in America."

Hughes snorted. "If he lives to do so."

"That's rather harsh, Pearsall," said his wife.

"It was meant to be."

"There are good people on both sides in this war."

"Not if they wear a red coat, Miranda."

A bellicose note had come into Hughes's voice and his jowls were wobbling. Proudfoot elected to change the subject. He glanced in the direction of the bookshop.

"Have you been busy today, Mr. Hughes?"

"No more than usual."

"What sort of books do people buy?"

"I know what they *ought* to buy," said Hughes censoriously, "but my customers do not always take my advice. What I sell most are copies of Samuel Richardson's novels. *Pamela* is still very popular, and so is *Clarissa*. They pander to the wrong kind of taste."

"Yet they are cleverly written," said his wife. "You must own that."

"We have American authors who are equally clever, my dear, and who do not find it necessary to titillate their readers by dwelling on sexual improprieties. I am not puritanical," he said, addressing himself to Proudfoot, "but I do like to observe the laws of decency."

Miranda was practical. "We can only sell the books people want."

"It's our duty to foster their reading habits, my dear."

"Unlike you, they can't all read Plato in the original Greek."

"More's the pity, Miranda."

"My husband is a classical scholar, Mr. Allen," she said. "Left to him, all our intelligence reports would be sent in coded Latin." She sipped her wine. "How do you find the King George?"

"Well suited to me, Mrs. Hughes," answered Proudfoot, "though its name was puzzling at first. Why preserve the name of a hated monarch in the rebel capital? I put it to Mr. Gilby and he explained that, in fact, he changed the tavern to the Black Horse and had a new sign painted."

"True," said Hughes. "Pontius is a shrewd businessman."

"Who?"

"Pontius. That's what we call him. Pontius Pilate."

"Why?"

"Haven't you noticed how he likes to wash his hands as he talks? He never stops. Pontius—Henry Gilby to you—is a pragmatist, so he kept the old sign-board. When the British entered the city, down came the Black Horse and up went King George again."

"It's a convenient disguise."

"Mr. Gilby is one of us," said Miranda.

"I gathered that."

"By the way," Hughes snapped suddenly, "what's *your* name?"

"Reece Allen," Proudfoot replied.

"And where have you come from, Mr. Allen?"

"Massachusetts."

"Your business in this city?"

"I'll looking to buy a small farm nearby. It will give me an excuse to travel in the area, you see," he told them. "I was reared on a farm. I know how to talk to countrymen."

"You've invented your story—that's good."

"When do I begin on the newspaper?"

"Tomorrow," said Hughes. "I'll take you to the place where we moved the press. You'll be able to work there."

"Do you have a copy of *The Pennsylvania Patriot*?"

"Not on the premises. It would be too dangerous to keep one here. British patrols are inclined to search houses that arouse their suspicion. In case that

71

should happen here, we have nothing that could be seen as evidence of our true convictions. Needless to say," he continued, "you'd not be advised to leave a copy in your room at the Black Horse."

"The King George," Proudfoot corrected him.

"I refuse to call it that, Mr. Allen. Among friends, anyway."

An hour in conversation with his hosts passed very pleasantly, then it was time for Proudfoot to leave. He had a last question to raise.

"How will you get copies of the *Patriot* to Valley Forge?"

"We have our couriers," said Hughes.

"General Washington wishes to see every issue."

"Then he shall—and so will all his officers."

"Only the officers?" said Proudfoot. "What about the men?"

"Many of them are illiterate, Mr. Allen. That's why your work is so important. You can speak to them in pictures. As for the officers," he went on, "they can read the *Patriot* to their men. That way, it reaches a much wider audience."

"I suppose it does."

"A sobering thought, is it not?" said Hughes, looking over the top of his spectacles. "When we win this war, the credit will not just go to educated officers who marshal their men in battle. It should also go to legions of courageous farm boys, who serve in the ranks but who can neither read nor write."

"They'll appreciate the prints of Ezekiel Proudfoot," said Miranda.

The visitor smiled. "I think that you mean Reece Allen."

They were in luck. None of them thought so when they were forced to spend the night on the fishing boat, huddled up together under a tarpaulin in wet clothing. Even the rough barracks on Prospect Hill were preferable to sleeping under the stars. Cabal Mears had tried to take them ashore, but he was hampered by the darkness, and when the bottom of the boat was scraped by a submerged rock, he decided that it was safer to drop anchor and bide his time. Snow continued to fall, but the wind had died down, and a tot of rum all round helped to keep out the cold. When dawn lifted the veil on a new day, they saw that they enjoyed some good fortune. Covered in a mantle of crisp, white snow was a long curve of coastline. Cabal Mears recognized it at once.

"Cape Cod Bay," said Mears. "This is what the Pilgrim Fathers first saw. We came further than I dared hope."

"Thanks to you, Cabal," Skoyles noted.

"You and the sergeant did your share of the work."

"Every time I eat a fish," Caffrey promised, "I'll think of people like Cabal Mears. You certainly earn your living the hard way."

"It's better than being shot at on a battlefield."

"I disagree. You can dodge musket balls. There's no escape from a storm." He looked up. "At least, it's stopped snowing."

"It's going to be a fine, dry day," said Mears, scanning the sky.

"Then we won't waste a minute of it," Skoyles announced. "Put us ashore and I'll pay you for your troubles. I expected you to be back home in your own bed last night, Cabal."

"So did my wife."

"Will she fret?"

"I doubt it," said the other easily. "We've been married a long time, so she's used to this kind of thing. Nancy knows that I'll get back to Cambridge sooner or later. Somehow, I always do."

"Did you tell her that you'd have passengers aboard?"

"No, Captain. Now, that *would* have worried her." He began to haul up the anchor. "You need to get ashore and find somewhere to dry off."

"Where would you suggest?"

"Barnstable."

"That's too far away," Caffrey argued. "Barnstaple is in Devon."

"I know, Tom," Polly added. "I was born there."

"When the Pilgrim Fathers came here," said Mears, yanking the rope, "they brought English names with them. Barnstaple changed to Barnstable, but it was so called after the town you mention. You'll find Truro, Chatham, Yarmouth, Sandwich, Rochester, and others here."

"We'll settle for Barnstable," said Skoyles, "however it's spelled."

Mears took command. The sail was hoisted to catch what little wind there was, and the fisherman took the tiller. Skoyles and Caffrey reached for the oars. Inspired by the sight of land and pleased with the relative calmness of the sea, they rowed with enthusiasm toward the distant harbor.

"We did it, Jamie," said Caffrey, grinning. "We escaped."

"There's a long way to go yet, Tom."

"Yes, but nothing could be as bad as being caught in that storm."

"Don't tempt Providence," warned Skoyles.

"What do you mean?"

"There could be worse to come."

The Indian name for the little port had been Cummaquid, but the settlers thought Barnstable more appropriate. A few isolated cabins had been built at first, and it was not until 1639 that the plantation had grown to a size where it could be officially recognized as a town. Barnstable had been founded by the Reverend Joseph Hull, minister and dairy farmer, drawn to the area by its salt-hay pastures. Covered in snow, some of the original timber houses were still there alongside later buildings. The Congregational church occupied a prime position.

It was still early, but people were already at work. As the bedraggled new-comers walked up the main street, they collected a lot of curious stares. Led by Skoyles, they trooped into the first tavern they found and were delighted to see a roaring fire in the grate. When they stood around it, steam began to rise from their wet clothing. The owner came bustling in, a stout, rosy-cheeked widow in her forties, wearing a plain dress with a white pinafore over it. Seeing the disheveled state they were in, she was immediately sympathetic.

"Oh dear!" she clucked. "Where have you been to get like that?"

"We were caught in a storm out at sea," said Skoyles.

"Poor things!"

"We were sailing to Dartmouth to visit friends but we were blown off course. After spending the night on board, we were put ashore here."

"You're a long way from Dartmouth, sir," she told him.

"No matter. We feel safer reaching it by land."

Skoyles had concealed their true destination from her. They were, in fact, making for Newport, Rhode Island, occupied by the British the previous year because, unlike New York, its harbor would not freeze over in the depths of winter. It was thus a much-needed all-weather naval base. Once they reached British territory, they could disclose their true identity and proceed on to New York to make contact with General Clinton. Fortunately, the woman accepted Skoyles's explanation without question. Her concern was for the two ladies.

"Leave the gentlemen here," she suggested. "Come with me and I'll take you somewhere even warmer. You can clean up a little and change into some dry clothes. And while you're doing that," she went on with a broad smile, "I'll make some breakfast for all four of you."

"Wonderful!" said Caffrey. "Thank you kindly."

"You toast yourself in front of that fire, sir."

"I will."

"Follow me, ladies."

She escorted Elizabeth and Polly into the adjoining room as if she had just decided to adopt them. The cordial welcome did much to help the men forget the exigencies of the voyage on the fishing boat. All that worried them now was how to reach their destination. Tom Caffrey held both hands out to the fire.

"It's a pity that Cabal Mears couldn't take us all the way, Jamie."

"He only agreed to get us well clear of Boston," said Skoyles. "To be honest, I never thought we'd sail this far with him."

"Do we have to walk from now on?"

"Unless we can find some other means, Tom."

"Which route do we take?"

Skoyles patted his pocket. "I've a rough map of the area that we can look at when we've thawed out. Otherwise, we take advice as we go. There'll be other taverns along the way. We just have to hope that everyone we meet believes our story."

"And if they don't?"

"Then we may have to leave certain places very rapidly," said Skoyles, turning around so that his back could feel the heat of the fire. "If anyone realizes that we've escaped from the Convention army, there could be serious trouble. And there'll be other dangers to contend with as well, remember."

"Wolves, bears, Indian tribes?"

"Put it this way, Tom, I think we'll be grateful that we're both armed. Before we set out, we must make sure that our powder is dry. And if anything should happen to separate us," he stressed, "make your way to Newport. We'll meet up again there."

Caffrey was dismayed. "Nothing is going to part us, surely?"

"You never know."

When the ladies rejoined them, they had had time to dry off and brush their tousled hair. After the night on the boat, they still looked weary, but they were much happier now.

"We've been talking to Hattie," said Elizabeth, glancing over her shoulder. "That's her name—Hattie Crocker. She's been running this tavern since her husband died, it seems. Anyway, she told us that the quickest way to get to Dartmouth is to go southwest to Falmouth and sail across from there."

"Not more time afloat!" groaned Caffrey.

"No," said Skoyles. "We'll stay on dry land. We'll head northwest and work our way around Buzzards Bay."

"Buzzards Bay—I don't like the sound of that!"

"After that, we follow the coast south until we reach Dartmouth."

Caffrey sighed. "If only it was the *real* Dartmouth."

"Yes," agreed Polly, "I'd give anything to be back home in Devon."

"You'll get there one day," said Skoyles.

"What about you? Aren't you dying to get back to England?"

He glanced at Elizabeth. "We have other plans, Polly."

Before Skoyles could enlarge on what those plans were, the door opened and Hattie Crocker came in, bearing a large wooden tray. On it were four bowls of hot broth and some hunks of bread.

"I thought you deserved something warm inside you," she said brightly, putting the tray down on a table. "Eat as much as you wish. There's plenty more in the kitchen. Here it is. Sit yourselves down and enjoy your breakfast."

They needed no more invitation.

An hour later, refreshed and restored, Skoyles searched the town until he found the one horse that was for sale. It was a bay mare, past her best years, but well able to carry the two women and the luggage. Skoyles also bought a sack of fodder. When they left Barnstable, they followed the track that took them in the direction of Buzzards Bay, some thirty miles or so away. With both women mounted and the men striding out purposefully, they were able to make good progress. The journey was uneventful at first, but Skoyles and Caffrey nevertheless preferred to carry their muskets. They were still in enemy territory.

Shortly after noon, they stopped beside a stream to rest the horse and eat some of the food they had brought with them. Polly Bragg took the opportunity to slip behind some bushes to answer a call of nature. Tom Caffrey went off to give the horse some of the hay. For the first time since they had made their escape bid, Skoyles and Elizabeth were alone.

"Why did you want me to carry most of the money?" she asked.

"Because you'll look after it."

"You could do that equally well, Jamie."

"No," he said. "If we are captured, I'll be searched and the money taken. A woman is less likely to be searched as thoroughly. Nobody will know just how much you have hidden away beneath your skirt."

"And how much is it?"

"You'll have to ask Major Featherstone."

Elizabeth grimaced. "I'd never do that!"

"Most of it came from him."

"He can afford to lose it. Harry comes from a wealthy family."

"He never let me forget that, Elizabeth."

"It's strange," she observed. "When I sailed from England, I was so determined to travel with him during a campaign, yet I can't even bear to think about him now. Harry belongs to another existence altogether."

"Are you happy with your new life?"

"Very happy. What about you?"

He kissed her. "There's no need to ask," he said. "Though I'll feel happier still when we get to Newport and see British uniforms again."

"How far will we go today?"

"As far as we can, Elizabeth."

The others rejoined them and they pressed on. Autumn had denuded some of the trees of their leaves and robbed the countryside of much of its color, but there was still a rustic beauty about the terrain. By midafternoon, they reached a village and bought fresh supplies. The others were content to linger, but Skoyles insisted that they move on. When they were well clear of the village, he explained why.

"I had a feeling that it was not safe to stay," he said.

"Why not?" asked Caffrey.

"Two women astride one horse, two men with muskets. We must present an odd sight, Tom. People were suspicious."

"They seemed friendly enough."

"They asked too many questions."

"At least, they told us where the next village is."

"Yes," said Skoyles, "but will we be allowed to reach it?"

At that moment, a shot rang out ahead of them. The horse shied and

Skoyles had to grab the bridle. Elizabeth and Polly were almost thrown to the ground. Disturbed by the report, a flock of geese took to the air and flew past them.

"Someone out hunting?" said Caffrey.

"Maybe, Tom. Then again, maybe not." Skoyles looked around. "Take cover while I go and see. Don't move from here."

"Would you like me to come with you?"

"No. Tether the horse and stay with the ladies. I'll not be long."

They were in a little clearing. The women dismounted and moved quickly to the shelter of a pine tree. Leading the horse, Caffrey followed them. Skoyles, meanwhile, checked that his musket was loaded, then went off at a steady lope. Sound was deceptive in woodland but he felt certain that the shot had been fired off to his right. When he left the track to go into the undergrowth, he kept low and moved more stealthily. His instincts had been sharpened by many scouting expeditions, and he sensed that somebody was nearby, somebody who now had plenty of time to reload his weapon. What he could not tell was whether the man was alone.

Time went slowly by. Ears pricked and eyes peeled, Skoyles crept deeper into the undergrowth. He was almost half a mile from his friends now and wondered if he should turn back. Then he heard the snap of a dry twig as someone trod on it. He ducked even lower. Inching forward, he kept his musket at the ready, his finger poised over the trigger. Something flashed across his path and startled him, but it was only a small animal of some sort. He waited several minutes before moving on again, choosing the trees with the largest girths as brief hiding places.

Eventually, he came to a clearing and paused, hardly daring to breathe. No hunter had fired the shot earlier. He was certain of that now. They were being stalked. Someone was deliberately leading him away from the others so that he was isolated. In spite of the cold, beads of sweat began to form on his brow. His lips went dry. Another twig snapped and it was much closer this time. It came from the other side of the clearing. Skoyles decided to draw the man's fire.

Stepping out in the open to offer a target, he suddenly dropped to the ground and lay flat on his stomach. The ruse worked. A musket was fired and the ball passed harmlessly over his head before embedding itself in a tree. The man had not only missed his target, he had given his position away. Skoyles had seen the weapon poking out at him. His own shot was more deadly, hitting the invisible enemy and causing him to fall backward with a grunt. Skoyles got to his feet, but before he could move, he heard another sound.

Footsteps were running away through the undergrowth. Having killed or wounded one man, he was still not safe. There were two of them.

CHAPTER SIX

The first thing that Skoyles did was to take cover again and reload. As an officer, he was entitled to carry a sword and a pistol, but he had never lost his skill with a Brown Bess musket. Stolen from the guard he had killed in Cambridge, it had been among the arms surrendered by the British at Saratoga. Skoyles was grateful to have a familiar weapon in his hands again. Though twelve separate actions were involved, including tearing off the end of the paper cartridge with his teeth, he was able to reload the flintlock musket in less than twenty seconds. Longer-barreled, muzzle-loading American flintlocks often needed the best part of a minute. It gave the British infantryman a distinct advantage. When Skoyles had served in the ranks, his ability to reload quickly in the heat of battle had saved his life several times.

He was not in combat now. Skoyles was up against a single enemy, a local man, in all probability, who knew the woodland far better than he did. The fellow had fled from the scene, but he might still try to ambush Skoyles. Before he went after him, however, it was important for Skoyles to find out what had happened to the man who had fired at him. If he had only been wounded, he might still pose a danger. Instead of crossing open ground and offering himself as a target again, Skoyles picked his way carefully around the clearing until he came upon an inert body. The man lay on his back, his mouth wide open in disbelief. Pierced through the eye, he had died instantly as the bullet went into his brain and straight out through the back of his skull. The empty eye socket was dribbling with blood.

Skoyles looked down at him. He could not be sure, but he fancied that it was one of the people they had met in the village, a hefty man with a beard, who had been chopping firewood when they asked for directions. To get ahead of them, he and his companion must have ridden horses. That thought spurred Skoyles on. If the second man were allowed to return to his mount, he could reach Tom Caffrey and the two women long before Skoyles could. He had to be caught quickly. Keeping low, Skoyles trotted after him, following a path that had been trampled by the other man. There were no more sounds of reckless flight. His quarry had gone to ground somewhere.

Slowing to a walk, Skoyles picked a way through the trees. He was quietly confident, unafraid of someone who had fled in panic without even trying to avenge the death of his confederate. That argued youth or inexperience. It might even be that the second man was unarmed. Skoyles took no chances. If the man had simply lost his nerve, he would have had time to regain his composure now. Safe in a hiding place, all that he had to do was to wait until his target got close enough.

Skoyles knew that he was there somewhere, and he kept his musket at the ready, using its barrel to move bushes gently aside so that he could peer around them. The woodland was thinning out now and cover was not so easy to find. Skoyles had to hide behind one trunk before making a run for the next temporary refuge. He sensed that he was getting close, but he could still see no sign of the man. Nor could he spot any more telltale footprints in the snow. Skoyles soon realized why. As he darted on toward another tree, a shot rang out behind him and a musket ball grazed his arm. Though he felt no pain, he pitched forward onto the ground as if he had been badly wounded, and lay prostrate for a moment.

Skoyles heard a whoop of triumph, followed by the sound of running feet. He rolled over and sat up in time to see someone sprinting toward him with a musket in one hand and a knife in the other, clearly intent on finishing his victim off. Delay would have been fatal. Skoyles took immediate aim and fired, hitting him in the chest from a range of ten yards, making him drop the musket as he staggered forward. One hand clutching his wound, the attacker came on, barely able to stand, still brandishing the knife. Skoyles saw that he was a mere boy, no more than thirteen or fourteen years old. Blood was soaking through his coat and tears were streaming down his face.

"You killed my father!" he cried.

He made a desperate lunge with his knife, but Skoyles dived swiftly out of the way and the blade sank into the ground. On his feet in an instant, Skoyles turned him onto his back to see how bad the wound was. The boy's eyes were already glazing over. He was still trying to mouth obscenities at Skoyles as his life ebbed away. Skoyles was sad to have been forced to kill someone so young, but he had been given no choice. Dragging the body to a hollow, he covered it with branches and dead leaves to give it a semblance of burial.

The musket ball had inflicted a small flesh wound on his arm, but the blood was hardly staining his coat. Skoyles decided that he would take the precaution of letting Tom Caffrey inspect it when he got back to the others. There was no point in traveling with a surgeon if he did not make use of him. Skoyles looked around to get his bearings. Something then dawned on him with the force of a blow.

He was completely lost.

The printing press was hidden away in the cellar of a house in Walnut Street, and Ezekiel Proudfoot wondered how they could have transported such a heavy piece of equipment there without being seen. Adam Quenby, the printer, treated his press as if it were a household pet that had to be cosseted, and he was forever cleaning it and making minor adjustments. Quenby was a short, skinny man in his early forties with a face like a diseased potato. Unprepossessing though his appearance was, the printer was a master at his trade and Proudfoot admired examples of his work. The copies of *The Pennsylvania Patriot* that the newcomer was shown were clear, legible, and well written.

"We need more illustrations," Quenby admitted.

"That's why I was sent here."

"Our troops must be rallied somehow."

"I have a few ideas of how we might do that," said Proudfoot.

"Be sure to discuss them with Mr. Hughes first," the other warned. "Nothing goes into the *Patriot* until the editor approves of it."

"He made certain I understood that."

"Not that I criticize him, mark you. He does a fine job. It's a privilege to work with such an educated man. But he can be sharp in his judgments," he explained. "More than one person has submitted ideas and had them thrown back in his face. Mr. Hughes does not suffer fools gladly—not that I regard you as a fool, of course," he added hastily.

"Thank you, Mr. Quenby."

"It's an honor to have Ezekiel Proudfoot here."

"Forget that name. He does not exist in Philadelphia. It's Reece Allen who will be helping to produce the *Patriot.*"

"Of course, Mr. Allen." He glanced around disconsolately. "I just wish that we could offer you better conditions in which to work. The light is poor, the place is damp, and it can get infernally cold."

"I make no complaint," said Proudfoot. "This is a paradise to what our soldiers will endure at Valley Forge. According to Mr. Hughes, they will be exposed to the very worst of the winter."

"That, alas, is true."

"There are bound to be many desertions."

"It will certainly test the army's loyalty—and that of Congress."

"You cannot doubt the commitment of Congress, surely?"

"No," replied Quenby, rubbing the press with an old rag. "They are as dedicated to the aim of independence as ever, but I would question their loyalty to General Washington."

"I'm afraid that you have good reason to do so."

"To retain such a large army at Valley Forge will be a difficult undertaking. Our commander needs to feed, clothe, house, and keep them warm. Let's hope that Congress votes him the necessary funds."

"Can we not speak up on his behalf in the *Patriot?*"

"Pearsall Hughes will be certain to do that."

A day spent with the printer had been instructive for Proudfoot. With meager resources, and in constant danger of arrest, Adam Quenby was determined to make his contribution to the rebel cause. His wife and family had fled the city, and his house had been taken over by British officers. All that he had left was his press and his professional pride, but they were enough to sustain him. His visitor rose to leave.

"I'll see you again tomorrow, Mr. Quenby."

"We'll be here," said the other, patting his beloved press.

Proudfoot was surprised. "You *sleep* down here?"

"Where else, Mr. Allen? I no longer have a house."

"Could you not stay with friends, or at a tavern like me?"

"And leave my press unguarded?" asked Quenby. "Never."

The notion of the little man protecting the press against a British patrol was ludicrous, but Proudfoot made no comment. He bade his new friend farewell and let himself out into the fading light of late afternoon. When he returned to the King George Tavern, the first thing that greeted him was a song that grated on his ears, less for the raucous voices of the singers than for its boastful sentiments.

Britannia's good genius appear,
Appear from your green, briny bed.
In your hand freedom's scepter you bear,
And commerce encircles your head;
Your harbinger, terror, send out,
To your side conquest buckles his sword;
Hark the Fleet fills the air with a shout:
Ohio! Ohio's the word.

Half a dozen young British officers were enjoying a drink and raising their voices in celebration. As they launched into the next verse, Proudfoot walked past them and went up the staircase to his room. He met a scowling Henry Gilby on the landing.

"Listen to them!" said the landlord. "Crowing like cockerels."

"It must be an old song if it talks about the Ohio Valley," noted Proudfoot. "That issue was resolved in the French and Indian War."

"They are still bragging about their victory, Mr. Allen."

"What has put that into their minds?"

"The play."

"Which play?"

"The one they performed last night," said Gilby. "I think it was called *The Kept Mistress*. This song is taken from the play because it obviously caught their imagination." He sucked in air through his teeth. "I'm sorry that you have to hear such hateful words."

"On the contrary, Mr. Gilby, I'm rather glad."

"Glad?"

"Yes," said Proudfoot thoughtfully. "It's caught my imagination as well. I'd be interested to see a copy of this song."

"Why?"

"The words may repay study."

"I fail to see how, Mr. Allen."

84

"The Kept Mistress, you say? Perhaps it was dedicated to Mrs. Loring."
Gilby gave a mirthless laugh.

Jamie Skoyles was worried. He had not realized how far he had come from the track where he left Tom Caffrey and the two women. He had to find them soon. An overcast sky was starting to squeeze the last bit of light out of the day. He did not wish to be caught in the woodland in the dark. Once more, however, he took the precaution of loading his musket before moving. A dusting of snow covered the ground, and he was able to make out a trail of footprints at first, but they vanished when the trees thickened because the snow had been unable to penetrate the branches. Relying on guesswork, he broke into a run, weaving a way through the undergrowth with more hope than confidence. At one point, he had the distinct feeling that he was going in a wide circle.

When he reached a clearing, he thought that it looked familiar and charged across it, only to come upon the dead body of the first man he had shot. That meant he was going in the wrong direction. Turning around, he retraced his steps and tried to find the route that he had taken when he first left the main track. The darker it got, the more confusing everything seemed. He increased his speed, then tripped over some roots that had pushed up through the earth. Skoyles fell heavily and bruised himself on the hard ground. Hauling himself up, he moved on with more circumspection.

His mind was racing. In killing a father and son, he had solved an immediate problem but, in doing so, had created others. Since they came from the village, they would be missed and, in time, someone would come out looking for them. It was vital for Skoyles and his party to get as far away as possible, but they could not do that until they were reunited. He was now panting for breath and blundering about in the half-dark. Skoyles paused for a brief rest and wondered if he should risk yelling out to his friends. It then occurred to him that the two men who had tried to waylay him might not have been on their own. They might have brought someone with them. He was still pondering when he heard a distant cry of pain, a yell of agony that made the hairs on the back of his neck stand up. It had sounded like a man's voice. He was afraid that it might have belonged to Tom Caffrey.

At least, he had a rough idea of the direction in which to go. The cry had come from well over to his left, so he changed the angle of his walk and strode

85

on. In the denser part of the woodland, light had all but disappeared, and Skoyles had to feel his way gingerly forward. Questions buzzed in his brain like a swarm of insects. Who had yelled out and why had he done so? What had happened to his friends? How far away were they, and in what state would he find them? Why had the men from the village followed them in the first place? Skoyles was utterly bewildered.

Where *was* he?

Alert to every tiny sound, he trudged on with growing disquiet. Of all his many anxieties, the greatest was that some harm had befallen Elizabeth Rainham. In agreeing to let her escape with him, he had taken on a huge responsibility, yet he could hardly have left her in Cambridge. Apart from anything else, she would have been vulnerable to the attentions of Major Featherstone. He and Elizabeth were pledged to each other. Skoyles had simply had to rescue her, but, in doing so, he had given himself an additional problem. Elizabeth, like Polly Bragg, was not able to defend herself properly. Instead of devoting all their energies to their own escape, Skoyles and Caffrey had to act as protectors of the two women. It was a severe handicap.

Skoyles felt an upsurge of guilt. Should he have left the others and plunged off into the wood? Was he exposing them to attack by doing so? Had the two men he killed simply been acting as decoys to get him away from the others so that they could be more easily overpowered? It was a thought that preyed on his conscience as he groped his way along. Having survived the storm in the Atlantic, had they now foundered on land? Were the others now captives? If that were the case, he had failed them badly. His remorse deepened.

Desperate to hurry, he was compelled to take his time, using the barrel of his musket yet again to push back any bushes that got in his way. Eventually, he stumbled out onto what seemed to be the track that he and the others had been traveling along. Skoyles was in a dilemma. Which way should he go? Was he behind or ahead of them? Taking a chance, he swung right, but he soon realized his mistake when he encountered a large boulder beside the track. He had certainly not passed it before. That meant the others must be behind him, in the direction of the village.

Finding himself on a wide track, albeit covered in a thin layer of snow, he was able to jog along at a steady pace. He had left the others beside a pine tree in a clearing. In the darkness, however, every clearing looked the same. He wondered how he would find the one where they were waiting—if, indeed, that was what they actually were doing. They might have been apprehended and spirited away elsewhere. Or they might even have gone looking for him. Skoyles had been away from them for some time, and they would have heard the four shots in the woodland. If they believed he had been killed, the most natural thing would have been to search for his body. Is that what they had done?

He had gone almost a quarter of a mile when he came to another clearing with a stand of pine trees around it. Skoyles was certain that this was the place. They had come up a gradient to reach that point and he could just make out the hill, starting to go downward. Yet there was nobody about. If they were nearby, they must have heard his approach. Skoyles cupped his hands to his mouth.

"Tom!" he called. "Are you there?"

His voice rang out, but there was no reply. He shouted louder.

"Elizabeth! Polly! Where are you?"

There was still no response. He walked across the clearing to the far side and stared into the gloom. Among the trees, it was almost pitch dark. He went a few more yards, then accepted that it was a hopeless exercise. His friends would never be found in the black interior of the woodland. Skoyles was about to return to the clearing when his foot touched something solid. It jerked along the ground. He was so startled that he backed away and raised his musket, thinking it might be a snake or a small animal of some sort. When he bent down and looked more closely, however, he was given another shock. Protruding from the bushes was a pair of feet.

Valley Forge lay at the junction of the Schuylkill River and Valley Creek, over twenty miles northwest of Philadelphia. It was a tiny farming community, consisting of a few houses and a forge that the British army had wrecked two months earlier. George Washington, commander in chief of the Continental Army, had chosen the two-mile-long site because it was protected by the creek itself and by a peak called Mount Joy. The sloping hill was also selected because it was thickly wooded, thus providing the timber with which the troops began to build their log town.

Even in the gloom of early evening, axes could still be heard at work. Washington strolled along between the rows of cabins that were beginning to grow up in serried ranks. His companion, Major John Clark Jr., was not sanguine about the operation.

"We have nothing like the number of axes and saws needed," he said. "We'll never be able to accommodate twelve thousand men."

"We must, Major. I want them under cover before the first snow."

"Then we need Congress to supply better equipment."

"I write to them daily," said Washington wearily, "but in vain. Frankly, I am less worried about housing the men than about feeding them. The British camped here first and plundered much of the stock in the surrounding area."

"Then we'll have to search further afield."

"Even then, our needs are not answered. Farmers would prefer to sell their produce in Philadelphia, where they can get paid in coin. All that we can offer them is printed money, and they distrust it completely."

"They should be *forced* to sell to us," argued Clark. "If they supply the British, they are conspiring with the enemy."

Washington nodded. He broke off to watch two men lifting another length of timber into place on their future home. Divided into groups of twelve, the soldiers were building cabins to an identical specification. They had to be sixteen feet long, fourteen feet wide, and have walls that were six and a half feet high. Three bunks, one above the other, were to be built in each corner. Roofs were made of saplings covered with earth and straw. Doors were constructed from split slabs, and windows were made of whatever could be found. Gaps between the logs were daubed with handfuls of clay.

Major Clark was impressed with the men's readiness to work on by the light of fires. He was a handsome man with a suppressed energy about him. A former aide to General Nathanael Greene, he had been chosen as the army's head of intelligence, having already gained valuable experience of espionage in the New Jersey campaign. Washington was convinced that he had made a good appointment.

"It was a clever idea to offer rewards for the best cabins," said Clark. "Competition always makes men work harder."

"True, Major. It also helps them take a pride in their work. Some of the cabins will even have a stone chimney."

"If only the British had not destroyed the sawmill."

"You can hardly expect them to help us."

"They've made things so difficult for our army."

"Then you must make things difficult for them, Major," Washington told him. "War does not stop in wintertime. It continues by other means. We need to mislead and perplex the enemy."

"I've already set plans in motion to do that."

"Do you have enough men in Philadelphia?"

"Yes, General," replied Clark. "And women, of course. Never let us forget that it was Lydia Darragh who warned us about the British attack at White-marsh. We owe a huge debt to Mrs. Darragh. And the beauty of it is that the British would never suspect her of being a spy because she is a devout Quaker. The Friends are supposed to refrain from war."

"Mrs. Darragh is an exception to the rule," observed Washington, drily, "and so is her son. Lieutenant Charles Darragh has given us good service. Be sure to tell her that when you next visit Philadelphia."

"I will, General."

"And pay a call on someone I have just planted in the city."

"Who might that be?"

"Ezekiel Proudfoot."

"The silversmith?"

"Yes, Major," said Washington. "He's a sound man. I have every expectation that he will turn out to be one of our most potent weapons."

Working by candlelight, Ezekiel Proudfoot was hunched over the table in the room at the King George Tavern. He had drawn several versions of the cartoon before he completed one that satisfied him. Proudfoot sat back to study it. Then he reached for the piece of paper on which he had written the words of the song he had heard earlier. Choosing one part of the refrain, he added it to his sketch by way of a caption.

His initial fear was unfounded. The dead man was not Tom Caffrey. When he pulled the corpse out of the bushes, Jamie Skoyles felt a gush of relief coursing through him. The man was a stranger, lying on his back after being stabbed through the heart. Blood made his coat sticky to the touch and Skoyles had to wipe his fingers clean in the grass. Whoever had killed him had not taken the man's musket. Still loaded, it lay in the bushes beside him.

Skoyles decided to get away from the place at once. After taking the opportunity of stealing the man's powder and ammunition, he set off back up the track. There was no telling if Caffrey and the others were in any way involved in the man's death, but one thing was certain. They would not have headed back toward the village they had passed earlier. They would have pressed on in the opposite direction.

Breaking into a trot again, Skoyles hoped that no more than three men had come in pursuit of them. He was sure that the earlier trio had been working together, and that he had been deliberately lured away from his friends. Since two of the men had tried to kill him in the wood, it was obvious that they were not there to capture what they thought were fugitives from the British army. They were common thieves, bent on shooting their prey before taking their horse and their valuables. It was an open question as to whether the women would have been spared.

Time was impossible to calculate accurately, but Skoyles reckoned that it was at least half an hour since he left the others in the clearing, perhaps even longer. They could be anywhere. He could not believe that they would have deserted him without a very good reason. All that he could do was to keep going forward in the hope that he would eventually catch up with them, assuming that they had actually continued along the track. Had they struck off at some point, then there was absolutely no possibility of finding them in the dark.

There was one small bonus. Apart from his musket, he had nothing else to carry. Unencumbered by a knapsack or any luggage, he could maintain a reasonable pace. It was getting colder. A stiff breeze started to blow in his face. Every so often, he would stop, listen intently, then call out. The only answer he ever got was the muffled cry of an animal. It served to remind him how dangerous it was to stay out after dark. The woods were full of predatory creatures.

Skoyles refused to believe that his friends had been killed. No shots had been fired apart from those exchanged with his two victims. The stabbed man in the clearing could hardly have accounted for the death of three people when he had not even discharged his musket. They had to be ahead of Skoyles somewhere. It was only a question catching up with them. After a mile or more, his hopes began to fade. Tom Caffrey and the two women seemed to have disappeared completely. Coming to a halt, Skoyles tried a last, desperate shout, but it did not reach the ears of his friends. He began to lose heart.

Before he could set off again, however, he heard a distant sound. It took him a few moments to make out what it was. A horse was coming toward him, moving at a brisk trot along the track. Skoyles wondered if it belonged to a confederate of the other men. If that was the case, the rider had to be waylaid and questioned. He might know what had happened to Skoyles's friends. As the clip-clop of the hooves came closer, Skoyles bided his time, choosing a point where the track narrowed and concealing himself behind a tree.

When the rider got close enough, Skoyles leapt out from his hiding place and pointed his musket, barking an order at the same time.

"Stop there—or I'll shoot!"

The horse was brought to an abrupt halt and slithered in the snow.

"Put that bloody thing down, Jamie!" said a voice. "It's me."

Sergeant Tom Caffrey let out a peal of laughter.

"It's good," he said, scrutinizing it. "It's very good, Mr. Allen. Thank you."

"Will you be able to use it?"

"Naturally."

"Then I'll do an engraving of it," said Proudfoot, looking over his shoulder at the drawing. "I'm not sure how accurate a portrait it is of General Howe because I've never actually seen him, but I've tried to make it clear who the man in bed with Mrs. Loring is."

"Well, it's certainly not her husband, I can vouch for that."

They were in the bookshop and Pearsall Hughes was taking a first look at the cartoon that Ezekiel Proudfoot had drawn. It showed a bloated British general, still in uniform, caressing a half-naked woman of ample dimensions, who had a hand down the front of his breeches. In the balloon that sprouted from his mouth were the words "In your hand freedom's scepter you bear, Mrs. Loring." Around the bed was a series of British soldiers, gambling, drinking, brawling, or molesting women, a scene of corruption that would have been revolting had it not been so comically drawn. The caption was below: *Conquest buckles his sword.*

"It's not something I'd care to show to one of my daughters," Hughes admitted, "but it will give our soldiers something to smile about."

"That was my intention," said Proudfoot.

"It will also make them more determined to regain their city. When they see what the British are doing to Philadelphia, they will want to march down here in the spring and chase every last redcoat out."

"Might they not go of their own accord, Mr. Hughes?"

"What do you mean?"

"Occupying the city was a severe blow to our pride," Proudfoot commented, "but it has no real strategic value to the British. As long as they remain here, they weaken their hold on New York."

"Is that what General Washington says?"

"He's counting on the fact. Even the British army does not have infinite resources. The further they are stretched, the more weak points will begin to appear."

"You are quite the military man, Mr. Allen," said Hughes, removing his spectacles to clean them with a handkerchief. "That time you spent on the field of battle was clearly not wasted."

"I take the same view as General Washington."

"And what is that?"

"The credit for our victory at Saratoga must not go entirely to the Continental Army and the militia. General Howe should not be forgotten."

"But he was not even there."

"Exactly," said Proudfoot. "He was too busy pursuing an adventure here, and fighting the battle of Brandywine. Had he kept his army in New York, he could have sent a sizable force up the Hudson Valley to meet with General Burgoyne at Albany." He brought both palms slowly together. "We'd have been squeezed flat between them. I raise my hat to General Howe. Thanks to his folly, we triumphed in the field."

"Otherwise, you'd be languishing in a British jail somewhere."

"Oh, I think they'd have strung me up from the nearest tree."

Hughes held up the cartoon. "They'll certainly want to do that when they see this," he said, chuckling. "I'll make sure that a copy of the *Patriot* is delivered to General Howe so that he can admire your work." He handed the drawing back. "What gave you the idea in the first place?"

"*The Kept Mistress.*"

"Who?"

"It's the title of a play that was performed here last night, apparently.

92

When I got back to the tavern, I heard some of the officers singing a song from the piece."

"And you memorized the lines?"

"No," explained Proudfoot. "When I realized that I could make use of the words, I went downstairs and joined the officers for a drink. They were only too ready to help me learn the song, and thought me a splendid fellow for appreciating it."

"I did tell you to ingratiate yourself with them."

"And that's what I did, Mr. Hughes. In point of fact, the song trumpets the virtues of the British navy, but the lines I took from it serve my purpose admirably."

"Hurrah for *The Kept Mistress*!"

"What's all this about a mistress?" asked Miranda Hughes as she tripped into the room. "Oh, good evening, Mr. Allen. So nice to see you again. I hope that you are not leading my husband astray."

"*The Kept Mistress* is a play, Mrs. Hughes," said Proudfoot.

"A low farce, my dear," added Hughes. "It was staged here last night. England has produced dramatists such as Shakespeare, Marlowe, and Ben Jonson, geniuses whose talent will thunder down the ages. Yet what does the British army prefer to offer its soldiers—theatrical dross!"

"Next week they have a comedy called *Polly Honeycombe*."

"Why not a famous tragedy such as *Hamlet* or *Macbeth*?"

"I can answer that, Pearsall," his wife interjected. "It's because we've had enough tragedy from the other side of the Atlantic as it is."

"Well said, my dear."

"But why were you talking about plays at all?"

"That was my doing, Mrs. Hughes," said Proudfoot, holding up his cartoon. "A song from *The Kept Mistress* helped to inspire me."

"Really? Oh, do let me see."

"Perhaps not," said Hughes, stepping between them. "It's a trifle indelicate, my dear. It verges on the indecent."

"Out of the way, Pearsall. I can make up my own mind what's decent or not." She extended a hand. "May I, Mr. Allen?"

"Of course," replied Proudfoot.

Ignoring the warning glance from the bookseller, he passed the drawing over to her. Miranda Hughes moved it closer to the candelabrum so that she could see it more clearly.

"My goodness!" she exclaimed with mild outrage.

But the smile stayed on her lips for several minutes.

Jamie Skoyles was so overjoyed to see that Elizabeth Rainham was safe that he hugged her for a long time. It was only when he finally broke away that he became aware of Polly Bragg's presence. Kissing her on the cheek, he embraced her warmly. The four of them were in an abandoned cabin a few miles along the track from the point where Skoyles had met up with Tom Caffrey again.

"When we heard those other shots," Caffrey explained, "we were very worried. I decided to come looking for you."

Skoyles frowned. "You left the two ladies alone?"

"As it happened, that turned out to be the wisest course of action. Not long after I'd gone, someone rode up and held a musket on them."

"It was frightening," Polly recalled.

"He demanded any money and jewelry we had," said Elizabeth. "He also told us that we could expect no help because he had two friends who would take care of both of you."

"That proves they were from the village," Skoyles remarked. "They saw the four of us traveling together—rich pickings."

"Luckily," Caffrey resumed, "I got horribly lost. The next thing I know, I heard voices not far away and recognized one as Polly's. I must have worked my way back to them somehow. Anyway, it didn't take me long to realize what was happening, so I crept up slowly on them."

"You had a musket, Tom. Why didn't you shoot the man?"

"Because I was afraid that I might have hit someone else."

"So you stabbed him instead."

"It was gruesome," said Polly, a hand to her throat. "He let out this terrible cry as he went down. I'll never forget that sound."

"I heard it myself," said Skoyles. "I thought it might be Tom."

Caffrey grinned. "I've got a few more years in me yet, Jamie. Anyway, I felt it was important to get the ladies to a place of safety, so we took the man's horse and came here." He looked up at the gaping hole in the roof. "It was not the ideal place, but it was better than standing among the trees and waiting for another of those robbers to turn up. Once we got here, I rode back in search of you."

"Thank heaven we found each other!"

"You gave me a scare, Jamie—standing there like Dick Turpin."

"I had no idea who was coming out of the dark at me," said Skoyles, "and I had to make sure he stopped. It could easily have been a friend of those other men."

"They won't be bothering us again," said Caffrey bluntly. "And one of them was kind enough to give us his horse. From now on, we can move much faster."

"And that's what we have to do, Tom. Those men were from that village we came through. When they don't return tonight, someone will come out searching for them. We don't want to be caught here with a stolen horse."

"No," agreed Elizabeth, remembering their earlier failed attempt at escape. "They hang horse thieves without even giving them a trial."

"Nobody will search until daylight, surely?" Caffrey argued.

"Probably not," said Skoyles, "but we can't stay here in any case. This place is falling to pieces. We need to ride on until we can find another village. There may be a tavern where we can stay."

"Polly can ride behind me."

"Then Elizabeth and I will take the other horse."

"Tom and I should have the one we bought in Barnstable," said Polly. "It will remind us of Devon, won't it, Tom?"

"You're the only reminder of Devon I want, my love."

She laughed. "Get away with you!"

"It's that whiff of cider you always bring."

There was a dull ache in Skoyles's arm where it had been grazed by the musket ball, but this was neither the time nor place for him to ask for medical attention. That could come later. For the time being, he could willingly stand the discomfort.

"Let's be on our way," he declared. "We'll feel a lot happier when we're a long way from here. Are you all ready?"

"Yes," said Elizabeth. "Especially if we're riding that stolen horse. I keep thinking of that man they hanged in Cambridge."

"I can't get the one that Tom stabbed out of my mind," Polly confessed with a grimace. "That look on his face when the knife went in will haunt me forever."

"Not when I'm around," said Caffrey jauntily. "Mount up, my love."

Sharing the bundles between the two horses, they rode off along the track. Skoyles led the way, with Elizabeth clinging to his waist. At a steady canter, they soon began to eat up the miles, but there was no sign of any village or even of a farm. Buzzards Bay could not be too far ahead. They were all hoping to reach it soon when Skoyles tugged on the reins and brought the horse to a sudden halt. Tom Caffrey did likewise with his mount.

"What's up, Jamie?" he asked.

"Listen."

"I don't hear a thing."

"Well, I do," said Skoyles. "Listen more carefully."

Caffrey strained his ears and the women followed suit. The three of them soon heard the sound. It was the faraway drumming of many hooves, beating out a menacing rhythm somewhere behind them. Riders were heading their way. Skoyles was alarmed. Since their horses were slowed down by having to carry two people each, there was no hope at all of outrunning pursuit. He made a decision at once.

"Take cover!" he ordered. "They may be coming after us!"

CHAPTER SEVEN

Dismounting quickly, they led their horses off the track and into the cover of the trees. They did not have long to wait. A dozen riders soon appeared, dark phantoms that came out of the gloom for an instant only to be swallowed up by it again. It was an eerie sensation and it left them slightly jangled. Jamie Skoyles waited until the thunder of hooves began to die away.

"Militia," he decided.

"How can you tell?" asked Tom Caffrey.

"By the way they rode—one man in the front, the others in pairs."

"They could have been Continentals."

"I doubt it, Tom. The Northern Department prefers to keep its troops together in chosen locations. A dozen full-time soldiers would not be released to patrol this part of Massachusetts. My guess is that those men were part of a local militia."

"Were they after us, Jamie?" asked Elizabeth Rainham.

"I hope not."

"They would have come through that village where we stopped."

"That's true," said Skoyles, "and if they asked people whether they had seen anything suspicious, I'm sure that we'd have been mentioned. But they were definitely not searching for us because of what happened back in the woods. Those three dead bodies will not be discovered until morning at the earliest."

"So what do we do?" Polly Bragg wondered.

"We obviously can't go back," Skoyles replied, "and going forward will not be as easy as we thought. I've no wish to meet up with those riders in the next village."

"Where will we spend the night?"

"We'll find somewhere, Polly."

"I've been wondering if we should split up," said Caffrey.

Skoyles was taken aback. "Are you serious, Tom?"

"Two people attract less attention than four, and Polly and I would stand more chance of finding a room for the night on our own. So would you and Elizabeth."

"I take your point, Tom. But two people on one horse will always get us noticed, whether we travel in pairs or all together."

"We can explain that away."

"Can we?"

"Yes," said Caffrey airily. "We simply claim that we had a second horse, but that it had to be put down when it was injured in a fall."

"Both of us would not get away with the same excuse."

"That's why it might be better for us to travel separately."

"But Jamie has the only map of the area," said Polly.

"We'll get by. I've got a good sense of direction."

Polly nodded her assent. "What do you think, Elizabeth?"

"To be honest, I'm not sure," said the other woman.

"Four of us are bound to be noticed more easily."

"But it does feel safer if we travel together."

"I agree," said Skoyles. "Look at what happened earlier on. If we'd been coming along that track in pairs, those men could have picked us off at will. On the other hand," he went on, thinking it through, "if a posse is sent out after us tomorrow, they'll be looking for four people."

"That's why I believe we should split up," argued Caffrey. "I reckon we'd have a much better chance of dodging them."

"Possibly."

"We would, Jamie. And it would also ease my conscience."

"What do you mean?"

Caffrey hesitated and shot a glance at Polly before speaking. "Well, I do feel that we're imposing on you," he said.

"That's nonsense!" retorted Skoyles.

"No, it's not. All that you really wanted to do was to escape from Cambridge with Elizabeth. Then we barge in."

"We were delighted to have you with us, Tom."

"Yes," said Elizabeth with enthusiasm. "You were so helpful. We could never have managed without you in that fishing boat. You and Jamie rowed us through the storm."

"We're back on land now," Caffrey pointed out, "and the situation has changed. You got us this far, Jamie, and we're very grateful. But if we make our own way from now on, I'll feel less guilty."

"So will I," added Polly.

Skoyles gave a shrug. "Well, if that's the way you both feel."

"It is, Jamie. I agree with Tom."

"At least, sleep on the decision."

"If you wish."

"Yes," said Caffrey. "If we can find somewhere to lay our heads tonight, that is. Staying here is asking for trouble. There'll be wolves on the prowl before long."

"Then let's move on," resolved Skoyles, putting his foot in the stirrup. "Those men will be far ahead of us by now." He hauled himself into the saddle, then offered a hand to Elizabeth. "We'll stay together for the time being, then discuss this again in the morning."

George Washington had spent his first few days in a marquee, but he had now moved his headquarters to a little stone-built house, owned by Isaac Potts, situated near the junction of Valley Creek and the river. It was there that he was busy writing letters when Major Clark called on him that evening. The visitor was touched to see his commander working in such modest surroundings. Washington was a wealthy man who lived in a palatial house on his Virginia plantation, and who believed, in his own words, that farming was the most delectable of pursuits. Instead of being able to indulge his passion for hunting, shooting, and fishing, he was forced to share the deprivations of the Continental Army.

Clark stepped into the room and Washington looked up.

"News already, Major?"

"Yes, General."

"But we only spoke a couple of hours ago," said Washington.

"These tidings will not keep, especially as they come from someone whose name we mentioned earlier."

"Mrs. Darragh?"

"The very same," confirmed Clark, taking some tiny pieces of paper from his pocket. "Her younger son brought these and handed them over to his brother. Lieutenant Darragh gave them straight to me."

"What do they portend?"

"Place them in the right order, sir, and you will see."

He laid the pieces of paper out on the table and Washington examined them by the light of the candle. Leaning over his shoulder, Clark translated the neat shorthand messages for him. Washington's interest was sparked off at once.

"So General Howe is to send out a foraging expedition, is he?"

"With almost half their total men," said Clark.

"If our estimates are correct, that would put the number of those in the party around five thousand—too many for us to do more than harass them. They hold the advantage, Major," he conceded. "Their men are healthy and well fed while ours are sick and hungry. I'm told that almost two thousand of our soldiers are unfit for duty. They are either ill, wounded, or lacking shoes in which to walk. We are fighting this war with scarecrows."

"Even scarecrows can give the foraging expedition a fright."

"And I'll make sure that they do so." He looked down at the pieces of paper. "How is Mrs. Darragh's intelligence always so accurate?"

"Her house in Second Street is virtually opposite General Howe's headquarters. Lydia Darragh sees all their comings and goings. But she also has British officers lodging in her house," said Clark. "That was how she overheard the plan to surprise us at Whitemarsh."

"Forewarned is forearmed."

"Indeed, sir."

"You say that her younger son brought this message?"

"Yes, General, and by an ingenious means. It's one that I would never have fathomed. The boy has mold buttons on his coat."

"Nothing unusual in that."

"There is in this instance," explained Clark. "The buttons are covered with cloth, and these pieces of paper are hidden beneath them. All that the lad has to do is to cut off the buttons and hand them over to his elder brother. If stopped, he runs no risk of discovery by the British."

"But he puts his mother to some trouble," observed Washington. "Every time she sends intelligence by that means, she has to sew on a fresh set of buttons."

"Mrs. Darragh is an accomplished seamstress by now."

"Then we could certainly use her services here, Major—and that of a hundred good ladies like her. There's enough sewing and darning to keep them all busy. Some of our men are dressed in rags."

"I know. It's a pitiful sight."

"We have eighteen brigades of infantry, a brigade of artillery, and a brigade of artificers. Not one of them has enough uniforms to wear," said Washington, "let alone enough arms and ammunition. When you look at the brigade of local militia and the three regiments of dragoons, then the situation is even worse. We've men with nothing but a blanket to wrap around them."

"And we know who's to blame for that," said Clark with vehemence. "The very people who should help us—Congress."

"They've neglected us badly."

"Shamefully, sir."

"However," the commander went on with a tired smile, "there is one thing from which I gain satisfaction."

"What's that, General?"

"Our army is drawn from eleven of the thirteen colonies. The only exceptions are South Carolina and Georgia, though we do have a few officers from both. In short," said Washington, "we are facing the British with a truly *American* army. I take pride in that."

"So do I, sir."

"As for this intelligence, thank you for bringing it so promptly."

"It's not the only news I have to deliver, alas."

"Oh?"

"It seems that Mother Nature is against us as well."

"Mother Nature?"

"I fear so," said Clark. "As I was walking toward the house, I am sure that I felt the first few flakes of snow."

The men spent the night in a barn, curled up on hay and trying to block out the lowing of the cows nearby and of the distant howling of wolves. Alerted by the approach of dawn, Jamie Skoyles was the first to wake up. He nudged his companion with an elbow. Tom Caffrey sat up at once, reaching out instinctively for the loaded musket that lay beside him.

"No need for alarm," said Skoyles, pushing the weapon aside. "I just wanted to be on the road as early as possible."

"So do I, Jamie."

"Did you get any sleep?"

"A little. I missed Polly too much to sleep for long."

"She and Elizabeth were far better off in the farmhouse. Since the farmer only had one room to offer, we had to make do with the barn."

"That proves my point."

"What does?"

"If there had been just the pair of you on the road, then you and Elizabeth would now be snuggling up together in bed. How does that sound?"

"Very enticing, Tom."

"That's why we must go our separate ways."

"You've not changed your mind, then?"

"No, Jamie. We'll get to Rhode Island on our own." He gave his friend a playful jab. "And I'll wager we'll be the first there."

"You're a bold man to make such a foolish claim."

"We'll see."

They had slept in their clothes and left the horses saddled so that they could make a quick departure. Rolling off his makeshift bed, Skoyles brushed the strands of hay from his clothing. His wounded arm was now bandaged. He had a first look at the day. It was cold but dry. There was only a faintest breath of wind. When he glanced across at the farmhouse, he saw that there was already a light in the window.

"It looks as if they were up before us, Tom," he said.

"And they'll be fresher, too, having slept in a proper bed."

"Let's join them for breakfast."

They went across to the little farmhouse and found that the front door had been unlocked for them. Everyone was in the kitchen with its warm fire crackling away, its flames reflected on the rough stone walls. The farmer was a sprightly old man with white hair and beard, pleased to have had two attractive women staying in his humble dwelling. His wife, a plain, shuffling, taciturn creature, looked less happy to have had visitors, but she prepared a frugal meal for them as they chatted. The farmer was inquisitive.

"Where are ye headed?" he asked.

"Dartmouth," replied Skoyles.

"Then all ye need to do is to stay on the same road."

"Is that the only way there?" said Caffrey.

"It's the best, my friend."

"But there is another route?"

"Aye."

"Could you show us where it is, please?" said Skoyles, taking the map from his pocket and laying it on the table. He pointed with a finger. "My guess is that we're around here somewhere."

"No," said the old man, exposing bare gums in a grin. "You've come farther than you think." His skeletal finger tapped the map, then moved as he spoke. "We are right here. Now, you can either follow the coastline around Buzzards Bay—like this, you see—or take another road that snakes off in that direction."

"How far is it to Dartmouth?"

"Not much above thirty miles."

"Is that all?" said Caffrey. "We can do that in a day."

"As long as ye don't waste any of it. This time of year, it gets dark a mite early." The farmer looked up as his wife began to put food on the table. "Thankee, Mother."

"Eat up, all," she grunted.

Sitting down at the bare wooden table, they ate their breakfast quickly and washed it down with some hard cider. All four of them thanked their hosts for their hospitality. Caffrey and Polly Bragg then went out to the barn, but Skoyles stayed behind to offer the farmer some money. The old man waved it away, insisting that it was his Christian duty to take strangers in from the cold and to look after them. He refused to charge them anything. His wife, however, had no inhibitions about taking the coins. Grabbing them from Skoyles, she thrust them into a pot on the shelf. There was a heated argument between the old couple, then the farmer eventually conceded defeat. He smiled fondly and patted his wife on the rump.

"Mother always knows best," he said.

Skoyles shook him by the hand. "You've earned it."

"Yes," said Elizabeth. "We were exhausted."

"Goodbye."

"Good luck go with ye!" said the old man.

Skoyles thanked him again and led Elizabeth Rainham outside. After several hours' sleep, she looked bright and refreshed. Given some vigorous brushing, her hair had recovered its beautiful sheen. Skoyles paused to have a quiet word alone with her.

"How did they treat you?" he said.

"Very well."

"The wife seemed very surly."

"She thought her husband was paying too much attention to us."

"Who can blame him?"

"Yes, it must get very lonely out here."

"We found a bed for you. That was the main thing."

"Not if it meant your sleeping in the barn," said Elizabeth with concern. "It must have been very uncomfortable in there."

"I was fine once I got used to Tom's snoring," said Skoyles. "And it was a big improvement on spending a night in a fishing boat."

"Did you have an opportunity to talk to him about splitting up?"

"I thought we'd do that now, Elizabeth."

"Polly is still keen to strike off alone with Tom."

"I'm not altogether happy with that notion."

"Nor am I, Jamie."

"Apart from anything else, Tom is no horseman. Unlike us, he's never really learned to ride properly. I'd feel better if I was there to keep an eye on him."

"That's my view as well."

"Then let's get across there and talk them out of it. Come on!"

He took her by the hand and they walked around the corner of the farmhouse to the barn. When they went inside, however, they saw that it was too late to hold any kind of discussion with their friends. Tom Caffrey and Polly Bragg had made up their own minds.

They had already left.

They were everywhere. Ezekiel Proudfoot had never been in a city that was so fully occupied. Having eaten breakfast with the redcoats staying at the King George Tavern, he saw more of them as soon as he stepped into the street. Four privates were standing idly outside a house, taking part in a girning contest, twisting their faces into such distorted expressions of joy that Proudfoot thought they must be in extreme pain. At a corner, he met a patrol on the march. Farther along the street, some officers were tumbling out of a house with their arms around each other, still not fully sober after a night of heavy drinking. And so it went on. By the time he reached his place of work, Proudfoot had counted over seventy British soldiers. He told Adam Quenby about his mathematics.

"I've seen far more than that," grumbled the printer, indicating the window that was half below street level. "I've watched hundreds of pairs of army boots as they strut past. The British think they own the place."

"Might is right in their view."

"This city is *ours*."

"And will be so again, I'm sure."

"But what state will it be in? They've changed Philadelphia out of all recognition. From morn till night, it's filled with loud noise, and it's not safe for a decent woman to be abroad on her own."

"What about an indecent woman, Mr. Quenby?"

"There are far too many of those about," said the other darkly. "I sometimes think that whoring and gambling are the chief occupations of the British. Not that the German mercenaries are any better," he added with a sniff. "The Hessians run a gambling table where only high stakes are permitted. It's iniquitous, sir."

"I'm sure that Mr. Hughes has pointed that out in the *Patriot*."

"Regularly."

Proudfoot could not believe that the little man had spent the whole night in the dank cellar. Quenby seemed too spry and animated. He was already hard at work when the silversmith arrived, setting type with painstaking care. The printing press, as ever, was quite spotless. Opening his satchel, Proudfoot took out the sketch he had made the previous evening.

"I showed this to Mr. Hughes," he said, handing it to Quenby, "and he would like it to appear on the front page of the *Patriot*."

"Let me see."

"I hope that it won't cause offense."

"I very much hope that it will, Mr. Allen. Causing offense to the British is one of our ambitions." Holding the cartoon only six inches from his face, he studied it for a long time as if not able to believe what he was seeing. "Good Lord!" he exclaimed at length. "You've been very daring, I must say."

"Is that good or bad?"

"Neither, Mr. Allen. It's excellent!"

"Thank you."

"It has a crude simplicity that will make anyone take notice. Just look at that ogre, General Howe!"

He threw back his head and burst into laughter, savoring the detail in the cartoon. Grateful for his approval, Proudfoot took it back from him and glanced at it again.

"Drawing this was easy," he said. "Making a plate of it will be far more difficult. Everything will have to be the other way round."

"Leave the caption to me. I'll print it in large letters."

"It's a line from a song I overheard some redcoats singing."

"They'll think twice about singing it again when they see this. You have a quick brain, Mr. Allen. There's wit and savagery here."

"I've always been an admirer of William Hogarth."

"You are a worthy successor," said Quenby.

"I'm flattered that you think so."

"Like Hogarth, you use your talents to mock the follies and vices of the English. The *Patriot* is blessed in having you."

"When will the next issue be printed?"

"As soon as you have engraved the plate for me."

"How many copies will you produce?"

"Not nearly as many as I would like," Quenby admitted. "Paper is getting scarce, so we have to conserve it. But there'll be enough copies to reach all the people who need to see it."

"Mr. Hughes wants General Howe to be one of them."

"I'll deliver it to his headquarters in person."

"I'm told that his own soldiers sing bawdy songs about him and Mrs. Loring. He must be heartily tired of the ridicule by now."

"That cartoon is more than ridicule," said Quenby. "It's symbolic of all that's wrong with this city. The audacity of it! General Howe has the nerve to talk about freedom's scepter when the only reason he came to this country is to deprive us of our liberty."

"I tried to point out the cruel irony of that situation."

"You hit the mark, Mr. Allen."

"I'm glad that you think so."

"And you even managed to win over Pearsall Hughes at the first attempt. Nobody has ever done that before."

"Except, perhaps, Mrs. Hughes."

"Ah, yes. A divine creature and an editor in her own right."

"She was gracious enough to praise my work as well."

"Then you have conquered man and wife," said Quenby as he continued to set type. "There is only one more judge whose good opinion you must now seek—General Washington."

Wearing a cape over his uniform, George Washington set his hat on his head and stepped out of the house. Snow had stopped falling but it had already made its mark. The grass was covered in a carpet of thick white snow. Wherever he looked, there was a cold, unyielding, wintry scene. He felt a tremor of alarm as he thought of the additional problems that would be created for his men, most of whom were still living under canvas while they were building their log cabins.

He could hear them at work. Axes were already thudding into the trunks of trees. Saws were already cutting timber to size. But the bad weather would impede progress and make conditions very unpleasant. It would also increase the likelihood of desertions as soldiers shivered in their inadequate clothing. Washington was dismayed. When he looked up at the sky, there was no comfort to be found. Clouds hung low and full. There was more snow to come.

"Hell!" he cried in exasperation. "What else do we have to endure?"

Jamie Skoyles could not understand it. Though they traveled at a steady speed, they made up no ground at all on the others. Tom Caffrey and Polly Bragg had either ridden harder than they or turned off the main track at some point. After a while, Skoyles gave up all hope of catching them. Since the horse was carrying two riders, it was important to rest him at regular intervals. They had covered almost five miles when the animal was tugged to a halt for the first time. Skoyles dismounted, then helped Elizabeth Rainham to the ground. Tethering the horse to a bush, he walked to the edge of the precipice and gazed down. From their high eminence, they had a perfect view of the majestic sweep of Buzzards Bay and its rugged coastline and countless inlets, coves, promontories, necks, and rocky outcrops. Small craft were mere specks on the sea.

"It's beautiful," said Elizabeth, coming to stand beside him.

"It would be if we had time to admire it."

"We can spare a few minutes at least."

"Of course," he said, putting an arm around her shoulders. "This is a view to take your breath away. Look at those boats down there. Going about their business as if a brutal war never existed."

"We know differently," she said. "When will it end, Jamie?"

"Oh, there's a lot more blood to be spilled yet."

"But we will triumph in the end, won't we?"

He was uncertain. "I think so."

"Harry told me that it was something he took for granted."

"That was before Saratoga," he reminded her. "Things can change, Elizabeth. General Burgoyne's invincible army was beaten hollow. Major Featherstone was unwise to be so overconfident. There was a time when he made the mistake of taking *you* for granted, and we know how foolhardy that was."

"Only because you rescued me from that silly dream." She became reflective. "Except that it did not seem so silly at the time. In fact, it was the only dream a young woman like me could have had. I grew up in a military family, remember. My father served with General Burgoyne in Portugal. I could think of no better life than marrying a British officer."

Skoyles grinned. "I hope that delusion still holds."

"You told me that you'll not be staying in the army."

"Not forever, anyway. I have my silly dreams as well, Elizabeth. As you know, I want to buy land here and settle down." He pulled her to him. "If I can find the right woman, that is."

She smiled up at him. "I've come this far."

"No regrets?"

"I had a few when we saw that horse thief swinging from a tree."

"What about that squall we were caught in?"

"I was far too scared to have any regrets then," she said. "I kept trying to fit my thoughts for death. At least, we'd have been together. What about you, Jamie? Do you have regrets?"

"Plenty of them."

"Really?"

"I regret that I trusted Otis Tapper. I regret that I've put you in jeopardy by bringing you with me. I regret that I'll have to go on fighting for a long time before we can be together. And I regret that—"

She put a hand to his lips to silence him. "That's enough for now. Let's enjoy this moment while we can."

"Of course."

Turning to face her, Skoyles pulled her close, but their moment together was brief. Over her shoulder, he could see three horsemen approaching, and he was forcibly reminded that they were still in a colony where rebel feeling was at its strongest. He and Elizabeth stood apart and waited for the riders to reach them. They were three in number, well-built farm boys, not yet in their twenties, sitting astride animals that looked as if they belonged between the shafts of a wagon. Each rider had an old musket.

When they came to a halt, Skoyles gave them a friendly wave.

"Good morning to you, lads," he called.

"And to you," replied the biggest of the three, eyeing them shrewdly. "Do you only have the one horse between you?"

"Yes, my friend."

"Where are you bound?"

"Dartmouth."

"Why, so are we," said another of the men, ogling Elizabeth. "If the lady would care to jump up behind me, I'll gladly take her there."

"We'll get there ourselves, have no fear."

"Where are you from?" the first man asked.

"Boston," said Skoyles.

"You've come all that way with one horse?"

"No, we thought to travel by sea, but we were blown off course and our boat was washed ashore near Barnstable. We decided to travel the rest of the way by land. There was only one horse for sale."

Skoyles could see that the man was suspicious and wanted to give him no excuse to use his musket. He was not only outnumbered, his own weapon was ten yards away, resting against a tree. The other two men were more interested in Elizabeth, grinning at her inanely and blowing her kisses. Their spokesman, however, a hulking youth with a ragged beard, was appraising Skoyles with palpable mistrust.

109

"You've the look of a soldier about you," he said.

"I served my time in the 11th Massachusetts Regiment."

"Who was in command?"

"Colonel Turbott Francis."

"He was killed at Hubbardton."

"I was lucky to escape myself," said Skoyles. "Had we only fought the British, we'd have sent them running, but their hired killers from Germany came to their rescue. We had too few men to hold them all off."

"Who else fought on our side?"

There was a note of respect in the young man's voice now. He had heard a great deal about the heroic resistance given by his countrymen at Hubbardton, and wanted more detail. Skoyles supplied it willingly, and all three men listened intently. Elizabeth was forgotten. From the way he described the battle, there was no doubting that Skoyles had actually taken part in it. What he did not tell his rapt audience was that he had fought on the other side.

"We're joining the militia," said the youngest of the men. "They say there won't be much fighting during the winter, but I'll find some redcoats to kill." He lifted his musket and fired into the air. "There goes one!"

"Why did you do that, you idiot," the big man scolded.

"I have to practice, Abner."

"Wasting a shot like that is madness."

"He's right," Skoyles agreed. "If you want to be a soldier, learn to keep your powder dry and bide your time. Every shot must count. Our army is desperately short of ammunition. Only fire when necessary."

"Yes, sir," said the youngest man, penitently.

"You're heading for Dartmouth, you say?"

"We are," their spokesman replied. "Ethan, Jude, and me, we mean to enlist, and we were told to get ourselves to Dartmouth. We'll ride with you, if you like. You could tell us about other battles you've been in."

"That would only bore my wife," said Skoyles, a protective arm around Elizabeth. "Besides, we'd hold you lads up. I can see you have red blood in your veins, and the militia needs people like you. Ride on and we'll get there at our own pace."

"Are you sure, sir?"

"Yes, we're in no hurry."

"Then we'll leave you." He turned to the youngest man. "And don't you go loosing off another bullet, Ethan, or I'll wrap that damn musket around your stringy neck, so help me." He smiled apologetically at Elizabeth. "Excuse my bad language, ma'am, but my brother needs to be kept in line." He touched his hat. "We wish you both good day."

After a flurry of farewells, the three men rode off. Relieved to see them go, Skoyles retrieved his musket and walked back to the horse. He looked after the departing farm boys.

"That changes our plans a little," he commented.

"Does it?"

"Yes, Elizabeth. If Dartmouth is going to be crawling with militia, it might not be the safest place to go. It's a pity that Tom and Polly are not aware of that. They could be riding into trouble."

"What about us, Jamie?" she asked.

"We'll find another way."

When the first copy of *The Pennsylvania Patriot* was peeled off the press, Adam Quenby folded it, then examined the four pages with meticulous care. Only when he was satisfied with his handiwork did he pass the newspaper over to Pearsall Hughes. The bookseller laid it down on the table so that he and Ezekiel Proudfoot could study it together by the light of the candle. The two men were looking at different things. Hughes was only interested in checking his elegant prose for printing errors while Proudfoot's gaze was fixed solely on the cartoon.

Dominating the front page, and notwithstanding a few black smudges around its perimeter, it had remarkable clarity. The figures were almost life-like. A cursory glance was enough to tell any reader of the *Patriot* that General William Howe, distinguished commander in chief of the British army in America, was being well and truly lampooned. Proudfoot wished that he could be there when the man himself first set eyes on the cartoon.

The artist was not allowed to admire his work for long. Hughes turned over the page so that he could read his article about the various outrages committed by the occupying force in Philadelphia. By allowing himself a degree of exaggeration, the bookseller felt that he could more easily arouse the wrath of those members of the Continental Army whose families had either been forcibly evicted from the city, or were still living there in the long shadow of the British army. His aim, as an editor, was to make Americans proud enough of their country to want to fight hard to liberate it. He felt that the latest issue of the *Patriot* would achieve that objective.

"It's fine, Adam," he said. "Print more copies."

"Yes, Mr. Hughes."

"And make sure they are distributed by the usual means."

"I will, sir," said Quenby.

He set about his task at once, ready to work all evening and well into the night. Hughes, meanwhile, turned back to the first page and chortled merrily as he looked down at the cartoon. After a few minutes, he swung round to face Proudfoot.

"A thousand thanks, Mr. Allen," he said, shaking his hand in congratulation. "Admirable work. You've given the newspaper a completely new bite."

"I hope that it will draw blood."

"Most assuredly."

"Then I've done what I came to do."

"I'd suggest that you keep this first copy as a souvenir but that would only imperil you. There are too many prying eyes at the King George Tavern. The only man you can trust there is the landlord."

"I've already found that out, Mr. Hughes."

"In any case," the bookseller went on, "copies are like gold dust. We need every single one for our readers."

"Each one will be seen by several people," said Quenby over his shoulder. "They pass the *Patriot* around so that it has a wider impact."

"Except in the case of General Howe," said Proudfoot. "I venture to suggest that he'll not pass it around. As soon as he sees it, he'll most likely toss it in the fire."

Quenby cackled. "He'll certainly not let Mrs. Loring look at it."

"You can hardly blame him," said Hughes. "Mr. Allen will, without question, draw blood from the general. That's why we must steel ourselves against the consequences."

"Consequences?" said Proudfoot.

"General Howe will be deeply insulted. He'll demand revenge. Extra patrols will be sent out to search for the press. More to the point, Mr. Allen, the redcoats will come looking for you."

"But the cartoon is unsigned."

"You're too modest."

"It has your signature all over it," Quenby confirmed.

"And even Howe will be able to read it. He'll have seen examples of your art before. Your prints of our victories at Trenton and Princeton were sold everywhere. So were those you drew at Saratoga. In British eyes," he continued, "you are an enemy weapon. They take note of you."

"I didn't realize that I had such notoriety," said Proudfoot.

"It will increase tenfold when this cartoon is seen."

"And General Howe will know that it's my work?"

"The moment he sees it," Hughes warned. "He'll also know that you're somewhere in the city. That will infuriate him, and he'll act at once. Redcoats will come after you, my friend. British spies will join the chase. They'll hunt you day and night until they catch you. Beware!"

Ezekiel Proudfoot's mouth went dry, and prickly heat disturbed him. For the first time since he had been in Philadelphia, he felt a distinct quiver of apprehension.

"You've never done that before," said Elizabeth Rainham.

"Done what?"

"Called me your wife. When those three men stopped to speak to us on the road, you told them that talking about battles with them would only bore your wife."

"Did you mind?" asked Skoyles.

"Not at all. I loved it."

"I had to use the same pretense to get a room here."

She kissed him. "I enjoyed that, too."

The village was a few miles north of Dartmouth, and they had taken an upstairs room for the night in its only tavern, a small, cramped, drafty establishment that smelled in equal proportions of drink, tobacco, and mold. They consoled themselves with the fact that, whatever its defects, they had somewhere to stay. Both of them were also quick to realize that they had never shared a bed before. The prospect excited them.

"You were so convincing, Jamie," she recalled.

"Was I?"

"Yes. Those three men were quite menacing at first, but you soon talked

113

them around. I watched their faces. By the time you'd finished telling them about Hubbardton, they did more than admire you. It was a kind of hero worship."

"Only because they thought I'd fought on the rebel side."

"That was the amazing thing."

"What was?"

"You talked about the battle as if you'd really wanted the Americans to win. You were so convincing that you even had me fooled for a time. You were one of *them*."

"I have great sympathy for the rebel cause."

She was startled. "Even though you're in the British army?"

"Yes, Elizabeth. These men want freedom enough to fight for it."

"But they're in open revolt against the Crown."

"The king and his government did provoke this quarrel."

"They had every right to impose taxes on the colonies."

"People who have to pay those taxes disagree," said Skoyles.

Elizabeth was hurt. "You sound as if you're taking their part."

"I'll bear arms against them whenever I have the chance, Elizabeth. But that doesn't mean I can't understand their point of view."

"Harry always talked about them as if they were mere vermin."

"That was another mistake of his," said Skoyles coldly. "If you do not respect an enemy, you underestimate them, and that can be costly. I suspect that even Major Featherstone will have revised his opinion of the rebels by now. He's a proud man. He'd never admit that we lost on the battlefield to an army of mere vermin."

It was ironic. They had both yearned for a time when they were alone together without any impediments. All that they had enjoyed before were stolen moments of pleasure in an army encampment. Since their escape from Cambridge—until that day—they had always had company. Now they were together, able to express their feelings at last, and yet they were arguing about the basis of the war. A slight rift had opened up between them. Skoyles tried to close it by stretching out a contrite hand. She needed some time before she reached out to take it.

"The war is outside," he whispered, "and we are in here together."

"I know."

"That's all that matters, isn't it?"

"Yes, Jamie."

He took her impulsively in his arms and kissed her. Elizabeth responded with equal passion, holding back nothing as she tried to banish the memory of all the setbacks they had so far encountered. Easing her toward the bed, Skoyles began to unhook her dress so that he could slip a hand inside it. His gentle caresses on her bare skin gave her such a thrill of delight that she pulled him down on the bed and started to help him off with his hunting shirt. Before he had even got it over his head, however, they were interrupted by noises from below.

Horses approached at a gallop before being reined in. Someone dismounted and banged on the tavern door. Skoyles was worried. Letting go of Elizabeth, he crept to the window and looked down. Three mounted men waited below while a fourth hammered relentlessly on the door until the landlord eventually opened it, holding a lantern.

"We're looking for four people," the man told him. "Two men and two women. Are they staying here?"

"We've only two guests here tonight," said the landlord.

"Who are they?"

"A man and a woman."

"Young or old?"

"The wife is young, the husband a little older."

"What are they riding?"

"They share a horse between them."

"Where is it?"

"In the stables," said the landlord. "Why are you asking?"

"Because murder's been committed and a horse has been stolen." The man turned to his companions. "I'll look in the stable. The rest of you can stay here. I think we may have found them."

CHAPTER EIGHT

Jamie Skoyles had heard enough. Reacting with speed, he dragged the bed across to the door to act as a barricade, then he quickly pulled off the blankets.

"What are you doing?" cried Elizabeth.

"Get your things together. We must leave."

"*Now?*"

"There's not a moment to lose," he said, knotting the blankets together before tying one end to a low beam. "They've found those men we killed. We have to get out of here."

Trembling with fear, Elizabeth did as she was told, gathering all her possessions into a bundle, then putting on her cloak and hat without even bothering to hook up the back of her dress. Skoyles, meanwhile, was piling every piece of furniture in the room onto the bed so that it would delay entry and gain them precious time. Four armed men were outside with vengeance on their mind. They would not bother with the refinement of a trial. Immediate flight was essential.

There was one saving grace. Because they occupied a room on the corner of the tavern, they had a window that looked out on the side of the building as well as one on the front. It was the side window that Skoyles now opened, peering out to make sure that nobody was below. When he saw that the coast was clear, he dropped one end of the knotted blankets through the window. He then grabbed his own belongings and reached for his musket.

"How many of them are there, Jamie?" Elizabeth asked.

"Too many."

"Do we take the horse?"

"There's no chance of that."

"Then how can we possibly outrun them?"

"Leave everything to me," he said, moving her toward the window. "We must hurry. They'll be here any moment."

The man who had banged on the tavern door was impatient. When the landlord took him around to the stables at the rear of the premises, he did not wait for him to open the door. Snatching the lantern from him, he pushed him aside, then pulled back the bolt himself.

"Hey!" the landlord protested.

"Keep out of my way!"

"This is my property, sir."

"I must see those horses."

Diving into the stables, he held the lantern up as he walked along the stalls. There were five horses in all, and they were disturbed by the sudden intrusion. They neighed in protest and shifted their feet in the straw. After checking each one, the visitor stopped at the last stall and spilled light onto the animal, running his hand along its flank as he did so. Having inspected the horse, he looked at the saddle that was resting over the side of the stall. It was all the proof that he required. He thrust the lantern back into the landlord's hand.

"That's it," he declared. "It belonged to him."

"Who?"

"My brother."

"But another gentleman brought it here," said the landlord.

"He won't ride it again."

"Do not be so hasty, sir."

"Move over!"

Shoving him aside once more, the man rushed out of the stables and round to the front of the tavern, yelling to his men to join him. They dismounted quickly and tethered their horses. When the landlord came waddling up to them, the four men stood around him in a circle. The one who had identified the horse jabbed him in the chest.

"Which room are they in?" he demanded.

"Not so fast, sir," said the landlord. "There may be some mistake."

"That was my brother's horse. It was stolen after he'd been stabbed to death. We found his body this morning. We want his killer."

117

"It was dark in the stables. How can you certain about the horse?"

"Take us to their room."

"Stay calm," urged the landlord, not wishing his tavern to be invaded. "Why not let me ask the gentleman to come down and speak to you out here?"

"No. We'll go to him."

The barrel of a musket was pressed hard against the landlord's forehead, and his nerve failed. He indicated the front door of the tavern.

"This way, if you please," he said.

Still holding the lantern, he led them into the building and up the staircase, their feet resounding on the hard wood. They went along the landing until they came to the room at the end. The landlord tried to rap on the door with his knuckles but the men were in no mood to wait. One of them lifted the latch and pushed hard. He met resistance. When he kicked the door, it still refused to budge. He used the butt of his musket to hammer on the timber, then put his shoulder to it. The bed inside the room moved a few inches. A second, more concerted shoulder charge forced it back another foot and the door opened wide enough for them to burst through.

The lantern was again ripped from the hands of its owner. It was lifted high so that it illumined the whole room. They saw the open window at once and ran to it. The knotted blankets were dangling down the side of the tavern and swaying in the breeze. They were incensed at having lost their prey.

"They've gone!" one of them exclaimed.

"They'll not get far on foot," said another, heading for the door. "Spread out and search for them. We'll soon catch the bastards and they'll wish they were never born."

Elizabeth Rainham could hear the voices clearly and they struck terror into her heart. Skoyles wrapped a consoling arm around her. It was no use telling the men that he had not, in fact, stabbed anyone to death. He would be caught in possession of the dead man's horse, and that was fatal. Fleeing from the village on foot would have been suicidal. The four riders would have hunted down the fugitives within minutes. Skoyles had therefore chosen the one hiding place where they might be safe. Instead of running away from the tavern, he had clambered up on to the roof and hauled Elizabeth after him. Lying flat on the tiles near the ridge, they were completely invisible to anyone below.

Afraid that she might fall, Elizabeth clung on for dear life. The cold wind made her shiver, and she was in extreme discomfort, but she knew that it was preferable to capture. Skoyles would be summarily hanged or shot, but she would be kept alive for sport. The four men would surely take their pleasure before they put her to death. She could still hear them, roaring with anger as they searched the village. It was only when their voices began to die away that she dared to speak.

"What are we going to do, Jamie?"

"Stay here until they've gone."

"That might take hours," she said with trepidation.

"Then that's how long we'll have to wait."

"I'm not sure that I can manage it."

"You'll have to manage, Elizabeth," he said, tightening his grip on her. "I dread to think what would happen if they caught us."

Skoyles was lying full length against the steep roof, his musket slung from his shoulder. Their two bundles had been tied together and straddled the ridge tiles beside the chimney. Neither of them dared to look down. Skoyles cursed himself for landing them in such a dire predicament. He had not thought that anybody would catch up with them when they had such a head start. He was wrong. The chasing pack, he decided, had probably tracked them to the farmhouse where they had spent the previous night, and learned that they were on the road to Dartmouth. Having looked in vain for them there, the four men had shifted their attention to the nearest village.

"What will they do?" asked Elizabeth.

"Give up in time."

"And then?"

"We get down from here."

"How?"

"I'm not sure," he admitted, risking a glance downward, "but I'll find a way somehow. Take heart, Elizabeth."

He leaned across to kiss her cheek and heard her teeth chattering.

The Honorable William Howe was a tall, dark, well-featured man in his late forties, renowned as a disciplinarian yet popular with officers and men alike. His resounding victory at Brandywine had helped him to secure the rebel seat of government, Philadelphia, and he was still basking in his success. He celebrated it with bouts of heavy drinking, interspersed with nocturnal delight in the arms of Betsey Loring. It was after one such night of adulterous pleasure that he and his mistress finally descended for breakfast. She smiled at him across the table.

"I'll miss you when you return to England," she said.

"It will be months before I do that, Betsey, and I intend to see a great deal of you beforehand. You have made my time in America not only bearable but—when we are alone together—positively rapturous."

"Thank you."

"I'm grateful that you have such an understanding husband."

"Joshua will always do what's best for me."

"Sensible man."

They tucked into their breakfast with relish. Betsey Loring was a pretty young woman with a vivacity that had attracted him the moment they first met in Boston. The husband was a wine merchant with loyalist sympathies, and Howe had secured the favors of his wife with the lure of higher profits for Joshua Loring. Once the corrupt bargain had been struck, the general took the couple with him to New York, where he appointed the husband as his commissary of prisons, a post that carried a high salary and gave its holder endless opportunities for graft.

Mrs. Loring picked at her food and shot him another smile.

"I never knew that military life could be so pleasurable."

"It's not all blood and thunder on the battlefield," he said, dabbing at his lips with a napkin. "There'll be a long cessation from hostilities during winter. Even the dauntless General Washington is not so rash as to mount an attack at this time of year—unless he means to pelt us with snowballs, that is."

She tittered happily. "We can devote ourselves to the gaming table and the bedchamber."

"Do not forget the dancing. Another ball is being held soon."

"Then we will be the first on the floor, Betsey."

"I will hold you to that," she said, sitting back as a servant arrived to clear the plates. "Your brother must be very jealous of you."

"Jealous?"

"Yes. While the admiral is cooped up on a ship, you have the freedom of a city where you are treated like a conquering hero. Some people have fled, it's true," she said, "but Philadelphia always had more Tories in it than rebels. With the British army here, they have been able to show their true colors."

"That gratifies me more than I can say," he told her. "But do not trouble yourself on my brother's account. The navy is well able to indulge itself when it chooses to do so. Within his reach, Richard has all the luxuries that I have." He raised his cup to her. "With one significant exception, of course."

She giggled at the compliment. "Do you think that your brother would take to me?"

"He'll not get the opportunity, my dear."

"Why, are you afraid that he'd steal me away from you?"

"Oh, no," replied Howe with a laugh. "Richard is the finest seamen in the world, but his talents are strictly confined to naval matters. Let me put it this way. I am considered by some to be reticent and inarticulate. Yet compared to my brother, I am the very soul of eloquence."

"Then I've clearly chosen the better of the two."

"Indubitably."

There was a tap on the door and a manservant entered with a newspaper. He handed the copy of *The Pennsylvania Patriot* to Howe, then left the room. Wiping the moisture from around his lips, the general saw the title of the newspaper and got ready to sneer. Rebel publications always aroused his disdain. This issue, however, was different. In a prominent position on the first page was a large cartoon in which he and Betsey Loring were featured. After looking at it with horror, he tore the paper to shreds and threw it on the floor in a fit of anger.

"Whoever's upset you?" she asked in consternation.

"His name is Proudfoot," he growled. "Ezekiel Proudfoot."

Days later, at his headquarters in Valley Forge, George Washington was still diverted by the cartoon. He congratulated Proudfoot, and they speculated at length on how it would have been received by its intended target. Major Clark then arrived at the little house, anxious to meet the silversmith for the first time and eager to add his own words of praise. After introductions had been made, the three of them sat down for a discussion.

"What brings you to Valley Forge?" Clark asked.

"Discretion," Proudfoot replied.

121

"Exchanging the city for the bleak countryside is hardly discreet."

"I felt it safer to get out of Philadelphia until General Howe's ire died down a little. Troops were scouring every street and alleyway for me. Besides, I had intelligence to pass on to General Washington and was keen to see what progress you had made here."

"Very little, alas."

"Not so, Major," said Washington. "The outer fortifications improve with each day, and the redoubts give us additional protection. What is taking more time than I anticipated is the building of the cabins."

"There's no shortage of wood," Proudfoot observed.

"We lack sufficient means to cut it down and shape it, Ezekiel."

"What about food supplies?"

"The men have eaten no meat since we've been at Valley Forge."

"It's a scandal," said Clark fervently. "We have no succor here. The Commissary and Quartermaster Departments are in total disarray. We are desperate, Mr. Proudfoot. Christmas Day will soon be here and they will have nothing to eat but fire cake. A mixture of flour and water, baked before an open fire, will hardly keep body and soul together."

"We are short of fodder for the horses as well," Washington added solemnly, "but there are even greater worries than that. Twenty officers have already resigned, and, in spite of threats of execution, desertions mount daily. The demand for furloughs is never ending. If I granted them all, we'd lose a thousand men or more." He picked up the copy of the *Patriot.* "That's why your cartoon was so welcome, Ezekiel. It gave us a rare smile."

"Indeed, it did," said Clark. "Your work may not have the force of a cannon, Mr. Proudfoot, but its echo will last a deal longer."

"I'll ensure that the copies we were sent are passed out among the officers. They need something to cheer them."

"There'll be many more cartoons like that," Proudfoot promised.

"Good," said Washington. "Keep at it, Ezekiel. By the way," he went on, leaning back in his chair, "how did you find Pearsall Hughes?"

"Exactly as you described him, General."

"Intelligent, fearless, committed to independence?"

"And as prickly as a hedgehog."

"That's the fellow," Clark agreed with a smile. "But he's a godsend to us.

Not only does he edit the *Patriot,* he picks up so much useful gossip from British officers who patronize his bookshop."

"But it is merely gossip," Washington cautioned, "and, therefore, not altogether reliable. I mean this as no criticism of you, Major, because your sources in Philadelphia have given us invaluable information, but what we really need is someone within General Howe's circle."

"That's more difficult to contrive, General."

"Is there nobody who can be bought for money?"

"I've not found the ideal person as yet," Clark confessed. "That's why all of our intelligence comes second-hand."

"Keep looking," Washington advised. "The right man in the right place would be invaluable."

"And what did you do then, Captain Skoyles?" he asked. "Once you had reached Dartmouth under cover of darkness."

"We stole a boat from the harbor."

"A musket, a horse, a boat—you are an accomplished thief, sir."

"I prefer to see it as a case of serendipity, Major. I've always been adept at picking up a good thing when I found it. When we were on foot with four riders on our tail, the only way that we could possibly escape was by sea."

Captain Jamie Skoyles and Elizabeth Rainham had finally reached the headquarters of the British army in New York via the naval base at Newport, Rhode Island. They had been welcomed at both places and, for the first time in days, enjoyed the comforts of good food and warm beds. Major Walter Doel was now interviewing Skoyles on his own in a dining room that was used as an office. They sat either side of a long oak table. The major was a fleshy man with a round face, dimpled cheeks, and a habit of closing one eye when he asked a question. Even though he was senior in rank to Skoyles, he was all of six years younger. He was fascinated to hear about the escape from Cambridge and the subsequent adventures along the way, marveling at the sheer effort that was involved.

Skoyles's account was lucid but concise, omitting many details in the interests of speed. He did not describe the bitterly cold hours spent with Elizabeth on the roof of a tavern, or their hazardous descent in the dark down the side of the building. Nor did he dwell on the long time spent rowing the stolen boat in the choppy waters of the Atlantic before they were eventually picked up by a British frigate and taken to Rhode Island. The trials and tribulations of the past week had not weakened Skoyles's readiness to fight. While most officers in his position would want a rest, all that he craved was further action.

"General Clinton has something in mind for you," said Doel.

"Really?"

"Yes, Captain. He was very impressed with the report you gave us on the conditions our soldiers endure in Cambridge. It was commendably thorough and confirmed all our fears. Congress means to tear up the convention treaty as if it never existed."

"Unhappily, that's true," said Skoyles.

"Our hopes are dashed. General Howe sent transports to Boston on the understanding that, instead of taking the men to England, they would bring them here, where they are sorely needed."

"Did he intend to release an equivalent number of rebel prisoners?"

"That's immaterial."

"I disagree, Major. It was the third article of the convention."

"So?"

"There was a specific mention of an exchange of prisoners."

"We're extremely careful whom we release from custody."

"But it's a question of honor, sir."

"Honor goes by the board in certain circumstances," said Doel glibly. "We'd have felt no obligation to set thousands of those damned rebels free so that they could do their best to kill us again."

"Custom demands it."

"Then custom would have been flouted on this occasion."

Skoyles looked at him with growing distaste. Major Doel was an able man, but he was irredeemably complacent and he showed an utter contempt for the enemy. Like the majority of officers, Doel had bought his commission, and that immediately set him apart from Skoyles, who had worked his way up from the ranks on merit. There was a social gulf between them that could never be closed. With his smugness and his air of well-bred arrogance, the man was beginning to remind Skoyles uncomfortably of Major Harry Featherstone.

"You've come to us too late, Captain," said Doel.

"Too late?"

"Yes, you've missed all the fun. When we drove the rebels out of the city, General Howe declared his policy in four words: *Toujours de la gaité*. We had such merrymaking," he went on with a braying laugh. "We had plays, concerts, and dances. Do you know what the trouble is with these benighted revolutionaries?"

"They refuse to give in."

"No, Captain. They don't know how to enjoy themselves. New York was full of long faces and narrow minds. We taught them the meaning of recreation. That's why you should have been here in the summer."

Skoyles was curt. "I was too busy fighting the enemy, sir."

"We had horse racing at Long Island, billiards at the King's Head Tavern, cricket at Bowling Green, swimming parties, of course, and even some golf. Do you play golf, Captain?" He wrinkled his nose slightly. "No, I suppose that you don't. It's a wonderful game."

"What about now, Major Doel?"

"Oh, we still have lots of ways to amuse ourselves."

"I was thinking of more serious matters, sir," said Skoyles. "I did not go to all the trouble of escaping simply to sit in the playhouse every evening. I'm hungry for a new assignment."

"Your enthusiasm is a tonic for us all, Captain," said Doel, getting to his feet. "And nobody could hear the tale of your escape without realizing what a brave and resourceful officer you are."

"Then use me, sir."

"We intend to."

"Give me work that will test me."

"General Clinton has already done so."

Skoyles was pleased. "Indeed?" he said. "Where must I go?"

"To prison."

Ezekiel Proudfoot was astonished at the ease with which Major Clark got into the city. They traveled from Valley Forge together and passed the forward posts that had been set up by Washington to control the roads into Philadelphia.

Once they got near the city, however, Clark led his companion down a track that looped around the British patrols and allowed them to enter from the south without ever once being properly challenged. Having shed his uniform, Clark was dressed in the sober apparel of a Quaker.

"It's only one of many disguises that I use," he explained.

"How often do you come to Philadelphia, Major?"

"As often as I can. There's nothing much that I can do at Valley Forge beyond shivering in the cold and railing at the patent shortcomings of Congress. Here, at least, I can gather intelligence from my agents. I'm pleased to call you one of them, Mr. Proudfoot."

"Allen," corrected the other.

"Of course. You, too, have a disguise—Reece Allen."

"I hope that it will be effective enough."

"Where will you stay?"

"At the King George Tavern."

"I'll meet you there this evening to share a drink."

"Yes, Major."

"Uh-uh," the other warned. "Now it is your turn to slip up. Do not give me away so easily. There are no soldiers in the Society of Friends. I am simply John Clark here."

"Then you will feel at home among your fellow Quakers," said Proudfoot, as a group of people in the familiar plain garb went past. "It must distress you beyond measure to see this fine city occupied. Henry Gilby never ceases to moan about it."

"Given the chance, Pontius Pilate would moan about anything. Does he still wash his hands in the air?"

"Constantly." They laughed together. "According to him, the British have turned Philadelphia into a sewer of depravity."

"There's a grain of truth in that," said the other, "but it's not a fair reflection of what has happened. There's strong loyalist support in the city, Mr. Allen. What upset me was the welcome that the British army was given when they moved in. Suddenly, there is life and levity here. The Quakers may take a dim view of it all, but speak to the daughters of any Tory and you'll hear a different tale."

"In what way?"

"Scores of attentive young officers have appeared on the scene. There are plays and dances to attend. Young ladies here are spoiled for choice," he admitted tartly. "They love all the excitement."

"So they would like the British to stay?"

"They will certainly do nothing to aid our return here."

"That could be a long way off," said Proudfoot with a sigh.

"A very long way, Mr. Allen. Our men are in no condition to fight."

"Why are we so shabbily treated by Congress?"

"You may well ask."

"They must realize the privations the men suffer at Valley Forge. Surely, they should take proper notice of them," said Proudfoot earnestly. "At the very least, they should appoint an inspector general."

"They've recently done so."

"Oh? Who is the man?"

"Major General Conway."

"I've heard that name before."

"You'll hear it many times again, I assure you," said Clark with rancor. "General Washington opposed the appointment strongly and with good reason. Thomas Conway is no friend of our commander. He has been intriguing against him behind his back."

Proudfoot was shocked. "Why?"

"Because he believes that the general should be replaced."

"By whom?"

"Horatio Gates."

"Never!" said Proudfoot with unconcealed dismay. "I'm no soldier, but I can tell the difference between a commander in chief and a mere subordinate. I was at Saratoga when General Gates was in command. He conducted the whole operation from his tent and actually tried to keep Benedict Arnold off the field of battle."

"Nobody in his right mind would do something like that."

"He would not be denied," said Proudfoot, who had vivid memories of Arnold's inspirational bravery in combat. "He disobeyed orders and helped to win the day for us."

"That allowed General Gates to take all the credit."

"Yes, a man who stayed in his tent throughout and let others do the fighting for him. He should have seen the example our commander set at Trenton."

"How true!"

127

"General Washington led from the front where his soldiers could see and follow him." Proudfoot was emphatic. "He is by far the better soldier and unquestionably the finer man."

"You've no need to convince me, Mr. Allen."

"Nobody else is fit to take command."

"I agree," said Clark, "but ambition can warp minds. It's produced the last thing that General Washington needs."

"And what's that?"

"Enemies within."

"George Washington is damnably deficient," he asserted. "His brain is too slow, his judgment too unreliable, and his experience of commanding an army is negligible."

"Yet he is held in such high regard by his men," said Skoyles.

"Not by me, Captain. When I tried to save this province, he left me without guides, cavalry, money, medicines, or support. Some of my men had no shoes and stockings to wear."

"Was he aware of your plight, General?"

"Of course. I sent him letters every day. But he dithered as usual, and because of that, I was captured."

"You blame him for your arrest, then?"

"Of course. Responsibility lies entirely at his door."

It was not what Jamie Skoyles had been told, but he did not disagree with his fellow prisoner. His task was to befriend the man and probe him for information when he was off guard. To that end, Skoyles had been given a complete history of Major General Charles Lee, late of the Continental Army. Born in Ireland and raised in England, Lee was the grandson of a baronet. When he entered the army as an ensign in the 44th Regiment, his own father had been in command, and they had shared in the vicious suppression of the Jacobite rebellion in 1745. Lee had been no more than a callow youth of thirteen at the time.

He was now in his midforties, a tall, lean, ugly man with a nose so large and bony that it earned him some unflattering nicknames. He was not one to hide his light under a bushel.

"I have ten times the experience of Washington," he boasted. "I fought in all the campaigns that led up to the conquest of Canada. I won laurels in Portugal. I was appointed major general in the Polish army and saw action in the Russian war against the Turks. I'm a *soldier,* Captain. Hell's teeth—it's in my blood."

"What brought you to America again?"

"King George."

"You returned with the British army?"

"No, my friend," said Lee, eyes igniting with resentment. "The king had vowed to offer me a commission when I returned to Europe. In his wisdom, however, His Majesty did not do so."

"Is that why you left England?"

"Indeed it was—so that King George would never have the chance of breaking a promise to me again."

A suite of rooms in City Hall, New York, was serving as a temporary prison. Jamie Skoyles had been locked up with Lee in very comfortable surroundings. As their most important captive, the general was being treated with respect. The fact that fifty men guarded him showed how determined the British were to hold on to the man. Lee was shrewd, watchful, and highly intelligent. It had taken Skoyles over an hour to convince him that he, too, was a prisoner of the British army. The general searched for more detail.

"You say that you were in the 24th Foot."

"That is so, sir."

"Under the command of Major Acland."

"No," replied Skoyles, knowing that he was being tested, "under Brigadier General Fraser. Major Acland belonged to the 20th Foot and commanded a grenadier battalion." He gave a nostalgic smile. "I was fortunate enough to play cards with both of them on several occasions."

"I heard that Simon Fraser was killed at Bemis Heights."

"Shot from his horse by a marksman."

"We could do with more sharpshooters like him."

"He was one of Daniel Morgan's riflemen."

"How did you feel when the battle was over?"

"Relieved that the better side had won," said Skoyles, "but keen not to show it. My orders were to remain with the British army to gather what intelligence I could from Gentleman Johnny."

"He's a slippery customer."

"He's also very fond of gambling. That's where I picked up all my information—at the card table. It was clear from the start that he had no real commitment to the terms of the convention. He talked of a secret letter from General Howe at one point," Skoyles continued. "I'm quite sure that it contained instructions to divert the transports that were supposed to take the men back to England. General Howe wanted them in New York, and I have it on good authority that the British would not have released a single prisoner in exchange."

"On good authority?"

"Major Walter Doel. He questioned me when I came to New York."

"Yes, I've met the major. A tall, thin man with a mustache."

"No, sir. He's fat and clean-shaven."

"And far too stupid to interrogate prisoners. I tied him in knots."

"He could not make up his mind about me," Skoyles explained. "I invented a fanciful story about how I'd escaped from Cambridge, and he seemed to believe me at first. But he wanted to confirm certain details about me by writing to General Burgoyne."

"So they're keeping you under lock and key?"

"Until they are satisfied that I'm telling the truth. I'm being sent to Philadelphia. They think that General Howe will be interested in what I can tell him about the situation with the Convention army."

"Only if he accepts that you're loyal to the British army."

"Quite," said Skoyles. "If he does not, I'll be hanged as a spy."

"You seem extraordinarily untroubled by that possibility," said Lee, struck by his calmness. "Have you no fear of the rope?"

"None—because they'll never get me to Philadelphia."

"Are you so confident of escape?"

"I've done it many times before."

Skoyles had been so prompt and confiding that Charles Lee was slowly won over. He believed that Skoyles was working for the rebel cause and that he had been assisted in his flight from Cambridge by guards who knew where his true allegiance lay. Skoyles had not dared to mention that Elizabeth Rainham, Tom Caffrey, and Polly Bragg had been with him at the time.

Lee rose from his chair and walked restlessly around the room. In an old shirt and torn breeches, he looked very slovenly. Skoyles noticed that he had not shaved properly that morning. Lee suddenly winced as if he were in pain, then he turned angrily on his companion.

"I don't deserve to be here!" he exclaimed with passion. "Congress should be doing everything in their power to get me exchanged."

"The Continental Army has nobody of your rank in captivity."

"Nobody of my rank or tactical genius."

"That goes without saying, General."

"The British wanted to shoot me as a deserter, but even they could not bend the law sufficiently. I resigned my commission before I came to America so I did not desert." He put out his chest. "I simply found a worthier cause for which to fight."

"And you've done so with immense success," said Skoyles honestly. "Your reputation on the battlefield is second to none, sir. No wonder the British are so pleased to capture you. Your grasp of strategy is unparalleled."

"Do you know what John Adams said when he first met me?"

"No, sir."

"That he had never expected to find a man who had read more military history than he. More of everything," he said, gesturing toward a pile of books on the table. "They have at least had the good grace to let me have my library." He picked up a book. "Have you read Rousseau?"

"Not in the original French," said Skoyles.

"But you are familiar with his ideas?"

"I've heard much about the *Social Contract*. I find its notions very appealing. Democracy has so many advantages. It treats everyone as an equal and not mere subjects of a higher power."

"Precisely," said Lee, standing over him like a teacher with a pupil. "For a start, it does away with the immoral institution of kingship. There is no place for monarchy in the ideal society that Jean-Jacques Rousseau envisages. Such a society could never exist in England."

"It's too mired in prejudice, General."

"Prejudice, corruption, folly, and injustice!" yelled the other with a show of anger. "God's blood! I'd not care if the whole bloody island sank into the sea and took that stinking, brown turd of a king with it. Yes, and those feckless, prattling, lying politicians can drown as well—two-faced, frigging rogues, that they are!"

He ranted on for several minutes. Skoyles heard him out. He had been warned that Lee was inclined to lose his temper on occasion and resort to obscenity. It was odd to hear such bad language coming from the mouth of a man who could read French and whose little library included texts in Greek and Latin. When he had finished his tirade, Lee collapsed into a chair and glared sullenly around the room. Skoyles waited a long time before initiating conversation.

"How have you been treated here, General?" he asked.

"What?" snapped the other, jerked out of his reverie.

"The British seem to have given you some privileges at least."

"But not the ones I requested, Captain. My dogs, for instance."

"Dogs?"

"Splendid animals," said Lee ardently, "and capable of a loyalty that no human being can match. You can trust dogs. They do not break their promises." He became sentimental. "I travel with a whole pack of them, Captain Skoyles. They are my family. When I first came to America, I bought a Pomeranian as big as a bear, but they will not even let me see him. One little dog is all that I am permitted—Caesar."

"What else do you miss?" asked Skoyles.

"Giuseppe."

"Another of your dogs?"

"No, man. Giuseppe Minghini is my servant."

"Oh, I see."

"A person like me needs someone to look after him, but Giuseppe's time with me is restricted. It's humiliating to do things for myself."

"You fare much better than our rank and file, sir."

"And so I should. Damnation—I'm a major general!"

"Conditions in New York are deplorable," said Skoyles with genuine sympathy. "Major Doel bragged about it. He was proud of the way they maltreat their prisoners. He told me of four hundred men crowded into a French church so small that they cannot all lie down at the same time. Since they were refused firewood, they burned the pews and doors to keep warm. And they eat their pork raw."

"I am allowed decent meals," said Lee, grudgingly.

"That's not the case in the prison ships."

"You've no need to tell me that, Captain. When we exchanged prisoners with the British, the poor wretches they released from the hulks were walking skeletons. Instead of getting soldiers, we got hundreds of miserable invalids, unfit for service of any kind."

"At least they survived their ordeal," said Skoyles. "Many of their fellows died in chains of starvation or disease. They were supposed to be given wholesome meals to keep them alive, but the food never reached them and they were given scraps."

"Do you know who was responsible for that?"

"Yes, sir—the commissar of prisoners."

"A certain Joshua Loring," said Lee with contempt. "While our men waste away from hunger, that monster pockets the money that should have bought them provisions. And when thousands of them die," he went on, waving an angry fist, "Mr. Loring has the gall to invoice the army for the food he pretends to supply to men who are no longer alive. He's nothing but a vulture, pecking at the bones of dead men who lie in their own excrement."

"Everyone knows how Joshua Loring secured the appointment."

"Between the thighs of his pretty wife."

"General Howe felt the need for companionship."

"So he condemns thousands of our soldiers to a hideous death."

"I doubt if he saw it quite like that."

"Yet it's exactly what has happened, Captain Skoyles."

"I regret it as much as you, sir."

"I've written to Howe to complain about the inhuman treatment of our prisoners of war," said Lee scornfully. "He's never had the time to fashion a reply. He's too busy fucking Mrs. Loring and making that egregious husband of hers rich. That's the British commander in chief for you, Captain—a cunt-struck buffoon in gold braid epaulets!"

With the orchestra playing a reel, General William Howe swept into the room that evening with Mrs. Loring on his arm, and collected a battery of obsequious smiles, polite nods, and mild applause. His fellow officers saw nothing unusual or outlandish in the sight of a married man in the company of someone else's wife when he was three thousand miles away from home. Howe was by no means the only soldier in the room who was enjoying an adulterous liaison with a gorgeous young woman.

Tory citizens of Philadelphia took a more critical view of Howe's behavior, but they hid their feelings behind fixed expressions of approval. In expelling the revolutionary government, the British army had restored loyalty to the Crown as a guiding precept and lifted the gloom that had pervaded the city when it had been under the control of Congress. The Tories felt that Philadelphia had been handed back to them, and they were deeply grateful for that.

The room was full, the reel lively, and the floor filled with whirling dancers. Betsey Loring watched them with envy from beside a pillar.

"We must join in the next dance," she insisted.

"We will," said Howe, patting her gloved hand. "We will, we will,"

"I came here to be *seen*."

"There's not a man in the room who can take his eyes off you."

It was true. Mrs. Loring was wearing a dress of pink taffeta with a low-cut bodice, side hoops under the skirt, and echelle trimming that consisted of tiny bows. She wore dainty, high-heeled shoes on her feet, and her hair was piled high on her head in an oval shape and kept in place with wire frames. The whole effect was quite dazzling.

"You are truly the belle of the ball," he whispered in her ear.

"As befits a general's lady."

"I have always had an eye for beauty."

"I am grateful to be its beneficiary," she said.

"You can show me the extent of your gratitude later."

They exchanged a conspiratorial smile. The reel was coming to an end and Betsey was keen to take her turn on the floor. The general, however, had just seen someone enter the room. He excused himself and went across to speak to Lieutenant Hugh Orde, a gaunt young man in his early twenties. Howe took him aside.

"Well?" he asked.

"There's no sign of him, General."

"There must be."

"We've searched everywhere," said Orde, "but in vain. The problem is that we don't really know what Ezekiel Proudfoot looks like, so we are hunting for a ghost. It may be that he's not even in Philadelphia."

"Oh, he's here," Howe insisted. "I feel it."

"He might be at Valley Forge with General Washington."

"The printing press is in the city, and that's where Proudfoot will be. Find one and we find the other."

"Both are proving confoundedly elusive, sir."

"Then double the number of men you have—treble it, if need be."

"It's not simply a question of numbers," said Orde reasonably. "If the fellow is in the city, he can keep on the move. When he has so many hiding places at his disposal, a brigade could not flush him out. The same goes for that press, General. That, too, can be shifted when they see us approach."

"Proudfoot must be caught somehow," said Howe petulantly.

"Then perhaps I might make a suggestion."

"Go on."

"This man is not here by accident," Orde explained. "He was sent here for a purpose by General Washington. If we want to know where we can find Ezekiel Proudfoot in Philadelphia, we must go to Valley Forge to ask about his whereabouts. Washington will know exactly where he is."

"He's hardly likely to tell us, Lieutenant, is he?"

"He'd confide in those closest to him."

"How does that help us?"

"It doesn't at the moment," Orde confessed. "But it might if we could get someone inside the camp who could win Washington's trust. If we chose the right person, he could, in time, learn the precise location of the printing press and of Proudfoot's lodging. A clever spy could save us weeks of futile searches, General."

Howe ruminated. "You are right," he said. "We need such a man."

"Choosing him will be a difficult exercise," cautioned Orde.

"I don't care how difficult it is—find him!"

A day in the company of Charles Lee was fatiguing. He was so fond of discussing ideas and so ready to criticize his fellow officers that he talked for hours on end. It was not until late at night that Jamie Skoyles was finally able to get to bed. He and his fellow prisoner were conducted to an upstairs room that was completely bare except for the two mattresses on the floor. Four guards were posted outside the door, and when he looked through the window, Skoyles saw that four sentries were on duty below. The British were determined not to let their prize catch escape.

"Good night, sir," said Skoyles, lying on his mattress and pulling the blankets over him. "I'll see you in the morning."

"Yes," replied Lee sardonically. "I'm not going anywhere."

They lay side by side in the dark. Lee soon drifted asleep, but Skoyles was plagued by thoughts of Tom Caffrey and Polly Bragg. He had no idea what had happened to them since their premature departure from a Massachusetts farmhouse. Had they been recaptured? Were they, in fact, still alive? Their fate troubled him for a long time. It was only when his thoughts turned to Elizabeth Rainham that he was soothed. Still in New York, she was safe and sound, taken in by a major and his wife, and able to recuperate after the hardships of their escape. Fond thoughts of Elizabeth gradually helped to lull Skoyles to sleep.

He was soon trapped in a nightmare, reliving the horrors of being caught in a storm at sea and having the additional problem of being the only person in the fishing boat this time. It was completely out of control. As a colossal wave hit the vessel, it was tossed high into the sky and Skoyles was thrown headfirst into the turbulent sea. As he came to the surface, he looked upward and saw his boat spinning down toward him through the air. Striking him hard, it pinned him down like a ton weight and made it impossible for him to breathe.

Skoyles began to choke. He came out of his dream to find that Charles Lee was sitting astride him, trapping his arms under the blanket so that he could not move them. Strong hands were around Skoyles's throat. They slowly tightened.

"Now, then, Captain Jamie Skoyles of the 24th Foot," he said with mocking politeness, "what are you *really* doing here?"

CHAPTER NINE

Taken completely by surprise, Skoyles was in a desperate situation. Charles Lee was a strong man, and he had a firm grip on his victim's throat. There was no doubting his ability or readiness to kill. He released the pressure slightly so that Skoyles could actually speak.

"I'm exactly who I say I am," gasped Skoyles.

"Oh, I'm quite sure that you are. What I'm not so certain about is why you've been incarcerated here."

"I told you. They're suspicious of me."

"And so am I," snarled Lee. "With good reason, too. I don't trust you, Captain Skoyles."

"Everything I said was the truth."

"You told me what you thought I wanted to hear and, I admit, I was taken in at first. Then it occurred to me that you might have been put in here with me for a purpose."

"Yes," said Skoyles. "They wanted me locked up."

"If they don't believe your story, why not keep you in the jail on the Common? It seems strange to me that, of all the places they could have sent you, they chose here. Why did they do that?"

"Ask them."

"Was it to give you a chance to worm information out of me?"

"No!"

"How do I know that?"

"Because I swear it."

"With your life in danger, you'd swear to anything."

He tightened his hold, but Skoyles was not going to be threatened again. His retaliation was swift and decisive. Putting all his energy into the move, he

137

pushed himself up hard then twisted to one side, toppling his attacker and freeing his hands from the blankets. He was on Lee in a flash, grappling with him and rolling over on the floor. Now that he could fight on equal terms, Skoyles soon began to master his opponent. Lee was older, slower, and patently unused to a brawl. A year in captivity had made him indolent. Skoyles, by contrast, had been hardened in battle and toughened by constant exercise. His superior strength and fitness were self-evident. It was not long before Major General Charles Lee was pinned to the ground on his back with Skoyles's knees across his arms.

"So that's why you're here," said Lee, breathing heavily. "They've paid you to murder *me*."

"No, sir. I just want to prove that I'm on your side."

"By wrestling me into submission?"

"By showing you that I can get the upper hand, if I wish," said Skoyles coolly. "Now, I think we've had enough fighting for one night, don't you? I'll let you go on one condition—that you give me your word you won't try to strangle me again."

Lee gave a dry laugh. "You're far more likely to strangle me."

"Do I have your promise?"

"You do, old chap," said Lee, relaxing. "Now, please get off me."

"With pleasure, sir."

Skoyles stood up, but he remained on the alert in case the other man tried to overpower him again. His caution was unnecessary. It soon became clear that Charles Lee had had enough. Shaken by the tussle, all that he wanted to do was to recover. He sat up and rubbed his arms. Skoyles lowered himself to his own mattress. Their eyes had become used to the darkness now. Lee stared at him with a new respect.

"I'll wager that you've killed men before with your bare hands."

"Only when I was forced to," said Skoyles.

"I'm sorry that I mistrusted you, Captain."

"I didn't ask to be put in here with you, sir, believe me. I would much rather have ridden on to Philadelphia. I stand far more chance of escape on the road. This place is like a citadel."

"They guard me well," said Lee. "I take it as a compliment."

"Then let me give you another compliment. When the word spread that the famous General Lee had been captured, cheers went up throughout the entire British army. It was felt that Washington had been deprived of his best tactician," said Skoyles with sincerity, "and it was a cause for celebration."

"The man who caught me celebrated royally, I know that. In taking me from the battlefield, he seemed to think that he'd won the whole war. Do you know who the wretched fellow was?"

"Lieutenant Colonel Banastre Tarleton."

"A black-hearted fiend from the depths of hell."

"Yes," agreed Skoyles. "He's not known for his tenderness."

"He's a ruthless butcher."

"Yet he spared your life."

"Only because he thought I'd be more use to them alive than dead," said Lee bitterly. "I'm a trophy. They can display me like an animal in a cage." He snorted. "It was only by sheer luck that Tarleton caught me in the first place. I'd been careless. I was in a tavern without my usual bodyguards. The redcoats happened to ride up—God rot their guts!—and that was that. Since then, I've spent a year twiddling my thumbs in captivity."

"You've had Rousseau and the other books."

"But only one dog—and limited use of my manservant."

"You'll have everything restored when America wins this war."

"How can it do that without me?" Lee demanded.

"You made it more difficult for them by being captured," Skoyles conceded, "but the Continentals are bound to win in the end by wearing the enemy down. Britain simply doesn't have an army big enough to subdue thirteen colonies."

"Even that imbecile, General Howe, realizes that."

"Then why does he not sue for peace?"

"That's what he was ready to do," said Lee irritably. "His brother, Admiral Howe, was charged with initiating peace negotiations, and they wanted me to broker them. Nothing, alas, came of it. Since the brothers were uncertain of winning—fearing that the French might, in time, support us openly—I even took the trouble to show them how victory could be achieved in a mere two months."

"Indeed?" Skoyles was startled. "And how was that?"

"First, by severing the colonies along the line of the Hudson. Second, by sailing to Chesapeake Bay and cutting the southern colonies off. Third, by occupying Annapolis, Baltimore, and Alexandria."

"You actually agreed to *help* the enemy?"

"Of course not, man."

"That's what it sounds like, sir."

"I was trying to bring the conflict to an end so that we—the rebel army—could have peace with honor. I gave them no details about the size and disposition of our forces," he stressed, "and in urging them to disperse their men over a wide area, I was ensuring that there would be no major battle for us to fight. In a large-scale encounter, the British would always have the advantage."

"Let me understand you aright," said Skoyles, wrestling with the implications of what he had just heard. "You advised the British?"

"It was in our interest for me to do so."

"By letting them win the war?"

"By bringing it to an end in such a way that favorable terms could be offered to us. I loathe monarchy," Lee affirmed, "and I despise the way that King George has treated the colonies. On the other hand, I'm not entirely convinced that a republic is the ideal form of government."

"But that's what you were fighting for—independence."

"Yes, and a peace treaty of the kind that I envisaged would have guaranteed us a fair amount of independence."

"A country is either independent or it is not."

"You are just playing with words."

"No," said Skoyles with passion, "there's a serious point at issue here. Thousands of men are ready to lay down their lives in the hope of creating a republic. You'll not find one who bears arms so that he can achieve what you call a fair amount of independence."

"These things are relative, Captain Skoyles," said Lee blandly. "Nobody would be more delighted than me to see the British driven from these shores, and the thirteen colonies wrested from the tyrannical grasp of King George. But it may have to be done in stages."

"We must agree to differ."

"The war has gone on too long. We need peace."

"On our terms," Skoyles pressed. "American independence."

Lee laughed. "And to think I questioned your sincerity," he said. "It's all too obvious which side you are on now."

Skoyles was glad to have convinced him, but he was also troubled by the ardor with which he had spoken. Ideas that should have been anathema to a

British soldier had come tumbling so naturally from his lips that he surprised himself. The discussion had roused him, but his sense of invigoration was tempered by unease.

Lee yawned. "Is it safe for me to go to sleep now?"

"I might ask the same of you, sir."

"Oh, there's no danger from me, Captain."

"I'm very glad to hear it."

"You not only proved the stronger man in a fight, you showed me that you've got revolutionary blood in your veins." He pulled the blankets over him. "Good night, my friend."

"One last thing, sir."

"Yes?"

"You spoke very slightingly to me of General Washington," Skoyles recalled. "I have more respect for him as a commander. Do not despair of him yet. Against all the odds, he might still lead us to victory."

George Washington deployed his men with skill. They were ready for action. Heavy rain had dispelled the first snowfall at Valley Forge and left a quagmire in its wake. Instead of trudging through thick mud as they built their cabins, the soldiers were given a chance to close with the enemy and gain something even more precious than military victory. They could get food.

Washington was ready for the British. Forewarned by intelligence from Philadelphia, he sent his men out in various directions, covering all districts where the British army was likely to forage. He gave strict orders that his troops were to watch and wait. It was important to let the redcoats round up what animals were available. Because they could pay for them in coin, rather than with fiduciary money issued by Congress, the redcoats would find farmers more ready to sell to them.

The foraging expedition involved thousands of redcoats and, even though they divided into groups and set off in different directions, some detachments were still too large for the rebel soldiers to take on. Others, however, were not. One regiment of Continental soldiers lay in ambush for hours until they saw their opportunity. When the British troops were heading back toward Frankford with the supplies they had managed to acquire, the rebels fired on them from concealed positions, killing a few but wounding many more.

To save their skins, the redcoats fled the field, and the delighted attackers were able to assess the day's haul—cattle, oxen, sheep, and hogs, together with dozens of squawking chickens, imprisoned in wicker baskets. They carried their booty back to Valley Forge as if they had just captured the colors of an enemy regiment. George Washington was the first to congratulate them on their success.

"We'll be able to eat meat for a change," he observed.

"Yes," said his adjutant, "and the beauty of it is that we did not have to pay a single penny for it. The British picked up the bill."

"That contents me more than I can say. There are few things more pleasurable than sending bad tidings to General Howe."

Elizabeth Rainham was perplexed. Now that she was in New York City, the main base of the British army, she ought to be feeling relieved and reassured. Instead, she was increasingly nervous and succumbed to moments of real fear whenever she reflected on the perils that she and Jamie Skoyles had come through. Events had happened so quickly that she had had no time to appreciate the full danger involved. Elizabeth had been borne along by a wild excitement such as she had never known before. Recollecting it all now, she saw how close to death they had come during their escape, and it left her thoroughly shaken.

The city was a haven. It was not only the sight of so many red uniforms in the streets that rallied her. She had been taken in by Major Donald Wright and his wife, a delightful couple who had given her a room in their house in Queen Street and acquainted her with some of the luxuries she had not known for a long time. Elizabeth was able to take a bath and wash her hair. Because she and Georgina Wright were of the same age, height, and build, she was able to discard the soiled dress she had worn all the way from Cambridge and put on one that Mrs. Wright kindly lent her. To someone as fastidious as Elizabeth, it was a joy to return to a degree of normality. And yet those occasional shudders kept disturbing her. Safe at last, she now was haunted by her brush with terror.

New York City had allowed her another indulgence. She had an opportunity to read again, to lose hour upon hour in the magic of a novel and be transported into an engaging fictional world. Elizabeth was halfway through her latest book that afternoon when she heard someone knock on the front door. Since both her hosts and the servants were out of the house, she went to answer the door herself and was thrilled to find that it was Jamie Skoyles. As soon as he stepped over the threshold, they embraced warmly. Elizabeth then conducted him into the parlor.

"I did not expect you this early," she said.

"There's been a change of plan."

"You were due to call this evening when Major Wright and Georgina will be here."

"That may not be possible," he told her. "I've been summoned to meet General Clinton to get my orders."

"What sort of orders?"

"I'm being sent to Philadelphia."

"Oh, Jamie—no!"

The thought of being separated from him jolted her. She flung herself into his arms and held him tight. Skoyles hugged her to him. Like Elizabeth, he had been able to wash off the grime of travel and put on clean apparel once more. Instead of being a nameless fugitive, he was Captain Jamie Skoyles again, wearing his uniform with pride and enjoying the privileges that came with his rank. One privilege of their escape, however, had had to be sacrificed, and it was a severe loss. Since they were not married, he had had to surrender Elizabeth to the care of Donald and Georgina Wright. Those precious days together on the run were behind them. Convention set them apart. Feeling her in his arms again, he realized how much he had missed their intimacy. Skoyles held her by the shoulders so that he could appraise her.

"You should be happy for me, Elizabeth," he said.

"Happy that you're going away?"

"It's a form of promotion. General Clinton is very pleased with what I've been able to do since I've been here."

"I want you to stay, Jamie."

"I know, and part of me hates the idea of having to leave you behind. But I have the consolation of knowing that you are completely safe and staying with good friends. Besides," he went on, "Philadelphia is not all that far away. I'll be back in due course."

"What if something should happen in the meantime?" she asked. "I'll be worried that you might get yourself injured or even killed."

"There's little chance of that, Elizabeth. The Continental Army has gone off to winter quarters and we shan't see any major engagements until next spring."

"Then why are you being sent to Philadelphia?"

"I'll know the full details this evening."

"When do you leave?"

"At first light tomorrow."

Elizabeth blenched. "Tomorrow? Why so soon?"

"General Clinton must have a reason."

"Does that mean this is the last time I shall see you, Jamie?"

"Probably. But I'll send word of where I'll be. And we'll be able to keep in touch by letter." He glanced around. "Where's Major Wright?"

"He and Georgina are visiting friends?"

"What about the servants?"

"I'm all alone in the house."

Skoyles grinned. "Oh, no, you're not, Miss Rainham." He kissed her full on the lips. "I'm here as well."

"I've missed you so much, Jamie," she said, clinging to him.

"I know."

"Have you missed me?"

"Of course."

"How much?"

"Let's go upstairs," he said, easing her into the hallway.

"I asked you a question."

"Then I'll give you an answer, Elizabeth."

"When?"

"Afterward."

With an arm around her, he led her up the steps to her room.

General Howe was almost apoplectic. As he paced up and down his office at the British headquarters in Philadelphia, his cheeks were red and he was grinding his teeth audibly. Coming to a halt, he turned on Hugh Orde with a face of thunder.

"They *stole* our animals?" he said, subjecting the young lieutenant to a full glare. "British soldiers allowed the enemy to take food supplies for which *we* had paid?"

"That is the report I received, general."

"Zounds! This is insupportable! We have enough trouble feeding our army without provisioning theirs."

"It was unfortunate, I grant you."

"Unfortunate!"

"But," said Orde quickly, anxious not to provoke him, "I have news that may help to take away the sour taste a little. General Clinton has sent a Captain Skoyles to us with the highest recommendation. The captain managed to escape from the Convention army that is being held at Cambridge and made his way to New York by land and sea."

"A capable man, obviously. He'll be able to give us accurate information about the plight of General Burgoyne and his men."

"He can do more than that, sir. General Clinton was so impressed with him that they locked him up with Charles Lee for a day. Captain Skoyles was able to persuade Lee that he was a rebel spy and, having won his confidence, drew all sorts of intelligence out of him."

"Splendid," said Howe, rubbing his hands. "I long to hear it."

"The captain is waiting outside."

"Then send him in, man. I'll speak to him alone."

The lieutenant nodded and opened the door. Inviting the visitor in, he first introduced him to General Howe, then left. The general studied the newcomer. Back in uniform, Jamie Skoyles had the assurance and military bearing of someone who had spent over half his life in the British army. Howe indicated a chair, then resumed his own seat behind the desk. Skoyles sat opposite him.

"Your reputation comes before you, Captain," said Howe. "When the lieutenant first mentioned your name, I thought it sounded vaguely familiar. You are Captain Skoyles of the 24th Foot, are you not?"

"Yes, General."

"You've been mentioned in dispatches."

"That's very gratifying."

"General Burgoyne holds you in high esteem. How is he?"

"In low spirits, sir," replied Skoyles, slipping a hand into his pocket. "At General Clinton's request, I prepared a written report on the frightful conditions that the Convention army faces." He reached forward to put some sheets of paper on the desk. "I've brought a copy of that report for you. It makes rather sad reading, I fear."

"Yes, the rebels have betrayed us yet again."

"Congress always disliked the terms of the convention."

"That does not mean they have the right to rescind them. But enough of that," he continued, glancing at the report. "I'll read this with interest, Captain, and question you further on its detail. What I'd really like to hear about is the time you spent with Major General Lee. I can't say that I would relish being locked up with such a spiky individual."

"He's not the most endearing bedfellow," said Skoyles.

"What did you learn?"

"A great deal, sir."

Skoyles gave him a full account of his discussion with Charles Lee but said nothing about the man's attempt at strangling him. An attentive listener, Howe jotted down a few notes with his quill pen, dipping it into the inkwell on his desk at intervals. When he had finished, Skoyles felt obliged to add a comment.

"Other rebel prisoners do not live in such luxury," he said.

"Charles Lee has special privileges."

"They are denied to the men I saw at the jail on the Common. Conditions there are inhuman. There are filthy dungeons in which prisoners of war suffer solitary confinement for months."

"Those who raise their hands against us must be punished."

"Prison ships are even worse, I am told."

"They are meant to be, Captain," said Howe abruptly. "If you make imprisonment unbearable, you gain new recruits for the navy. What would you do, if given a choice between rotting in chains or fighting against your own side?"

"I'd try to escape, General."

Howe chuckled. "Yes, to be sure. But most men have neither your skill nor your determination, Captain. Some prefer to desert."

"While the majority are left to starve or die."

"Do I detect a note of sympathy?" asked Howe sharply. "We did not ask for this war, remember. I love this country and its people. It goes against the grain for me to fight Americans. But if they entertain these absurd notions of independence—and if they persist in killing or maiming thousands of our soldiers—they must be taught a lesson. Harsh treatment of prisoners of war is part of that lesson."

"I understand, General."

"Then let's have no more criticism."

"You have my apology, sir."

"Accepted." Howe stood up and regarded him with interest. "You come at an opportune moment, Captain Skoyles. If you can convince as astute a judge of character as Charles Lee that you are really a rebel spy, then you might be able to bamboozle General Washington."

"What do you mean, sir?"

"The enemy has moved to Valley Forge, northwest of here. We need someone to get inside their encampment, to win their confidence by supplying intelligence about our army while, at the same time, collecting information about theirs."

"You must already have agents of some sort."

"Yes," said Howe. "There are plenty of Tories hereabouts who are only too ready to tell us everything they know about enemy movements. But we have nobody close to Washington himself. We must find a man to penetrate his inner circle, and I believe that I may be looking at him now."

"Thank you, sir. I'm flattered."

"Are you tempted by the assignment?"

"More than tempted," said Skoyles, thrilled at the prospect. "It has great appeal to me, General. I've been idle too long."

"Idleness is a vice that nobody could accuse you of, Captain. Some of the details of General Burgoyne's reports are coming back to me," Howe said with a smile. "You fought with distinction at Hubbardton, Bennington, and in both Saratoga battles."

"I was only one of many who did that, General."

"And the moment they imprison you at Cambridge, you not only escape. You somehow contrived to bring a young lady to safety as well."

"There were four of us involved in that escape," Skoyles said with sadness. "Two are still unaccounted for."

"The misfortune of war, Captain Skoyles." He came around the table to stand beside him. "Naturally, we will provide you with plenty of intelligence to feed to the enemy, accurate in some cases, deliberately misleading in others."

"I've done this kind of work before, General."

"Oh?"

"I posed as a new recruit in order to get inside the rebel camp at Bemis Heights. I was so helpful to them that I had the personal approval of General Gates."

147

"How did you get away afterward?"

"Very quickly, sir."

"I don't blame you," said Howe, chortling. "But we'll need you to stay in place for much longer this time. The rebels have their own spies in Philadelphia, and they are extremely competent. When we tried a surprise attack on Whitemarsh some weeks ago, Washington's men were waiting for us. And when I sent out a foraging expedition yesterday," he went on, grinding his teeth once more, "rebels ambushed one of our detachments and made off with all the animals our men had bought."

"Is that my main aim, sir—to discover who their spies are?"

"It's one of them."

"What are the others?"

"Get as close as possible to General Washington. Find out what his plans are. Search out his weaknesses."

"Yes, sir."

"In a month's time, Valley Forge will be a snowbound wilderness. I want to know how the rebels will survive. I want the numbers of those men fit for service and the details of any desertions. It will be pure hell up there in the dead of winter," said Howe, "and it will be difficult for Washington to maintain his control. His soldiers will complain. His officers will carp and bicker. Bring back any remarks you hear to the detriment of their commander. We may be able to use them."

"I will, sir, though I believe that he still has the full support of his army at this juncture."

"We must alter that situation," insisted Howe. "We must do all we can to blacken the name of George Washington. I made a start when we occupied New York. Do you know what I did?"

"No, sir."

"I commissioned a play in which he appeared. It was a satire called *The Battle of Brooklyn,* and the noble General Washington was shown as a dangerous fanatic, an inveterate whoremonger whose mistress charged him thirty dollars a night for her services."

"But, in truth, he's a man of high moral principle."

"That's an image we must seek to destroy." Howe's wrath stirred. "The rebels have no scruples about traducing *my* character," he said. "They publish all kinds of lies about me in a disgraceful newspaper called *The Pennsylvania Patriot*. That's something else you need to establish."

"What is, General?"

"The name of the editor and the location of the printing press."

"Are they here in Philadelphia?"

"Most certainly. And so is that viper of a silversmith. He is the man I'm most anxious to track down. His name is Ezekiel Proudfoot."

"Proudfoot?" repeated Skoyles with a smile of recognition.

"You know the man?"

"Only by reputation."

"He drew the most offensive cartoon about me."

"He's a talented artist," said Skoyles, pleased to hear that he might meet Proudfoot again, but careful to hide the fact that they were friends. "I've seen a lot of his work."

"I've seen far too much of it," said Howe.

"And you think that he is in the city as well?"

"He must be, Captain Skoyles."

"How do you know?"

"Because I can *smell* the rogue."

"You want me to find out his whereabouts?"

"I want you to do far more than that."

"Oh?"

"I want you to discover where Ezekiel Proudfoot is hiding," said Howe vengefully, "then cut off both his hands."

When he finally got back to Valley Forge, looking tired and travel-stained, Major John Clark reported at once to his commander at headquarters. Washington could see the fatigue etched into his features.

"You push yourself too hard, Major," he said.

"Circumstance demands it."

"You go to and from Philadelphia far too often."

"My horse picked up a stone and went lame," Clark explained. "I had to walk most of the way. What's a mere twenty miles?"

"Enough to wear out any man. Tell me your news."

They were inside the room that the commander used as his office, and Clark was relieved to be sitting down at last. Having made contact with most of his agents in Philadelphia, he was able to pass on a lot of intelligence. Most of it depressed Washington—especially that fact that the British army was ever more comfortably ensconced in the city—but some of the tidings brought pleasure. The general laughed aloud when he heard how upset General Howe had been at the ambush of one of his foraging parties.

"How much did our men get exactly?" asked Clark.

"Plenty of hay, for a start. Our horses were in sore need of that."

"What else?"

"About forty animals and dozens of chickens."

"A tidy amount."

"Not when we have to feed nearly twelve thousand men," said Washington, shaking his head, "though that number is slowly decreasing."

"More desertions and soldiers on furlough?"

"Disease is turning out to be another worry, Major. When you pack so many men together, sickness spreads more easily. Typhoid, typhus, dysentery, and pneumonia can be killers if patients do not get good medical attention. We've had to transfer some of our worst cases to hospitals in places like Yellow Springs, Ephrata, and Bethlehem."

"What about smallpox, sir?"

"The situation is more encouraging there."

"How many men have been inoculated?"

"About a third of our army," Washington told him. "Many of them were skeptical about the whole notion, but one prick of a needle may save their lives. A smallpox epidemic in camp would be a catastrophe."

"We must keep our men fit enough to fight."

"I need to keep *you* healthy as well, Major. The man who controls our intelligence operation is far more important than a private soldier."

Clark smiled bravely. "I'll be fine when I've rested, sir."

"Have some of our meat while it's still available."

"Yes, please," said the other, licking his lips. "But you've not been sitting on your hands here, I see. In the short time I was away, you've established some more signal trees. I noticed them as I came toward the camp."

"Lookout posts are vital," Washington emphasized, "which is why those lines of chestnut trees are a boon to us. We cut out the tops and install a platform instead. From a tree on the summit of Mount Joy, a lookout can see for miles and send a signal to the next post."

"It must be freezing up there in those trees—especially at night."

"The posts must be manned twenty-four hours a day."

"The men will be blocks of ice," said Clark, with compassion. "Sentry duty is likely to produce even more deserters in due course."

Washington was crisp. "They know the punishment. If enlisted soldiers try to leave Valley Forge, they'll be shot or hanged. And I'll not hold back from flogging any malingerers, either. We must exert control. But," he went on, adopting a more pleasant tone, "let's talk of other things. Did you see Ezekiel Proudfoot in Philadelphia?"

"No, sir."

"But I thought the two of you entered the city together."

"I traveled with a man named Reece Allen."

"My apologies," said Washington with a half smile. "I'd forgotten that our silversmith has been christened again. How is Mr. Allen?"

"To be frank," admitted Clark, "I'm rather worried about him."

"Worried?"

"The work he does for the newspaper is above reproach, and they are delighted to have him. Pearsall Hughes described him as a blessing from above, and there very few people who earn that kind of comment from our pugnacious bookseller."

"So why do you have qualms about Mr. Allen?"

"He has had no experience of this kind of work."

"Nobody had until the war broke out, Major."

"I agree," said Clark, "but some take to it more naturally than others. Reece Allen is a silversmith and not a trained spy. My fear is that he may sooner or later give himself away."

"Not if Pearsall Hughes keeps an eye on him."

"He's being protected by Pontius Pilate as well."

"Who?"

"The landlord of the King George Tavern, sir. That's his nickname."

"I hope that's all it is," said Washington. "We don't want any of our sympathizers to wash his hands of the whole business. And I do hope that your fears about Reece Allen are groundless. He's already fired one artistic broadside at General Howe and secured a direct hit."

"He was working on another when I left."

"Will this one feature the ever-compliant Mrs. Loring?"

"I think not."

"Then what's its subject?"

"Brotherhood, sir," replied Clark. "I think that he intends to aim a few barbs at Admiral Howe as well this time."

"Well done, Mr. Allen!" she said. "You excelled yourself."

"Thank you, Mrs. Hughes."

"I don't believe the cartoon should be confined to the *Patriot*. It should be printed on its own and put up all over Philadelphia."

"With a copy sent to Admiral Howe," Proudfoot suggested.

"Of course."

"See to it, Pearsall," she ordered.

Hughes was jocular. "Your word, Miranda, is my command."

"Mr. Allen will bear witness to that promise."

The three of them were having supper together in a room at the rear of the bookshop. Although no copy of *The Pennsylvania Patriot* was on the premises, Miranda Hughes had seen the latest issue when it first came off the press and she praised Ezekiel Proudfoot's cartoon time and again. Its caption was simple: *Brothers-in-Arms*. Distinguished by his admiral's hat, Richard Howe, the naval commander, was dancing a hornpipe on the deck of a frigate with his brother, General William Howe. Their arms were linked. In the hold below their feet, however, were dozens of rebel prisoners, fettered to iron rings and reduced to skeletons by starvation. In the background, sailors were callously tossing dead Continental soldiers overboard.

The message had an immediate impact. No magnanimity could be expected from the two brothers. Conquest, to them, meant utter subjection. While they did their dance of triumph on a British vessel, American soldiers died in agony beneath them. The success of the Howe brothers was thus built on the bones of prisoners of war. Throughout the thirteen colonies, thousands of families would never see their soldier sons, brothers, or fathers again. They would perish in captivity.

"My article on the state of the prisons will buttress the cartoon," said

Hughes through a mouthful of food. "General Washington has protested strongly, but nothing is done."

"It's heartbreaking," Proudfoot declared. "Congress should send money to alleviate their plight."

"They've done so, Mr. Allen, but it does not reach the prisoners. My guess is that it merely helps to line the pockets of the commissary of prisons—that odious creature, Joshua Loring. How could any man trade his wife for the chance to make money by such squalid means?"

"I trust that *you* would never do so, Pearsall," Miranda teased him.

"Why, has General Howe made advances to you, my dear?"

"Frequently."

"And did you encourage them?"

"Not unless he believes that being hit over the head with the *Encyclopaedia Britannica* can be construed as encouragement. Forgive me, Mr. Allen," she said, a hand on his arm. "I jest. Though we do possess the three-volume encyclopaedia, as it happens. The only set in America. It was published in Scotland a few years ago and is a mine of information."

"So is *The Pennsylvania Patriot*," Hughes noted.

"I could hardly hit General Howe over the head with that."

"Mr. Allen has done so—figuratively speaking."

"Twice in succession."

Proudfoot had never met a married couple like Pearsall and Miranda Hughes. They were stimulating company, bubbling with ideas and taking a delight in verbal fencing. It was a far cry from Proudfoot's own domestic life. His wife and children had been massacred by some of the Hessian soldiers hired by the British army. While she had been alive, however, Selina Proudfoot had been a quiet, conscientious, God-fearing woman whose reading was limited entirely to the Bible. She had not been as educated or outspoken as Miranda Hughes, but her husband had loved her dearly.

"Now, what news on the Rialto?" Hughes asked.

Proudfoot was baffled. "I beg your pardon?"

"My husband was quoting from Shakespeare," Miranda explained.

"*The Merchant of Venice,* in fact." said Hughes. "I wanted to know the tidings from the King George Tavern?"

"It continues to do good business," Proudfoot answered.

"What of Pontius?"

"Still sedulously washing his hands."

"Have you befriended any of the British officers?"

"Yes," said Proudfoot. "There's a lieutenant who can't hold his drink, so I make sure that I buy him plenty of it. When he's in his cups, he'll tell me anything. Most of his news is worthless, but he did mention something of interest about a play—not Shakespeare this time."

"Then who is the author?"

"One of the officers stationed in New York, apparently. It's a play that was staged there with much success."

"Does it have a title?"

"The Battle of Brooklyn."

"I can see why it appeals to the British," said Hughes sourly. "They seized Brooklyn Heights and Governors Island so that they were in position to invade Manhattan and capture New York City."

"How can you put a battle on stage?" asked Miranda.

"Shakespeare did it all the time, my dear."

"Even he might have difficulty portraying the action in Brooklyn."

"From what I gathered," said Proudfoot, "the play is an excuse to attack General Washington and drag his name through the mud. It's a cruel satire and—according to the drunken lieutenant—it's very comical. He saw it when his regiment was stationed in New York."

Hughes was pensive. "Cruel and comical, eh?" he said. "Slander against George Washington. Perhaps the performance should not go ahead uninterrupted. *We* can be cruel and comical, if we choose."

The picket squads at Valley Forge were placed half a mile apart and a sentry would patrol the intervening space until he met his counterpart from the next squad. The men would exchange a greeting, talk for a few minutes, then head back to their respective posts. Private Novus Kane hated picket duty. It was cold, lonely, unrewarding work. Kane, a short, undernourished, lantern-jawed youth from Virginia, had left his job on a farm for the promise of excitement in battle, and regretted his decision ever since. He had experienced more terror than excitement on a battlefield, and seemed to have spent his whole army career in retreat. It made him despondent.

When dawn came that morning, he was plodding back to his post yet again, body sagging and mind vacant. The first time the thickets rustled, he did not even hear the noise. It was louder the second time and Kane could not ignore it. Unslinging his musket, he pointed it in the direction from which the sound had come.

"Who goes there?" he demanded in a quavering voice.

Nobody replied but the thickets began to shake slightly.

"Come out or I'll shoot!"

Isolated from his companions, and exhausted by the long night on duty, Kane barely had the strength to hold his weapon still. But he knew his duty and he knew what his sergeant would say if he failed in it. He swallowed hard, then tried to put some firmness into his tone.

"This is your last warning—come out now!"

The thickets shook more violently, as if in mockery. Kane could stand no more suspense. Finger around the trigger, he pulled hard, only to hear a dull click as the flint failed to ignite. He looked at his musket in despair, then he backed away from the thickets. After he had gone a few yards, a pistol was thrust against the side of his head.

"Where is General Washington?" whispered a voice.

"At his h-h-h-headquarters," stuttered Kane.

"Take me there," said Jamie Skoyles. "And afterward, I'll show you how to load that musket properly."

George Washington had just finished an early breakfast when his servant brought word of an unexpected visitor. The general was so intrigued by what he was told that he put his napkin aside and went to the door himself. Outside, in the fresh morning air, was a curious sight. Watched by the anxious young private in a tattered uniform, a man in hunting clothes and a wide-brimmed hat was loading a musket with remarkable dexterity. He handed the weapon back to the open-mouthed sentry.

"There, my friend," he said. "You'll be able to kill me next time."

"Thank you, sir," mumbled the other.

Becoming aware of Washington's presence, the man doffed his hat.

"Captain Jamie Skoyles at your service, General," he said.

Washington studied him. "From a British regiment, I am told."

"The 24th Foot."

"And what are you doing here, Captain Skoyles?"

"Testing your security," said Skoyles, "and finding it wanting. Because my young friend here knew the password, we were able to get past every guard to the very door of your headquarters. Do not blame him, sir," he continued, extracting the pistol from his belt, "because he had this in his back all the time." He offered the butt of the weapon to Washington. "Take it, General—as a show of good faith on my part."

"What other weapon do you carry?" asked the other warily as he received the pistol. "Do you have something else concealed about you?"

"Nothing." Skoyles lifted both hands in the air and turned in a circle. "Let this young fellow search me, if you wish."

"I do wish." He flicked a glance at Kane. "Search him."

"Yes, General," said the private.

Flustered at being in the presence of his commanding officer, Kane tried to rest his musket against the side of the house but it fell over. He then patted Skoyles hesitantly as he felt for a hidden weapon.

"Nothing, sir," he confirmed.

"Thank you," said Washington. "What is the purpose of your visit, Captain Skoyles? Am I to take it that you have come here to surrender?"

"No, General," replied Skoyles, "but I hope, in time, to effect the surrender of the British army—with your assistance, of course."

"I was informed that you had come to help me."

"And so I can."

"How?"

"For a start, I bring you greetings from Major General Charles Lee."

"You've *seen* him?"

"I spent a day and night with the fellow."

"How can I be sure of that?"

"He began by making disparaging remarks about you, sir."

Washington stifled a smile. "That sounds like him," he conceded. He looked at Kane. "Get back to your post and be more alert next time."

"Yes, General," said the sentry, backing away gratefully.

"And you had better come inside, Captain Skoyles."

"Thank you, sir."

Skoyles followed him into the house and had his first look at the headquarters of the Continental Army. Compared to the sizable house occupied by General Howe in Philadelphia, the place seemed ridiculously small and cluttered. With the pistol on the desk in front of him, Washington sat down. He deliberately kept Skoyles standing.

"Now, sir," he began. "Explain yourself. There are easier ways to reach me than by that little performance you staged out there. A letter would have been a more acceptable form of introduction, so that I knew what to expect."

"Letters can fall into the wrong hands," said Skoyles, "as I think you know only too well."

"I do not follow you."

"I have the highest respect for you, General, but Charles Lee does not share it. He is a man of intemperate language. Something he once wrote about you fell into your hands by mistake."

"True," said Washington, piqued by the memory, "but it told me nothing about him that I did not already know. Brilliant soldier he may be, but General Lee is an awkward comrade. He never gives credit to anyone but himself. We fought together in the British army many years ago. When he returned to America, therefore," he continued, "it was natural that he should first look to me for hospitality. Charles was a restless guest, to put no finer point on it, and he brought a pack of yapping dogs with him. When he finally left, he borrowed twenty dollars from me." He gave a wan smile. "I'm not sure that he ever paid it back."

"Having met him, I would doubt it."

"And where did this encounter take place?"

"In the suite of rooms he occupies in City Hall, New York City."

"Why were you given access to him?"

"Because I convinced Governor Clinton that I might be able to coax some useful information out of him. General Lee was far too cunning for his interrogators," said Skoyles. "They questioned him dozens of times and got nothing of value from him. I pointed out that he would only confide in someone he recognized as a friend."

"And did he recognize you as such?"

"Eventually, after he tried to throttle me."

"Yes," said Washington. "Charles does have a violent streak."

157

"He also has a gift for bad language. I served in the ranks, General, and met plenty of foulmouthed corporals and sergeants. None of them could have touched General Lee."

"And yet he is such a cultured man."

"I know. He talked at length about Rousseau, and he kept quoting Plutarch at me as if he had known the man personally."

"It's obvious that you spent time with him, Captain, but you haven't explained how you managed to gain his confidence."

"The easiest way possible," said Skoyles.

"And what is that?"

"By telling him the truth."

Skoyles repeated the story he had told Lee, inventing an escape from Cambridge made possible by the connivance of rebel guards. After his incarceration with Lee, he was able to divulge intelligence that the British army had failed to get out of the prisoners, but held back anything of real substance. Washington was still not persuaded. He had heard too many plausible tales from men who claimed to support American aspirations while really seeking to undermine them. Skoyles was aware of the general's misgivings.

"Do not take my word for it, sir," he said. "I know that you are able to smuggle letters to General Lee. Ask him to vouch for me."

"I will."

"And remind him that he owes you twenty dollars."

"He's hardly in a position to repay that particular debt," said Washington drily. "You're an enterprising man, Captain Skoyles, and not afraid to take risks. In entering Valley Forge the way you did, you could easily have got yourself shot."

"Not by a sentry whose powder was damp."

"You could not rely on that fact."

"Granted," said Skoyles, "but I had something else in my favor. A guard who had been on duty all night would be tired and easier to fool. All that I had to do was to create a simple diversion."

"There are more sensible ways to get my attention."

"I preferred a direct approach, General. I didn't wish to tell my tale to endless subordinates before I even got near you. I had to seize my opportunity," said Skoyles. "I'm on my way to Philadelphia to join the British army there. It was much better to meet you *before* I reach the city than afterward. General Howe may have work for me that precludes an early visit to Valley Forge."

"I'm certain that he will employ you, Captain," said Washington. "Everything tells me that you're a remarkably good soldier. My fear is that you may also be a remarkably good liar."

"You're right to have doubts about me, General."

"Can you give me one good reason why I should trust you?"

"Not until you put me to the test."

"Test?"

"Deeds speak louder than words," said Skoyles. "Wait and see what I'm able to do for you first, and then judge me. Is that fair?"

"Extremely fair."

"Then all I need is a means to get messages to you."

"Slow down, Captain," warned the other. "I'm not putting you in touch with anyone until I know much more about you. I can see that you're a trained soldier, through and through. How long have you been in the army, where have you served, and how did you rise from the ranks to get a commission?"

Skoyles gave him a succinct account of his military career, starting with the moment when, as a youth, he had left his home in Cumberland to join the army, and detailing every campaign in which he had taken part. Suitably impressed, Washington was also quizzical.

"Throughout your life," he said, "you fought for King and Country."

"I was a loyal servant of the Crown," Skoyles admitted.

"At what point did you cease to be one?"

"There was no point as such, General. My feelings slowly changed over a period of time. To begin with, I have a natural affinity with America. It calls to me. There's nothing for me back in England. When the war is over, I hope to buy land and settle here."

"You could still do that if the British force us to surrender."

"No, sir."

"Why not?"

"Because I'd not be a free man in a free land," argued Skoyles. "I'd be one more American colonist who had to pay taxes to a corrupt government back in England."

"Does that notion offend you?"

"It turns my stomach, sir. I believe in basic human freedoms."

"And where did you pick up these ideas?"

"From various friends I've met in America."

"What about your friends back in England?"

"I've been away too long for them even to remember me, General. My world is here now. I ran away to enlist in order to escape the future that was planned for me."

"By whom?"

"My father," replied Skoyles. "He was a country doctor, and so were his own father and grandfather. I was the next in line."

"Medicine is a worthy profession."

"But it offered no thrill for an exuberant lad."

"I think there's a greater thrill in curing people than killing them."

"That may be the case, but it's an argument that had no appeal for a lively boy of fourteen. Had I stayed in Cumberland," said Skoyles with no hint of regret, "I could have had a nice, comfortable, uneventful life and been respected in the community. But I'd never have felt my blood pulse at the sights I've seen in America. I'd never have been exhilarated."

"Is that the only thing turned your mind in our direction?" said Washington cynically. "A fondness for scenery?"

"It gave me a vision of what was possible, General."

"Only if we win the war."

"Oh, you will," Skoyles contended. "It may take time but you'll prevail in the end. General Howe has conceded that by tendering his resignation. Did you know that he's ready to go home?"

"Yes, Captain."

"You should see it as a small victory."

"Howe can easily be replaced."

"Not by General Burgoyne," said the other bitterly. "He blighted his chances forever of securing the supreme command. I was part of the army that invaded from Canada, and I watched him make mistake after mistake. In the end, I lost all confidence in him. He *squandered* men," Skoyles went on. "He sent them needlessly to an early grave. You try to protect your soldiers. You would rather hit and run than sacrifice too many lives pointlessly."

Washington sighed. "We lost a lot of men at Brandywine."

"But you've saved many more in other battles you fought."

160

"I had to, Captain. Our resources are very limited. I have to harbor them." Still undecided about his visitor's honesty, he picked up the pistol from the desk and examined it. "It's loaded."

"And the powder is dry," said Skoyles. "I also reloaded that musket for the sentry. In other words, I had two weapons with which I could easily have killed the commander in chief of the Continental Army." He met Washington's gaze. "If I'd been a loyal British soldier, do you think I've had missed such a glorious chance?"

"Probably not."

"What else do I have to do to convince you?"

"A lot of things."

"Put me to the test, General."

"Oh, I shall."

"See what intelligence I can muster for you."

"I'm a trifle more concerned about the intelligence you can gather here," said Washington cautiously. "You can't have seen much of our defenses so far. I'll have you led back through the lines blindfold."

Skoyles extended a hand. "May I have my pistol back?"

"No, Captain."

"Why not?"

"Because I'd like to keep it as a memento of this illuminating little conversation that we've had. And if—so be it—you turn out to be nothing but a British spy," said Washington with a cold smile, "then I'll use this pistol to blow your brains out. You have my word on that."

CHAPTER TEN

E zekiel Proudfoot had taken great pains with his appearance. He had washed his face, brushed his hair, trimmed his beard, and put on the one reasonably smart coat that he possessed. A minor transformation had taken place. He was about to leave his room at the King George Tavern when there was a respectful knock on the door. Proudfoot opened it to be greeted by the sight of his landlord. A perplexed Henry Gilby stared at his lodger.

"Is that you, Mr. Allen?"

"The very same. Come on in, Mr. Gilby."

"Thank you," said the landlord, stepping into the room. When the door was shut behind him, his manner became less formal. "It's good to have you back with us, sir."

"Thank you," said Proudfoot.

"You are going out, I see."

"One of my new acquaintances has invited me to a play."

"Oh, and who might that be?"

"Brevet Lieutenant Jenkinson. I've bought him so many drinks here that he sought to repay me by inviting me to the theater."

"And you accepted the invitation?"

"Naturally."

"What's the play called?"

"*The Battle of Brooklyn.*"

"Indeed?" said Gilby disapprovingly, rubbing his hands together as if holding an unusually large bar of soap. "I wonder that you should think such an entertainment a fit spectacle."

"I'll not be there to see the play, Mr. Gilby."

"Then why are you going?"

"To watch the audience," replied Proudfoot. "And to pick up any scraps of information that I can. When people are enjoying themselves, as you well know, they tend to be less guarded."

"Yes, that's why I eavesdrop on any revelers here. But I came to deliver a message, Mr. Allen," he went on, thrusting a letter into Proudfoot's hand. "It's from our mutual friend."

"Thank you."

"When next you see him, pass on a nugget of information."

"I'll do so readily."

"My wife overheard it earlier when some officers had dinner at the tavern." He gave an ingratiating smile. "Damaris has keen ears. When she was serving the meal, she did not miss a syllable."

"And what did she learn?"

"There'll be another foraging expedition two days after Christmas."

"Do you know where it will be going?"

"The southern end of Brandywine Valley."

"I'll pass the intelligence on to our mutual friend," said Proudfoot, "and it will reach interested parties in no time. Please thank your wife."

"I will, sir."

"And congratulate her on her cooking."

"Damaris will be delighted to receive a compliment."

"I've not eaten so well since my own wife was alive." His face clouded. "That seems such an eternity ago now. How long has this war been going on, Mr. Gilby?"

"Too long, Mr. Allen."

"Far too long."

Proudfoot went off into a reverie, thinking of earlier and happier days when he was a married man with a young family. Established as a silversmith in Albany, he had been looking forward to a prosperous and contented life when hostilities broke out between the thirteen colonies and the mother country. Everything had changed for the worst.

"Aren't you going to read your message?" Gilby prompted.

"What?" asked the other, then he remembered that he was holding the missive. "Oh, yes, of course."

Turning away from the landlord, he opened the envelope, found an unsigned note and read the single sentence written by the neat hand of Pearsall Hughes. He then put back his head to let out a peal of laughter.

"Good tidings?" said the landlord.

"I think so, Mr. Gilby," replied Proudfoot. "After reading this, I would not miss tonight's performance of the play for anything."

William Howe, commander in chief of the British army, was amazed.

"And you actually got to meet General Washington himself?"

"Face to face," replied Jamie Skoyles.

"How on earth did you contrive it?"

"By going directly to his headquarters."

"Were there no guards?"

"Dozens of them."

"How did you get past them?"

"That would take too long to explain, General," said Skoyles deferentially, "and I'd hate to hold you up when you have to get to the theater. Suffice it to say that I was able to offer my services to the enemy. Whether or not General Washington decides to accept that offer is, of course, still open to question. He's a perceptive man and not easily convinced."

"What did he decide to do?"

"Wait for me to prove myself."

"We'll give you any help you require, Captain Skoyles."

"Thank you, sir."

They were in the house that was used as the headquarters of the British army, and General Howe was resplendent in his dress uniform. Now that his resignation had been accepted, it was only a question of serving out his time until spring, when he could return to England. Meanwhile, he intended to enjoy himself to the full with a heady round of plays, dances, concerts, and extended drinking bouts.

"How did you find Valley Forge?" he said.

"Very chilly, sir."

"Winter will take all the fight out of the rebels."

"I'd not bank on that, if I were you," Skoyles warned. "Their commander's spirit is indomitable and that's bound to inspire his men."

"Were you able to see much of their camp?"

"No, sir. It was barely dawn when I arrived, and I was blindfolded before I was led back through the lines."

"So you have no idea of the size of their army?"

"Not yet—but I know that they underestimate *our* numbers."

"To what degree?"

"Washington seems to think that we have no more than ten thousand men in the occupying force."

"That's good to hear," said Howe, beaming. "It shows that their intelligence is not as good as I feared. In fact, we have around sixteen thousand soldiers, either in the city or in nearby encampments."

"So I was told by General Clinton."

"Keep them ignorant of our true size, Captain."

"I intend to, sir."

"It's a bad miscalculation and wholly to our advantage. If the rebels are foolhardy enough to offer us battle in the coming months, we can overwhelm them with superior numbers. Thank you," he went on, clapping Skoyles on the soldier. "I knew that I'd chosen the right man. Your visit to Valley Forge has already paid dividends."

"It will take time for me to insinuate myself properly."

"Move at your own pace, Captain. Move at your own pace."

The door suddenly opened and Betsey Loring swept into the room with the confidence of someone who was in her own home. In a light blue dress that shimmered as she moved, she was more arresting than ever, but her comely features were disfigured by a frown. When she saw that they had a visitor, she conjured up a polite smile. After placing a solicitous kiss on her gloved hand, Howe introduced her to Skoyles.

"I'm pleased to meet you, Captain Skoyles," she said.

"The pleasure is all mine," he returned.

"Are you joining us at the play this evening?"

"I'm afraid not."

"That's a pity. It's such a jolly little piece, and it pokes the most wondrous fun at George Washington. I saw it first in New York City and it made me laugh so. It was called *The Battle of Brooklyn* then."

"General Howe has mentioned it to me."

"It's been cleverly rewritten," explained Howe, "to reflect the latest developments in the conflict. The new title is *The Battle of Brandywine*."

"Not a play that the rebels would care to see, then."

"No, Captain. It mocks them from start to finish."

"They deserve it," said Betsey, pouting, "for they are ready enough to laugh at us." She held up a piece of paper. "This was sent to me, and I found it in extremely bad taste."

"What is it, Betsey?" asked Howe.

"A cartoon about you and your brother, the admiral."

"Let me see it."

"I did not find it the least bit amusing," she said, handing it over, "and I think that the man who drew this should be severely punished."

"He will be," promised Howe, recoiling as he studied the print. "His name is already on the list of people we need to arrest immediately. Ezekiel Proudfoot is living on borrowed time."

"Proudfoot?" Skoyles was interested. "May I see it, General?"

"Yes, it shows a warped and macabre sense of humor."

Skoyles took the proffered cartoon and saw the two brothers dancing their hornpipe on the deck of a ship. Proudfoot's technique was inimitable, and Skoyles felt a rush of pride at his friend's artistic skill. It was mixed with a feeling of profound sadness, a recognition that they were fighting on opposite sides. Though the two brothers in the cartoon were drawn with comic exaggeration, Skoyles was not in the least tempted to smile. He had too much sympathy for the message that Proudfoot was trying to send.

"The man deserves to be hanged, drawn, and quartered," said Howe, peevishly. "Where did you get this piece of filth, Betsey?"

"It was delivered to me not ten minutes ago," she answered.

"Who sent it?"

"I've no idea. One of your servants said that he found it by the door. My name was on it, but, for the life of me, I cannot see why."

"No more can I."

"What happens in the war is none of my doing."

"No, Mrs. Loring," said Skoyles, giving the print back to Howe, "but it does concern your husband, so, indirectly, there is a link with you. As commissary of prisons, Mr. Loring has a responsibility for the way that rebel captives are fed and treated."

"Joshua would never let men be abused like that."

"Nevertheless, General Washington has protested strongly about the care of rebel prisoners of war."

"My husband is a man of integrity."

"I don't mean to suggest otherwise."

"He's too kind and considerate to do such a thing."

"And he's very efficient at his job," said Howe testily, not wishing to be reminded of a husband whose wife was his mistress. "This must not be allowed to go on," he continued, scrunching up the paper and hurling it into the fire. "Find him for me, Captain Skoyles."

"Yes, sir."

"I want this scheming devil caught *now!* Hunt down this scoundrel who goes by the name of Ezekiel Proudfoot."

"Good evening, Mr. Allen," he said. "I'm so glad that you could join me."

"I've been looking forward to it all day, Lieutenant."

"Did you know that George Washington appears in the play?"

"In person?" asked Proudfoot, jokingly.

"That would be priceless fun, were it possible."

Brevet Lieutenant Matthew Jenkinson had a high-pitched laugh. He was a tall, spare young man with a pair of bulging brown eyes set in an otherwise pleasant face, and a prominent Adam's apple. Long before the play started, he had been drinking. Like most of the men present at the theater, he was in uniform, and it made Proudfoot feel both underdressed and rather more obtrusive than he wished to be. In fact, he aroused very little curiosity. It was the legion of pretty young women who commanded the attention of the soldiers. As Jenkinson and Proudfoot took their seats, nobody even bothered to look in their direction.

"I thought it was called *The Battle of Brooklyn*," said Proudfoot.

"So did I, Mr. Allen."

"Is this a new play in its stead?"

"It's the old one, newly fashioned," said Jenkinson. "But no less full of hilarity, I am sure. Ah, here's the general."

There was a buzz of interest and a round of applause as General Howe sailed in with Betsey Loring to take up a place of honor. Everyone talked excitedly.

The sense of expectation was tangible. When the little orchestra began to play, there was loud clapping for the musicians.

"Where are the actors from?" asked Proudfoot.

"Various regiments. As it happens, I was in a play myself once."

"Really?"

"Yes," said Jenkinson, Adam's apple bouncing up and down like a billiard ball as he spoke. "It was the first play we staged when we moved into Manhattan."

"What was the title?"

"*The Life and Death of Tom Thumb the Great.*"

"And what role did you take, lieutenant?"

"That of Noodle, one of the courtiers. I made everyone laugh."

"I'm sure you did," said Proudfoot with an irony that went unnoticed by his companion. "I'll wager that you were Noodle to the life."

The music stopped and an actor stepped out onstage in the uniform of a British general. Doffing his hat to the audience, he earned a generous round of applause and several shouts of encouragement. There was also some concerted stamping of feet. Proudfoot was fascinated. Never having been to a play before, he was surprised at the amiable rowdiness among the spectators. As the good-natured tumult faded, the prologue began.

Tonight, good friends, to satisfy your taste,
We'll offer you a downright English feast,
A tale of love and loss and loyalty,
Of dedication to our royalty.
While rebels shiver up in Valley Forge,
Here sit we in the warm and gorge on George,
That's George the King of Britain's empire great,
Not George the Traitor, who has sealed his fate
By standing up against a redcoat line
And getting drunk on too much Brandywine!

Hoots of joy greeted the first mention of the battle, and it was some time before the noise died down sufficiently for the actor to continue. More and more opprobrium was attached to the name of George Washington, and each time it was welcomed with cheers and gibes by the spectators. Proudfoot was squirming in his seat at the patent injustice and ridicule that was being meted out to a man he venerated. In the company of Matthew Jenkinson, however, he was forced to add his own small contribution to the waves of laughter. At the end of the prologue, there was a near ovation.

"Isn't it magnificent, Mr. Allen?" said Jenkinson.

"I've never seen anything like it, Lieutenant."

"I must have a copy of that prologue. It delights me so."

"The playwright has clearly got the measure of his audience," said Proudfoot grimly, looking around at the happy faces. "He obviously knows what is the order of the day."

His last remark went unheard beneath the thunderous applause for the parting of the curtains. The row of candles that acted as footlights illumined a backdrop on which a valley had been painted. Two British officers entered and discussed the forthcoming battle, taking the opportunity to vilify the rebel commander even more. But it was during the next scene that Proudfoot began to doubt his wisdom in agreeing to attend the play. To an explosion of abuse and catcalls, a bogus George Washington, in full uniform, came onstage with his mistress, a buxom wench who had a bewitching swing of her hips. Describing herself as the Whore of American Independence, she set off howls of delight.

When he tried to woo her, she reminded him that her favors were not given freely and they began to haggle over the price. What gave the scene additional sparkle for most of the audience was that they knew that the couple onstage were really man and wife. The British major in the luckless role of Washington was married to the lady who was now trying to charge an entrance fee to her boudoir. It provoked some ribald humor among the less sober members of the audience, all of which increased, in the eyes of Ezekiel Proudfoot, the derision heaped upon Washington. The scene soon descended into such lewd comedy that he could bear to watch it no longer.

The Battle of Brandywine was well into its second act before he was compelled to open his eyes. The alternating cheers and mockery that had accompanied every scene suddenly changed to fear and perturbation. Proudfoot looked up and witnessed an extraordinary performance. Five small furry animals were darting about wildly onstage, creating havoc and forcing the actors, playing a detachment of brave redcoats, to drop their muskets and take to their heels in disarray. Proudfoot realized that someone had just introduced five frantic squirrels into the action, producing a very different result to the Battle of Brandywine.

Utter pandemonium followed. One squirrel leapt into the orchestra, landing on a drum and ripping it open with its sharp claws. Another tried to climb up the leg of the Whore of American Independence, making her screech in panic and forcing the erstwhile General Washington to resume his duties as a husband and burrow beneath her dress. The three other animals sought to escape by jumping into the audience, causing men to roar with anger, women to faint, and those near the door to quit the scene with undignified haste. Five squirrels had completely rewritten the play. As they dived between legs, hopped onto chairs, and, in one case, even climbed nimbly up a curtain before urinating over the horrified wife of a colonel, they scattered the audience here, there, and everywhere, turning entertainment into sheer frenzy and ruining the evening beyond recall.

A broadside from forty cannons could not have cleared the theater so quickly. Spectators fought each other to reach the door first. Amid the shrieks, bellows, curses, and random collisions, Ezekiel Proudfoot was alone in being highly diverted by the spectacle.

"You are so right, Lieutenant," he said to a white-faced Jenkinson. "The play is hilarious. I've never enjoyed an evening so much before."

Miranda Hughes was reading a book by the light of a tallow candle when her husband returned. The broad smile on his face was confirmation that his jape had been successful.

"Well?" she asked. "What happened, Pearsall?"

"We emptied the place in under ten minutes," he replied, sweeping off his hat. "I did not see what happened inside, mark you—we'll have to wait for Reece Allen to report on that—but I watched them tearing out of the exit as if the hounds of hell were biting at their heels."

"And all because of five tiny animals."

"Five tiny, fearless, native-born, American squirrels. They scattered the British army and won the Battle of Brandywine for us."

"How did you get them into the theater?"

"The only way that I could, Miranda," he said. "I paid a lad to bring the animals out of hibernation for me, then I diverted the man at the door of the theater so that my little accomplice could sneak in. All that he had to do was to open the sack behind the scenes and shake out the squirrels. They were not happy at being woken up."

"Did the boy get away safely?"

"Yes, he escaped in the confusion, and judging by the way that the audience poured out into the street, the confusion inside the building was akin to chaos."

"I doubt if they'll try to stage that particular play again."

"With or without the squirrels."

"Such a droll idea of yours, Pearsall," she said fondly. "Who would suspect that an upright bookseller could be capable of such a thing?"

"The one place they will not search for the malefactor is here."

Miranda wanted more detail, and he sat beside her to describe at length the exodus from the theater. Nobody had stood on ceremony, he told her. General Howe had had to elbow a way out for himself and his greatly disheveled mistress. Hats had been discarded, wigs surrendered, shoes cast off, purses abandoned willy-nilly, clothes torn indiscriminately, and all decorum forgotten. The audience had been like a routed army, beating a hasty retreat.

"Those five animals were symbolic," he claimed.

"Of what?"

"A small American army up against a much larger British force."

"It will take more than squirrels to defeat the redcoats."

"I know that, Miranda, but we struck a blow at them tonight."

"A powerful one, by the sound of it," she said. "The last place they expected danger was in a theater. But if there was such a mad rush to get out of the building, people will have been hurt. I hope that Mr. Allen was not one of them."

"I warned him beforehand of the disruption."

"Did you mention the squirrels?"

"No," said Hughes. "I did not wish to give the game away. Besides, I was not entirely sure that we would be successful."

"But you were, Pearsall. You were triumphant."

"Yes, Miranda," he agreed with a chortle. "I think I can say, without undue modesty, that I was."

"As long as you were not seen and followed."

"There was no fear of that. I hid in a doorway throughout."

171

"And nobody saw you slipping away afterward?"

"Who would have noticed me in that crowd? If I'd yelled out, at the top of my voice, that I was responsible for the attack, my confession would have gone unheard. People were too busy running away at full pelt to bother about me."

"What about that lad you employed?"

"He was well paid to keep his mouth shut."

"Who was he?"

"Simon Chatfield's son," said Hughes. "He was glad to help. His father was killed by the redcoats at Harlem Heights."

"We can rely on his loyalty, then," said Miranda, reassured. "Well, it has been quite a day for us. We upset Mrs. Loring by sending her a print of that latest cartoon, and you stampeded General Howe and his officers out of a play. I think we can be well satisfied."

"Satisfied, but not complacent. There's still so much to do."

"I know, Pearsall. It's going to be a long, hard, bitter winter."

He chuckled. "We must see how we can help to enliven it."

Their laughter was short-lived. The doorbell rang to jolt them out of their merriment. They traded a worried glance. When the bell rang again with some insistence, Hughes took off his coat and put it away in a cupboard with his hat. Miranda did not need to be told what story to tell. If questioned, she would swear that he had been with her all evening.

As the bell rang for the third time, Hughes walked quickly toward the front door, wondering if he had, after all, been recognized outside the theater. Having lived in the city for many years, he was a well-known figure. It was not impossible that one of his Tory neighbors had attended the play that evening. His heart was pounding as he reached out for the door. He was being forcibly reminded of how perilous a game he played. No mercy would be shown to him if his guilt were proven.

Hughes unlocked the door with apprehension, ready to dispute that he had even ventured out that evening. His face was impassive but his mind was in turmoil. Had he been careless? Had someone spotted him as he sneaked away from the scene? Was it possible that the boy had been arrested and forced to surrender the name of Pearsall Hughes? Could his bold and unremitting campaign against British occupation be about to come to a premature end?

As the door swung open, he prepared himself for robust denial.

"Congratulations, Mr. Hughes!" said Ezekiel Proudfoot, shaking his hand warmly. "That was a brilliant device."

"Thank you."

"I just had to come and tell you."

"Then do so inside," suggested Hughes, glancing up and down the street to make sure that nobody was about. "Come in, Mr. Allen."

"Gladly," said Proudfoot, going into the house.

The bookseller was relieved. "You gave me such a fright."

Christmas Day was marked in Philadelphia with all kinds of celebrations, but Jamie Skoyles did not attend any of them. He was missing Elizabeth Rainham badly, and took the time to write another letter to her, assuring her of his love and hoping that they could be reunited soon. He then changed out of his uniform into the hunting apparel that he had worn so often when on scouting expeditions. Armed with a musket and a knife, he left the city and took the road northwest, using the appropriate password to get past the British pickets.

As he rode on in the direction of Valley Forge, he wondered what Elizabeth would be doing on Christmas morning, and he also spared a thought for the missing Tom Caffrey and Polly Bragg. On that day of all days, he hoped that they would be safe and well somewhere. Though light snow was falling, he made good time. Twenty miles passed without incident, but he remained alert. Soldiers rarely took a rest on Christmas Day. He had spent too many of them exchanging fire with an enemy. It had been on Christmas night the previous year that George Washington had crossed the Delaware River with his army and inflicted an important defeat on the British at Trenton.

Since it was broad daylight, there was no hope of surprising one of the sentries again and using him as a guide through the encampment. Skoyles therefore intended to ride on until he reached the enemy pickets, then offer himself as a new recruit to the rebel army. His plan did not, however, meet with approval. No sooner did he get within sight of the first picket squad than a shot was fired. It passed too close for comfort and made Skoyles leap from the saddle.

He raised his arms in a gesture of surrender but that only provoked a second man into firing. The musket ball kicked up the dust at Skoyles's feet and he jumped. It was no time to present himself as a target for a third marksman. Pulling the reins, he took his horse off the road and quickly tethered it in the bushes. Then he ran hard to the right, keeping low and listening for the approach of any pickets. His musket was loaded, but he could hardly take on the seven men he had seen at the post. Shooting even one of them was a poor way to convince them that he had come to enlist in their army. Negotiation was his only hope.

Having worked his way round to the side of the squad, he stopped to peer through the trees. Only three pickets remained. Evidently, the others were searching for him. Hand to the side of his mouth, he called out as loud as he could.

"I come in peace!" he yelled.

"Show yourself!" demanded one of the sentries.

"I'm a new recruit. I want to join you."

"Throw down your weapon and come out where we can see you."

"First give me your word that nobody will shoot."

But no promise came and Skoyles heard rustling in the bushes to his left. Abandoning one hiding place, he went swiftly off in search of another. Entry into Valley Forge for the second time was clearly going to be a more hazardous business. Skoyles ran, stopped, listened for sounds of pursuit, then moved on again. Dressed like a hunter, he was now himself the quarry. One thing was certain. The men who were tracking him were not imbued with the Christmas spirit. They scented blood.

Reaching the cover of a large tree, he flattened his back against the trunk and paused for a respite. If the men were determined to shoot before he could even explain why he had come to Valley Forge, only two courses of action were left to him. He could either find another way to penetrate the defenses, or he could simply turn tail and head back to the city. The problem with the second option was that his horse had probably been discovered by now, so his return would have to be on foot. Even in relatively mild weather, that was not an appealing notion. As it was, neither possibility remained for long.

Skoyles heard footsteps approaching. Someone was trampling his way through the undergrowth nearby. Risking a peep around the tree, Skoyles caught a fleeting glimpse of a man in a shabby uniform, musket held in front of him and head twisting from side to side as he looked for his prey. He was so close that there was no chance of getting away easily. Skoyles therefore decided to reason with him. Resting his Brown Bess musket against the tree, he edged his way slowly around the massive trunk. As the man moved past, Skoyles jumped out behind him and clapped one hand over his mouth, using the other to disarm him and drop his weapon to the ground. Though the picket struggled hard, he was held tight in an iron grip.

"I've come to join you, friend," said Skoyles earnestly. "Don't you understand? I want to fight the redcoats alongside you."

The man stopped struggling and Skoyles released him, turning him round so that they were face to face. The picket was surprisingly old, a wizened grandfather with hollow cheeks and sunken eyes. He gazed at Skoyles with mingled suspicion and wonder.

"Who are ye?" he croaked.

"A recruit for the Continental Army."

"Where did ye come from?"

"Philadelphia," said Skoyles. "I'm a friend." He bent down to retrieve the fallen musket and held it out to him. "Go on—take it."

The old man took the weapon, an ancient rifle with a long barrel, and looked at it as if seeing it for the first time. Skoyles was relieved that his companion made no attempt to shoot him. Daring to believe that he might now be safe, Skoyles was soon deprived of that illusion. The butt of a musket struck him hard in the small of his back and he sprawled on the ground, rolling over to see other weapons pointing at him. The old man found Skoyles's rifle leaning against the tree.

"This is a Brown Bess musket," he announced, spitting on the ground. "It's what the redcoats carry. He's from the enemy."

"Then he's another British spy," said one of the other men.

"No," Skoyles asserted, trying to get up.

"Stay there," ordered the third man, kicking him down. "Let's shoot the bastard and have done with it."

"Me, first!" said the old man, lifting his rifle. "I've always wanted to kill me a lousy redcoat."

Skoyles was trapped. Three muskets were trained on him and he had no means of defense. All that he could do was to cover his face with an arm and wait for the noise of gunfire. Miraculously, it never came. Running feet approached at speed and a new voice was heard.

"Don't shoot him!" cried Private Novus Kane.

"Stand back," the old man told him. "He's a spy."

"For the British," said another man. "He deserves to die."

"No!" Kane insisted.

He jumped between them and their victim, protecting Skoyles by holding out both arms. The other pickets were annoyed.

"Out of the way, Novus!" howled the old man. "Then that pesky varmint can get what's coming to him."

"But I *know* him, Jed. I've met him before."

"What are ye talking about?"

"I recognize this man," said Kane, offering a hand to help Skoyles up from the ground. "I took him to General Washington. He's on our side. He taught me how to load a musket properly."

"Are ye sure of this?"

"I swear it. Let him go."

Reluctantly, the others lowered their weapons. Skoyles gave his young savior a smile of thanks and patted him familiarly on the back.

"When you've got the time," he promised, "I'll teach you how to shoot that musket properly as well."

Betsey Loring was delighted with the Christmas present that General Howe had given her. It was an expensive gold necklace that he had had specially made for her, and she put it on at once, preening in front of a mirror and twisting from side to side so that she could view the necklace from different angles. They were in the bedroom that they had shared since the occupation of Philadelphia. Before going down to the dining room for Christmas dinner with senior officers, Howe had bestowed his gift.

"It's wonderful!" she said. "It's just what I wanted, William."

Howe kissed her cheek. "You deserve it, Betsey."

"I can't wait to show it off."

"It's something by which you can remember me when I leave."

She flicked a wrist. "Oh, I don't even want to think about that now. It's months before you have to go, and I intend to make the most of every single second."

"I think we're both agreed on that."

It was a few days since the fiasco at the theater, and they had both recovered their composure. Howe's hat had been knocked off in the surge for the exit, and one of Mrs. Loring's shoes had been lost in the melee, but they had put those petty humiliations to the back of their minds on Christmas Day. The general had received a welcome present of his own.

"More good news," he told her, holding up a letter delivered to him earlier. "Some battalions moved further down the Chester road to cover the wagons below Darby Creek. They were harried by rebels but sustained no losses. The Light Horse killed three, wounded two, and captured five. That's ten more rebels put out of action."

"When *will* they realize that they are beaten?" she asked.

"Not during my time here, alas."

"But you have a professional army; they are raw recruits."

"The rascals hold out well," Howe admitted. "I have to give them credit for that. And some of those untrained farm boys helped to defeat Burgoyne at Saratoga. They can fight, Betsey."

"Yet you will win."

"Ultimately."

"And when will that be?"

"Let's forget this war for one day, shall we?" he suggested, offering his arm. "It's a time when we should count our blessings—and I regard you as one of mine."

"Thank you," she said, looping her arm in his.

"We make such a handsome couple."

"I think so, William. Not everyone agrees, however. I know that we caused a lot of adverse comment, particularly in New York City."

"Pah! Whoever listens to adverse comment?"

"Some of it was very hurtful."

"People can be so small-minded," he said with a gesture of dismissal. "Ignore them. Puritans are their own worst enemy. Because they try to suppress normal human passions, they resent those of us who enjoy them. The Declaration of Independence talks about life, liberty, and the pursuit of happiness, yet most of the damn fools have no idea what true happiness is."

"I like to think that you've found it with me," she said.

"Time and again, Betsey."

"I just wish that some people were less censorious."

"Jealousy, my dear, pure jealousy."

"There was no jealousy in that drawing I was sent," she recalled. "That was a case of simple malice. And I heard a rumor that there was a scurrilous drawing about us in that rebel newspaper. Is it true?"

"Yes," he said through clenched teeth, "but it's not something I care to be reminded about—least of all, on Christmas Day. If they can't beat us with bullets, the rebels will use any other weapon at their disposal, as we know to our cost."

"Why can't you stop them, William?"

"I will, in due course."

"I loathe it when people snigger at us."

"It's all that our enemies are able to do."

"That cartoon of you and your brother was hateful."

"Someone will pay dearly for that," he vowed, moving her to the door. "Our problem is that the rebels have many friends inside the city. But we have our spies as well."

"I'm sure that you do."

"In fact, one of them is paying a visit to Valley Forge this very day. I'll be most interested to see what he finds out."

Captain Jamie Skoyles was disappointed. Instead of being taken to see the commander in chief, he was handed over to Major John Clark. They met in the drafty log cabin that was Clark's home for the winter.

"I hear that you have volunteered to help us, Captain Skoyles," he said, assessing his visitor with a prolonged stare. "Is that not so?"

"It was the case until today, Major."

"Has something occurred to change your mind?"

"Indeed, it has," said Skoyles. "Before I could even explain who I was, your pickets tried to kill me. I think they should be taught the difference between friends and enemies."

"Everyone is regarded as an enemy until his loyalty is proven."

"Does that mean you have to shoot holes in them before you even find out who they really are?"

"No," said Clark. "But pickets are warned to show caution."

"There's not much caution in a musket ball, Major."

"Those men on duty this morning were overzealous. They'll be duly reprimanded. On the other hand, their conduct is understandable. Skirmishers attacked some of our pickets yesterday. Four of our men were killed and two wounded. Had we been forewarned, of course," he went on pointedly, "lives would have been saved."

"I can't advise you about every soldier who's sent out on duty. That sort of information does not reach me. So many regiments are involved," said Skoyles reasonably, "and each has different orders to follow. I do not have access to them all."

"Then what do you have access to, Captain?"

"Privileged intelligence."

"Such as?"

"A large foraging expedition will leave the city in two days, sir. It will be going to the southern end of Brandywine Valley."

"This news is stale."

Skoyles was checked. "You already *know*?"

"We have eyes and ears in Philadelphia."

"Clearly."

"We know all about the debacle at the theater as well."

"Yes," said Skoyles with amusement, "I gather that you enlisted some squirrels into your ranks. It was a cunning jest. I spoke to some of the officers who were there, and they said it was like bedlam. I'd like to meet the man who thought up that prank."

"There's no need for you to do so."

"It must have been someone in the city."

"But all it achieved was an evening's discomfort for General Howe and his fellow playgoers. We need to strike a more telling blow than that." He stepped forward to look Skoyles in the eye. "How can you help us to do that?"

Skoyles could see that he was not yet accepted. Having made an impression on Washington, he had not convinced him of his sincerity and had now been referred to Clark for a more thorough examination. It was obvious that the major would not be easily won over.

"Well?" said Clark.

"Your estimate of our troop numbers is awry, sir."

"Too low?"

"Too high," said Skoyles briskly. "General Washington spoke of ten thousand men. There are rather less than that. The British may have won the battles of Brandywine and Germantown but they sustained heavy losses—something in the region of twelve hundred were killed."

"That's almost as many casualties as we suffered."

"And there were hundreds of men wounded and not fit for duty."

Skoyles had deliberately exaggerated the number of British dead, almost doubling the exact figure. He was interested to learn the scale of American losses during the battle of Brandywine, in sheer size, even bigger and bloodier than the two in which he had fought at Saratoga.

"What are General Howe's plans?" asked Clark.

"To strengthen his defenses and sit tight, Major. He'll send out foraging parties and skirmishers, but he has no inclination to do anything more than that. He's bored with the war and he's grown lazy."

"How close have you been to him?"

"Very close," replied Skoyles. "General Washington will surely have told you my story. General Clinton sent me to Philadelphia because he thought I might be of use there."

"In what capacity?"

"Whatever role General Howe chooses for me."

"Has he given you an assignment yet?"

"He made me prepare a full report of events at Saratoga, and a detailed account of what happened to the Convention army. It will come as no surprise to you that he intended to divert the transports that were sent to take the men back to England. He desperately wanted those soldiers for himself."

"We suspected as much."

"I heard it from his own lips. And there was something else."

"Go on."

"If he acquired Burgoyne's army," explained Skoyles, "then he was bound, by the terms of the convention, to release an equivalent number of your prisoners in exchange. General Howe did not even consider it."

"So much for British honor!"

"The conditions in which your prisoners of war are held are indescribable. Disease and starvation are rife. Cruel punishments are inflicted for minor offences. The provost marshal at the prison on the Common in New York City glories in his brutality."

"We know, Captain," said Clark. "General Washington protested so vehemently that the British agreed to an inspection. Elias Boudinot was sent as a special envoy. What he found beggared belief. Animals are cared for better than our prisoners of war."

"Did he visit the prison ships?"

"No, he was barred from them."

"With good reason, sir," said Skoyles with frank disapproval. "By repute, they are even more hellish."

"Elias Boudinot saw enough to disgust him. Out of the goodness of his heart, he advanced almost $27,000 of his own money to buy bread, beef, shirts, suits, and blankets for the prisoners." Clark pulled a face. "How much of that will actually reach the prisoners is another matter."

"Was he able to meet Joshua Loring?"

"The commissary of prisons accompanied him on the inspection. We are told that, afterward, he reported to General Howe that everything was satisfactory."

"Satisfactory for Mr. Loring no doubt! He's making a fortune."

"And we all know how he secured the post as commissar," said Clark with asperity. "But we digress, Captain. I've still to hear about this privileged information you mention."

"Then here it is, Major."

Skoyles had been well prepared. All the details that General Howe had given him were rattled off, most of them quite correct and easily verifiable, a few of them artfully misleading. Clark was astonished at how much his visitor had learned in such a short time. Yet he was still not entirely persuaded of Skoyles's trustworthiness.

"You have obviously been close to Howe."

"That fortunate situation is set to continue," Skoyles told him.

"If you are such an intimate of his," said Clark, "the wonder is that he did not invite you to share Christmas dinner with him."

"The same could be said of you and General Washington. You obviously have a position of great significance in his army."

"We have little time for any celebration, Captain. While your commander is feasting with Mrs. Loring, ours is holding a council with his generals to determine the future direction of this war. For soldiers like us, Christmas does not really exist."

"It's the same for me," said Skoyles. "Had I been invited to General Howe's table, I would have declined. I thrive on action—even if it's confined to ducking the bullets of your pickets."

"That will not happen again," said Clark.

"Will I be given the appropriate passwords?"

"No, Captain."

"How can I get here with safety, then?"

"We will save you the trouble of coming anywhere near Valley Forge. When you have fresh information, you can pass it on by letter. I'll give you instructions in how to use a code."

"But I was hoping to report directly to your commander," Skoyles confessed, dismayed at the news. "Some of the things I may discover will be for his ears alone."

"We will see. In the first instance," Clark went on, "everything will come through me. My task is to sift intelligence carefully so that General Washington is not burdened with contradictory information."

"How will I make contact?"

"I'll give you an address where you may leave correspondence."

"Am I to deal with anyone in particular?"

"Only me. Nobody else will read your reports."

"But you are stuck here in Valley Forge."

"Temporarily," said Clark. "I will soon be back in the city. In case I have any instructions for you, I'll need your address."

"I have a room at a house in Spruce Street. Number 10."

"I'll remember that."

"Will you put me in touch with your other agents?"

"No, Captain."

"Why not?"

"Because you are still on trial," warned the other. "Besides, most of the people I use are kept unaware of each other. If they are caught, no list of names can be beaten out of them."

"What of *The Pennsylvania Patriot*?" asked Skoyles.

"What of it?"

"The editor must live in the city; so must the printer."

"You'll not be allowed to meet either of them."

"But I may hear juicy gossip that they could use to effect in their newspaper. Is there no address where I can drop such information?"

"Send it to me and I will pass it on."

"It will be quicker if I deliver it in person to the editor."

"How do you know that you are not looking at him?" said Clark with a teasing smile. "Here," he continued, taking a sheet of paper from the table to give to Skoyles. "This is the only address you need, along with details of the code you must use. Commit both to memory, then destroy the paper. Whatever happens, it must not go astray."

"Of course not." Skoyles glanced at the address on the paper and raised his eyebrows. "A funeral parlor?"

"Run by a Quaker," explained Clark, "who allows us to pick up mail from there even though he has no idea what it might contain. He is not a patriot—indeed, he abhors the very notion of war—so he would never be suspected of helping us."

"I see. He is simply a friend."

"In both senses, Captain."

Major John Clark was much more relaxed with him now, and Skoyles was grateful. He felt that he had passed a first important test. Getting close to Washington again might take longer than he thought, but he would be patient. In a volatile situation, where betrayal was an everyday event, it was vital to build up trust slowly. If he could win over the man who was in charge of the espionage system of the Continental Army, then the name of Jamie Skoyles would be looked upon favorably by the commander in chief. That was the best way to proceed.

"I don't envy you this cabin, Major," said Skoyles, looking around.

"It is much more comfortable than some."

"How many do you have here?"

"Not nearly enough. Our men are building away like beavers."

"Yes, I saw them as I was brought here. But you already have a large number ready for use—a thousand at least, I'd say."

"We need twice that number, Captain."

"Then you will have to fell a small forest. Do you have the right equipment for such a task?"

"Unhappily, no," said Clark, chewing his lip. "Congress is dilatory. The Board of War refuses to give us all that we need."

"That may be so," said Skoyles, "but Congress is now in York, close enough for you to harry. When General Howe wants additional supplies or reinforcements, he has to send a letter three thousand miles across an ocean. And even then he rarely gets what he wants."

"I can see why he tendered his resignation."

"He is anxious to get back home to his wife."

"His wife!" repeated Clark. "He behaves as if he doesn't have one."

"Only when he is a long way away from her, Major."

"Decent people are shocked at the way Howe carries on."

"Soldiers are soldiers," said Skoyles tolerantly. "I'm one myself, so I'll not criticize another for enjoying the favors of a woman. In any case, I don't believe that immorality is restricted solely to the British army."

"No, Captain."

"When I spent some time with General Lee in New York City, he made no bones about his fondness for the company of women even though he is, apparently, already married."

"Charles Lee wed the daughter of a Mohawk chief," said Clark levelly, "and he never considered it to be a real marriage. That's to say, it was not one that precluded a regular dalliance with other ladies."

"I formed the same impression, sir."

"Because he was so restless, and talked to himself, the Indians used to call him Boiling Water. It was very appropriate. I think that they had the true measure of the man."

"So do I. He was always bubbling. But, even omitting him, I daresay that you have your fair share of lechers and adulterers."

"We have no saints in the Continental Army."

"Then do not censure General Howe so readily. In one sense, his friendship with Mrs. Loring is a boon to you."

"A boon?"

"Yes. From what I can gather, *The Pennsylvania Patriot* is able to make much of it. I heard mention of a cartoon that pilloried the pair of them unmercifully. The general and his mistress were shown in bed to grotesque effect. Is it true?"

"Very true. The artist has a singular talent."

"I know, Major," said Skoyles coolly. "General Howe was so furious that he's given me a direct order—I am to kill the man."

184

Ezekiel Proudfoot had never had a Christmas quite like it. Born and brought up on a farm in Massachussetts, he was accustomed, as a boy, to spending the day with his parents and his brothers, eating dinner around the long table in the kitchen before returning to his chores outside. When he followed his instinct and became apprenticed to a silversmith, he fell in love with the man's daughter and eventually married her. From then on, a Christmas dinner was shared with Selina's family until Proudfoot's own children came along. His wife then took over the cooking and her parents became guests at the Proudfoot table. They had been very happy occasions.

Proudfoot was sharply reminded of past delights when he sat down to eat more humble fare with Adam Quenby. He had invited the printer to the King George Tavern, but Quenby had refused to go, vowing that he would never enter an establishment with a portrait of King George on its inn sign. Proudfoot had therefore joined him in the cellar, eating at a grubby little table and celebrating with a cheap wine. It was not the most enjoyable meal he had ever had, but he felt sorry for Quenby, who would otherwise have spent Christmas alone, too frightened to leave his beloved printing press in order to ride the thirty miles that separated him and from his wife and children.

"What will we have from you next, Mr. Allen?" asked Quenby.

"A cartoon about the play that was abandoned, I think."

"It must have been wonderful to be there."

"It was," said Proudfoot. "I'll savor it for the rest of my life."

"And did General Howe really scamper away in fear?"

"I hadn't realized that he could run so fast."

Quenby laughed. "I wish I'd been there to see it," he said. "It was one battle of Brandywine that ended in defeat for them. Pearsall Hughes is a genius to come up with such an idea."

"I trust that he will have several more of the same quality."

Proudfoot had his back to the window while the printer sat opposite him. They were still relishing the memory of the wrecked performance when Quenby suddenly froze in his seat. His eyes bulged, his mouth fell open, and every muscle tensed. Looking over Proudfoot's shoulder, he could see someone staring back at him through the window. Another face appeared there. The two British soldiers were on their hands and knees to peer into the cellar, but they soon got back to their feet. Quenby leapt up from the table.

"Get out, Mr. Allen!" he cried. "They've found us."

CHAPTER ELEVEN

A dam Quenby pushed him through the door, then slammed it behind him before shooting home the bolt. He scoured the room and removed the most glaring evidence that it was where *The Pennsylvania Patriot* was based, thrusting the two stray copies of the newspaper into the fire. When the blaze died down, the plates from which Proudfoot's cartoons had been printed were quickly hidden up the chimney. He heard soldiers coming down the stairs and banging on the door. Grabbing a piece of cloth, Quenby began to give his press a valedictory cleaning.

Ezekiel Proudfoot, meanwhile, had raced up the steps and, as redcoats were coming in through the front, he made for the back door of the house, letting himself out into a small garden. He did not get far. As he tried to open the gate to the street, he felt the point of a musket at the base of his spine. A rough hand then swung him round. Two soldiers stood over him with stern expressions on their faces.

"Search him," snapped one of them to his companion.

"I'm not armed," said Proudfoot.

"We're not looking for weapons."

Proudfoot was thoroughly searched, but nothing suspicious was found on him. He was pushed back into the house and down to the cellar, where three other soldiers had forced their way in. Hands on hips, Quenby was standing beside his printing press, like a father ready to shield a favorite child from attack. Lieutenant Hugh Orde, who was in charge of the raid, looked around the cellar with a mixture of interest and satisfaction. He clicked his fingers.

"See what you can find," he ordered.

While two of the soldiers began a rigorous search, the others stood guard over the captives so that Orde could question them. He began with the printer.

"What's your name?" he demanded.

"Adam Quenby," replied the other staunchly, "and this is my workplace. I'm a printer, pursuing a legitimate trade. You have no right to barge in here like this."

"Why didn't you open the door when we knocked on it?"

"I didn't hear you."

"Half of Philadelphia would have heard us," said Orde flatly. His eyes swiveled to Proudfoot. "Who are you?"

"Reece Allen," said Proudfoot.

"And why were you here?"

"He's my nephew," said Quenby.

"Let him answer for himself."

"Uncle Adam is right," said Proudfoot, taking his cue from the printer. "I knew that he was spending Christmas Day on his own, so I agreed to have dinner with him." He indicated the table. "That's all that's left of it or you'd have been welcome to join us."

Orde looked at the mattress. "You *live* down here, Mr. Quenby?"

"Yes," said the printer. "Times are hard."

"Perhaps you're not very good at your trade."

Quenby's chest inflated. "I'm the best in the city, sir."

"Then why do you have such mean premises?" asked Orde. "Could it be that you are printing something in secret—a newspaper, perhaps?"

"Do you *see* any newspapers?"

"No, but I think I've caught the men who produce one."

"I'm no printer," said Proudfoot, displaying the roughened palms of someone who grew up on a farm. "Look at these hands. They've seen hard work. I'm a farmer and I'm looking to buy land in Pennsylvania. That's what brought me to the city in the first place. I took the chance of seeing Uncle Adam while I was here."

"Then why did you run away as soon as you saw us?"

"I was frightened, Lieutenant."

"I'm sure," said Orde smoothly, "and I'll wager that you had good reason to be frightened. It's the same reason why your uncle—if that's what he really is—refused to open the door to us."

Quenby stepped forward. "We've nothing to hide."

"Is it a crime to have dinner on Christmas day?" said Proudfoot.

"That depends, Mr. Allen," said Orde.

"On what?"

"What you happened to be celebrating."

"I've found something, sir," said one of the soldiers. He kicked out some of the logs in the fireplace so that he could reach up the chimney without getting burned. "Yes, here it is!"

He brought out the soot-covered plates from which Proudfoot's two cartoons had been printed. Hugh Orde took them from him and cleaned them off so that he could see them properly. He barked a command.

"Take these men away," he ordered.

A smile of triumph spread across his face. The lieutenant had not only redeemed himself. He was certain that he had just found the ideal Christmas gift for General Howe.

Captain Jamie Skoyles missed nothing. As he walked through the camp at Valley Forge, he took note of its layout, its defenses, and the disposition of its soldiers. During his lengthy conversation with Major Clark he had managed to remove most of the reservations that the man had about him. He had also demonstrated his quick brain by memorizing the code that he had been given and writing some notes for the major there and then to prove that he had mastered it. Since he was highly unlikely to forget the name of a Quaker funeral parlor, the sheet of information that he had been given could be torn to shreds on the spot.

Before he left, Skoyles sought out Private Novus Kane, the young soldier who had saved his life earlier on. Now off duty, Kane was lying on his bunk in the cabin that he had helped to build. He was on the point of dozing off when Jedediah Elliott, the old man who had been part of the same picket squad, stood on tiptoe to prod him with the stem of his pipe.

"Wake up, Novus!" he said.

"Not another inspection, is it?" groaned Kane.

"Ye got company, lad."

"What?"

"Down ye get."

Elliott reached up to pull him by a trailing arm, and Kane almost fell off the top bunk of the three. When he had finished complaining to the old man, he saw Skoyles standing in the doorway.

188

"I came to thank you," said Skoyles, offering his hand.

"It's me should thank you," returned the other, accepting the handshake willingly. "You taught me how to load my musket."

"If you've time, I'll show you how to fire it."

"Ammunition is scarce," said Elliott. "We don't waste it."

Skoyles looked round the cabin. Apart from Kane and Elliott, ten other men were there, some playing cards, others snatching a few hours' sleep after sentry duty, and one of them cleaning his rifle. They looked cold, tired, and dejected. None of them had a full uniform on. Skoyles noticed that some had bare feet streaked with blood.

"Let's step outside," he suggested.

"Yes, sir," said Kane.

Collecting his musket, he followed Skoyles out through the door. Jedediah Elliott went after them, sucking hard on his pipe even though there was no tobacco in it. He and Kane represented two extremes of the Continental Army, the old and the young. One was a grizzled warrior who refused to use his advanced age as an excuse not to join the conflict, while the other was a bewildered farm boy, still wondering why he had been misguided enough to enlist in the first instance. They were not untypical soldiers. Skoyles saw an opportunity to garner intelligence from two people who could not possibly suspect his motives.

"How long have you been here?" he asked.

"A couple of weeks," said Kane.

"You did well to build your cabin so quickly and so solidly. A lot of them are nowhere near finished."

"We've Jed to thank for that."

"Yes," said the old man, removing his pipe to spit on the ground. "I'm a carpenter by trade. I know how to cut and work wood. Without me, these ignorant fools would still be sleeping under canvas."

"Where are you from, Jed?" said Skoyles.

"Charlottesville, Virginia."

"You're a fair distance from home."

"I wanted to be where the fighting was fiercest," boasted the other. "I served in the French and Indian War, and I wasn't going to be left out of this one."

"Most men of your age would be sitting at home by the fire."

"More fool they! I joined up to teach young whippersnappers like Novus here how to fight. Someone has to knock sense into their heads."

189

"Do you really want to spend a winter at Valley Forge?"

Elliott stood at attention. "I'll do whatever General Washington asks of me," he said loyally, "and so will every man jack of us here."

"That's not true, Jed," Kane asserted spiritedly. "A lot of us would rather give up and go home until spring."

"Fair-weather soldiers!"

"All that keeps me here is the fear of being shot for desertion."

"Ye'll not run away while I'm here, Novus," the other warned. "Or I'll come after ye and put a bullet in that yellow belly of yours."

Skoyles encouraged the argument between them, throwing in an occasional remark whenever it began to falter. In the process, he learned a great deal about the lot of the common soldier, and the steady decrease of numbers since they had arrived at Valley Forge. When they were on the verge of trading blows, Skoyles stepped in to calm them down.

"Go easy," he said, holding them apart. "You're comrades in arms, you fools. Save your strength for the enemy."

"He started it," Kane alleged, pointing at the old man.

"No, I didn't," cried Elliott. "It was ye, Novus Kane. I'm ashamed to sleep in the bunk below ye."

Kane grinned inanely. "You're only there because you didn't have the strength to climb to the top bunk—not without a ladder!"

Elliott reacted angrily to the gibe, but Skoyles pushed them apart.

"Let's have that lesson in shooting, shall we?" he said firmly. "Is your musket loaded, Novus?"

"Yes, sir."

"Then let me see you hit that post."

He pointed to a wooden post that marked the end of a row of cabins. It was less than thirty yards away, but, since it was no more than three inches wide, it was not an easy target. Kane was honest.

"I'm not sure that I can, sir."

"Then give me the musket," said Elliott, trying to take it from him. "I could hit that post with my eyes closed."

"In that case, you need no further instruction," said Skoyles, easing him away. "Leave it to Novus. He's the one I promised to teach." He patted Kane on the shoulder. "Go on—in your own time."

Kane shifted his feet uneasily. Knowing he was a poor marksman, he was

190

made even more nervous by the fact that several other soldiers had drifted across to watch him. The last thing he wanted at that moment was an audience. If he missed, Elliott and the others would taunt him unmercifully. He felt sick. Even in the cold, the palms of his hands began to sweat.

"Ignore everyone else," Skoyles cautioned him. "Just shoot."

"Imagine it's a redcoat, Novus," Elliott called out.

Kane tried to block out the various gibes, comments, and pieces of advice that the other soldiers threw at him. He did not even hear the bets that were being laid on his chances of success. The firing of one shot had taken on the significance of an event. Getting down on one knee, he put the stock of the musket into his shoulder and took aim. His hands were now running with moisture and his eyesight was blurred. It took him a long time before he felt able to pull the trigger.

There was a flash, a popping sound, and the musket ball shot out and missed the target. Jedediah Elliott led the howls of derision. Skoyles raised a hand to stop the noise.

"This is how it should be done, Novus," he said.

After his meeting with Major Clark, his own musket had been returned to him, and Skoyles now lifted it into position and took aim. It was only a second before he fired, scoring a direct hit on the post and sending splinters of wood spinning in the air. The men broke into spontaneous applause.

"Load your musket, Novus," said Skoyles. "The way I showed you."

Kane did as he was told. Skoyles, meanwhile, loaded his own weapon with such speed and precision that the soldiers were struck dumb. It took Kane over three times as long to reload. Skoyles looked around the group and picked out the youngest of them. He beckoned him over with a crook of his finger.

"You look as if you can run, lad," he said, whisking off his own hat to hand to the boy. "Set it up on the post so that Novus has something bigger to aim at."

Taking the hat, the boy raced off and put it on top of the post before darting back to the others. When it was evident that Kane would fire again, more wagers were immediately offered.

"Do I *have* to, sir?" Kane protested.

"I hit the post," said Skoyles. "Show them that you can do it."

"But you have a better weapon."

"Then use it instead."

Skoyles handed him the Brown Bess and took the other musket in exchange.

He whispered something in Kane's ear. Heartened by the advice, Kane went through the same routine again, getting down on one knee and waiting until he had steadied himself. When he fired this time, he had more success, grazing the side of the post and earning some grudging cheers from the audience. After congratulating him, Skoyles took aim with the other weapon and fired, hitting the top of his hat and sending it flying through the air.

"You see?" said Skoyles over the sound of appreciative clapping. "It's not the musket, it's the man firing it that makes all the difference."

"I wish that I could do that, sir," said Kane, awestruck by the demonstration. "What am I doing wrong?"

"I'll show you, Novus."

"Thank you."

"First, tell me this. Which musket did you prefer?"

"This one," said Kane, patting the weapon that he held.

"Then it's yours to keep," said Skoyles with a smile. "As long as you promise not to fire it at me next time I approach the camp."

The interview was held in the parlor of the house where Lieutenant Hugh Orde was staying. Sitting at a table with pen and paper before him, he was flanked by two armed redcoats. Ezekiel Proudfoot stood in front of the table. To ensure that *The Pennsylvania Patriot* was never published again, Orde was more than happy to miss the Christmas festivities. He was questioning the men separately so that he could pounce on any discrepancies in their respective answers.

"I knew that I would catch you sooner or later," said Orde smugly.

"But I have nothing to do with the newspaper," Proudfoot insisted.

"I only have your word for that, Mr. Allen."

"Why should I lie to you?"

"Your uncle did. In fact, he told me nothing but lies. He kept denying that he knew anything about the newspaper even though we found those two plates in his possession, and a printing press that was set up for the next issue."

"Until today, I'd never heard of *The Pennsylvania Patriot*."

"Oh, I think you did. I fancy that you're one yourself."

"I come from Massachussetts, Lieutenant."

"Then what are you doing here?"

"I told you," said Proudfoot. "I'm looking for land to buy. When my father died, my elder brother, Silas, inherited the farm. I was left some money to start up on my own and I decided to look in this area."

"Why?"

"My wife was born in Reading, sir. She always hankered after coming back to Pennsylvania one day."

It was not true, but Proudfoot spoke with such apparent sincerity that it sounded as if it were. Blending fact and invention, he went on to talk about his life on the farm, giving details of crops he had grown, and animals he had reared, that could only come from someone with firsthand experience of both. He was pleased to hear the first sign of doubt in the voice of his interrogator.

"It seems that you really are a farmer, Mr. Allen," he conceded. "But the fact remains that you were caught with the printer responsible for the publication of a rebel newspaper."

"He's my uncle, Lieutenant."

"Then you must have been aware of his political sympathies."

"Of course," said Proudfoot, "but I certainly didn't share them."

"Did he talk about *The Pennsylvania Patriot* to you?"

"No, Lieutenant. We were too busy discussing family matters. He wanted to hear news of my mother and my two brothers."

"Why did you make a run for it when we arrived?"

"You scared the daylights out of me."

"If you were innocent of any crime, you could have stayed."

"Uncle Adam pushed me away," Proudfoot explained. "He said that you'd be after him, and that there was no need for me to be tarred with the same brush. He more or less threw me out of there."

Hugh Orde wrote something down on the paper in front of him. He looked up at the prisoner again, weighing him up and trying to decide if he was dissembling or telling the truth.

"You say that Lieutenant Jenkinson will vouch for you?"

"Yes," Proudfoot replied.

"How did you come to be acquainted with him?"

"We met at the tavern where I'm staying."

Orde glanced at his notes. "The King George?"

"That's it. He was kind enough to take me to the performance of a play the other evening—*The Battle of Brandywine.*"

"Yes," said the other, grimacing slightly. "I was there myself."

"I'm sorry that it was cut short. I liked the play."

"So you enjoyed the fun that was poked at General Washington?"

"Very much."

"I see."

"It was a real treat for me," said Proudfoot. "The truth of it is that I'd never been to a theater before. When you work on a farm, you have no time to see plays—not that I saw all of this one, mind you."

"A most unfortunate turn of events."

"People charged out like a herd of wild horses."

"You were obviously present at the performance, Mr. Allen," said Orde, "but I'd like to hear confirmation from Lieutenant Jenkinson that he actually took you. I've also sent a man to the King George Tavern to see if you really are lodging there."

Proudfoot was worried. He hoped that Jenkinson would speak up for him, and he knew that Henry Gilby would defend him to the hilt. What disturbed him was the thought that soldiers might search his room at the tavern and find his engraving tools. They were hardly the sort of items that a farmer would be carrying. If his true identity were revealed, Proudfoot had no doubt that he would be either hanged or shot. The same fate would surely befall Adam Quenby.

"Did your uncle, by any chance, mention a man named Ezekiel Proudfoot?" asked Orde.

"No, Lieutenant."

"Have you ever heard the name before?"

"Never. Who is he?"

"A silversmith who has lent his meager skills to the rebel cause. His cartoons appeared in that newspaper. They were very offensive."

"It pains me to hear that my uncle was involved in this business."

"He gave you no hint of it?"

"None at all, Lieutenant."

Orde scrutinized his face and did his best to read his mind. Proudfoot remained calm under his searching gaze. Before the questions could continue, there was a tap on the door and Brevet Lieutenant Matthew Jenkinson was shown into the room. After being introduced to Hugh Orde, the newcomer, clearly inebriated, turned to shake hands warmly with Proudfoot. He put a companionable arm around him.

"Mr. Allen is a splendid fellow, Lieutenant," he said. "He's a farmer, looking to buy land nearby. We've had some good times together."

"Really?" said Orde.

"Yes, I'm happy to speak up on his behalf."

"You've never had any cause to suspect him?"

"Of what?"

"Siding with the enemy."

"Good Lord, no! Reece Allen is a deep-dyed Tory."

"Are you certain of that?" Orde pressed.

"Bet a month's pay on it, old chap."

Jenkinson emitted his high-pitched laugh. Proudfoot could smell the alcohol on his breath, and he knew that the arm around his shoulder was not merely evidence of friendship. Jenkinson needed someone to help him stay on his feet. Orde opened the door and showed him out.

"There you are," said Proudfoot, gaining in confidence. "One of your own men is ready to speak up for me."

"A more sober testimony would have been preferable."

"It is Christmas Day, Lieutenant."

"Is there nobody else who could vouch for you?"

"Henry Gilby, the landlord at the King George Tavern."

"My men will talk to him," said Orde. "If you've been in the city for some time, you must have met other people who will remember you."

"Pearsall Hughes would certainly do that."

"And who is he?"

"A bookseller. I've been to his shop a couple of times."

Orde's eyebrow lifted. "A farmer so interested in books?" he said. "Isn't that rather unusual, Mr. Allen?"

"Not at all, lieutenant. We are always trying to keep abreast of the latest farming methods. The first thing my father did when he took over a farm was to write to England for a copy of *Horse-Hoeing Husbandry*."

"What's that?"

"A book by Jethro Tull. It explains the advantages of sowing crops in lines. My father made us all read it from cover to cover, and it was not the only book in his little library."

Proudfoot listed several titles before Orde waved him into silence. There was another knock on the door. A soldier entered and spoke to the lieutenant in a corner of the room. The man had just returned from the King George Tavern and Proudfoot wished that he could catch what he was saying. When both of them stared at him with muted hostility, his stomach heaved. He felt certain that his engraving tools had been found. Hugh Orde dispatched the soldier, then came to confront Proudfoot.

"Well," he said with manifest disappointment, "it appears that you may, after all, be the person whom you claim to be, Mr. Allen. When my men searched your room at the tavern, they found nothing untoward."

"Does that mean I'm released, Lieutenant?"

"For the time being."

"Thank you, sir."

"Make sure that you stay in Philadelphia," Orde warned him. "We may well wish to talk to you again in due course."

"I'll be here until well into the New Year," said Proudfoot, already planning to leave that very day. "You know where you can find me."

As he set out on his return journey, Jamie Skoyles had plenty of time to reflect on his second visit to Valley Forge. There had been gains and losses. The real loss had been the severing of his direct link with George Washington, and he was dismayed that he would not even be allowed to go to the encampment again. His only contact with the Continental Army would be by means of coded letters. As a consequence, he would be providing information while getting none in return. Skoyles resolved that he would find another method of gathering intelligence about the enemy.

The gains were numerous. He now had a much clearer idea of the structure of the camp and its fortifications. But it was his conversation with some of the rank and file that had yielded the best results. After his display of marksmanship, they had been only too keen to talk to him. Skoyles learned that the choice of Valley Forge was essentially that of the commander in chief, and that his generals had strongly advocated other sites for the winter cantonment. Many had favored Wilmington, while some had argued that a line between Lancaster and Reading would be the easiest to defend against a surprise attack.

Skoyles was intrigued to hear frank opinions about the various commanders. Major General Wayne, a wealthy Pennsylvania tanner, was respected, though it was felt by all that his nickname of Mad Anthony was well deserved. There was praise, too, for Major General Henry Knox, a bookseller from Maine, who had no knowledge of artillery when he was put in charge of it, but who had learned with surprising speed. And so it went on: Nathanael Greene, John Sullivan, Enoch Poor, Baron de Kalb, George Weeden, William Maxwell, Charles Scott, James Mitchell Varnum, and John Armstrong of the Pennsylvania Militia—all were discussed and compared. There were also some derogatory comments about Charles Lee, the man with whom Skoyles had been earlier incarcerated.

There was patent dissension among the generals, and that could only get worse as conditions at the encampment deteriorated. None of the rank and file wanted to spend winter at Valley Forge. They lacked real spirit. It was news that would bring immense pleasure to General Howe. The man about whom Skoyles would like to have heard more was the Marquis de Lafayette, an intrepid French adventurer, who had inherited a fortune, then spent some of it buying a ship so that he could sail to America and join what he saw as a fight for freedom. Still only twenty, and serving entirely at his own expense, the young officer had fought with distinction at Brandywine until he was shot in the leg.

All in all, Skoyles decided, the Continental Army was a demoralized collection of men with no shortage of courage or determination. But it was weakened by a Board of War that was unable to supply them adequate food and clothing, and had a commander in chief who was being hampered by quarrelsome colleagues and sniped at by ambitious rivals. It would be cheering news to take back to General Howe. On balance, Skoyles concluded, his visit had been a success. The gains outweighed the losses substantially.

He had traveled over ten miles before he encountered anyone else. Cresting a hill, he rode down the slope toward a stand of trees. A man was sitting idly on a fallen trunk, eating something. When he got closer, Skoyles saw that it was a hunk of bread. The man picked up a flagon that stood beside him and offered it to Skoyles.

"Will you share a drink with me, friend?" he asked.

"No, thanks," said Skoyles.

"Where are you heading?"

"Philadelphia."

"Do you live there?"

"No, I'm visiting friends for Christmas."

Skoyles kept one hand on his musket. The man was young, fresh-faced and affable, but there was something about him that alerted the British soldier. He wore a tattered cape over his hunting shirt and breeches, and his hat was set back on his head. Though he had a broad smile on his face, his eyes were cold and watchful. Skoyles was being sized up. The man got slowly to his feet.

"Have you time to stop and talk?" he inquired.

"No, I'd best be on my way."

"You can spare me five minutes."

"I've a long way to go," said Skoyles.

"That's for us to decide, my friend."

The man suddenly reached out, grabbing the reins with one hand and trying to snatch the musket with the other. Skoyles was too fast for him. Taking a foot from his stirrup, he kicked his attacker hard, then, as the man reeled away, he used the butt of his weapon to knock him senseless with a single blow. When he tried to ride off, however, a shot was fired from the trees, and his horse let out a loud neigh of agony before collapsing in a heap on the ground. Skoyles had to dismount rapidly before he was crushed under the heavy body. The animal was not dead. It was twitching frenziedly on the grass.

"Put him out of his misery!" a voice ordered.

Two burly figures had come out of hiding to cover Skoyles with their muskets. The man who had shot the horse had slung one weapon over his shoulder so that he could train a second on their prisoner. He sounded angry.

"Shoot him!" he demanded.

Skoyles did as he was ordered, more out of pity for an animal that was clearly in great pain than because he was obeying a command. Aiming at the head, he put a bullet through the horse's brain at close quarters. After some more frantic convulsions, the animal finally lay still.

"Good," said the man who has issued the order. "Now we know that your musket is not loaded. Throw it down, then see to Ira. Be careful with him. He's my brother."

"Who are you?" Skoyles asked.

"We'll ask the questions."

The two men came slowly forward, keeping their weapons trained on Skoyles. The bigger of the two was clearly the leader, a tall, thickset man in his thirties with a rough beard, chewing tobacco as he spoke. His companion was much shorter but equally stocky, a swarthy individual in his forties with protruding brown eyes. Skoyles bent down to look at the fallen man, who was still unconscious. Blood had seeped from a wound on the side of his temple, but he was breathing normally.

"How is he?" asked the leader.

"He'll live," Skoyles replied.

"In that case, so will you."

He lashed out with his foot and knocked Skoyles on to his back, then he held the end of his musket inches away from his face. Skoyles looked up into a pair of green, unforgiving eyes. He then turned his head away as a stream of tobacco and phlegm was spat contemptuously at him. A second kick made him double up.

"Search him, Aaron," said the leader.

The swarthy man took Skoyles's knife and relieved him of the small amount of money he was carrying. The other man, meanwhile, was examining the injury to his brother, dabbing away at the blood with a handkerchief, before tying it around the head of the unconscious man to prevent any further bleeding. He shook his brother with tenderness.

"Wake up, Ira," he said gently. "It's me, Jack. Wake up."

Ira let out a low moan, and it was enough to convince his brother that he would soon recover. Crossing to the dead horse, he took the water canteen from the pommel and removed the stopper. When he poured the water over Ira's face, it produced a few drowsy curses.

"He'll be fine," said Jack with a laugh. He stood over Skoyles. "Now we can see to you. What's your name?"

"Dan Lukins," Skoyles replied.

"Where are you from?"

"Lancaster."

"Where are you going?"

"Philadelphia."

"I think you're lying."

"I'd never lie to someone holding a musket on me," said Skoyles.

He had deliberately concealed his name, using instead that of a private who had once served in his regiment. Skoyles was not going to admit that he was a captain in the British army. If the men were members of a local militia, they might shoot him out of spite. They would not believe for one second that he had been to Valley Forge to receive his instructions about providing intelligence. Skoyles had wounded one of them. If provoked, the men would have no compunction about killing him.

Rubbing his stomach where he had been kicked, he took stock of his captors. Ira was still badly dazed but the other two were vigilant. They glared at him as if he were an animal caught in a trap.

"What do you want?" asked Skoyles. "I've nothing on me."

"I heard you claim you was visiting friends," said Jack with a sneer. "What sort of a guest turns up on Christmas Day without any gifts? Would you do such a thing, Aaron?"

"Not me, Jack," answered the other.

"Nor me. Nor Ira, for that matter."

"He's lying to us."

"That leads me to one conclusion, Daniel Lukins. You didn't come from Lancaster at all, did you? I think you escaped from Valley Forge."

"No," said Skoyles.

"You're one more lousy deserter from the Continental Army."

"I'm a hunter. I live in Lancaster."

"Tell that to the firing squad when they shoot you."

"Who *are* you?"

"Me," returned the other. "I'm Jack Bedford. That's there's my brother, Ira. And this here," he went on, pointing to the swarthy man, "is our cousin, Aaron Pask. We catch deserters, you see. It's how we make a living. They fetch a good price."

Skoyles was disgusted. "You're bounty hunters!"

"It's an honorable profession," said Bedford.

"Only for cowards. Honorable men prefer to fight."

"Then why are you running away from the army?"

"I'm on furlough from the Pennsylvania Militia."

"Think we haven't heard that excuse before?" asked Bedford with a cackle. "Only last week, we had two lads who tried to talk their way out of a noose with the same story. But we were not fooled. We took them back to Valley Forge and got our blood money. General Washington will always buy deserters off us. He can make an example of them."

"So can General Howe," Pask added.

"Yes, he pays even better. But redcoats are harder to find. Why should they desert when they're nice and snug in Philadelphia? No," Bedford went on, "Valley Forge is where our money will be made."

Skoyles did not relish the idea of returning there, especially as he would have to walk the ten miles on foot. It would not help his standing with General Washington or Major Clark if three ruffians dragged him back to Valley Forge. Something else concerned him. When Ira Bedford became fully conscious again, he would have a blinding headache and a desire to avenge himself on the person who had given it to him. If they believed him to be a deserter, they would not worry about the condition in which they handed him over.

His escape had to be made soon. Skoyles waited for his chance.

"Come on," said Bedford. "Let's tie him up."

"I'd rather string him up from a tree," said Pask.

"So would I, Aaron, but we don't get paid for dead deserters. They want him alive." He kicked Skoyles once more. "Or half alive, anyway."

"On your feet!" Pask snarled.

Taking hold of Skoyles's collar, he showed his strength by hoisting him up from the ground. Retrieving his hat, Skoyles dusted it off and put it on his head. Bedford jabbed him with his musket and the three of them walked into the trees. They came to a clearing where the horses were tethered. Pask rested his musket against a trunk and took a coil of rope from his saddlebag. By way of a jest, he tossed one end up over a sturdy bough and pretended to make a noose. It was the moment that Skoyles had waited for, and he sprang into action immediately. With one man distracted, he leapt quickly on the other, seizing Bedford's loaded musket and wrestling for possession.

Skoyles brought his knee up hard into the man's groin, causing him to release the weapon and yell with fury. Swinging the musket deftly, Skoyles caught him on the point of the chin and dropped him like a stone. The whole exercise had taken seconds. Caught by surprise, Pask tried to make amends by grabbing his own musket. Before he could aim it, however, it was knocked upward by Skoyles, and the bullet was discharged harmlessly into the air. Pask screeched with rage and pulled out his knife, lunging at Skoyles with a ferocity that would have cut his stomach to ribbons.

Years of training with a musket and bayonet now came into play. Skoyles parried the thrust expertly, moved smartly to one side so that Pask was thrown off balance, then stuck out a leg to trip him. As soon as his adversary hit the ground, Skoyles struck the back of his head with the butt of the musket and sent him into oblivion. It was not a time to linger. Untying two of the horses, he slapped them on the rump to send them galloping off, then he collected his knife and his money from Pask. With the loaded musket still in his hand, he mounted the remaining horse.

One hand to his aching head, Ira Bedford came swaying drunkenly through the trees. He looked down at the motionless bodies.

"Have you killed them?" he cried in dismay.

"No," said Skoyles, "but the next time they cross my path, I will."

And he rode off hell for leather toward Philadelphia.

"When was this?" asked Pearsall Hughes, hoarse with anxiety.

"A couple of hours ago," said Proudfoot.

"And where is Adam now?"

"Still in custody. I was lucky that they didn't keep me locked up as well. We were caught like fish in a net, Mr. Hughes," he went on. "There was no hope of escape. When they discovered those plates up the chimney, I knew we were done for."

After his release, Ezekiel Proudfoot had hurried to the bookshop and interrupted a family gathering. Hughes and his wife took their visitor into the kitchen so that they could talk in private. Sounds of jollity came from the drawing room to provide an incongruous descant to the solemn discussion that was taking place.

"How ever did they find the press?" asked Miranda Hughes.

"By accident," said her husband. "It was so well hidden."

"It was no accident," Proudfoot corrected him. "Lieutenant Orde boasted about it to me. When he couldn't locate the press with a series of random searches, he tried something else. He began to look for the source of our paper, and he eventually ran our supplier to earth."

"Linus Arrowsmith," said Miranda with sadness.

"Yes," Hughes added. "Linus is the one owner of a paper mill in Philadelphia who is not a Tory. Ironic, isn't it? This city is the center of the papermaking industry, yet nobody else would dream of providing us with paper on which to print the *Patriot.*"

"Linus would never give us away, Pearsall."

"He's like Adam Quenby—he'd die sooner than betray us."

"It was one of the men who worked for Mr. Arrowsmith," Proudfoot explained. "He actually delivered the paper to us, so he knew the house where the press was kept. Lieutenant Orde bribed the fellow."

"Traitor!"

"What will happen to Linus?" wondered Miranda.

"I have no idea, Mrs. Hughes," said Proudfoot.

"If they know he was our supplier, he'll surely be arrested."

"That may well be the case. I just wanted to tell you what happened and warn you to be on guard."

"Why is that, Mr. Allen?" said Hughes.

"Because I had to use your name," replied Proudfoot, "and there's a possibility that someone may come here to ask questions about me. I told the lieutenant that you were one of the few people in the city whom I'd met, and that you would identify me as Reece Allen."

"Gladly. Did you tell them how we met?"

"I said that I came to the shop, looking for books about farming."

"Then that's the same tale *I'll* tell, if it comes to it."

"Thank you, Mr. Hughes."

"You be on your way, Mr. Allen," urged Miranda. "I think that you're very wise to get out of the city for a while."

"We'll be in touch," said Hughes. "Once we find another press, we'll start to print the *Patriot* once more."

Proudfoot waved a farewell. "Count on me for another lampoon."

"Thank you for the warning, Mr. Allen."

"Yes," said Miranda. "God bless you!"

It was only as he was taking his leave of them that Proudfoot realized how fond he was of the bookseller and his wife. In spite of their many eccentricities, they were a wholly admirable couple, brave, talented, and dedicated to the notion of a republic. As he strode briskly along the street, Proudfoot hoped that it would not be too long before he was able to see them again. No such hopes could be entertained about Adam Quenby. Since he had played a crucial role in the publication of the newspaper, summary execution would soon follow. Deeply upset at the prospect, Proudfoot felt that the best way to serve the printer's memory was to ensure that *The Pennsylvania Patriot* was soon revived.

Acutely aware that he was still in danger himself, he hurried on. When he got back to the King George Tavern, he found the landlord waiting for him. Washing his hands more strenuously than ever, Henry Gilby followed him up the stairs and into his room. The first thing that Proudfoot did was to reach under the bed and take out the satchel that was concealed there. His engraving tools were untouched.

"They told me that you'd been arrested," said Gilby worriedly.

"Yes," replied Proudfoot. "Fortunately, they let me go. I've decided to leave the city while I still can."

"Very wise, Mr. Allen. What about our mutual friend?"

"I've spoken to him."

"Good."

"How many redcoats came here?"

"Three," said Gilby. "They demanded to search your room."

"Then why didn't they find my satchel?"

"I can't answer that, sir."

"They must have looked under the bed."

"They did. I was there when they conducted their search."

"Then how did they miss this?" said Proudfoot, tapping his satchel.

"Very easily."

"Were all three of them *blind*?"

"No, Mr. Allen," said the landlord. "They were simply misled."

"Misled?"

"Yes. When they burst into my tavern and ordered me to take them to the room occupied by Reece Allen, I showed them to the one that you had on your *first* visit here." He grinned happily. "It's further along the landing. I gave you a different room this time."

"Thank heaven you did, Mr. Gilby!"

"The gentleman staying in there at the moment is a merchant from

Brunswick, New Jersey. They found nothing in his belongings that made them suspicious."

Proudfoot shook his hand. "That was very clever of you."

"You learn a few tricks in my occupation, sir."

"I can't tell you how grateful I am, Mr. Gilby."

"Shall we see you back here some day?" said the landlord.

"Oh, yes," promised the other. "But not until you change the name of the tavern and burn that detestable signboard. King George will not rule over this city forever. You have my word on that."

By the time Jamie Skoyles got back to Philadelphia, it was early evening and darkness was falling. Tired and bruised after the day's escapades, he first rode to his lodging so that he could wash off the dust of travel and change into his uniform. The more he thought about the three men who had ambushed him, the angrier he got. Soldiers on both sides were risking their lives every day. Thousands had died, others had been hideously maimed. All that Jack Bedford and his confederates saw in the war was an opportunity for profit, rounding up those who felt compelled to desert and taking them back to certain and ignominious death. Skoyles had nothing but contempt for such ruthless parasites.

General Howe had insisted on hearing any new intelligence as soon as possible. Skoyles therefore went off to call on him, even though he expected that the commander would still be celebrating Christmas. He found Howe in his headquarters, sharing a drink with Hugh Orde and smiling with delight as if he had just won a major battle. Howe rushed across the room to greet the newcomer.

"Come in, Captain," he said cordially. "We've splendid tidings."

"Really, sir?"

"Lieutenant Orde will tell you his news. He's done it at last."

"Yes," said Orde, pleased at the opportunity to earn more praise. "I managed to track down the press on which that deplorable newspaper, *The Pennsylvania Patriot,* was printed. The odious publication is no more. The printer—one Adam Quenby—is locked up in chains."

"Well done, Lieutenant," said Skoyles.

"Thank you."

"How did you discover the location of the press?"

Orde went on to repeat what he had told General Howe, gaining a fresh batch of compliments from his happy commander. Skoyles was interested to hear that two people had been arrested in the cellar.

"Who was the second man?" he asked.

"Mr. Reece Allen," said the lieutenant.

"Was he the editor?"

"Alas, no. That villain is still on the loose."

"We'll soon catch him," Howe affirmed confidently.

"Mr. Allen is a farmer from Massachussetts," continued Orde. "He's the nephew of the printer. He's in the city because he wishes to buy land in the vicinity. His wife hails from Reading, it seems, and has always wanted to return to Pennsylvania." He hunched his soldiers. "It was a big disappointment, really."

"Why is that?" said Skoyles.

"Because I had the feeling that he might be Ezekiel Proudfoot."

"Oh?"

"What a stroke of good fortune that would have been!"

"Yes," said Howe. "I could have hanged him beside the printer and danced around the pair of them with glee. Proudfoot is the man I despise most. The insolent rogue had the gall to ridicule me, and nobody does that with impunity."

"I'll get him one day, General," said Orde.

Skoyles was curious. "What made you think that you'd already done so, Lieutenant? Was it because you found him in that cellar?"

"It was the fact that he tried to run away."

"Did he have an explanation for that?"

"Yes, Captain. He said that his uncle bundled him out of there because he knew that he was in trouble himself, and did not wish his nephew to be arrested as well, when he was in no way connected to the newspaper."

"Can you give me a description of Reece Allen?"

"Why do you ask that?" said Howe.

"Because I once caught a glimpse of Ezekiel Proudfoot," said Skoyles, careful once again not to reveal that he and Proudfoot were old friends. "He was captured at the battle of Hubbardton, and we held him prisoner for a short while until he escaped."

"Reece Allen did not look like a silversmith," admitted Orde. "He was a tall, rangy, round-shouldered man with a pockmarked face."

"Age?"

"In his thirties."

"What color hair?"

"Brown."

It sounded remarkably like a description of Ezekiel Proudfoot, but Skoyles did not say so. He needed more detail to be certain.

"You say that he was a farmer, Lieutenant?"

"Yes," answered Orde. "He grew up on a farm in Massachussetts—no question about that. He told me how they grew crops and raised cattle. When his father died, his elder brother inherited the farm. Allen was left some money, and he was going to use that to buy his own land and start up in Pennsylvania."

"Did he happen to mention his brother's name?" said Skoyles.

"He did, Captain. I think it was Silas."

"Are you sure about that?"

Orde thought it over. "Yes," he said, "I'm certain of it."

Skoyles was convinced. Having heard the name, he knew that Reece Allen was indeed Ezekiel Proudfoot. Of the three brothers, Silas was the eldest and the one in line to take over the farm. Skoyles had met the whole family when he had been billeted with them, as an untried young soldier, during the French and Indian War. Ezekiel had been his best friend. Reuben, the youngest of the brothers, had fought for the rebels in a Massachusetts regiment and died at the battle of Bemis Heights. It still troubled Skoyles greatly that he had been the one who killed him. As a result, his involvement with the Proudfoot family had taken on a new resonance.

"Well, Captain?" prompted Howe. "Does it sound like the man?"

"No, sir," said Skoyles.

"Then what did Proudfoot look like?"

"As I said, I only had a brief look at him. All I can remember is that he was of middle height with thick, black hair and a beard."

"Reece Allen had a beard," said Orde. "A brown one."

"Then he is who he says he is."

"A pity."

"Hardly," observed Howe tartly. "You wouldn't want to be told that the man you released earlier today is actually the one we'd most like to capture. That would be unforgivable, Lieutenant."

"Quite, sir," Orde agreed.

"I'm pleased to hear that it never happened."

Skoyles kept silent and wrestled with competing emotions. He was glad that the printing press had been found, and that the newspaper would not be able to direct any more attacks at the British army. At the same time, however, he was relieved that Ezekiel Proudfoot had not been identified. The thought that his friend came so close to being hanged was so disturbing to Skoyles that he had deliberately given a false description of the man. If the silversmith were ever caught again, and stripped of his alias, Skoyles could be called to account for lying to his fellow officers. Yet he did not feel in any way penitent. He wondered why.

"Right," said Howe, clapping his hands. "Lieutenant Orde has brought me some heartening news today. I look to you to do the same, Captain Skoyles. I assume that's why you're here."

"It is, General. I've not long returned from Valley Forge."

Orde was astounded. "You went there on Christmas Day?"

"Yes, Lieutenant, though I was not exactly made welcome."

Skoyles gave them a straightforward recital of the facts, adding no embellishments and saying nothing about his proficiency with the Brown Bess musket. What the general wanted to hear was detail about the encampment and the state of readiness of the Continental Army. For that reason, Skoyles did not touch on his encounter with Jack Bedford and the others. They were scavengers in a war-torn country, and Skoyles had met many like them over the years.

"Thank you, Captain," said Howe when he had heard the report. "I'm sorry that you will henceforth be kept away from Valley Forge, but I'm sure that you will find a way to return there eventually."

"Oh, I will, sir," said Skoyles. "It's simply a question of earning the right to do so in the eyes of the enemy."

"Meanwhile, you need to supply intelligence to them."

"Details that their other spies could not possibly get."

"That will be no problem. Call on me again tomorrow."

"Morning or afternoon, sir?"

"Oh, afternoon," said Howe with a chuckle. "We'll be drinking well into the night. I daresay that you'll be doing the same." He reached for a piece of paper on his desk. "Have you met Captain Tillman yet?"

"No, General."

"Roderick Tillman is a member of my staff. Excellent man. Salt of the earth. An exemplary soldier. You and he should get on well together."

"Why am I to meet the captain?" asked Skoyles.

"He'll tell you when you get there. Here's the address."

Skoyles took the paper from him. "I'll call in the morning."

"Oh, I think that you should do that this evening."

"Any particular reason, sir?"

"Tillman will explain. Off you go, Captain."

It was a brusque dismissal though Skoyles thought he detected a ghost of a smile around Howe's lips. After bidding them farewell, he let himself out of the building and walked the three blocks to the address that he had been given. Still mystified, he rang the bell. When the door was opened, Skoyles could hear sounds of a party from somewhere deep inside the house. The servant spoke deferentially.

"Can I help you, sir?" he said.

"I was told to speak to a Captain Tillman."

"Then please come in."

The man stepped back so that Skoyles could enter the house. Someone came tripping along the passageway toward him and Skoyles understood why he had been sent there. The young woman who threw herself into his arms was Elizabeth Rainham.

George Washington had found no time for leisure on Christmas Day. He had spent most of it in a long and contentious meeting with his generals. Liberated from that, he had toured Valley Forge to inspect the camp and to offer his men the compliments of the season. It was not until evening that he was able to have a private conversation with Major John Clark. They were in the little stone house that served as the army headquarters.

"This place is far too small," said Washington, "especially since I've started the practice of inviting the field officers of the day here so that I can become better acquainted with them. I'm having a dining room built in order that we can eat in a modicum of comfort."

Clark was skeptical. "Valley Forge and the idea of comfort do not sit easily with each other," he said. "Will they build in stone?"

"Timber. We'll be eating in a log cabin."

"Just like the men, sir."

"Not quite, major. They're confined to a diet of fire cake, and they'll remain so unless we can intercept another British foraging expedition."

"Captain Skoyles confirmed that it would take place in two days."

"Did he now? What did you make of him?"

Clark collected his thoughts before he replied. Seated in a wooden chair, he was close enough to the fire to feel its warmth against his legs. Candlelight was throwing an array of shifting patterns onto the walls. Washington sat opposite him.

"I was uncertain of him at first, sir," admitted Clark.

"So was I."

"He seems too good to be true. The person we most need is someone close to General Howe and one suddenly volunteers himself."

"We've had deserters from the British army before, Major."

"Granted," said Clark, "and they've been very welcome. Captain Skoyles is not exactly a deserter, however. He's acting as a spy within his own camp. It takes courage to do that."

"He has that in abundance," said Washington. "You only have to listen to him, talking about the campaigns in which he's been involved. He lives to fight and he's been taught how to do it effectively. He's also a natural leader."

"I had the same impression."

"The question is, do we trust him?"

"I'd *like* to," said Clark, "and nine-tenths of me is willing to do so. But there's a nagging doubt at the back of my mind. It's the reason I'm keeping him well away from Valley Forge for a while."

"How did he take that news?"

"Not well, General. He had hopes of dealing directly with you."

"Then he'll be disappointed. I have other fish to fry." He gave a dry laugh. "If only I did, Major! If only I was back on my plantation where I could shoot, hunt, fish, and eat everything that I caught." Washington sighed. "Will those days ever come back, I wonder?"

"Yes, General."

"I miss my family so much."

"And they'll be missing you—especially today."

"Martha will join me here in time, but not just now. We've too much to do at the moment. There are defenses to be strengthened and the cabins to be completed. Winter is knocking on our door."

"I take it that we'll be staying put, then?" said Clark.

"Yes, Major. That was the theme of the endless debates we had today. Should we forget about the war or try to stage a surprise attack on one of the British encampments outside Philadelphia? Thankfully," said Washington, "and after an eternity of bickering, they came round to the view that major hostilities should be well and truly suspended."

"Our men are simply not ready to fight."

"I know. Brandywine knocked the stuffing out of them. We need to nurture them a little, and train them properly in the art of war. We've still far too many lads with strong hearts but a weak knowledge of soldiering." Washington put another log on the fire. "Well, we've had one reprieve today," he continued. "The weather improved. Let's hope that the snow holds off a little longer."

"Yes, sir. It will make my job so much harder. I won't be able to reach Philadelphia if the roads are blocked."

"When are you returning to the city?"

"Tomorrow."

"So soon?" said Washington. "You're always on the move. You must not overdo the traveling, Major. It's starting to tell on your health."

"My health is an irrelevance," returned Clark. "I've too many things to do in Philadelphia to stay away. In the light of what we talked about a moment ago, one task is particularly important."

"What's that?"

"Keeping an eye on Captain Jamie Skoyles."

"When did you get here?" asked Skoyles breathlessly. "How ever did you travel? I thought you were still in New York City. Why didn't you tell me that you were coming? What happened to Major Wright and his wife?"

"They can manage perfectly well without me," said Elizabeth.

211

"I assumed that you'd spend Christmas with them."

"That's what I wanted you to assume, Jamie."

"Why?"

"So that I could surprise you."

Skoyles laughed and pulled her to him. "You certainly did that!"

They were in the front room of the house to which he had been sent, and Skoyles was still wondering if he were caught up in some sort of dream. All was soon explained. It transpired that Major Wright, with whom Elizabeth had been staying in New York City, had a close friend on General Howe's staff. When he wrote to the man and explained the situation, his friend, Captain Roderick Tillman, was delighted to help. He offered board and lodging to Elizabeth and promised to look after her as carefully as the major and his wife had done. Riding with an escort, it had taken Elizabeth almost three days to reach Philadelphia.

"And you intend to stay?" asked an excited Skoyles.

"Of course." `

"This is more than I dared hope for, Elizabeth."

"I couldn't leave you all alone for Christmas."

"Thank you!"

He tightened his embrace and kissed her on the lips, trying to forget all the sorrow and loneliness of being apart from her. Overjoyed to see her again, Skoyles wanted to know if she had brought him news.

"Any word of Tom Caffrey and Polly?" he asked.

"None, I'm afraid."

"They would have reached New York City long before now."

"I wondered if they'd come on here, Jamie," she said.

"No. I made inquiries as soon as I arrived. They must have gone astray somewhere. Or been captured by those men who came after us."

"Don't even think that. We must never give up hope."

"You're right."

"We're together again," she said joyously. "Safe in the bosom of the British army, and nothing can touch us."

"No," he said with a fond smile.

"It's the start of a new life for me, Jamie."

"And for me."

"I want to put the old one firmly behind me. I want to get rid of all the silly ideas that brought me to America. I'm yours now. Nobody else matters. I'll never see Major Harry Featherstone again."

The attack was swift and decisive. The garrote was slipped around the man's neck and pulled tight. Within a minute, he was dead. As his victim fell to the ground, the killer stole his musket, powder, and ammunition, then ran to the man's horse. Having made his escape at night, Major Harry Featherstone was soon riding away from Cambridge in the dark.

CHAPTER TWELVE

The selected regiments left Valley Forge with severe misgivings. The march to the Brandywine Valley meant a return to a battlefield where they had been soundly defeated in September by a British force possessing numerical and tactical superiority. Over twelve hundred soldiers of the Continental Army and its supporting militias had given their lives or been badly wounded at Brandywine Creek. In the headlong retreat, many of the dead had to be left unburied. Just over three weeks later, even though they had matched the courage and tenacity of the redcoats, the rebels had been hounded from another battlefield near Germantown. It left them with unhappy memories.

"We seem to have been marching forever," grumbled Novus Kane.

"That's what we do in the infantry," said Jedediah Elliott. "We march, we rest, we march, we rest, we march, we fight."

"Then, as like as not, we run for our lives."

"No, we don't!"

"Well, that's what happened at Brandywine, Jed. And it was even worse at Germantown. I've never run so fast in my life.

"That was General Stephen's fault."

"He nearly got us all killed."

"And I was shooting so well that day," bragged Elliott, tapping his chest with his pipe. "I spilled a lot of redcoat blood at Germantown."

"The only thing I hit was one of our own men," Kane confessed mournfully. "When General Stephen pulled us out of the attack, he ordered us to support General Sullivan. Next thing we know, we bump into Mad Anthony's men coming from the other direction. We thought they were the enemy."

"Those blockheads thought *we* were the enemy as well," Elliott recalled

214

with scorn. "Two divisions of the same army, firing at each other! No wonder those pesky redcoats chased us from the field."

Kane was fearful. "And it will happen again, Jed. I feel it."

"Not while I'm around, it won't!"

The Brandywine Valley was a patchwork of rolling countryside and thick woodland. Since the valley was thirty-five miles long, the Continental Army had set out the previous day in order to reach the southern end of it in time. Caught in heavy rain, they had spent a cold, wet night bivouacking under trees. Like most of the rank and file, Kane and Elliott were chilled to the bone and tetchy on the following day. During a break in what seemed like an interminable march, they gobbled down their frugal rations. Kane was seated on a tree stump, but Elliott preferred to stay on his feet so that he could see what was happening all around them as he puffed on his clay pipe.

"Why did we have to come all this way?" Kane wailed.

"To get some decent food for our empty bellies."

"The redcoats won't hand it over without a fight."

"We'll take them by surprise," said the old man, "as we did last time. Never known a chicken so good as the one we sneaked off them before Christmas. We only had a tiny mouthful each, I know, but I could taste it for days."

"Anything is better than fire cake!"

All the time he had been speaking, Kane had been cleaning the Brown Bess musket that Jamie Skoyles had given to him. It was his most prized possession, and the way he nursed it was irritating Elliott.

"Leave the blessed thing alone!" he said harshly. "Ye fondle that damned musket as if it was a naked woman—not that ye'd know what to do with one of those! Put it down, Novus."

"Mr. Skoyles said I was to take care of it."

"He didn't mean that ye had to sleep with it in your hands."

"Treat your musket with respect, he told me, and it won't let you down." He held up the weapon proudly. "Since I've had this, I've begun to feel like a real soldier."

Elliott was contemptuous. "It's about time, too!"

Scouts came galloping back into camp to report a sighting of redcoats only a couple of miles away. They had been seen herding a large number of animals. Once that information was passed through the ranks, the men stopped complaining about their freezing bodies and their aching limbs. Getting quickly into formation, they marched off with a spring in their step. The scouts had done well to locate the enemy so soon. The Brandywine Valley was all of fifteen miles wide, big enough for two armies to pass without even being aware of each other's presence.

Moving east, the Americans eventually took up their position on a wooded slope from which they could intercept the foraging party. Rough estimates put the number of redcoats at five hundred, only half of the size of the force about to ambush them. Hundreds of animals were being driven in the direction of Philadelphia. Long before they were seen, they could be heard. The sound of sheep, cattle, and hogs whetted the appetite of the men hiding in the trees.

"I can almost *smell* that pork!" said Elliott, smacking his lips.

"Do you think they'll have any geese or turkeys?" asked Kane.

"I don't care what they have, lad, as long as we can eat it."

"We have to capture the animals first, Jed."

"And we will. We haven't come all this way to go back hungry."

When the foraging party finally came into view, the Americans waited impatiently for the signal to attack. A sizable herd was moving forward, kept in check by outriders on the flanks and in the rear, and followed by the infantry. Evidently, the redcoats had had a successful visit to various farms in the valley. People who refused to sell to the rebels were more than ready to accept money from the British army. The foragers got closer and closer. It was time to relieve them of their stock.

The signal was at last given and a first volley was discharged. Novus Kane could not believe his luck when he knocked a rider from the saddle. He let out a yell of triumph and began to reload. A few of the redcoats had been shot dead, and many more wounded, but they did not quit the field. Instead, they guided the stampeding herd in a half circle, driving it in the direction from which the attack had come. Expecting to be able to round up the animals and take them back, the rebels saw the crazed beasts charging directly at them.

There was worse to come. A cavalry regiment that had been lurking well behind the foraging party now spurred their horses forward. The thunder of hooves and the sight of raised swords in the distance induced further panic in the trees. Though their officers bellowed at them to hold their positions, several of the rebels lost their nerve and fled. Many who stayed were buffeted and trampled by the bolting herd. Those who dodged the animals found themselves facing a concerted volley from the redcoat infantry and the threat of a cavalry charge. The situation was hopeless. All control was lost. Abandoning any hope of success, they fired for a second time, then ran off in all directions.

Young and nimble, Novus Kane was able to climb the slope with relative ease. He soon became aware that Jedediah Elliott was not with him and he looked back to see the old man laboring up the incline. He ran downhill to offer him a helping hand, then he more or less dragged Elliott behind him. The higher they went, the thicker the trees became, giving them a degree of safety at last from the pursuing cavalry. Retreat was always a humiliation, but one element of it was particularly irksome this time. When they reached the top of the hill, the Americans had to run past the very animals they had come to catch. Lost and bewildered, cattle, sheep, and hogs were wandering aimlessly around, looking for something on which they could graze.

The rebels kept going for half a mile before they felt able to stop for a rest. All of them were panting for breath, but Elliott was wheezing noisily as he flung himself down on the grass. Putting his musket aside, Kane sat down beside him.

"What happened, Jed?" he asked.

The old man needed minutes before he was able to answer.

"They were expecting us," he gasped.

Coming to Philadelphia had given Elizabeth Rainham two wonderful sources of pleasure. She was reunited with Jamie Skoyles, and she had found, in Lucy Tillman, the sort of female friend she had lacked since she had left England. Married to Captain Tillman of the 17th Dragoons, Lucy was a charming young woman in her early twenties, bright, talkative, and eminently trustworthy. Elizabeth felt that she could confide in her and, by the same token, Lucy knew that she could entrust secrets to her new friend. Both women came from military families, grew up in cathedral towns—Elizabeth in Canterbury, Lucy in Winchester—and had a passion for riding. And they shared many other common interests.

Days after her arrival in the city, Elizabeth was being introduced to its array of shops by Lucy Tillman. They began with a milliner and went on from there. As they looked in the window of a dress shop, Lucy chose the moment to probe into her companion's private life.

"Captain Skoyles is such a daring man," she said with a smile of appreciation, "and you showed courage as well, Elizabeth. I don't know that I'd have been brave enough to escape the way you did."

"I had complete faith in Jamie."

"I have complete faith in Roderick, but I'd think twice if he told me that I had to sail along the Atlantic coast in a fishing boat. I can't swim."

"Neither can I," admitted Elizabeth.

"Then you're even braver than I thought. It must have been an amazing experience—frightening as well."

"It was, Lucy, but it brought us closer together."

"You make such a handsome couple."

"Thank you."

"Marrying a captain is something that I can recommend."

"It obviously suits you."

"It does, Elizabeth. I love army life. I was born to it." She gave Elizabeth a sly nudge. "Have you set the day yet?"

"No, Lucy. There's no chance of a wedding in the near future."

"Why not? There are plenty of churches here."

"That's not the problem."

"The army has dozens of chaplains to choose from. Look at me—I was married in Boston when it was still in British hands. I simply couldn't bear *not* to be Roderick's wife."

"Our opportunity will come in due course."

"Ah," said Lucy with a smile, "I understand. You want a wedding in Canterbury Cathedral with all the accoutrements. You and Captain Skoyles would rather wait until you can get back to England."

"Not at all," said Elizabeth. "When the war is over, we intend to stay here and buy land. It could be many years before I return to Kent again. Jamie and I will be married in America."

"Just like me and Roderick."

They went into the shop and inspected the various fabrics that were on display. It was something that Elizabeth had not been able to enjoy for over six months. After all the dangers she had come through, she found it strangely refreshing to do something as pleasant and ordinary as visiting a shop. Lucy waited until they came out into the street again before she picked up the conversation.

218

"Roderick thinks the war will be over by next spring," she said.

"I wish that I could be that sanguine," remarked Elizabeth.

"The rebels are on their knees. Roderick came back from a foraging expedition in the Brandywine Valley yesterday. According to him, when the rebels tried to ambush them, his dragoons responded so swiftly that they chased the enemy away. They ran like startled rabbits."

"But they always come back to fight again somehow, Lucy."

"A lot of them won't be doing that. Deserters are coming in all the time. The town jail is full of prisoners of war. General Washington is so short of food in Valley Forge that all he could afford to send to the prisoners here for Christmas was one cow and a supply of flour."

"Yes," said Elizabeth, "Jamie has been to Valley Forge."

Lucy was astonished. "How ever did he manage that?"

"He went on a special mission."

"You mean, he actually got inside the enemy camp?"

"Twice, Lucy. The first time, he even spoke to General Washington himself. It's quite primitive there, apparently. They've had to build a log town. Jamie says that living there will be an ordeal when winter really starts to bite."

"That will teach them to take up arms against us."

"I still don't believe that it will break their spirit."

"Then I hope you're wrong," said Lucy airily, "because I want to be there when you and Captain Skoyles get married. The sooner this war can be brought to an end, the sooner the pair of you can become husband and wife."

"I'm looking forward to that moment very much."

"How will your parents take the news?"

"I haven't told them yet," Elizabeth confessed. "All that they know is that I broke off my engagement to a major in the 24th Foot. Letters take such a long time to reach England. My parents will not even be aware that I escaped from the Convention army yet. It was in a letter I sent from New York City."

"That, at least, will bring them great cheer."

"It will, Lucy, though I gave them no details."

"No flight at dawn on a boat? No thrilling escape from that ambush? No hiding on a roof from men who were trying to kill you? Honestly," said Lucy with a giggle, "I'd have described every last second of it. My parents would have had a dozen pages to read."

"My situation is a little different."

They had been strolling along the street as they spoke, attracting many admiring glances from passing men. When they came to another shop, Lucy put out a hand to stop Elizabeth.

"Oh, we must go in here," she said. "It's my favorite bookshop. It's run by a dear man called Pearsall Hughes, and he knows exactly what to recommend for light reading. Come in and meet him, Elizabeth."

It was New Year's Eve before Jamie Skoyles made his first visit to the funeral parlor. General Howe had provided him with information to pass on, and he had transposed it into the code that he had learned. Skoyles set out on the frosty morning of Wednesday, December 31, 1777, to deliver his letter. The funeral parlor occupied a corner site. There were stables at the rear, and as Skoyles approached, he could hear the horses neighing and whinnying as they were being harnessed for another funeral. While the war had brought ruination for many businesses, undertakers were among those who had prospered most. The Quakers who ran the establishment might espouse peace, but it did not prevent them from helping to bury the countless victims of war.

Skoyles had expected to slip the letter through the door. When he got there, however, it opened and a middle-aged woman in the distinctive attire of the Society of Friends gave him a quiet smile of welcome.

"Good morning, sir," she said.

"Good morning?"

"Can we help you?"

"I'd like to leave this, if I may," he said, offering the letter.

"Thank you," she said, taking it from him.

"Have you any idea when it might be collected?"

"No, sir. Will that be all?"

"Yes, thank you."

The woman closed the door gently in his face. He had written no name or address on the envelope, but was assured that it would nevertheless reach its destination. Skoyles had been wrong to ask for details of collection. Those who worked at the funeral parlor clearly exercised great tact. Turning on his heel, he walked away, knowing that he might be watched from inside the building. As soon as he turned a corner, however, he stopped and waited. If someone came to pick up his envelope in the next couple of hours, Skoyles was eager to know who it was.

Every so often, therefore, he would take up a position from which he could see the front and side entrances to the premises. When the funeral procession began, Skoyles stepped out of sight and waited until the cortege has passed on its way to the church. While he maintained a long, lonely, vigil in the cold, he had plenty to occupy his mind. The unheralded arrival of Elizabeth Rainham had delighted him at first, but two slight drawbacks had now appeared.

The first was that they had to live apart. For the sake of propriety, and in order to preserve Elizabeth's reputation, they had to remain in their separate lodgings. The days spent together during their escape had included nights in each other's arms, albeit in fraught circumstances. That intimacy was now denied them. In a city where General Howe openly flaunted his mistress, Skoyles and Elizabeth had to behave with more decorum. Private moments together were scarce. It was vexing.

The second drawback was one he had not foreseen. As long as Elizabeth had been in New York City, he had taken risks with his usual audacity. Now that she was in Philadelphia, awaiting his return every time he left, he felt a slight sense of restraint. Her presence reminded him to take more care. Fear of upsetting Elizabeth had also made him suppress certain facts about his adventures. Though he had told her about the two visits to Valley Forge, he did not divulge the information that he had almost been shot dead by pickets, and that he had been caught by bounty hunters who had mistaken him for a rebel deserter.

Instead of remaining in one place all the time, he strode up and down the street at intervals, making sure that there were no significant gaps of time in his surveillance. A few people did visit the funeral parlor, but they always seemed to be potential customers, in mourning for dead family members or friends. It occurred to him that one of the distressed people who entered and left the parlor could easily have collected his envelope, but he did not think so.

After almost two hours, Skoyles felt someone touch his arm. Then a small boy thrust a note into his hand before scurrying off down the street. Skoyles opened the slip of paper. The message was terse.

GO AWAY. WE WILL CONTACT YOU.

He had been seen.

Major General Marie Joseph Paul Yves Roche Gilbert de Notier, Marquis de Lafayette, was a slight young man, rather unimpressive in appearance, yet having the unmistakable air of a French aristocrat. As he entered the headquarters at Valley Forge on New Year's Day, his wounded leg was still heavily bound and he needed a walking stick. Ezekiel Proudfoot had met him before and been impressed by everything that he did. Like George Washington, the French adventurer insisted on undergoing the same suffering as his men. At the start of another year of possible conflict, Proudfoot had come to see if there were any tidings of a press that could print *The Pennsylvania Patriot* once again. He arrived on the heels of Lafayette, who was treated with an almost paternal affection by the commander in chief. The two guests occupied chairs around the fire in the office. Washington sat between them.

"Do you have news for me, General?" asked Proudfoot.

"Indeed, I do," Washington replied. "You are to make your way to Germantown as soon as possible."

"Germantown? But it's crawling with redcoats."

"So was Philadelphia, but it took them a long time to find you."

Washington broke off to explain to Lafayette how the printing press had finally been located and put out of action. Proudfoot had escaped, but the printer had not been so fortunate. Unrepentant to the last, Adam Quenby had been hanged the day after Christmas.

"We must print the *Patriot* again," Washington went on, reaching for a drawing on his desk, "if only to gain a wider audience for Ezekiel's latest work." He handed it to Lafayette. "This is what happened at a play that was staged in Philadelphia."

"I call it 'Redcoats in Retreat,'" said Proudfoot.

Lafayette looked at the drawing and laughed. "I like it," he said, pointing to the central figure in the unceremonious exit from the theater. "This is General Howe, I think. Is very funny."

"The lady being pulled along behind him is Mrs. Loring, his mistress. They ran past me as if they were leaving a powder magazine that was about to explode. I didn't have to invent anything," Proudfoot went on with a grin. "That's exactly what happened."

"Then we must show it to the men."

222

"We will," said Washington, "now that we have another press. If the *Patriot* is printed in Germantown, I'm sure that Major Clark will find a way to smuggle copies into Philadelphia. He's a real magician."

"Major Clark is a fine man," said Lafayette. "He has many spies. We are lucky, I think. The British, they do not have a Major Clark."

"He's incomparable. My only concern is that he never knows when to stop. He has great energy but it has limits, and I'm afraid he may push himself beyond those limits."

"The same might equally be said of you, General," Proudfoot pointed out. "Nobody at Valley Forge works as hard as you."

"Is true," agreed Lafayette. "Even you must rest."

Washington shook his head. "When there is so much to do?" he said. "I have no time for leisure. Someone has to keep shouting at Congress or they will forget that we are here."

"The way we've been neglected is deplorable," said Proudfoot. "If it were not for the generosity of people like the marquis, who have paid out of their own pockets for food, clothing, and blankets for the men, our situation would be desperate."

"The Board of War, it has let us down," said Lafayette.

"Badly."

"Do they want us to *lose?*"

"I sometimes think so," said Proudfoot with passion. "If this war has taught me nothing else, it's taught me to despise politicians. They not only do all they can to hamper the army, they even have the gall to criticize its commander in chief." Fearing that he had spoken out of turn, he glanced at Lafayette. "Excuse me. I didn't mean that."

"No, no," insisted Washington. "Do go on, Ezekiel. I have no secrets from the marquis. It might interest you to know that he was approached by Thomas Conway as well."

Proudfoot was shocked. "Really?"

"I was one of many," said Lafayette.

"It's a proper cabal, then."

"That's what we call it, Ezekiel," said Washington resignedly. "The Conway Cabal. He denies it, of course, but General Conway is at the heart of it. He wants me replaced by General Gates, so he has been intriguing with certain members of Congress."

"He try to draw me into it," said Lafayette with a gesture of disgust. "He promise me that, if I speak up for General Gates, I will lead a division into Canada when the time comes. I tell them, already we have a commander, who is the best man."

"Thank you, Marquis."

"How can Congress appoint such a disloyal character as inspector general?" asked Proudfoot angrily. "He should be dismissed for daring to plot against his commander in chief."

"It's one more cross to bear," said Washington, his jaw tightening, "and it's very tiresome. Unfortunately, General Gates is by no means the only man who would like to supplant me. There's even a candidate from Europe who wants to unseat George Washington."

"Oh—and who is that?"

"The Comte de Broglie. The marquis knows him well."

"He was my teacher," said Lafayette with obvious embarrassment. "Everything I learned about war came from him."

"He is a veteran soldier," Washington explained, "and a former head of the French secret service. Then Silas Deane, one of our envoys in Paris, started whispering in his ear, and told him that *he* could be the new commander in chief of the Continental Army."

Proudfoot was aghast. "A Frenchman in charge of the fate of the American colonies?" He raised an apologetic hand. "I'm sorry, Marquis. We are honored to have you with us, but I do not think our soldiers would fight for someone they have never heard of. The French are not even involved in this war."

"At the moment," said Lafayette. "That could change."

"Yes," Washington added. "Benjamin Franklin is in Paris at this moment, trying to get some kind of commitment from them."

"I pray that he does," said Proudfoot. "His hand must have been greatly strengthened by our victory at Saratoga."

"Unquestionably. Franklin will know how to exploit that to the full. He's a wily old character. If we could count on French allies, the progress of this war will change dramatically."

"We would win even sooner," said Lafayette, stabbing the floor with his walking stick. "My country will not let you down, General."

Washington was philosophical. "Let's take things one day at the time. Even if it comes," he said, "French assistance may be months away, and I have more immediate concerns. I have to feed, clothe, and train a whole army. And I have to prevent epidemics breaking out here."

"The weather, General, is another enemy. It will be a killer."

"It's already started to mutilate our soldiers. Only yesterday, there were two men whose feet had to be amputated because they had turned black with frostbite. They start the New Year on crutches. However," Washington continued, trying to inject a note of optimism, "we'll come through the winter somehow, and we'll not be dormant."

"No," said Proudfoot, "I'll pepper the British with cartoons until they are sick of me, and there'll be lots of other ways to harass them."

"We must peck away at them all the time," said Lafayette.

"No opportunity will be missed to do that, Marquis," vowed Washington. "British skirmishers will be sent out tomorrow, and we will give them a warm reception."

"Do you know when and where they'll be?" asked Proudfoot.

"We have a good idea, Ezekiel."

"How on earth do you get such intelligence?"

"From the indefatigable Major Clark."

"But where does he get it from?"

Washington smiled. "We have an impeccable source," he said.

When, in his coded letter, he gave the Continental Army advance warning of the attack, Captain Jamie Skoyles did not realize that he would be asked to lead the skirmishers. His experience fitted him for the work, and his knowledge of the terrain around Valley Forge made him the ideal choice. It was an assignment that he could not refuse. The object of the exercise was simply to strike, draw blood, then pull out. No territory would be secured. All that Skoyles and his men needed to do was to remind the enemy that the British army would not let them rest. It would put the rebels back on the defensive.

After spending the night at Germantown, the skirmishers set out before dawn in crisp, dry weather. A relatively small, compact, handpicked group of men, they were expert marksman, able to cover ground quickly on foot and adapt to unexpected situations. Skoyles had taken the trouble to learn as many of their names as possible and to win their confidence. His escape from the Convention army had already given him some kudos in the eyes of the men, and the decisive leadership that he showed from the outset further enhanced his standing. As they marched northwest in the direction of Valley Forge, the skirmishers were happy to be under his command.

All that the coded letter had revealed was the approximate time and place of the attack. Skoyles had deliberately misled the rebels. Though he gave some idea of the size of the skirmishing party, he made no mention of a second, larger force that came up behind it in support. Once they had struck, the intention was for the skirmishers to flee in the hope of pulling rebel soldiers behind them toward a concealed line of reinforcements. The pursuing men could then be picked off at will.

The assault was on one of the forward posts, some miles southeast of Valley Forge. Its isolation made it a potential weak spot. When they got within reach of their target, Skoyles gave the order for his men to fan out and use the cover of the woods. As an officer, he carried a sword and a pistol. The skirmishers all had Brown Bess muskets primed for action. It was still morning when they caught a first glimpse of the enemy.

To survey the post, Skoyles used a telescope, running it along the redoubt and estimating how many men might be behind it. Several pickets were already visible, patrolling a line that stretched out for hundreds of yards. Still hidden by the trees, the skirmishing party was well within range of its target. Skoyles's pistol would be no use at that distance but the muskets could be deadly. Putting the telescope away, he waved a hand to the nearest man and the first shot was fired, dropping one of the pickets beside the redoubt. The rest of the skirmishers immediately fired a volley, downing four more men and wounding others.

Skoyles had expected some return fire from the rebels, followed by some reloading before they charged toward the woods. By that time, the skirmishers would already have reloaded their own weapons, and they had been instructed to unleash a second volley before breaking cover and running back toward their reinforcements. Events, however, did not unfold as planned. Stung by their reverse in the Brandywine Valley, the rebels were not going to be caught out a second time. A much larger body of men than anticipated surged out from behind the redoubt and sprinted toward the attackers. At the same time, a detachment of light horse emerged from behind a hill to the far left.

Even with their support line, the skirmishers were outnumbered. Though they had reloaded swiftly, they were not shooting at stationary targets now.

226

The men running toward them were spread out wide and zigzagged their way across the grass to make it more difficult for the redcoats. When the second volley came, the rebels dived flat on the ground, then leapt straight up again and continued their run. They had the advantage now. Their muskets were still loaded, and their cavalry was galloping up to join the fray.

Skoyles took a split second to make his decision.

"Pull back!" he yelled.

The skirmishers turned and fled. Sword in one hand and pistol in the other, Skoyles went with them. A first hail of bullets was discharged behind them. Most of them bounced off trees or went far too high, but one skirmisher was wounded in the shoulder. A second man tumbled to the ground with a musket ball in his thigh. He was picked up by two of the others and hauled along behind them. When they reached open ground, they had the best part of a hundred yards to go before they could find cover, and link up with their reinforcements.

It was here that the cavalry attacked. Skirting the wood, they came in from the flank and kicked their horses on. Some of the skirmishers stopped to reload and fire at the oncoming horde, unsaddling two men and bringing one horse crashing to the ground. All that they could do from that point was to use their muskets to parry the slashing swords of the light horse. Skoyles was in the thick of it, shooting one rider between the eyes, then ducking under a flashing blade before thrusting with his own sword at the rider.

The victim yelled in agony. As the man held his wounded stomach and pitched sideways onto the ground, Skoyles tossed away his pistol and grabbed the reins of the horse so that he could mount it. At least, he could fight on equal terms now, wielding his sword with manic fury and riding to the aid of any of his men he saw in jeopardy. The second line of skirmishers had emerged from cover, but they held their fire, afraid that they might hit their own men in the confusion. Having reloaded their weapons, the rebels who had pursued them through the woods waited for the chance to discharge another volley at the fleeing redcoats.

Skoyles kept on the move. All too aware that officers were singled out as targets, he swung his horse in a series of sharp turns as he hacked away with his sword. It was only when he saw that most of the skirmishers had reached cover again that he felt able to retreat himself. His reinforcements, meanwhile, shot for the first time and toppled seven men from their saddles. They then had to contend with sporadic gunfire from the rebels on foot. On a command from Skoyles, they fled back into the woodland.

There was no more pursuit. The light horse wheeled away and the soldiers from the redoubt melted back into the trees. After waiting until he was certain that it was safe, Skoyles instructed his men to collect the wounded and count the dead. Of the skirmishers in the front line, over half had been killed or injured. The rebels had trounced them. It was a salutary lesson for Skoyles. George Washington and his men could no longer be duped. The coded letter had been sent to entrap the rebels, but it was the redcoats who were caught in a snare. Skoyles felt that he had to take much of the blame for their failure.

As they trudged back to Germantown, he could sense that his men blamed him as well. Confident of success with only limited casualties in their own ranks, the skirmishers were instead limping away with their wounded. The dead had been left behind them. When he returned to Philadelphia, Skoyles would have uncomfortable letters to write to their families back in England. He had surrendered the stolen horse so that it could carry two of the wounded men, but they gave him no thanks. Their brooding silence was like an accusation.

When they entered Germantown, they were tired and dispirited. As they plodded down the main street, Skoyles happened to glance up at the window of a tavern. A face appeared and, for an instant, his eyes met those of someone whom he thought he knew. Then the man vanished from the window. Refusing to believe what he had just seen, Skoyles decided that his mind was playing tricks on him.

It could not possibly have been Ezekiel Proudfoot.

They had known each other only ten days, yet Lucy Tillman felt able to confide something very personal to her new friend. Elizabeth Rainham was delighted for her.

"That's wonderful news!" she said. "When is the baby due?"

"Not until June."

"You and your husband must be thrilled."

"We are," said Lucy, "but we haven't told anyone else yet. You're the first person to know, Elizabeth—apart from the doctor, that is."

"I feel honored."

"I know that I can count on you to keep our little secret."

"I won't tell a soul, Lucy."

"What about Captain Skoyles?"

"That's up to you."

"I'm sure that he can be trusted."

"Then I'll pass on the good news," said Elizabeth. "But, in your condition, you shouldn't be doing anything as energetic as showing me around the town."

"I must have some exercise. Besides, I enjoy being your guide."

"You certainly know your way around Philadelphia."

They were sitting together in the bedchamber that Elizabeth had been given, a small, snug room at the back of the house with just enough space for a bed, a cupboard, a little table, and two chairs. On the table was the novel that Elizabeth had bought from Pearsall Hughes. In the cupboard, with her clothing, were the other items that she had bought during their shopping expedition. Her accommodation could never hope to compete with the two large rooms she occupied back home in England, but it was a vast improvement on living under canvas during a long campaign, or being held in captivity with the Convention army. Elizabeth was now warm, safe, and among friends.

"Well," said Lucy, feeling that their relationship had moved on to a new level, "now that I've shared my secret with you, I think that it's your turn, don't you?"

"What do you mean?"

"I'm still waiting to hear why your betrothal came to an end."

"Oh, it's not a very interesting story," said Elizabeth uneasily.

"Everything about you is interesting. It took me all my time to find *one* man who proposed marriage to me—you've already found two."

"I'm not looking for a third, I assure you."

"Let's just talk about the first one, shall we?"

Elizabeth was reluctant. "If you wish."

"This is strictly between us. Nobody else will ever know." She sat forward on her chair. "Did you love him?"

"I thought so at the time, Lucy."

"And was he dashing?"

"Yes," said Elizabeth. "Harry was the epitome of a dashing soldier. When I first met him, I thought that he would make a perfect husband."

"Love at first sight, then."

"Far from it. That would have been quite unseemly. I was far too young even to think about such things. Major Featherstone was engaged to marry my sister, Cora, you see. He hardly noticed me. When he came to the house, he only had eyes for Cora. They seemed so *right* for each other. Wedding plans were quite advanced by the time she became sick."

"Oh dear! Don't tell me that your sister died."

"After a long, lingering illness," Elizabeth recalled sadly. "When she realized that she could never marry him, she wanted me to do so in her stead. 'Love him for me, Elizabeth,' she said. I found that very easy to do. Then, in time, when the shock of Cora's death began to wear off, Harry started to take an interest in me."

"Where did he propose?"

"On horseback."

"Horseback!" Lucy shrieked. "That's not very romantic."

"It felt like it at the time. We'd been out riding on Chartham Downs that afternoon. When we got back, he leaned over to take my hand and asked me to marry him."

"I made Roderick go down on one knee."

"Harry Featherstone was not that kind of man. Anyway," Elizabeth went on, eager to bring her tale to an end, "he sailed for America and I followed him in due course. It was only when I saw him here that I had an insight into his real character."

"Was he so beastly?"

"He did things that were quite unforgivable, Lucy."

"Such as?"

"For a start, he paid two men to assault Jamie."

"Why?"

"Harry had grown to hate him," said Elizabeth. "Luckily, Jamie was warned about the plan, and he was able to fight off his attackers. From that moment on, Harry was his implacable enemy. He did all he could to malign Jamie. During the battle at Bemis Heights, he even tried to . . ." Eyes filling with tears, she choked back the words. "What he did was nothing short of evil. And it did not end there, Lucy. After the battle, Harry got drunk and . . . tried to molest me."

Lucy was appalled. "I can see why you turned against him."

"It was a nightmare." She conjured up a brave smile. "So let's think about happier events, shall we? I can't tell you how pleased I am. But you must get plenty of rest," she insisted, wagging a finger. "I'll take it upon myself to see that you don't overtax yourself."

"I'm not an invalid, Elizabeth. I'm with child, that's all."

"You can't take any chances."

"Stop sounding like the doctor."

"He knows best, Lucy."

"Who is carrying this baby—him or me?" She gave a brittle laugh. "It's the main reason we're not announcing anything at this stage. The moment we do that, everyone will urge me to take to my bed."

"I can't imagine you ever doing that. You're far too lively."

"I'm young and strong and at the right age for childbirth."

"Do you want a boy or a girl?"

"We'll love the child, whatever it is. Though, in his heart, I think that Roderick would like it to be a boy—someone to carry on the Tillman tradition. Roderick comes from a long line of soldiers."

"Jamie's father was a country doctor in Cumberland."

"Hardly a typical military background," Lucy opined. "By the way, where is he today? The gallant Captain Skoyles usually calls on you every afternoon."

"He's involved in a raid somewhere," said Elizabeth. "Jamie wouldn't tell me the details until afterward. I'll see him later on."

"Then you'll be able to hear about his latest triumph."

General Howe was irritated when he was called away from the supper table, and annoyed when he learned the reason. The report that Skoyles delivered to the commander in chief was not an inspiring one.

Howe goggled. "You lost half your men?"

"Killed or wounded, sir."

"How many of them did you account for?"

"A rather smaller number," Skoyles admitted. "They had the whip hand over us, sir. We were lucky to get away with our second line almost intact. They'll not be so easily tricked from now on."

"Nor will I, Captain. My trust in you may have been misplaced."

"I did what any officer would have done in my place, sir. I cut my losses and withdrew. They harried us vigorously. With respect," said Skoyles, meeting his glare boldly, "I could not have foreseen the size of their response."

231

They were in Howe's office at headquarters. Hands behind his back, the general paced restlessly up and down, trying to absorb the bad tidings. The successful foraging expedition in the Brandywine Valley had been given an additional luster by the complete rout of the rebels. Some of the sheen had been taken off the event by the failure of Skoyles and his men. It did not help Howe's digestion.

"A setback like this will give them confidence," he said ruefully.

"It was only a very minor reverse, sir."

"They beat us, Captain. I take that very seriously."

"So do I," said Skoyles, "especially as my own life was at risk. I am sure that General Washington will be pleased to have got the better of us for once, but it will hardly prompt him to order a full attack. The time to do that would have been in December, when our forces were more scattered than they are now."

"That's true. He was a fool not to lead an assault on the city."

"It was concern for his men rather than folly, sir. His soldiers are, for the most part, young recruits with no real experience of warfare. They still bear the scars of the battles at Brandywine and Germantown. I think he was wise to avoid another major engagement."

"I'd question that wisdom," said Howe, adjusting his wig. "He's made so many mistakes, the wonder of it is that he's still in command."

"That's another problem that dogs him," Skoyles pointed out. "He's worshiped by his soldiers, yet sniped at by envious colleagues and their political allies. Major Clark told me all about the Conway Cabal. How can you command an army properly when so many people are waiting to stab you in the back?"

"Soldiering would be so much easier without politicians."

"They'd argue that politics would be so much easier if there were no soldiers telling them what to do."

Howe gave a hollow laugh. "Fair comment, Skoyles." He put a hand to his brow. "I'll be so glad to get away from all this. Some years ago, in a moment of honesty, I said that I'd never fight against Americans because I respected them too much. I meant it as well," he said. "But when the opportunity came, I was too much of a soldier to follow my inclinations. And I could not resist the lure of glory—not that there's been enough of that, alas."

"We'll be sorry to see you leave, General."

"I'll be here till the spring at least. Knowing the speed at which the colonial secretary moves, I do not expect a successor to be appointed before April, if then. I do not envy him his task."

"The Continental Army will have had time to recover."

"Meanwhile, their much-vaunted commander will be laughing at us over today's little farce."

"That's a very unfair description, sir," Skoyles returned.

"Is it?"

"Our men fought bravely and I'd like you to understand that."

"I do, Captain Skoyles. But, as we both know, bravery is not always enough, is it? Ah, well," he said with a sigh, "we must let General Washington have his brief moment of triumph. There'll be precious few of those for him this winter."

Pearsall Hughes read the newspaper with his customary attention to detail, making sure that the printer had allowed no errors to creep into the bookseller's polished sentences. When he had studied all four pages of *The Pennsylvania Patriot,* he allowed himself to dwell on the cartoon that adorned the front page. He chortled with pleasure.

"This is magnificent," he said. "If only I'd been there!"

"What you see is what actually happened, Mr. Hughes."

"General Howe and his concubine on the hoof."

"You put the whole audience to flight," said Ezekiel Proudfoot.

They were in his room at Neale's Tavern in Germantown. Hughes had made the journey from Philadelphia to inspect the latest issue of the *Patriot,* and to take some copies back with him to the city. It was the first time they had met since Proudfoot's arrest on Christmas Day, and they were delighted to see each other again. The silversmith was interested to hear the latest news from Philadelphia.

"Did anyone ever make inquiries about me at the bookshop?"

"Yes," said Hughes. "A young lieutenant asked if I knew a Reece Allen, and I told him that you were a customer of mine. Since you had only been into the shop twice, I insisted, our acquaintance was, of necessity, only a fleeting one."

"Did he accept that?"

"I think so. I've not seen him since."

233

Proudfoot bit his lip. "I still feel so guilty about Adam Quenby," he said, running a hand through his hair. "We were both caught in that cellar. Yet, while I was released, he was sent to the gallows."

"Yes," said Hughes sorrowfully, "Adam was a great loss. He was a master of his trade, and nobody believed more passionately in freedom than he did. On the other hand," he continued pragmatically, "his death was not without its benefits. It brought us in someone to take over the printing from Adam."

"Raphael Dyer."

"He was apprenticed to Adam Quenby, and when he wanted to set up in business on his own, it was Adam who lent him the money to do so. Raphael feels indebted," Hughes went on. "When he heard what had happened to his old employer, he got in touch with me."

"He doesn't have the same burning commitment."

"No matter, as long as he's prepared to help us. Raphael Dyer has done what many of us have been compelled to do—pretend to be a Tory in order to stay in our homes. But he's no loyalist at heart."

"Neither is his assistant," said Proudfoot. "I get on well with both of them. And the fact that they still carry on their normal business is to our advantage. It's a perfect disguise. All that Mr. Quenby did in that cellar was to print the *Patriot.*"

"That was the raison d'être of his press."

"It's not the case with Raphael Dyer. In addition to our newspaper, he prints dozens of other things. Nobody is going to track him down by finding out which mill supplies his paper. We have that consolation. As for this place," added Proudfoot contentedly, "it's every bit as welcoming as the King George Tavern, though I must confess that I do miss the landlord."

"Pontius Pilate sends his regards."

Encrusted by a light fall of snow, Germantown was a remote country retreat, a place of clean, clear air that made it an ideal refuge for people from Philadelphia, whether fleeing from an outbreak of yellow fever or escaping from the city's oppressive summer heat. Houses tended to be large, and its population tended to be wealthy. It was a pretty town, in a delightful rural setting, with none of the bustle or cosmopolitan feel of Philadelphia. Although a large number of redcoats were stationed there, Proudfoot did not feel in any danger.

"How is Mrs. Hughes?" he asked.

"Miranda is well. You must come and see us some time."

"When the weather improves."

"That may not be for some time yet," said Hughes, glancing through the window as more snowflakes began to fall. "You may find yourself cut off for weeks out here."

"As long as I'm able to work," said Proudfoot.

"Nothing would stop you doing that. You and Adam Quenby were well matched—you both thrived on hard work."

"His family must have been distraught when they heard what happened. He had a wife and children, didn't he?"

"Yes, they left when the British army arrived on their doorstep. I wrote to his wife with the details, and I told her what a Trojan her husband had been in the fight for liberty." He exhaled through his teeth. "I expect no reply from her."

"It's one of the most heartbreaking things about this war."

"What is?"

"Letters like that."

"I've had to write quite a few," said Hughes. "Adam was only one of a number we've lost since the British took over the city. And, of course, it must be even worse for our commanders."

"There's no doubting that," said Proudfoot. "General Washington told me how much he hated writing letters after a battle, informing people that their fathers, husbands, or sons had died. He could not bear to tell them the truth—that, in some cases, the dead bodies had had to be abandoned where they lay."

"A letter signed by him might still be something to cherish."

"My fear is that he'll be writing a large number of them this winter. Valley Forge is no place to be when the snow really falls. Some of those poor devils are going to freeze to death."

The eleven soldiers who shared the log cabin with him looked upon Jedediah Elliott as a disagreeable grandfather. He was the oldest man in the ranks and easily the most ornery. Yet it was Elliott who had made sure that their dwelling was built faster than any other in the regiment, thus winning a monetary prize that was divided equally between them. Though they resented his unending complaints, and his constant boasts about his part in the French

235

and Indian War, some of his companions turned to him with gratitude. They were illiterate.

"What else do ye want to say?" asked Elliott.

Novus Kane scratched his head. "I don't know."

"Well, make up your mind, lad. I need my sleep."

"What have I said so far, Jed?"

"How cold the weather is," replied Elliott, reading by the light of the candle. "How poor the food, how hard the beds, how tired ye are, and how ye share this hut with the worst, smelliest, and most cowardly band of rascals in the Continental Army."

"I didn't tell you to write that," said Kane over the loud protests from the other men. "Did I mention how awful that beef soup was today?"

"Your parents don't want to hear about beef soup."

"What *do* they want to hear?"

"That their son is doing his duty—like me—without whining."

"You never *stop* whining, Jed," another man called out to a chorus of agreement. "First thing I hear when I wake up of a morning is that griping voice of yours. It's also the last thing I hear before I fall asleep."

"Be quiet, Euclid," retorted the old man, looking over the top of his spectacles. "I'm trying to write this blessed letter for Novus, and it needs all my attention."

It was late evening and most of the men had already retired to their bunks in the smoky interior of the cabin. A few flames still flickered in the little fire, but they gave off scant warmth. Everyone who was still up had a blanket wrapped around his shoulders. Novus Kane was not the only farm boy there. Four others had been recruited. Elliott was a carpenter, and there was also a stonemason, a rope maker, a baker, a brewer, and a leather worker. Euclid Rawson was a schoolmaster, but, unlike Elliott, he was not so willing to write letters for his comrades. Three of them played cards by the light of a guttering candle. Kane was the only correspondent there. Wanting to tell his parents good news, he could think of none.

"I know," he said, snapping his fingers. "Write about that foraging party we ambushed. Tell them that I knocked a redcoat from the saddle."

"That was my shot, not yours," Elliott asserted.

"It was *mine,* Jed."

"Ye couldn't hit a barn door from five yards."

236

"You couldn't even *see* one from that distance."

"There's nothing wrong with my eyes."

"Then why are you wearing spectacles?"

"I killed that rider and there's an end to it."

"No!" Kane yelled. The old man held up the piece of paper as if about to tear it apart. Kane gave in. "Say nothing about it," he conceded. "Maybe it *was* your bullet that hit him."

"Ye might tell your parents what a help I've been to you."

"For all I know, you've already put that in the letter. It's so maddening not being able to read or write." He turned to the card players. "Why don't you teach me, Euclid?"

"I'm a soldier now," said Rawson, "not a schoolmaster."

"Pretty soon, ye'll be neither," said Elliott, chewing on the stem of his pipe. "Ye'll be like the rest of us, Euclid—a block of ice."

"You think this is *cold?*"

"My pizzle is frozen solid."

"I was born and bred not twenty miles from here," said Rawson, "and, in these parts, we'd call this weather mild."

"Then I'd hate to see it when the temperature really falls."

"Finish my letter, Jed," Kane urged.

"I have finished. Sign it."

"I don't know how."

"Then make your mark," said Elliott. "Your parents will know that you're still alive then." He offered the pen to Kane who put a cross at the bottom of the paper. "At least, ye were when this was sent. By the time the letter reaches them, ye might have died of starvation."

"Or poisoning," said Kane sourly. "I'm not eating any of that beef soup again. It tasted like horse piss."

"How do you know?" asked Rawson.

Elliott cackled. "That's all they drink on the farm."

"No wonder Novus stinks of it."

"I don't stink of anything!" cried Kane.

"Horse piss and cow shit. I can smell you from here."

"Shut your mouth, Euclid!"

"They ought to make you sleep in a stable."

Kane had been sitting beside Elliott on the latter's bunk. When he tried to

237

get up in protest, he banged his head on the bunk above him and let out a yelp of pain. Everyone still awake laughed at him. Rubbing his head with both hands, Kane decided that he had had enough argument for one night. He took the letter from Elliott and thrust it into his pocket before clambering up to the top bunk. After shivering under his blanket for a long time, he finally drifted off to sleep—with Jamie Skoyles's musket still clasped to his chest.

Winter was playing games with them. One day, it would send driving snow and biting cold; the next day, bright sunshine would set a thaw in motion, only for it to be countermanded a few days later. Sooner or later, the games would stop and the real winter would arrive. Meanwhile, Jamie Skoyles tried to take advantage of the milder spells. When the snow was melting away yet again, he and Elizabeth Rainham went riding out of the city. Anticipating no trouble, he nevertheless took his sword and a newly acquired pistol with him.

Elizabeth was an accomplished horsewoman and she was glad of the chance to go riding, even if the fields were still streaked with white, and the roads soggy. They had gone a few miles northwest of Philadelphia before they stopped in the shade of a tree. Skoyles leaned across to kiss her on the cheek.

"Alone at last," he said.

"We have so few opportunities. Lucy Tillman is a lovely woman, and I enjoy her company enormously, but she does hang on to me."

"That's understandable. She recognizes a true friend."

"And what do *you* recognize?" asked Elizabeth teasingly.

"Someone who's a lot more than that."

Skoyles reached out to squeeze her hand. She returned his smile, then looked at the tranquil scene ahead of them. Undulating fields stretched out toward an expanse of woodland. Through the low hills to the left, a stream was starting to flow again now that the ice had melted. In the sunshine, it was an appealing panorama.

"Is this the sort of place that you have in mind, Jamie?"

"For what?"

"Settling down."

"Something like this," he decided, surveying the scene, "though I can't say

238

that Pennsylvania was ever a possibility. If anywhere, I'm drawn to Massachussetts."

"But that's the heart of rebel resistance."

"At the moment, Elizabeth. I'm looking beyond the war."

"Do you think we'd be made welcome there?"

"Americans are very friendly if you don't try to push them around. In any case, I won't be wearing this uniform then. I'll be plain Jamie Skoyles, gentleman farmer."

"I'll believe it when I see it."

"What do you mean?"

"Fighting is in your blood," she said without any trace of criticism. "I have the feeling that you'll always be a soldier."

"Only until this war is over, Elizabeth."

He was about to explain why when his attention was caught by some figures in the middle distance. Two horsemen had come out of the woods to move slowly northwest, but it was not the riders that Skoyles had noticed. It was the two forlorn figures who were being hauled along by ropes behind them.

"Jack Bedford!" he exclaimed.

"Who?"

"Stay here, Elizabeth. I have a score to settle."

Kicking his horse into a canter, he headed for the quartet. With their human cargo in tow, the riders could hardly outrun him, and they had, in any case, no reason to flee from a single redcoat. If one of the horsemen was indeed Jack Bedford, then Skoyles expected him to brazen it out. The bounty hunter would have a plausible excuse why two men were being tugged along like stray animals.

Seeing him approach, the riders stopped and waited. One of them waved to the two captives, as if warning them to hold their peace. When he got closer, Skoyles saw that his guess had been correct. Jack and Ira Bedford were in business again. They had caught two rebel deserters and were taking them back to their death in Valley Forge. Skoyles brought his horse to a halt some ten yards from them.

"What can we do for you?" asked Bedford with a lazy smile.

"Tell me where you're going, for a start."

"That's *our* business," said Ira truculently.

"Don't be so unfriendly," his brother chided him. "The captain asked a question so he's entitled to an answer." He indicated the men, one of whom was black. "These were slaves on our plantation. They escaped three days ago, and we came after them."

Skoyles looked at the captives. "Is that true?

"Go on," said Bedford, watching them carefully. "Tell him. You worked for us, didn't you?" The men nodded. "There you are, Captain."

"Can we go now?" said Ira. "It's a long ride."

"Yes," said Skoyles pointedly. "All the way to Valley Forge."

"What are you talking about?"

"Jack and Ira Bedford, following the scent of blood money. The only people you ever chase are deserters from the Continental Army. These men were on the run from Valley Forge, and you're taking them back to sell their skins."

"Who the devil are you?" Ira demanded angrily.

"Take a closer look," his brother advised, recognizing Skoyles at last. "He's that man whose horse I shot, and who gave us so much trouble. He slipped through our fingers."

"Well, he won't do it again!"

He reached for his musket, but Skoyles already had his pistol trained on him. When Jack Bedford lifted his weapon, Skoyles turned the barrel of the pistol on him.

"Drop it!" he ordered.

"You can't shoot both of us."

"Then I'll start with you, Jack, before I slice your brother to pieces with my sword. Now, drop those muskets—both of you!"

The sharpness of his command gained him instant obedience. Both dropped their weapons. Still keeping them covered with a pistol, Skoyles made them dismount and walk several yards away from the muskets. He dismounted and drew his sword, using it to motion the two prisoners forward. They were miserable specimens, barefoot, clothed in rags, and bearing the clear signs of a recent beating.

"Are you deserters from Valley Forge?" asked Skoyles

"Yes, sir," gabbled one of them.

"Where were you going?"

"To Philadelphia, sir. We want to give ourselves up."

"Then at least you can ride there."

With two slashes of his sword, he cut the ropes that were tied to the pommels of the two saddles. Their hands were still bound, but they were no longer at the mercy of the bounty hunters. Skoyles ordered them to sit down while he dealt with the two brothers. Jack Bedford had never taken his eyes off him, biding his time until he could strike back. His brother was more impatient. Slipping a hand behind his back, he pulled a knife from its sheaf and held it in readiness.

"It's not these men who should be hanged," said Skoyles, looking from one to the other with utter contempt. "It's you two bloodsuckers, living off the proceeds of war. You're worse than vermin."

Ira Bedford had heard enough. Hand on the blade of his knife, he suddenly brought it from behind his back and hurled it at Skoyles. While it was still spinning through the air, Skoyles fired his pistol instinctively, and the bullet hit Ira between the eyes, sending him flat on his back. At the very same moment, the point of the knife burrowed into Skoyles's right shoulder with such force that he was knocked sideways, dropping the pistol from his grasp.

Jack Bedford came to life. Incensed at the death of his brother, and outraged that anyone should take his captives away from him, he charged at Skoyles with a bloodcurdling yell. There was a knife in his hand and he was going to plunge it deep into the heart of the wounded man. Skoyles heard him coming. Dizzy with pain, and feeling his energy ooze away, he summoned up the last of his strength and turned to face his attacker. As the enraged man lunged toward him, Skoyles went down on one knee and thrust out the sword with his left hand, so that the Bedford impaled himself on its point.

There was a howl of disbelief, followed by a stream of abuse that soon faded into a pathetic whimper. Eyes filled with hatred, Jack Bedford fell to the ground and lay motionless. Skoyles barely had enough energy to pull out his sword. His eyes were misting over, his legs were unsteady, and there was a searing pain in his right shoulder. Blood was already gushing out of the wound. Dropping his sword, he used his left hand to pull out the knife that was still embedded in his flesh. The blade felt red hot as it came out. Skoyles was weakening by the second. The last thing he remembered was the sight of two open-mouthed men from the Continental Army, watching him in sheer horror.

Then he dropped to the ground.

CHAPTER THIRTEEN

Time passed in a confusing blur. Captain Jamie Skoyles came in and out of consciousness to hear voices, see faces, and feel hands touching him. There was such a stab of pain in his shoulder at one point that he felt the knife was being buried in it all over again, and he took refuge once more in oblivion. When he finally emerged from it, he looked up into the tearful eyes of Elizabeth Rainham. One hand resting firmly on his wounded shoulder, she was kneeling anxiously beside him. Skoyles made a supreme effort to stay awake, fighting hard when his eyelids began to flicker again. As he tried to reach up to Elizabeth, his right shoulder seemed to be on fire.

"Lie still, Jamie," she advised softly.

"Where am I?"

"Don't move. I've sent for help."

Skoyles moved his head slightly to look around. He realized that he was on his back with her cloak over him. Out of the corner of his eye, he could see another body on the ground and his memory started to return. He had been confronting Jack and Ira Bedford when the younger brother had hurled a knife at him. There had been two witnesses. One of them, a black man in his thirties with a gash over one eye and a swollen lip, came into view behind Elizabeth.

"Who are you?" Skoyles asked.

"I'm Cicero, sir," replied the other, deferentially.

"You're one of the deserters."

"Yes, sir. You saved our lives."

"By the time I got here," said Elizabeth, "they'd used a knife to cut themselves free, but neither of them tried to escape, even though there were horses here. They say that you were a hero."

"I don't *feel* like a hero," admitted Skoyles.

"We needed help, so I asked the other man to ride to that camp we passed on our way here. It can't be more than a mile away and they must have surgeons there. Meanwhile," she explained, applying a little more pressure to his shoulder, "I tore my petticoat so that I could use it to stem the bleeding. It's a deep wound."

He forced a smile. "You don't need to tell me that."

"How do you feel now, Jamie?"

"Better," he said. "Much better."

"Cicero told me what happened. You took on both of those men."

"They were parasites."

"When they caught Cicero and his friend, they tied them up and beat them. They were very brutal."

"It's true, sir," said Cicero, edging forward. "Nathan and me, we'd been on the run from Valley Forge since dawn. When we got this far, we thought we were safe—then those men caught us."

"Is that your friend's name?" said Skoyles. "Nathan?"

"Nathan Petersfield, sir."

"You're not wearing uniforms. What regiment were you in?"

"The 10th Massachussetts."

"You're a long way from home, Cicero."

"I know that, sir," said the other. "If I'd been born this far south, I'd have been a slave. It's a different world here."

"Why did you leave Valley Forge?"

"Bad food. Terrible cold."

Skoyles suspected that there were other reasons for his departure. A black soldier would not have been popular among regiments from Virginia or the Carolinas, colonies where slavery was common and where Negroes were treated as a lower order of creation. There could well have been taunts, sneers, and worse to face on a daily basis.

"Is it true what they told us, sir?" asked Cicero, eyes bulging.

"That depends on what it is," said Skoyles.

"They told us that if we were captured by the British, we'd be sent to work on the sugar plantations in the West Indies. Is that what will happen to *me*?" said the other, shaking with fear.

"No, Cicero. That won't happen."

"You promise?"

"I do."

"Thank you, sir."

"They were telling you lies."

Skoyles heard the approach of distant hooves but he did not dare to sit up and look. It was Cicero who soon identified one of the riders.

"It's Nathan," he said. "I knew he'd come back."

"The two of you could easily have taken the horses and gone," said Skoyles. "Yet you stayed to help. I can't thank you enough. I'll make sure that goes into my report, Cicero."

"Hold this, Jamie," said Elizabeth.

She put his left hand on the sodden piece of material she had ripped from her petticoat. While he pressed it against the wound, she went off to welcome the newcomers. Skoyles heard the sound of two horses being reined to a halt, followed by an exclamation of surprise from Elizabeth. He had no idea why she had called out like that until a familiar figure bent over him.

"I'm getting tired of patching you up, Jamie Skoyles," said the man, smiling mischievously. "What have you been up to *this* time?"

It was Sergeant Tom Caffrey.

The fight came out of nowhere. One of the men had been chopping timber for firewood, while the other was gathering up the logs and putting them in bundles. They were chatting amiably enough until the ax bit into the wood once more and sent a chip flying into the other man's face. Striking him just below the eye, it produced a cry of anguish.

"What did you do *that* for?" he yelled.

"It was an accident," said the other.

"You could have blinded me."

"Then you shouldn't have been standing so close."

"Are you saying that it was *my* fault?"

"Well, it certainly wasn't mine."

The argument quickly intensified and tempers grew hotter. Words were soon replaced with blows. By the time George Washington came on the scene, the two men were trading punches as if they were mortal enemies. Their commander moved in swiftly, grabbing them by their collars and pulling them apart. He shook them hard.

"What's the matter with you?" he demanded. "We have a British army threatening us and all you can do is to fight each other. What kind of an example is that to set?"

The two men were shamefaced. One had blood trickling from his nose, the other had lost a couple of teeth in the brawl. To be reprimanded by a corporal would have been bad enough. To be caught fighting by Washington himself was humiliating. Still holding them tight, he towered over the pair, looking from one to the other with disgust.

"Have you nothing better to do than quarrel?" he said.

"Yes, sir," replied one of the men.

"Then get on with it."

"Yes, sir."

"If I catch either of you fighting again," cautioned Washington, letting them go, "I'll have the pair of you flogged. Do you understand?"

"Yes, sir."

"Then start to behave as comrades in arms. The day will come when you'll need to fight shoulder to shoulder against a real enemy. Save all your anger until then."

Completely abashed, the soldiers returned to their work. After watching them for a few minutes, Washington walked back to the man who was accompanying him on his tour of the Valley Forge encampment. Major John Clark was not surprised at what they had seen.

"The men are all on edge, General," he said. "Poor food, hard beds, and bitter weather have made them touchy. There'll be more brawls like this, I'm afraid."

"Not if we stamp on them hard, Major."

"You can't knock all their heads together."

"Good discipline is the first requisite of any army."

"But it needs strong officers to enforce it, sir, and we do not have a surplus of those. Some of our best men have resigned their commissions. As the weeks go by, more are likely to follow suit. When they are short of officers, the men become unruly."

"We must take steps to ensure that that doesn't happen."

"How?"

"By spending much more time drilling them," said Washington. "By instilling some pride into these men. While we have this long break from any major engagement, we must try to turn them into real soldiers."

"It will not be easy, sir. Some of our officers lack any experience of training men for battle. They are in need of instruction themselves."

"Then they may well get it."

"From where?"

"Europe. A certain Baron von Steuben is on his way here."

Clark was astonished. "A German? They usually fight against us."

"Not in this case," Washington told him. "The baron is a man of outstanding talents, it seems. He holds an important position at the court of the king of Prussia, and he comes to us with the highest recommendation."

"From whom?"

"Benjamin Franklin. According to him, we should make use of the baron's rare abilities. The fellow is an expert on military discipline."

"Franklin's opinion must always be respected," said Clark, "but I'm not sure how well our men will respond to the notion of taking orders from a Prussian."

"They took them happily enough from a Dutchman when Philip Schuyler was commander of the Northern Department, and nobody has refused to serve under the Marquis de Lafayette."

"He's an exceptional soldier."

"So is Baron von Steuben, if reports are to be believed. He has Silas Deane's approval as well."

"That news is not so comforting."

Washington smiled. "Have no fear, Major," he said. "I know that Deane would like to replace me as commander in chief, but even he would not choose a Prussian nobleman as my substitute. If, of course, that's what this fellow is. Franklin is the sort of character who would not hold back from inventing a title for someone if he thought it would make him more appealing to us. What he would not do is to embroider someone's military credentials. The baron could be just the person we need," he said hopefully. "I look forward to meeting him."

"And when will that be, sir?"

"Not until well into next month."

They strolled on through the swirling wind and passed a group of men who were at last finishing the roof on their cabin. When they recognized General Washington, the soldiers immediately put more effort into their work and only eased off once he had gone. Their commander believed in maintaining a visible presence at the camp. As well as keeping in daily touch with his field officers, he knew the importance of being seen by the rank and file. Washington was keen to destroy the myth that he was aloof and lordly. After strolling on for a while, he and Major Clark paused to inspect the artillery that lay behind the inner defenses on the western side of Valley Forge.

"General Knox has done a good job here," Clark observed.

"He's grown into an excellent artillery commander. Not that he needs to do any more growing, of course," said Washington, referring to Knox's excessive weight, "but you take my point."

"War brings out the best in some men."

"Then you are certainly one of them, Major. Since you took charge of our intelligence gathering, there's been a revolution. You've not only increased the number of our spies, you've found agents ready to help us because they actually share our aims, and not because they expect payment."

"There'll always be those we have to sweeten with a fee, sir."

"I keep an account of everything we spend on our spies. Some of it, alas, is a waste of money. But, in the main, we get what we pay for." He walked on and Clark kept pace with him. "Some of the best information came to us free, courtesy of Captain Skoyles."

"I agree."

"Has he stilled all your doubts yet?"

"Not entirely. I do wonder what his true motives are."

"I think that he has genuine sympathy for our cause. That warning he gave us about the skirmish party was timely. It enabled us to get the upper hand for once. That was proof enough for me of his readiness to aid us," said Washington. "What British officer would deliberately send some of his fellows to certain death?"

"I accept that point."

"Then why don't you have more faith in Skoyles?"

"I don't know," Clark confessed. "Perhaps I need even more proof."

"I'm sure that you'll get it, Major."

"Not for a while, sir."

"Why not?"

247

"Captain Skoyles has been wounded."

"Badly?"

"Enough to inconvenience him. When I saw him in Philadelphia yesterday, he had his arm in a sling."

"Did you speak to him?" asked Washington.

"No, General," Clark replied. "He did not even know that I was there. He was walking down the street with a pretty young woman. It was hardly the best moment for me to reveal who I was."

"I'd be interested to know how he came by his injury."

Clark nodded. "I'll find out for you, sir."

When he saw the cartoon on the front page of the newspaper, Tom Caffrey put back his head to let out a long, lusty, full-throated laugh.

"Where did you get this, Jamie?"

"It was pushed under my door," said Skoyles.

"Well, you can bank on one thing. It wasn't General Howe who put it there. If he sees this, he'll have a heart attack. Was there really such a scramble to get out of that theater?"

"So I'm told, Tom."

"This must be Mrs. Loring," said Caffrey, pointing at the buxom figure in the cartoon. "She won't forget *that* play in a long while. I wonder what she said to the general in bed afterward." He put the copy of *The Pennsylvania Patriot* on the table. "I know that I shouldn't enjoy a laugh at the expense of the British army, but this is so well drawn."

"It's by Ezekiel Proudfoot."

"That friend of yours?"

"Yes, Tom," said Skoyles. "Until Christmas, this newspaper was printed right here under our noses. Ezekiel must have been in the city as well. Then the press was discovered and the printer was hanged."

"What about Proudfoot?"

"They're still looking for him."

Skoyles did not tell him that he believed his friend had been released by mistake after he was arrested with the printer. Nor did he recall the instant in Germantown when he thought he saw Proudfoot's face at the window of a tavern. Caffrey and he were close, but there were some things that Skoyles

248

would not confide to him. It troubled his conscience that he somehow felt a deeper loyalty to one of the enemy. The latest cartoon in the *Patriot* established one fact beyond question. Ezekiel Proudfoot was back.

They were in Skoyles's lodging, a large, low-ceilinged room with a distinct odor of damp. He was propped up on the bed with his right arm in a sling. Tom Caffrey was standing near the window. Rain was pelting on the glass as if trying to force a way in. Caffrey remembered the main purpose of his visit to the city.

"How does your shoulder feel now, Jamie?"

"Still very tender."

"That knife must have been thrown hard. If it had hit a bone, it would have shattered it. You have a charmed life. Once again, you were very lucky."

"I was lucky that you were only a mile away. Why didn't you tell me that you'd come to join us in Philadelphia?"

"Because I had no idea that you were here."

"We thought we'd seen the last of you in Massachussetts."

"You won't get rid of us as easily as that."

"What made you decide to take the long route to New York City?"

"Common sense, Jamie. That little voyage from Cambridge nearly put the finish on us. There was no way that Polly and I would trust our lives to the sea again. That's why we looped around and came down the Hudson Valley instead. It took much longer," said Caffrey, "but we felt it was safer as well. When we finally got to New York City, and when they realized that I was a surgeon, they sent me on here to look after some of the wounded from the battles in the autumn."

"I was delighted to see you again, Tom, I know that."

"I should think you were," said Caffrey. "By the time I got there, you'd lost a lot of blood. What happened to those two deserters?"

"After what they did, they'll be treated leniently. Both men bore witness to what happened with those loathsome bounty hunters."

"You had to kill them in self-defense."

"The world is well rid of them, Tom. Cicero and his friend were also able to confirm how bad conditions really are in Valley Forge. I know that you're under canvas in that camp," he went on, "but you're in a much more sheltered position. Valley Forge is exposed to the elements."

"Then why did Washington choose it?"

"It's hard to attack, and he had to keep his army together somewhere. If he'd dispersed them for the winter, he'd never have got some of them back."

"As it is, a lot of his men are deserting like those two you came across." Caffrey's eye fell on a book that lay on the bed beside Skoyles. "What's that, Jamie?"

"A novel I bought yesterday."

"What! Did you defy my orders and go out?"

"I wanted some fresh air."

"You need a complete rest," Caffrey insisted. "That wound will take time to heal. Don't put any pressure on it."

"It was only a short walk," said Skoyles. "Elizabeth wanted me to see this bookshop she's discovered. Since she knew that I'd have to put my feet up for a while, she thought I might like something to read."

"What did you choose?"

"The bookseller chose it for me, Tom."

"Let me see," said Caffrey, picking it up to open it. "*The History of Tom Jones, a Foundling.* Henry Fielding—I've never heard of him."

"Then you must talk to Pearsall Hughes."

"Who?"

"The bookseller. He seemed to know everything that Henry Fielding had ever written. He thought I'd find it very diverting," said Skoyles, "but he did warn me that it was not suitable for ladies."

"What did Elizabeth think of that?"

"She didn't hear him. Elizabeth was too busy talking to his wife. Mrs. Hughes knows a lot about books as well." Skoyles sighed. "I can't say that I'm a reading man myself, but I'll need something to keep me occupied."

"Not suitable for ladies, eh? That sounds promising." He put the book aside. "Now let me get on with what I came here to do and change that dressing of yours."

"How long will I have to wear this sling?"

"Until I tell you to stop."

"Is there any chance I can take it off by Saturday?"

"Why do you ask that?"

"Elizabeth and I are going to watch a play," said Skoyles, "and I'd feel rather conspicuous like this. What do you say, Tom?"

Caffrey grinned. "All right," he agreed. "Go without it."

"Thank you."

"But if there's another mad dash out of the theater, put it back on again. I don't want my lovely sutures to be ripped out."

A break in the bad weather encouraged Ezekiel Proudfoot to come into Philadelphia again. Mindful of his earlier arrest, he took the precaution of shaving off his beard to change his appearance. When he stepped into the bookshop, Miranda Hughes did not at first recognize him.

"Is that really you, Mr. Allen?" she said.

"Yes, Mrs. Hughes."

"It's good to see you again."

"Your husband said that I should call in sometime."

"Well, you've come at the ideal moment."

"Have I?" said Proudfoot. "Why is that?"

"Because we have a visitor you know," she explained. "Go through and meet him. I have to look after the shop."

"We'll talk later."

Proudfoot pushed the hinged bookcase at the rear of the shop and, in response to an invitation from Pearsall Hughes, went through it into the parlor. Seated opposite the bookseller was Major John Clark. Both men got up to shake the newcomer's hand in turn.

"A timely arrival, Mr. Allen," said Clark.

"Your honor was but lately in our thoughts," added Hughes. "That's a quotation from Shakespeare, by the way. I was just telling the major what an impact your latest cartoon has made. Our supporters are still laughing, and General Howe is probably tearing his hair out."

"You sent him a copy of the *Patriot*?"

"Yes, with a separate one for Mrs. Loring. I thought that they both deserved a souvenir of a memorable evening."

Proudfoot was waved to a chair and the others resumed their seats. After an exchange of pleasantries, Clark told them about the hardship soldiers faced at Valley Forge and suggested to Proudfoot that he might reflect it in one of his cartoons.

"A group of our men," he explained, "knee deep in snow, yet nobly enduring the foul weather as they build their log cabin. They need something to hearten them, Mr. Allen."

"I understand, Major," said Proudfoot.

"Show them that they are not forgotten. Portray them as the heroes they are. We cannot simply laugh at the British all the time. Use your skills to inspire our men."

"I'll try."

"And so will I," decided Hughes, slapping his thigh. "I'll write an article about their dedication to duty that will invigorate everyone who reads it—or has it read to him. Mr. Allen is our master artist, but I'm a true magician with words."

"You've shown that many times," said Clark.

The major looked tired. There were dark patches beneath his eyes, and his face was drawn. Proudfoot was worried about the man's health. He knew that Clark was in constant movement between Valley Forge and Philadelphia, no matter how inclement the weather. Only a blizzard would stop him coming to the city to meet with his wide circle of agents. Aware of Proudfoot's shrewd gaze, Clark forced a smile.

"How are you enjoying life in Germantown?" he said.

"Not as much as my time with Pontius Pilate," replied Proudfoot. "The landlord at my tavern is a true loyalist. I dare not speak a word out of place for fear of offending him."

"At least, we have a printer for the newspaper again."

"Yes, Raphael Dyer is doing a fine job for us."

Hughes held up a finger. "When we needed a miracle," he said, "it came. Well, Mr. Allen, you're a prime example of that yourself. At a time when we required it most, you brought a new dimension to the *Patriot*."

"My humble talents are at your disposal."

"They are far from humble, sir."

"I agree," said Clark. "Pictures speak louder than words, and your cartoons—I mean no disrespect to you, Mr. Hughes—are more eloquent than any article."

"I endorse that sentiment wholeheartedly," said Hughes candidly. "Each of us contributes in his own way."

"Or *her* own way," added Clark. "Women must not be overlooked."

"No, they do splendid work—Miranda among them. The British may occupy our city, but they cannot douse the flame of liberty that burns inside so many of us."

"Without the help of civilians, we would be powerless."

"I heard about the way we routed those redcoat skirmishers," said Proudfoot. "That success was only made possible by you, Major. You obviously had good intelligence."

"That's what I always seek to provide," said Clark.

"General Washington told me that you have an impeccable source."

"He's certainly in the right place to assist us."

"Who is the man?"

"A British officer who shall remain nameless," said Clark. "Like you, he came to us at a critical moment. I expect to hear from him again very soon."

Captain Jamie Skoyles had shed his sling in order to wear his dress uniform without any encumbrance. His shoulder still ached and smarted, but he was used to coping with pain. As he and Elizabeth Rainham went to the theater that evening, he made sure that she was on his left arm. They attended the play with Roderick and Lucy Tillman, of whom Elizabeth had become increasingly fond. Captain Tillman was tall and slender with a handsome face set off by a chevron of a mustache. Though they held the same rank, he was seven years younger than Skoyles. Alert, personable, and devoted to his wife, Tillman was pleasant company, and Skoyles got on well with him.

Arriving at the theater, they noticed the many guards on duty outside. General Howe was clearly ensuring that there would be no interruption to the performance this time. No profit was made from the staging of plays. The receipts were always donated to charity. On this occasion, those who would benefit were the widows, or common-law wives, of redcoats killed in recent engagements with the enemy. The British army did not forget its casualties.

The four of them had seats near the middle of the auditorium and, like everyone else, they stood up when General Howe entered with Betsey Loring. It was the first time that Elizabeth had seen the notorious mistress, and she was torn between curiosity and disapproval. Lucy watched the pair of them take their seats.

"I think it's indecent," she said. "General Howe is married."

"So is Mrs. Loring," Elizabeth reminded her.

"What sort of husband lets his wife sleep with another man?"

"An ambitious one," Skoyles replied. "Joshua Loring has become a rich man as a result of this arrangement."

"Roderick would never dream of doing such a thing."

"No, my love," he said, taking her hand.

"How can she bear to let the general near her. He's *old.*"

"Old but still sprightly, if rumors are true."

"General Burgoyne had a mistress with him when we invaded from Canada," said Elizabeth, "but he didn't parade her in the same way. In that case, too, the woman had a husband."

"What happened to her marriage vows?" asked Lucy.

"They were conveniently forgotten."

Captain Tillman had taken the trouble to find out something about the play. It was a short farce called *A Will and No Will.* Written over thirty years earlier by the famous actor Charles Macklin, it was an adaptation of a French drama, and had the subtitle of *A Bone for the Lawyers.* In one respect, the performance would be unique.

"They've put back all the lines that were excised," said Tillman.

"What does that mean?" his wife asked.

"In England, the play was censored by the lord chamberlain. Certain passages were taken out because they were felt to be too salacious, or improper in some other way. You should enjoy it, Lucy."

"Why?"

"One of the characters bears your name."

Lucy giggled in anticipation. Skoyles liked her a great deal, and he was glad that Elizabeth had found such a good friend in Philadelphia. With her vivacity, Lucy Tillman was a positive tonic. The friendship had brought some stability into Elizabeth's life again and shown her that being married to a British officer had many advantages. Elizabeth was there to enjoy herself, and Skoyles wanted to share in her pleasure. It was a long time since he had seen a play of any kind, and he was in the mood for a lively and inconsequential romp. As someone sat next to him and nudged his right arm accidentally, he winced. The shoulder wound would not let him forget that it was there.

When the curtains opened and the play began, the hubbub in the audience was replaced by mild tumult on stage. The prologue to *A Will and No Will* was set in a pit, crowded with actors who whistled and banged their fists for the farce to start. Rattle and Smart got the first laugh within seconds.

RATTLE: *Curse catch me, Dick, if that is not a fine woman in the upper box there, ha!*

SMART: *So she is, by all that's charming—but the poor creature's married: it's all over with her.*

Since the lines were directed at Betsey Loring, they earned some knowing guffaws in the audience. Mrs. Loring was highly diverted, but General Howe merely scowled.

When the play commenced, it was Lucy Tillman's turn to feel self-conscious.

SHARK: *Good morrow, Lucy.*

LUCY: *Good morrow, Shark.*

SHARK: *Give me a kiss, hussy. (He kisses her.)*

LUCY: *Psha—prithee don't tousle and mousle a body so, can't you salute without rumpling one's tucker and spoiling one's things? I hate to be tumbled.*

Uncertain whether she should laugh or feel aggrieved, Lucy settled for a splutter of amusement. It was not long before she became reconciled to the fact that her namesake was a scheming maid, intent on being one of the beneficiaries of the will. The action bowled along at speed, keeping the spectators in an almost continual state of hilarity. What caught Skoyles's attention were three rhyming couplets that had, unbeknown to him, been struck out of the play by the lord chamberlain.

The statesmen's skill, like mine, is all deceit.
What's policy in him—in me's a cheat.
Titles and wealth reward his noble art,
Cudgels and bruises mine—sometimes a cart.
'Twas, is, and will be, to the end of time,
That poverty, not fraud, creates the crime.

There was a bald truthfulness to the lines that made them stand out for him. While the rest of the audience howled with delight at the rest of the play, Skoyles continued to think about the claim that had preceded the couplets.

255

SHARK: *On my conscience, had I been bred in court, I believe I should* *have made as great a figure as ever Oliver Cromwell did.*

The name of the Lord Protector was anathema to everyone else in the audience, but Skoyles fancied that it would not be unwelcome at Valley Forge. Oliver Cromwell had taken up arms against a king and, in time, replaced him as head of a commonwealth. Such ideals were not dissimilar to those that impelled the revolutionary forces. They, too, sought a republic. They, too, felt oppressed by a tyrannical monarch. Alone of the spectators, Jamie Skoyles had been given food for thought.

When the play was over, the actors received an ovation and took several curtain calls. It was an ideal entertainment for a cold evening in January, and everyone was in good spirits. Skoyles turned to Elizabeth.

"Did you enjoy it?" he asked.

"Very much," she said. "And you?"

"Oh, yes."

"Even the vulgarity was made comical."

"That was mostly Lucy's doing." Hearing the comment, Lucy Tillman looked across at him. "I meant Lucy in the play," he explained. "I don't think you'd be capable of any of the tricks that she was involved with."

"My wife can be quite wicked at times," said Tillman fondly.

"Only when you deserve it," Lucy retorted. "I didn't recognize myself at all in the play."

"How could you?" said Elizabeth. "You are a real lady, Lucy, whereas your namesake was nothing but an artful servant."

The audience was beginning to disperse, but Skoyles deliberately hung back, not wishing to be jostled in the crowd. He chatted happily with his companions until most spectators seemed to have gone, then he turned round to look toward the exit. He saw someone and started. Wearing the uniform of a major, a man in his thirties was standing near the doorway in conversation with a young woman. It was a person whom Skoyles had hoped never to see again, and he stared at him in disbelief. Elizabeth also caught sight of the man.

"It's Harry Featherstone!" she cried in alarm.

Skoyles felt as if he had been punched on his wounded shoulder.

George Washington pored over the map and jabbed a decisive finger.

"There," he said. "We'll attack there."

"But it's one of their larger camps," Major Clark argued. "It will be well guarded. We'd be taking unnecessary risks."

"I disagree, Major. There are times when the best way to surprise an enemy is to do the opposite of what they expect. The obvious place for us to strike is at one of the smaller camps, farthest from the city. The British will not be prepared for a raid here." He used a pencil to put a cross on the map. "We need food badly. If they have as many men there as we think, there should be rich pickings. The quartermaster will keep the camp well supplied."

Drenched by a sudden downpour, Major Clark had returned to Valley Forge with all the intelligence that he had gathered in Philadelphia. When he reached headquarters, dripping wet, he discovered Washington talking in his office to the Marquis de Lafayette. They had given him a cordial welcome, and the Frenchman had talked to him while Washington was sifting through all the material that had been delivered. It was a letter from Jamie Skoyles that had made him unroll his map to study it. The other men stood at his shoulder.

"How accurate are these troop numbers?" asked Washington.

"They accord roughly with what we already know," said Clark.

"Captain Skoyles has no reason to mislead us."

"Then we must believe what he tells us."

"Have you been to this camp, Major?" said Lafayette, indicating the cross that had just been put on the map.

"No, Marquis. I've only seen it from a distance. Captain Skoyles has been inside it, however. He has a friend stationed there."

"How do you know?"

"I had them followed to the camp from the city."

"Is his arm still in a sling?" said Washington.

"No, sir," answered Clark. "He's able to ride a horse now, so I presume that he's recovered. I've still not been able to find out how he came by the injury."

"It hasn't stopped him writing this letter, obviously. Thank you for decoding it, Major. I think that we should act on his intelligence."

"But he recommends a raid on one of the outlying camps."

"I deploy my men—not Captain Skoyles."

"I have heard this name so much," said Lafayette with interest. "Who is this man and why do you rely on his word so much?"

"I think that I place rather more reliance on it than Major Clark," said Washington. "Captain Skoyles is a British officer who is close to General Howe. What he has been able to tell us is invaluable."

"Yet you do not trust him, Major."

"I do and I don't," said Clark wearily. "Since we began to use him, Skoyles has done nothing wrong, yet I still cannot bring myself to put my full trust in him. It's probably a fault in my nature, Marquis. I'm suspicious of everyone."

"Even me?"

"At first."

"Mon dieu!"

"Your behavior did strike me as eccentric when you got here."

"I want to fight for liberty. What is eccentric about that?"

"Coming back to the attack," said Washington, taking a last look at the map. "My mind is made up. We strike here. Skoyles reckons that the camp has a large field hospital, so many of the men there are unfit for duty." He rolled up the map. "I'll pass on the word. Apart from anything else, it will give the men something to do. Inaction is bad for them."

"I feel that," said Lafayette, touching his injured leg.

"Every day this week, I've had to attend a court-martial for soldiers appearing on charges of attempted desertion, disobedience of orders, scandalous remarks, or conduct unbecoming a gentleman—a whole list of unnecessary offenses." Washington was bitter. "That's what happens when we simply sit here and wait."

"What is it you say about the devil?"

"He finds work for idle hands, Marquis."

"When will the raid take place, General?" said Clark.

"When the time is ripe."

"And the weather is kinder than today," said Lafayette.

"That goes without saying. Be sure to alert Ezekiel Proudfoot, Major," said Washington. "I have a feeling that he'd like to be present so that he can draw some sketches."

"The ones he did of Saratoga were superb."

"Compared to the battles there, this will be a mere skirmish. But it will be nice to have a record of it in the *Patriot*." Washington smiled as he put the map aside. "I'm sure that General Howe would enjoy seeing it."

Having basked in his triumph for weeks, Lieutenant Hugh Orde was now facing the full venom of his commander. It was a cruel change of fortune. Standing at attention in the office at British headquarters, he cringed inwardly as Howe delivered a blistering harangue. All that Orde could do was to keep apologizing, but that only enraged the general even more.

"I *know* that you're sorry, Lieutenant," he bellowed. "You've every reason to feel sorry for your lame-brained incompetence. But an apology will not atone for what you've done."

"I found the press and arrested the printer, sir," said Orde.

"What use is that when Ezekiel Proudfoot is still on the loose and able to hurl this piece of ordure at me?" He snatched up the copy of *The Pennsylvania Patriot* that lay on his desk. "Look at it!" he said, holding it the other man's nose. "I'm being pilloried yet again!"

"Nobody regrets that more than I, General."

"I tried to put that unfortunate business at the theater behind me, then this lampoon comes out to bring it all back to life again. I refuse to be laughed at, Lieutenant."

"Yes, sir."

"So what are you going to do about it?"

"Find the printing press that they are using this time."

"No," said Howe, flinging the newspaper aside. "That's not the answer. Destroy one press and they use another. When you put that out of action, a third will spring up somewhere. But—and listen to this carefully, Lieutenant— if you catch Ezekiel Proudfoot for me, if you put salt on the tail of that damn Yankee silversmith, then we can stop these libelous cartoons for good. That's your assignment: find him!"

"But he's like a phantom, General."

"Spare me your excuses. They're as irritating as your apologies."

"We still have no clear idea of what Proudfoot looks like."

"Yes, we do," said Howe, striding to open the door. "Come in, Major Featherstone. Thank you for responding so promptly."

"My pleasure, sir."

Harry Featherstone came into the room and was introduced to Orde. Taking a seat behind his desk, Howe invited the others to sit down. As he explained the situation to Featherstone in ponderous detail, he kept throwing in barbed criticism of the lieutenant. Hugh Orde writhed with embarrassment. It seemed an age since he had received unstinting praise from the same person in that very same room. His capture of Adam Quenby, it seemed, now counted for nothing.

When the general finally came to the end of his account, Harry Featherstone had his first question ready.

"You say that this other man—Reece Allen—was released?"

"Yes," said Howe. "Lieutenant Orde had no call to hold him."

"He was obviously what he claimed to be," Orde put in. "A farmer from Massachussetts, looking for land to buy."

"It's an odd time to search for a farm," said Featherstone.

"I put that point to him, Major."

"What was his answer?"

"That this was the only time of year when he could get away from his present farm without leaving them shorthanded. In spring, summer, and fall, he's working all day and every day."

"Could you describe him for me, Lieutenant?"

"Gladly, sir," said Orde. "He was a tall, lean, gangling man with a pockmarked face. Brown hair and beard."

"How old would he be?"

"Somewhere in his thirties."

"Did he stoop slightly?" asked Featherstone.

"He did, actually."

"And did it ever cross your mind that Reece Allen might really be someone else altogether—Ezekiel Proudfoot, for instance?"

"That was my original hope when I first arrested him."

"And mine," said Howe.

"But his story was sound, and we had a reliable witness who confirmed that it could not possibly have been Proudfoot."

"Oh?" Featherstone sat up. "Who was this witness?"

"Someone from your own regiment, as it happens," said Howe. "Captain Jamie Skoyles of the 24th Foot."

"Yes, I knew that he was here. He was at the theater last night."

"You've spoken to him, then?"

"No, General. We tend to keep out of each other's way."

"Brother officers should not fall out."

"In this case, it was inevitable."

"Captain Skoyles told me that he'd seen Proudfoot once before," said Orde, "when you arrested him after the battle of Hubbardton. The captain only had a brief glimpse of the man but he was adamant that he did not fit the description I gave him of Reece Allen."

Featherstone was astounded. "Is that what Skoyles told you?"

"Yes, Major."

"That he only met Proudfoot once before?

"That's right."

"And that all he got was a brief glimpse of the man?"

"You seem to find that testimony difficult to believe."

"General Howe," said Featherstone, turning to him, "I wonder if I might have a word in private?"

"But it was the lieutenant who interrogated Reece Allen."

"I beg leave to doubt that."

"It's a matter of record, sir," Orde protested.

"You questioned someone, that much is true. But I have a very strong feeling that the man was, in fact, Ezekiel Proudfoot."

"That's impossible, Major. Captain Skoyles vouched for it."

Featherstone spoke with disdain. "I, too, saw Proudfoot after the battle of Hubbardton," he said, "and, apart from the beard, he looked exactly like the man you described."

"How could he?"

"Are you certain of this?" said Howe.

"As certain as I am of anything," Featherstone affirmed. "That's why I prefer to talk to you alone, sir."

"Yes, yes, of course." He glared at Orde. "Lieutenant."

Orde jumped to his feet. "Excuse me, gentlemen," he said.

"Wait outside," Howe ordered, watching him cross to the door. "If I discover that you arrested the man we were after, only to turn him loose again, I'll want further words with you. Now get out."

Fearing retribution, Orde opened the door and made a hasty exit. Howe got up from his chair and came around his desk so that he could lean against the edge of it. His brow was furrowed.

"Well, Major?"

"Far be it from me to malign a fellow officer," said Featherstone suavely, "but I fear that you have been deliberately misled here. If Captain Skoyles claimed that he had only seen Proudfoot once in his life, he was lying outrageously."

"That's a very serious charge."

"But a well-deserved one."

"How do you know?"

"Because they are old friends."

"Friends?"

"Yes, General. When he first came to America with the army many years ago, Skoyles was billeted on the Proudfoot farm in Massachusetts. He and Ezekiel were only boys then. They became close friends."

"Skoyles said nothing of this to the lieutenant."

"It's easy to see why, sir."

"Only if your supposition is correct."

"Let me go back to the battle," said Featherstone. "When we captured Fort Ticonderoga, we chased the departing garrison all the way to Hubbardton. They turned and fought."

"Yes, yes. I read all this in General Burgoyne's dispatches."

"Some pertinent details were omitted from them. All the prisoners we captured at Hubbardton that day were sent back to Ticonderoga. There was, however, one exception."

"Ezekiel Proudfoot?"

"Precisely," said Featherstone. "At the instigation of Captain Skoyles, he returned with us to our new camp."

"On what grounds?"

"That he would be able to help us. Proudfoot had been close to General St. Clair at the fort, and knew all his plans, as well as details of the garrison. Given their friendship, Skoyles argued that he could get intelligence out of Proudfoot that might prove crucial. The two of them spent a long time alone together in Skoyles's tent."

"So much for only having a brief glimpse of the man!"

"Eventually, the prisoner was taken away under guard."

"Had he divulged anything of value?"

"Not really," said Featherstone. "The best evidence we had of the situation at Ticonderoga was in the form of his sketches. While he was there, Proudfoot did a series of drawings. He's an artist of some talent."

"Grotesquely misused talent," said Howe with distaste. "We should have hanged him when we had the chance."

"I understand that the fellow escaped from you."

"That's how it appeared at first, General, but I have a theory."

"And what's that?"

"Jamie Skoyles helped him to get away."

Harry Featherstone licked his lips like a cat that has just stumbled upon a saucer of cream. He had been given a heaven-sent opportunity to discredit Skoyles in the eyes of their commander, and he seized it. He knew perfectly well that Skoyles had not been instrumental in the escape of his friend, but it was an occasion when facts could be bent to the captain's disadvantage. Skoyles had unwittingly brought it upon himself. By deceiving them about his friendship with Proudfoot, he had laid himself open to a charge of assisting the enemy. Featherstone was quick to build on that.

"You believe that Skoyles was party to the escape?" said Howe.

"Without a shred of doubt."

"What evidence do you have?"

"That of my own eyes," said Featherstone. "When Proudfoot was put into a tent, his hands were bound and he was unarmed. Somehow, he managed to get free, overpower the guard, steal his uniform, and slip through our lines in disguise. Now," he continued, "my theory is this. Skoyles must have slipped him a knife during the interrogation so that he could later cut through his bonds."

"Did nobody challenge him to that effect?"

"I tried to do so, sir, but I was overruled by General Burgoyne. He always had an unduly high regard for Captain Skoyles."

"Quite rightly so. From what I've heard of his military record, Skoyles is an exceptional soldier. Would you contradict that, Major?"

"No, sir. He's a very brave man. I always felt that he was out of his depth as an officer, mark you," he said with condescension, "but, then, he was hardly born to it. To continue my story—when I learned that the prisoner had escaped, I sent Skoyles after him with a posse of soldiers and Indian scouts. They returned without Proudfoot."

"What construction did you place on that, Major?"

"The obvious one, sir."

"Which is?"

"That Captain Skoyles allowed his friend to get away."

"Surely not."

"He seems to have done exactly the same thing here."

"Only if the man we had in custody really was Ezekiel Proudfoot."

"He was caught red-handed on Christmas Day with the printer of that rebel newspaper," Featherstone urged. "What more proof do you need? The coincidence is just too great."

"Lieutenant Orde considered Reece Allen to be very plausible."

"He was taken in, General."

"What swayed him was Skoyles's categorical denial that the man we were holding could be this infernal silversmith."

"In short, he aided Proudfoot's escape yet again."

"I reserve judgment on that, Major."

Rubbing his chin meditatively, Howe tried to piece together in his mind all that he knew about Skoyles from personal experience. It was largely, if not overwhelmingly, in his favor. He liked and respected Skoyles. Apart from leading the skirmishers in a failed raid, the captain had done nothing wrong and a great deal that deserved commendation. Or, at least, it had seemed so at the time. In the light of Featherstone's comments, Howe had to revalue his opinion of the man. If Skoyles had indeed beguiled them, a worrying conclusion offered itself.

"He may have been working against us all the time," said Howe.

"I don't follow, sir."

"That's because you don't know how much faith I've placed in Captain Skoyles. I appointed him as my special envoy at Valley Forge."

"He's been in contact with the enemy?" said Featherstone, aghast.

"At my behest," explained Howe, "he offered his services to the rebels as a spy. He even managed to speak to General Washington himself. My reasoning was that Skoyles would not only be able to glean intelligence from inside the enemy camp, he could also feed them information that would mislead them."

"Is that what happened, sir?"

"At first."

"And then?"

Howe told him about the skirmishers who had been put to flight by the enemy, and how the survivors had limped back to Philadelphia to lick their wounds. Featherstone pounced on the news.

"There you are, sir—the proof you require."

"All that I saw was a bungled operation."

"They were waiting for your men," said Featherstone. "Skoyles was supposed to tell them that only a small body of skirmishers would be deployed, so that any retaliation could be drawn toward the supporting line that was hidden behind them."

"That was the plan, Major. They obviously guessed what it was."

"There's a much simpler explanation than that."

"Really?"

"Skoyles warned them that they were being tricked."

"But he *led* the expedition," Howe argued. "Why put himself into such terrible danger as that? He could easily have been killed."

"Not if the rebels had express orders to spare him. Others were shot, but Skoyles was allowed to get away unscathed."

"No, I can't accept that, Major. I've spoken to some of the men involved in that raid. They told me that Skoyles fought like a demon. If he was in league with the enemy, he would hardly attack them."

"That was only for show."

"Nobody cuts a man down with his sword simply for show."

"How was the intelligence communicated to the enemy?"

"Skoyles put it into code and passed on the letter."

"To whom?"

"He doesn't know," said Howe, "and he hasn't told me where he delivers his information. But they obviously received it because they had men ready to repulse the attack."

"Did you know what was in Skoyles's letter?"

"Of course. I drafted it for him."

"But you did not see the version that was sent?"

"What was the point? I could not decipher the code."

"Then you put yourself entirely into his hands," said Featherstone, "with fatal results. What I believe happened is this. The information that you gave to Skoyles was changed when he passed it on. He schooled them in what to do. Because they knew what to expect, the enemy took countermeasures."

"I just can't accept that Skoyles would do such a thing."

"He lied about his friendship with Ezekiel Proudfoot."

"So it appears."

"And he's in the ideal position to betray you."

"His orders are to confuse and misdirect the enemy."

"Has he supplied them with any more intelligence?"

"Naturally," said Howe. "A spy can only win the confidence of his masters if he keeps up a steady supply of information. I gave Skoyles false estimates of the number of soldiers in our various camps, making it clear that one of them was seriously under strength in the hope that it might lure the enemy out of Valley Forge. In fact," he went on, "I've sent heavy reinforcements from another camp, along with all its artillery. If the rebels attack, they'll be blown to pieces."

"Supposing that they were warned off by Captain Skoyles?"

Howe looked uncomfortable. "If that were the case," he admitted, "then the enemy would direct their efforts at the camp from which I've stripped two regiments and the whole of the artillery. I can't bear to think what would happen in that event. They'd be almost defenseless!"

Captain Jamie Skoyles was almost a mile away from the camp when the attack was launched. Instead of bringing Tom Caffrey into the city to change the dressing on his shoulder, he had chosen to ride out to see his friend in his camp, and to renew his acquaintance with Polly Bragg. As soon as he heard the resounding first volley, Skoyles realized that a sizable force was involved. Black smoke curled up into the sky as tents were set on fire, and the sound of frightened animals reached his ears. Though it caused a nagging pain in his shoulder, he kicked his horse into a gallop, desperately concerned for the safety of his friends. Realization hit him like a blow. Rather than attack the camp that Skoyles had recommended, Washington had sent his men against the one that had been severely weakened by the loss of men and artillery.

The pandemonium of battle filled the air. Volleys were fired in succession and cries of agony came from those who had been hit. Horses charged, swords flashed, orders were shouted. Above the sound of panic from inside the camp, came the drumming of hooves as its stock was rustled and driven away. Fire crackled merrily from a dozen burning tents. Enemy artillery sent more shot powering its way to disaster. Assaulted at the front, and on both flanks, those left in the camp were fighting for survival.

Skoyles arrived, brought his horse to a halt, and tethered it before running toward one of the redoubts. Redcoats were stretched along its length, firing and reloading with the precision they had been taught, but conscious that they were outnumbered. Facing them were regiments that did not follow the accepted rules of engagement. Instead of standing in ranks to discharge volleys, they scattered, took cover, and fired from sheltered positions before running forward to get closer. Difficult targets themselves, they were able to pick off the stationary redcoats with their sharp shooting. Several British soldiers had already been killed or wounded behind the redoubt.

To his intense relief, Skoyles saw that Tom Caffrey had not been hurt. Farther along the line, he was attending to a victim whose hand had been shot away, working quickly under fire, and looking to see where he would next be needed. When the injured man was bandaged up, Polly Bragg was on hand to lead him to the hospital at the rear of the camp. Caffrey had already scuttled along to his next patient, a corporal who had taken a bullet in his chest and who was begging for mercy.

Skoyles joined in the fight. Taking his place at the defenses, he picked up a discarded musket, then relieved a dead soldier of his powder and ammunition. He was in time to shoot an adventurous rebel who had crept to within thirty yards of the redoubt. He reloaded, discharged another accurate shot, then made his way toward Caffrey. When another hail of bullets came flying over the redoubt, he flattened himself against the timber while he reloaded his musket. His third shot only wounded a man in the arm, but it took the rebel out of the fight, and he scampered away in pain. After reloading yet again, Skoyles kept low and hurried toward the friend.

Caffrey was binding a hideous wound in a man's cheek when Skoyles eventually reached him. The surgeon was taken aback.

"What are you doing here, Jamie?" he asked.

"I could never resist a fight."

"Well, we've got a big one on our hands here. Half of the camp marched out yesterday, so we're very exposed. The rebels—damn their eyes—seemed to know that."

"How many men have you lost?"

"Too many. One of the officers asked me if there was anyone I could drag out the hospital to hold a musket. That's how desperate we are." He shuddered as artillery boomed again and shot raked a line of tents. "They're cutting us to bits."

"Then I'll not waste time talking, Tom. I'm needed."

He went back to the redoubt and lined up his next target. Fighting was fierce, and the smoke of battle obscured much of what was going on. The one consolation was that it was a remarkably short engagement. The rebels had struck, caught the redcoats napping, and stolen the animals they had come for. In every way, it was a highly successful raid. The drums sounded a retreat and the attackers drew back at once. So much damage had been done to the camp, and there had been so many casualties, that nobody even considered pursuit. They were simply grateful that the enemy had called off their attack.

Skoyles brought down one more rebel, but the others were now out of range, so he put his borrowed musket aside. Firing stopped along the line, and the redcoats were able to take stock of their losses. They were left shocked by the unexpected and savage assault. Like the other surgeons, Tom Caffrey would be kept busy for hours, and Polly Bragg was one of the many nurses who was giving their assistance with tireless devotion. When the departed regiments came back to their camp, they would be horrified to see what had happened to it in their absence.

Unable to use a weapon, Skoyles took out a telescope and scanned the line of retreating rebels. It was a rapid withdrawal, and the artillery had already been dragged out of sight over a rise. The Continental Army had come for food rather than blood, but they had helped themselves to both while they were there. Skoyles climbed onto the barricade to get a better look, letting his telescope sweep slowly across the landscape. It was when he looked toward the eastern end that he saw something that arrested his gaze. A lone figure was sitting on a horse, holding something that he put into a satchel. Watching the engagement from a safe distance, he had taken no part in it. He had simply been there to record a minor victory.

Skoyles remembered a face at a tavern window in Germantown.

CHAPTER FOURTEEN

Ezekiel Proudfoot rode back to Germantown at a canter, his excitement heightened by an awareness of his unique position in the drama. Having witnessed a small but meaningful victory over the redcoats, he would be able to record the event in a print that would put new heart into a dispirited Continental Army. It was a responsibility that he willingly embraced, and it gave him a sense of real significance. While he had enjoyed creating satirical cartoons for the *Patriot,* he now had a worthier subject for his talents—the celebration of a rebel victory, thrilling to watch and stimulating to recapture in an engraving.

When he reached Neale's Tavern, he stabled his horse and went straight up to his room. In the course of his return journey, he had already worked out in his mind the general shape that his print would take and the spirit that it would evoke. Sitting at his table, he set out the sketches he had made during the surprise attack on the British camp. Proudfoot was so keen to start that his hands were tingling. He took up a pencil and began.

Half an hour later, someone pounded on his door with a fist.

"Yes?" he asked, startled by the noise.

"I wish to speak to Reece Allen," said a man's voice.

Proudfoot recognized his caller at once. It was Jamie Skoyles. How he could possibly have been tracked to Germantown, the silversmith did not know, but the seriousness of his predicament was clear. The British army knew where he was. The only means of escape was through the window, but that would involve a long and perilous drop to the ground below, where armed redcoats might conceivably be waiting for Proudfoot. The pistol that he carried for protection while traveling would be little use against a bevy of

269

soldiers. Sweeping everything off the table, he thrust it into his satchel, then hid it hurriedly beneath the bed.

"Let me in," Skoyles demanded, banging the door.

"One moment, one moment."

"Come on, Mr. Allen. I won't ask again."

Unbolting the door, Proudfoot opened it, fully expecting to see his visitor with half a dozen soldiers at his back. Instead, astonishingly, Skoyles was on his own. As they stood there, face-to-face for the first time in months, there was an awkward silence. Neither quite knew on what precise terms they were meeting. The ties of friendship were loosened by the fact that they were on opposing sides in the war, but they still held firm. Proudfoot was the first to acknowledge this.

"Hello, Jamie," he said with a half smile.

Skoyles was more formal. "May I come in, please?"

"Of course."

"Thank you, Mr. Allen."

He stepped into the room. Proudfoot closed the door behind him. Before speaking, they took a long time to appraise each other.

"It's good to see you again, Jamie," said Proudfoot.

"Is it?"

"How did you escape from Cambridge?"

"By killing the guard who tried to stop us."

"I had a feeling that they'd not be able to hold you for long. Captivity doesn't suit a man like Jamie Skoyles." He pointed to the window. "Some while ago, I thought I saw you riding down the street outside here, but I could not be certain that it was you."

"It was me, Ezekiel," said the other, "or would you prefer to be called Reece Allen?"

"Call me whatever you wish."

"As a British officer, I ought to call you a damn Yankee and arrest you for aiding and abetting our enemy. I'd certainly win congratulations from General Howe. Your name—your real name, that is—is rarely far from his lips. He'd sooner hang you than General Washington."

"I take that as a compliment."

"It wasn't meant to be complimentary."

"Have my cartoons had that much effect on Howe?"

"He's certainly taken note of them."

270

"What about Mrs. Loring?"

"She's been equally displeased."

"That was my aim—to mock her and draw attention to the fact that her husband is a vile monster."

"Yes," said Skoyles coldly, "I saw something of Joshua Loring's work when I was in New York City. He squeezes every last penny out of his position as commissar of prisons. While he makes obscene profits by means of corruption, your prisoners of war suffer horrendous privations."

"The few who were lucky enough to escape have told the most gruesome stories about the conditions they suffered. I'm bound to admire some things about the British army," Proudfoot admitted, "but the way it maltreats its prisoners is not one of them. It's shameful."

"We don't have a monopoly on shameful actions, Ezekiel."

"No, we've committed outrages as well. I concede that."

"Yet you never put them into your prints."

"I find more inspiring subjects for those, Jamie."

"Like today's little escapade, for instance."

"What do you mean?" asked Proudfoot, feigning ignorance. "I've not been out of my room all morning."

"Then you clearly have a double," said Skoyles drily. "Either that, or my telescope let me down. I could have sworn that I saw you, sneaking away after the rebels raided one of our camps." He glanced round the room. "We can soon settle the argument. Where's you satchel? If you were there, you'd surely have drawn some sketches."

There was a lengthy pause. Proudfoot saw the folly of further denial. When he looked into his visitor's eyes, he quailed inwardly. Skoyles's gaze was noncommittal. Proudfoot could not tell if he had come to arrest him or simply to renew their acquaintance.

"How did you find me, Jamie?"

"While everyone else headed back toward Valley Forge," said Skoyles, "you rode off in the direction of Germantown. I recalled a face I thought I saw at a window in this tavern."

"Perhaps you confused me with Reece Allen."

"That's not a mistake that I'd ever make. I'm not young and naïve like Lieutenant Orde. Do you remember him? He was the man who arrested you and your printer on Christmas Day."

271

"Don't remind me. It was terrifying, Jamie. We were having dinner together when the redcoats descended on us without warning."

"Did you expect them to send calling cards in advance?"

"Adam Quenby paid a terrible price for what he'd done," said Proudfoot sorrowfully, "but I was lucky enough to be released."

"You took advantage of the lieutenant's inexperience."

"I talked my way out of a noose. It's amazing what lies you can tell when you're faced with the possibility of execution. I could almost feel that rope being put around my neck." He gave a mirthless laugh. "I just hope that Lieutenant Orde never realizes that he actually let Ezekiel Proudfoot slip from his grasp."

"I made sure of that."

"How?"

"By asking what you looked like," explained Skoyles. "I said that I'd had a glimpse of you after the battle of Hubbardton. When the lieutenant gave a description of you, I assured him that it could not possibly be Ezekiel Proudfoot."

"Thank you."

"At the time of arrest, I hear, you had a beard."

"I shaved it off," said Proudfoot, running a hand around his jaw. "I wanted to change my appearance so that I could go back to Philadelphia again without being easily recognized. So," he continued with a smile of gratitude, "you lied on my behalf, did you?"

"I threw the lieutenant off the scent, that's all."

"For my benefit."

"And his," said Skoyles. "If General Howe ever discovered that the most wanted man in the rebel ranks had been released from custody, he'd have torn Lieutenant Orde to shreds."

"Was that uppermost in your mind at the time?"

"No, Ezekiel."

"Then I thank you again."

"You'd have done the same for me."

"Yes," said Proudfoot after consideration. "I probably would."

"I may need to remind you of that one day."

Skoyles was in a quandary. Duty dictated that he should arrest Proudfoot and deliver him to army headquarters in Philadelphia, thereby assuaging General Howe's lust for revenge and taking the most potent contributor away from *The Pennsylvania Patriot*. In the wake of the successful attack on one of their camps, the British army would view the capture of Ezekiel Proudfoot as adequate compensation. Since he knew so much about Valley Forge and its high command, the silversmith would be ruthlessly interrogated before his execution. Proudfoot was not a rebel officer. He was still a civilian. There was no obligation on the enemy to treat him like a gentleman.

Yet it was not friendship that weighed heaviest with Skoyles. It was sheer practicality. If he handed Proudfoot over to Howe, he would lose all credibility at Valley Forge. Major Clark had an extensive web of spies in the city. The fact that Captain Jamie Skoyles had been responsible for the capture of Proudfoot was bound to reach the ears of one of them. In keeping his friend alive, Skoyles would also gain the complete confidence of George Washington and John Clark. More important, he would have successfully deceived Ezekiel Proudfoot himself, for, when he returned to Valley Forge, the latter would certainly report that it was Captain Jamie Skoyles who had let him go. Proudfoot would then be told that Skoyles was, in fact, operating as an agent for the Continental Army.

"What happens now?" asked Proudfoot.

"What do you think *should* happen, Ezekiel?"

"You should arrest me or you'd be failing in your duty."

"That depends on whom I owe the greater duty to," said Skoyles, face impassive. A memory nudged him. "How did General Washington know that that particular camp would be poorly guarded today?"

"He didn't, Jamie. It was pure luck on our part."

"Generals do not rely on pure luck."

"Maybe not," said Proudfoot, "but they're quick to make full use of it when it falls into their hands. We expected more resistance today. That's why such a substantial force was deployed."

"Who told you to be there?"

"I believe that it was General Washington's own decision."

"Did the assignment appeal to you?"

"Very much. I felt it an honor to be present." He looked quizzically at Skoyles. "Though I didn't expect you to be in the camp at the time."

"That was an accident," Skoyles told him. "I went to see my good friend, Tom Caffrey, who's stationed there. The last thing I bargained on was walking into a skirmish like the one I found. We were under sustained fire from the rebels. The one bonus was that I spotted Ezekiel Proudfoot."

"A bonus for you—or for me?"

"I'm not sure."

Proudfoot was worried. This was a situation he could not talk himself out of so readily. Jamie Skoyles was no gullible lieutenant. He was a shrewd man who could divine, better than anyone else, the way that the silversmith's mind worked. The fact that he had come alone was a hopeful sign, but Proudfoot did not attach too much importance to it. Other soldiers might be waiting downstairs in support, and Germantown was alive with redcoats. Reece Allen had been unmasked in one of the enemy strongholds. Only a personal favor could save him.

"I need your help, Jamie," he confessed.

"I know."

"It's time for Reece Allen to disappear."

"He's not the only one," said Skoyles. "If my guess is right, *The Pennsylvania Patriot* is printed here. What else would bring you to Germantown? Who is the printer, Ezekiel?"

"I can't tell you that."

"Then warn him to leave while he can or he'll be arrested. I may have obligations to you, but I've none to him. Get him out of the town before a search is instituted."

"Yes, Jamie."

"You can have three hours' start," decided Skoyles. "Then I'll have to report to General Howe that his least favorite rebel was sighted in Germantown. He'll have the place turned upside down in the search for you and your printer. Have the sense to be several miles away."

"I will." He offered his hand. "Thank you, Jamie."

Skoyles shook his hand. "Goodbye, Mr. Allen."

"Anybody else would have dragged me off to certain death."

"I have my reasons for not doing so."

"Friendship?"

"Partly that."

"Guilt over the way you killed my brother in battle?"

"Yes," said Skoyles with a sigh, "that, too, comes into it. But there's something else besides that I can't disclose to you."

"Why not?"

"Go to Valley Forge—and ask General Washington."

George Washington was lifted by the glad tidings. Ahead of the returning troops, a rider had galloped back to Valley Forge to deliver a report on the complete success of the mission. It made Washington change into his best uniform and collect the commander-in-chief's guard, the elite detachment formed in March 1776, to protect him, his family, and the rapid accumulation of documents at headquarters. He intended to ride out in style meet his soldiers so that he could signal his delight at their victory and accompany them back into camp. Before he could mount his horse, however, Washington saw the Marquis de Lafayette, hobbling toward him on his cane.

"The mission was a triumph, Marquis," said Washington.

"Did they steal any food for us?"

"They rustled every animal in the stock pen."

"That's good news," said the Frenchman, beaming.

"We'll all eat heartily tonight for a change."

"Did we lose many men, General?"

"Our losses were small compared to the enemy's," said Washington. "The camp was not as well defended as we thought. According to first report, we took them by surprise. They never thought we'd *dare* to attack such a target."

"Your decision was a sound one."

"I had a stroke of good fortune that was long overdue."

"I hope that you have many more like that," said Lafayette. He raised his cane. "But I hold you up, general. You will wish to go and welcome our heroes."

Washington hauled himself up into the saddle. "It's only a minor victory," he acknowledged, "but it will serve to bolster the men."

"What will it do to General Howe?"

"I don't think I'd like to be in his shoes at the moment."

"He does not like losing, does he?"

"No, Marquis," said Washington, smiling. "He hates it."

"They attacked the camp that we had deliberately weakened?" cried Howe in disbelief. "But they were supposed to strike elsewhere."

"General Washington had other ideas, sir."

"How could he possibly know that it was understrength?"

"I can't comprehend it," said Orde.

"Were there many casualties in our ranks?"

"Nineteen killed and over forty wounded."

"And the rebels?"

"They got off more lightly, it seems."

It had fallen to Lieutenant Hugh Orde to pass on the bad tidings, and it was not a task that he relished. Already in disgrace with his commanding officer, he was now the bearer of distressing news that had to be imparted at a particularly inconvenient time. Howe was seething. Hauled from the capacious arms of Betsey Loring, he had dressed in a hurry and descended angrily to his office. When he heard what Orde had to say, the general was infuriated.

"They rustled our stock?" he said.

"Apparently."

"But it would have kept the camp going for weeks."

"The rebels chose an opportune moment for attack," said Orde. "One has to admire General Washington's timing."

"Do not look for admiration from me," snarled Howe. "I despise this action. Was there any pursuit?"

"It seems not, sir."

"They were not hounded all the way back to Valley Forge?"

"Our men were outnumbered," said Orde reasonably, "and their first duty was to save the camp. There was untold damage. Several tents had been set alight. Patients in the hospital had to be rescued. That was their primary concern, General."

"Well, *my* primary concern is to find out how this happened."

"Rebel spies must have forewarned them."

"Yes," said Howe, tapping his desk as he pondered. "It's the only way that it could have happened. Someone betrayed us, Lieutenant, and I begin to think that it was someone in whom I unwisely placed trust."

"Do you have anyone in mind, sir?"

"Where is Major Featherstone lodging?"

"I can't say."

"Then find out at once."

"Yes, general."

"And bring him here immediately," ordered Howe. "I need him."

The meeting with his friend had left Skoyles's emotions in turmoil. As he rode back to Philadelphia, he turned over their conversation in his mind and tried to justify what he had done. To maintain the confidence of General Washington and Major Clark, so that he could continue to act as a spy for the British, he had allowed a wanted man to go free. It was not an explanation that his superiors would readily accept, and he would have to adjust the facts before he reported to General Howe. He wished that he could have met Proudfoot in less fraught circumstances. Neither had taken any real pleasure from the encounter. Once again, Skoyles had been given an illustration of the merciless cruelty of war. True friendship could only exist with someone who fought on the same side.

There had been fleeting moments during his confrontation at Neale's Tavern when he had felt a surge of hatred against Proudfoot for using the deaths of British soldiers as the subject of a print to hearten the rebels. Yet that hatred was tempered by fond memories of earlier times together. When they had first met each other, Skoyles and Proudfoot had been lively youths with questing minds and clear ambitions. They were natural allies. Ironically, however, Skoyles had ended up killing Proudfoot's brother in a battle that his friend had duly celebrated with his art, immortalizing a famous American victory. It made for hopelessly confused loyalties.

When he reached the city, Skoyles was still not entirely persuaded that he had done the right thing. The capture of Ezekiel Proudfoot would have been a powerful blow to the rebel cause, but Skoyles could not bear the thought of being the person who handed his friend over to the hangman. There was another factor that had to be taken into account. Proudfoot had once helped Skoyles to evade execution. Before the battle of Bemis Heights, Skoyles had joined the Continental Army as a recruit so that he could assess the strengths and weaknesses of the enemy camp. Spotted by Proudfoot, he could easily have been strung up as a spy, but his friend had kindly given him the opportunity to get away before he reported to his commander that he had recognized a redcoat officer in the camp.

To return the favor, Skoyles had to give Proudfoot time to warn his printer so that both could flee Germantown. Instead of going straight to army headquarters, therefore, Skoyles intended to return to his lodging and rehearse the story that he would tell General Howe. As it was, he got no further than the street in which he was staying. No sooner did he turn into it than six redcoat soldiers rushed to surround his horse and point their muskets up at him. Major Harry Featherstone strutted forward.

"I must ask you to surrender your weapons, Captain Skoyles," he said with a grim smile. "You are under arrest."

"On what charge?" demanded Skoyles in astonishment.

"Treason."

Elizabeth Rainham settled into a chair near the fire. Having enjoyed another shopping expedition with Lucy Tillman, she was glad to get back to the house for a rest. She was also concerned that her pregnant friend should not have too much exercise in her condition. After examining the various items that they had bought, the women turned to the subject that they most frequently discussed.

"Would you like the baby to be born in England?" asked Elizabeth.

"Of course," replied Lucy, "but the chances of that happening are very slim. Roderick may feel that the war will be over by spring, but that does not mean his regiment will be sent home. With my husband still in America, I'd never dream of going back to England."

"It would save you from making that dreadful voyage again."

"Yes, Elizabeth. I'm grateful for that."

"And they have excellent doctors here."

"Army surgeons can turn midwives, if necessary," said Lucy. "Look at Major Binyon's wife. Her twins were delivered in New York City by the regimental surgeon. Of course," she went on, "that's not a choice you'll have to make. If you wait until after the war before you marry, then your children will not come along until the army has left these shores. Have you talked with Captain Skoyles about raising a family?"

"Not yet, Lucy."

"It was the first thing that Roderick said when I accepted his proposal. Because he came from such a large family, he told me that he'd want at least four children."

"He might think differently if he had to give birth to them."

Lucy giggled. "That's true!"

"Besides," said Elizabeth, "I don't think that you can specify a number of children in advance. In the end, it comes down to luck how many times your union is blessed. I know that my parents wanted more children, but they had to settle for two girls."

"They only have one now, Elizabeth."

"Yes, and I'm on the other side of the world."

"Do you ever think of your sister?"

"All the time."

"In some ways, it was a fortunate escape that she didn't have to marry Major Featherstone."

"I don't know that I'd describe Cora's death as fortunate," said Elizabeth reflectively, "but I take your point. She was spared any future disappointment. The mistake that I made was in trying to live her life for her. It was only when I got to know Jamie that I found the courage to be myself."

"You are very much your own woman now," said Lucy approvingly.

"Coming to America helped me to grow up."

"It changes all of us, Elizabeth."

"It transformed me."

"Are you happier now?"

"Much happier, Lucy. These last few weeks have been bliss."

"It's been the same for me. Since you came to the city, everything has become that bit more enjoyable. Only yesterday, Roderick was saying how pleased he was that we'd become such friends. He thinks that you're good for me."

Elizabeth smiled. "I'd hate to be seen as a bad influence."

"I think I'm bad enough already," said Lucy with a grin.

"Fiddlesticks! You're an essentially good person, and you know it."

"You haven't seen my darker side yet."

"I refuse to believe that you have one."

Elizabeth looked up as she saw someone pass the window, then stop to open the front door. After a few moments, Roderick Tillman came into the room. He gave his wife a token kiss on the cheek, then turned to Elizabeth. She saw the unease in his face.

"Is something the matter, Captain Tillman?" she asked.

"I sincerely hope not."

"You look troubled."

"I am, Miss Rainham—on your behalf."

"Whatever do you mean?" said Lucy with a note of admonition. "I'll not have you upsetting my best friend, Roderick."

"I have no choice," he said sadly. "When I first heard the gossip, I refused to believe it but, apparently, it's quite true."

"What is?" said Elizabeth.

"Captain Skoyles has been arrested. He may face a court-martial."

Jamie Skoyles was in great discomfort. It was humiliating enough to be interrogated by General Howe in the presence of four armed soldiers. To have Major Harry Featherstone there as well made the whole experience both embarrassing and excruciating. He had been taken unawares and was now in a dire situation. Under the pressure of stern questioning, Skoyles was struggling to maintain his composure.

"I expected better of you, Captain Skoyles," said Howe.

"That's more than I'd ever do," added Featherstone, "but, then, I know the captain of old. His loyalties have a habit of shifting."

"I resent that, Major," Skoyles asserted. "I've served the British army dutifully for several years, and I'll not let you—or anyone else, for that matter—impugn my honor."

"You've done that for yourself."

"Leave this to me, Major," said Howe.

Eyeing the prisoner with a mixture of hostility and dismay, the general was seated behind the table in his office at headquarters. Featherstone occupied a chair to his right, but Skoyles was kept standing. His sword and pistol had been confiscated. Feeling at a distinct disadvantage, he made a strong protest.

"Why was I brought here like this?" he demanded.

"Because those were my orders," replied Howe.

"Did the major have to be involved?"

"He's a crucial witness."

"To what, sir?"

"Your treachery," said Featherstone.

Skoyles was vehement. "I strongly deny that charge!"

"Then let us examine the reasons for making it," said Howe coolly. "It's not an accusation that should be leveled against anyone without firm evidence to back it up. In your case, I regret to say, we appear to have that evidence."

"Allow me the courtesy of defending myself, General."

"I will, Captain Skoyles."

"Am I being accused by you or the major?"

"By both of us," said Featherstone.

"That is so," confirmed Howe. "It's only by chance that someone from your own regiment is here in Philadelphia, but his arrival has made me view your conduct in a very different light. According to the major, you and the detestable Ezekiel Proudfoot have been friends for many years. Is that true?"

There was an awkward pause. "Yes, sir," Skoyles admitted.

"Then why did you tell Lieutenant Orde that you had only seen Proudfoot once—enough, however, for you to be certain that the man arrested in the name of Reece Allen could not possibly be Proudfoot."

"There's no proof that it was."

"I disagree," said Featherstone. "The description tallies almost exactly with what I know of the man, except that he had grown a beard since I last saw him."

"I suspect that you *wanted* it to be Ezekiel Proudfoot," said Skoyles roundly, "whereas, in fact, the description could have fitted dozens of other people. You never saw this Reece Allen, Major."

"Neither did you, yet you insisted he could not be Proudfoot."

"I thought it unlikely."

"You're evading the point here, Captain," said Howe. "You and this fellow are friends. In other words, you told Lieutenant Orde a deliberate lie. Is that correct?"

"I may have misled him slightly."

"A lie is a lie, sir!"

"There are degrees of dishonesty."

"Damn it, man. Don't you dare argue with me! You obviously don't realize how critical your situation is. If you can't give me satisfactory answers, you'll face a court-martial that will hold the power of life and death over you. Does that mean nothing, Captain Skoyles?"

"It means a great deal," said Skoyles with dignity, "and I fervently hope that it will not reach that stage. Let me explain my conduct."

"Treason can never be excused," said Featherstone.

"But reputations can be vindicated, major."

"At this juncture, you do not *have* a reputation."

"As usual, I'm sure that you've done your best to besmirch it."

"Enough of this!" snapped Howe. "I did not bring the two of you here to

281

trade insults. Honor is at stake, and there is nothing that a soldier holds more dear than that. Captain Skoyles has offered to explain his conduct. I suggest that you permit him to do so without interruption, Major Featherstone."

"Of course, General. I apologize."

"You may continue, Captain."

Skoyles needed a moment to gather his thoughts. He could see only too clearly how his actions could be misconstrued and knew that he had only himself to blame. When he had misled Lieutenant Orde about the possible identity of Reece Allen, he had reacted on impulse. He now sought to account for that impulse.

"Because I did not see the prisoner," he began, "I could not be sure if he was Ezekiel Proudfoot or not. In any case—and I ask you to bear this in mind—he was not released at my command. The lieutenant took that decision."

"Unfortunately," said Howe.

"Even if I had seen him, and even if I could identify him as Proudfoot, I'd still have recommended that he be released."

"Release my tormentor! That would have been lunacy."

"No, General. It would have ensured that I won complete respect at Valley Forge when the news reached there. You wanted a spy in their camp, but I was denied ready access to it. Major Clark, who is in charge of their intelligence, would not trust me until I'd proved myself. In helping Proudfoot to get away," argued Skoyles, "I'd be doing just that. You may have lost a prisoner but you would have gained far more in return. I would have been given the freedom of Valley Forge."

"It sounds to me as if you already have it," said Featherstone sourly. "You're working for the enemy, Captain Skoyles."

"That's not true."

"Supplying them with vital intelligence."

"I sought only to confuse them."

"Then why did they attack our most poorly defended camp this morning?" said Howe. "Did you know that it was almost overrun?"

"Yes, sir," said Skoyles, "I was there."

Howe gaped. "What? During the attack?"

"I arrived shortly after it began."

"Eager to see that his betrayal had borne fruit," said Featherstone.

"No," retorted Skoyles. "I went to visit a friend, Sergeant Caffrey."

282

"Is he a party to this conspiracy as well?"

"There *is* no conspiracy."

"Then why else were you there at that precise time?" said Howe.

"Tom Caffrey is a surgeon. When I was wounded recently," said Skoyles, using his left hand to touch his right shoulder, "he took care of me. I went to have the dressing changed." He began to undo his coat. "If you do not believe me, I'll show you the wound."

"That won't be necessary, Captain Skoyles."

"Then please stop accusing me of base motives."

"You compel me to do so," said Howe sharply. "Consider the facts. When I wished to give the Continental Army a bloody nose, I tried to entice them out of Valley Forge by telling them that one of our camps had inadequate troops and suspect fortifications. In fact, as we both know, I sent reinforcements there who lay in wait for a possible attack. But when that attack came," he continued harshly, "it was launched against the very camp from which those reinforcements were taken."

"That was an unhappy accident, General."

"It looks more like design to me."

Skoyles was shaken. "You surely do not believe that I *told* them where to strike?" he said with passion. "The message that I sent to Valley Forge was the one that you instructed me to send."

"We only have your word for that," said Featherstone skeptically.

"I'd swear an oath on the Bible to that effect."

"You warned the enemy where to attack."

"That's a monstrous suggestion," said Skoyles vehemently.

"But it accords with the facts," Howe pointed out, "and it's not the first time I've had reason to wonder if the information I gave you was altered before it reached Valley Forge. Our skirmishers were routed because a larger force was ready to ambush them."

"I know, general—I was there at the time."

"Did you give them advance warning, Captain Skoyles?"

"Of course not!"

"Have you been feeding intelligence to the enemy?"

"Yes," said Featherstone. "It's as plain as the nose on his face."

"Well?"

"Ask him about the way that he let Proudfoot escape once before."

"I'm waiting for an answer, Captain," said Howe.

"Then you shall have one, sir," said Skoyles, mustering all his self-control. "But, first, let me place on record that I'm deeply insulted you should even put such a question to me. I've obeyed my orders to the letter. Every scrap of information you have given me has been sent to Valley Forge in code. If the skirmish failed," he insisted, "it was not because I forewarned the rebels. I came under fire during our retreat. Do you think I'd alert an enemy so that they were in position to kill me?"

"They could easily have been under orders to spare you," said Featherstone. "We know that the rebels aim first at our officers, yet you escaped without a scratch."

"I suggest that you talk to some of the soldiers in that skirmish party, Major. They will tell you whether I acted improperly or not. I shot one man with a pistol and hacked others to death with my sword. Do you think that General Washington would pay me to kill his own men?"

"Yes—if he thought them expendable."

"The Continental Army is desperately short of troops," said Skoyles. "General Washington hoards them like a miser. He'll not sacrifice one, if he can help it. He would never willingly provide me—or any other British officer—with target practice."

"Putting all that aside," said Howe, "let us look more closely at today's sorry episode. Foreknowledge *must* have been involved."

"Well, it did not come from me, sir."

"How can I be certain of that?"

"Because I give you my word," Skoyles affirmed.

"Only a fool would trust it," said Featherstone. "You lied about your friendship with Proudfoot, and you're telling further lies now."

"I did not warn the enemy, Major. I hoped that they would be tempted to attack the designated target, and find that they had bitten off more than they could chew. Once again," he went on, "I urge you to speak to people who were there today. They'll tell you how I joined in the defense of the camp with a borrowed musket."

"Shooting over the heads of the rebels no doubt."

Skoyles bridled. "That remark is unworthy of you."

"Yet close to the truth, I suspect."

"The truth is that I fought like any other British soldier, and there are countless witnesses to that fact—Sergeant Caffrey, for one. If I'd known beforehand that the attack would be made at that camp, why would I be reckless enough to risk my own life in going there?"

"I think that you went to admire your handiwork."

"Only you could place such a vile construction on it, Major."

"Scouts brought news of the attack hours ago," said Howe. "Why did it take you so long to return to the city, Captain Skoyles?"

"I first went to Germantown, sir."

"That would have taken you miles out of your way."

"There was a reason for that," Skoyles explained. "When the enemy withdrew, I watched them through my telescope. I noticed a man who had been observing the attack, and he went off along the Germantown road. I was fairly certain that it was Ezekiel Proudfoot."

"Even though you'd only had a brief glimpse of him," said Featherstone with heavy sarcasm. "What happened? Did you go after him so that you could collect your thirty pieces of silver?"

"No, Major. I tracked him to Germantown, and made inquiries at all the taverns. I eventually found one where a Reece Allen was staying."

"So he and Proudfoot *are* one and the same man."

"Apparently."

"Then why the devil didn't you arrest him?" Howe demanded.

"He was not there," said Skoyles, recalling what Proudfoot had told him about a man's capacity for lying when his life was in danger. "Besides, it would not have been politic for me to capture him. Had I done so, I'd have squandered the trust I'd so carefully built up at Valley Forge. I chose to report at once to you, General. If Proudfoot is in the town, the likelihood is that the man who prints *The Pennsylvania Patriot* is there as well. You have the opportunity to catch both of them. I urge you to institute an immediate search."

"You did not require my authority for that. Why did not you alert one of the regiments already in Germantown?"

"I knew that you had a personal interest in Proudfoot's capture."

"That much is undeniable," said Howe. He got to his feet, beckoned one of the guards, and whispered some orders to him. The man left the room quickly. "For your sake, Captain Skoyles, let's pray that Reece Allen is still in the town."

"There's no chance of that," Featherstone put in. "Skoyles will already have warned his friend to make himself scarce."

"Then why should I even mention that he was there?" said Skoyles. "I came back to the city at a gallop to report his whereabouts."

"You were not in any hurry when we arrested you."

"My horse needed to be rested."

"Why did you return to your lodging at all? If you had such important news, you should have come straight here with it."

"I intended to do so, Major."

"After you'd rested your horse?"

"I'd only have been a relatively short walk away."

"Nevertheless," said Howe suspiciously, "the major's point is a telling one. Speed was vital in this instance. What made you delay?"

"Was it to give Proudfoot time to escape?" Featherstone pressed him.

"Or did you have some other reason?"

"Are you working in collusion with your friend?"

"How did he come to be present at that attack in the first place?"

"Did you tell him that it was imminent?" said Featherstone.

"Have you known all along that Proudfoot was in Germantown?"

Jamie Skoyles remained silent. He had run out of answers.

Ezekiel Proudfoot had moved swiftly. Having warned the printer that redcoats would soon be searching the town, he gathered up his things and rode back to Valley Forge. The mood there was almost festive for once. A successful attack on a British camp had helped the beleaguered soldiers to forget their woes for a while. Proudfoot reported at once to General Washington, who was in his headquarters with Major Clark. Both men listened with disquiet to what they were told. They had lost yet another means of printing *The Pennsylvania Patriot*.

Washington decided to confide something to the silversmith.

"Jamie Skoyles is working for *us*?" said Proudfoot in amazement. "Why didn't he tell me that?"

"Because you probably wouldn't have believed him," said Clark. "He wanted the news to come from us. Until today, I own, I had a few doubts about Captain Skoyles, but not any more. He's demonstrated that he's truly on our side."

"You and Raphael Dyer would otherwise have been hanged," said Washington. "The captain saved your lives."

"I'm well aware of that, General," said Proudfoot. "That's the second time I've had a noose lifted from around my neck, and I don't think the trick will work a third time somehow."

"We'll keep you safe in Valley Forge for a while."

"Thank you. But I still find it hard to believe that Jamie Skoyles has volunteered to help us. I know that he had sympathy with our aims, but he's a British officer with a remarkable record of service."

"I sounded him out," said Washington, "and thought him sincere. Major Clark was less easily persuaded."

"I felt that he had to be put on trial first," said Clark, "so I watched him carefully for weeks. The way he helped Ezekiel has convinced me that he's trustworthy."

"We could not have found a better man."

"I agree," said Proudfoot. "Jamie is a huge asset for us. The wonder is that you didn't tell me he was providing us with intelligence, Major."

"How was I to know that the two of you were friends?" asked Clark. "In any case, my policy is simple. I prefer to keep my agents largely ignorant of each other's identities. That way, if they are caught, there's only a limited amount of information that can be wrung from them."

"Major Clark believes in being cautious," noted Washington.

"Then why does he visit Philadelphia so often?"

"Sheer bravado."

"Necessity," Clark corrected him. "Intelligence is being gathered every day. I like to be on the spot to be able to assess its value to us."

"And how do you assess Jamie Skoyles's value?" said Proudfoot.

"It's immense. We finally have someone inside the British army."

"Yes," added Washington, "and we can only hope that he stays there. Captain Skoyles is playing with fire. If he slips up, the consequences will be disastrous for him."

A whole day had passed since his arrest, and Elizabeth Rainham had still not been allowed to see him. For information about Skoyles, she had to rely, for the most part, on a succession of rumors that were coming out of headquarters. None of them was in any way reassuring. Captain Tillman tried to find out more detail, but Elizabeth had the impression that he was holding things back out of consideration for her feelings. At first, Lucy Tillman was very supportive, insisting that Skoyles was the victim of some dreadful mistake. When her friend's manner became more reserved, Elizabeth feared that she, too, was hiding something.

Out of desperation, she elected to challenge Harry Featherstone. Elizabeth knew that he was involved in the arrest, and that he would be aware of any charges brought against Skoyles. When she found out where it was, she visited Featherstone's lodging.

"Come in, come in," he said, shepherding her into his room. "This is an unexpected pleasure, Elizabeth."

"It's not a social call."

"What a pity!"

"I need your help, Major."

"Won't you at least sit down?"

He offered to take her cloak and hat. After some hesitation, she agreed. While she sat down, he hung the items on a door peg. The room was large enough to contain a table, two chairs, and a sofa, as well as a wardrobe and a chest of drawers. What worried Elizabeth was the proximity of the bed in the corner. She was grateful that Featherstone did not try to sit beside her on the sofa. He selected one of the chairs. She blurted out her request at once.

"Tell me what's happened to Jamie," she said.

"He'll appear before a court-martial in a couple of days."

"But he's done nothing wrong."

"General Howe thinks otherwise."

"On what possible grounds can he be charged?"

"I'm not at liberty to divulge all of the details," said Featherstone, "but I can give you a general impression of what occurred—on one condition, that is."

"Condition?"

"That you don't interrupt me."

"Very well," she conceded. "All I want is the truth."

"Then you shall have it," he promised.

Doing his best to conceal his deep hatred of Skoyles, he gave her an abbreviated version of the interrogation, the previous day, in General Howe's office. Elizabeth was increasingly distressed, unsure if she was hearing the full facts or only those detrimental to the prisoner. Of one thing, she was absolutely certain.

"Jamie Skoyles is no spy!" she argued.

"I found it difficult to believe myself."

"He would never betray anyone."

"He's been engaged in nothing but betrayal since he's been here," Featherstone told her. "General Howe asked him to court the enemy so that he could get behind the lines at Valley Forge. That's what he did, Elizabeth. He was there solely to betray the Continental Army. It now appears that he preferred to play false with us."

"No, Major!"

"The evidence against him is overwhelming."

"I refuse to accept that he's guilty," she said loyally.

"Then why will he not disclose the means by which he passed on information to the rebels?"

"I'm sure that he has a perfectly good reason."

"Yes," said Featherstone tartly. "It's to protect his friends. He claims that the people to whom he delivers his intelligence are quite unaware of what he gives them, and have absolutely no connection with the rebels. If that's the case, he has no need to conceal their identity." He leaned forward. "I don't suppose that he confided in you, did he?"

"Jamie is very discreet. I never press him about army business."

"So you have no idea where he delivers his correspondence?"

"None at all."

"I'm sorry to hear that," he said. "We've already exposed some of the lies he's told. Holding back information the way he does is merely another means of deception. Skoyles is not helping himself, Elizabeth."

"Let me see him."

"That decision is not mine to make."

"Then speak up on my behalf to General Howe."

"I can't guarantee that he'd listen to me."

"But you'll be called as a witness at the court-martial."

"It's my duty to appear," he said with a touch of pomposity. "Skoyles may have forgotten the meaning of that particular word, but I haven't. Duty is paramount."

Elizabeth was disconcerted. Although he tried to suppress it, she could sense the delight he was taking in the whole affair. It was nauseating to see him gloat. What she really wanted to do was to walk out of the room in disgust, but she could not do that. The only way she could find out about the man she loved was to humor one whom she loathed. She kept her poise with difficulty.

"What will happen at the court-martial?" she asked.

"Captain Skoyles will be cross-examined, then certain witnesses will be called to give their testimony."

"Will any of them speak in favor of Jamie?"

"No, Elizabeth. This is not a regimental court-martial. There's nobody here from the 24th Foot who can attest that he's a man of good character."

"*You* could," she challenged. He smirked. "No, that would be asking too much, wouldn't it? Jamie once rescued you from being shot by one of your own men. Anyone else would feel indebted to him."

He jumped up. "*Indebted*—to a man who stole you away from me?"

"You drove me away."

"That's not how I remember it."

"Well, that's what happened," she said forcefully. "No woman could be expected to put up with such atrocious behavior. A moment ago, you talked about the importance of duty. Jamie saved your life, Harry. Did you conceive it as part of your duty to thank him by trying to kill him during the battle at Bemis Heights?"

"No," he replied unashamedly, "but I can now have the satisfaction of achieving the same end by legal means. Skoyles is a traitor. He should be condemned to death."

"Not if he proves his innocence."

"What chance is there of that?"

"There's every chance—if he's given a fair hearing."

"General Howe will grant him that," said Featherstone, "and he'll probe into every lie that Skoyles has told him. Our men were betrayed yesterday, Elizabeth, and lives were sacrificed as a result. Do not look for any mercy from our commander in chief."

"Would I be permitted to speak up in Jamie's defense?"

"Your testimony would not be considered relevant."

"But I know what a decent and honorable man he is."

"He's forfeited any claim to honor."

"Is there *nothing* that could save him?"

Featherstone gazed at her intently. He had once loved her enough to want to marry her. In his eyes, the fact that she had spurned him for another man only made her more desirable. A thought stirred in his brain. He would never get such an opportunity again. Elizabeth was close to despair. He was in a position to relieve her anxiety, and to exercise power over her at the same time. Of her own volition, she had come to his room. The bed was yards away.

"There is one possibility," he said artlessly.

"And what's that?"

"I could speak to Brigadier General Malloby."

"Why should you do that?"

"Because he'll be sitting in judgement with General Howe and the others at the court-martial."

"Do you know this brigadier general?"

"Very well," said Featherstone. "He's my uncle. It's always a sensible idea for an officer to have at least one relation in the high command. I'm Uncle Arthur's favorite nephew."

"How could that help Jamie?"

"I could take my uncle aside beforehand, and tell him what a fine career Captain Skoyles has had in our regiment, and how highly General Burgoyne thought of him. Uncle Arthur is an old friend of Gentleman Johnny's," he confided, "so that will influence his view of the prisoner. I could also withdraw my accusation that Skoyles aided the escape that Ezekiel Proudfoot made from our camp in Skenesborough."

"But it's a false accusation in the first place."

"That's a matter of opinion."

"Jamie did nothing at all to assist his friend's escape."

"I'm prepared to make that very point, Elizabeth," he went on, "but not for *his* benefit. If Skoyles had turned to me, I'd not lift a finger to help him. Since the request comes from you, it's a different matter."

"What do you mean?" she said, becoming unsettled.

"In token of my admiration, I'm ready to do what I can."

"And what would you expect in return?"

"A sign of affection, that's all."

When he glanced toward the bed, she gave a shudder. Elizabeth was horrified at what he was suggesting. Blushing deeply, she rose to her feet. He took her by the shoulders.

"Let go of me, please."

"Not until you give me your answer."

"Let go of me, Harry!"

He released her but continued to stand uncomfortably close. She could feel his breath on her face. She could see the lust dancing in his eyes. Elizabeth was so outraged that he should suggest such a foul notion that she not could find words to express her revulsion.

"What's the matter?" he taunted her. "Don't you love him enough?"

She slapped his face hard. Then, without even bothering to grab her hat and cloak, she fled in panic from the room.

Though he was given the privilege of a cell on his own, Jamie Skoyles was very much aware of the other prisoners in the overcrowded jail. He could hear them coughing, spitting, arguing, and complaining about the lack of food or, in some cases, simply groaning in pain. Disease haunted the building. Its stink was in the air. During the night, a man had died of cholera and been dragged out of his cell. Skoyles was restless. He was locked up in the same jail as deserters, prisoners of war, common criminals, and disobedient redcoats who had transgressed once too often. He did not belong there.

Yet he had brought it upon himself. He knew that. When he claimed that he had only seen Ezekiel Proudfoot once, he never imagined that his claim would ever be questioned. Instead, it had been revealed to be a downright lie. Major Harry Featherstone had been his nemesis. The one thing that Skoyles had not allowed for was the appearance of his old enemy from the 24th Foot. As a result, his life was in the balance. Until the court-martial, he was doomed to spend his time in a tiny cell with an armed guard on the other side of the bars at all times. Because he had shown his proficiency at escaping from custody, they were taking no chances with him. Skoyles was being carefully watched.

The court-martial, he feared, would be a mere formality. While he had not betrayed his country, he was guilty of the lesser offense of helping an enemy, and that was enough to bring him down. Skoyles felt that he could have convinced Howe of his innocence, had Major Featherstone not already primed the general. No matter how eloquently he defended himself at the court-martial, Skoyles sensed that it would be in vain. The truth was painful. In saving Ezekiel Proudfoot, he had effectively signed his own death warrant.

When he heard footsteps coming along the corridor, he thought at first that his guard was about to be exchanged. Then, incredibly, the face of Elizabeth

Rainham appeared before him. Leaping up, he went over to welcome her, squeezing her hands through the bars. Skoyles looked at the guard who had accompanied her.

"Is privacy too much to ask?" he said.

"Yes, Captain," replied the man. "My orders are to remain with the lady. The visit will only last two minutes."

"Do not waste a second of it by protesting," said Elizabeth as she saw him about to do so. "I'm here, Jamie. Make the most of it."

"Major Featherstone swore that you'd not be allowed near me."

"General Howe has the ultimate authority. On our behalf, Captain Tillman appealed to him, and he relented."

"Thank him for me, Elizabeth."

"I will. He and Lucy have been my only succor. But how *are* you?" she asked, looking with distaste around the cell. "Is this the best that they can provide for an officer?"

"It will do."

"How could they even dream that you'd commit treason?"

"On my honor," he vowed, "I'm not guilty of the charge. But there's evidence of a sort against me and it may well bring me down."

"Harry Featherstone is confident that it will."

He was alarmed. "You've spoken to him?"

"Nobody else would tell me what was going on."

"Well, you'd be wrong to believe any account that he gave you. This is all his doing, Elizabeth—his opportunity for revenge."

"He's evil."

"Forget him."

"How can I when he's helping to condemn you?"

"It doesn't matter."

"It does to me, Jamie."

"No," he insisted, scratching the back of his neck. "If we have so little time together, I'd rather spend it in silence."

"But there's so much to say."

"It's too late, Elizabeth."

When his hand touched hers again, she felt something being slipped into her palm and she realized why he had scratched his neck. Having extracted some notes, hidden in the collar of his shirt, he had passed them on to her.

Words were pointless. With two guards standing behind her, she could not have a proper conversation with Skoyles. It was better simply to enjoy the feel of his hands and read the message in his eyes. The guard who had brought her was a stickler for punctuality.

"Time's up, lady," he announced. "You must go."

Pearsall Hughes was just about to close his bookshop for the day when he saw Major Clark coming toward him. The latter was dressed as a peddler and carried a pack on his back. Clark touched the brim of his hat deferentially.

"Is the lady of the house in need of anything, sir?" he inquired.

"Come inside and ask her, my friend."

Clark stepped into the shop and Hughes locked the door behind him. They went to the back of the room so that they could not be seen from the street. Taking off his pack, Clark set it down on the floor.

"It must be something important to bring you here," said Hughes.

"It is, believe me." He took a letter from his pocket and gave it to the bookseller. "What do you make of this?"

Hughes needed a little time to decipher the words. Clark did not hurry him. After a while, the bookseller looked up in surprise.

"Who is this fellow, Major?"

"Someone in sore need of help."

"What shall we do?"

"Exactly what he suggests," said Clark. "He deserves it."

Hughes returned the letter. "Where was this delivered?"

"To the usual place."

"By whom?"

"A beautiful young woman."

Sergeant Tom Caffrey marched along the corridor at the jail with a guard at his heels. When he reached the cell, he was saddened to see the state that Skoyles was in. Wearing only a shirt, breeches, stockings, and shoes, the prisoner was sitting on the edge of the crude wooden bed with his head between his hands. He looked desolate. Caffrey tried to cheer him up with an amiable greeting.

"Wake up, Captain," he said, "I've come to change that dressing."

Skoyles raised his head. "Thank you, Tom."

"How is the wound now?"

"Still seeping blood from time to time."

"We'll soon stop that," said Caffrey, turning to the guard. "Let me in, then lock the door again. Neither of us is going anywhere."

He was let into the cell. Watched by the two guards, he put down the satchel containing his medical kit. Then he peeled back Skoyles's shirt so that the bloodstained bandaging was revealed. He began to unwind it. As he did so, Caffrey made sure that he was between his patient and the two men on the other side of the bars. The wound had started to heal but a scar remained. Taking fresh bandages from his satchel, Caffrey put a pad on the wound and used the bandages to keep it in place. Skoyles pretended to wince.

"Does it still hurt?" said Caffrey.

"A little."

"This shoulder of yours seems to attract trouble. Didn't I once remove a musket ball from it?"

"You did," said Skoyles. "That was even more painful."

Caffrey bent down to close his satchel, giving something to Skoyles in the process. The guards saw nothing. As Skoyles hid the object in the back of his breeches, the sergeant blocked the view.

"Thank you, Tom."

"I'll change that dressing again in a few day's time, sir."

"I may not be here then."

"No," said Caffrey, "I expect that you'll be a free man once again."

"God willing!"

"Get out of there, Sergeant," barked a voice behind him. "You've done what you came for. Don't linger, man."

Caffrey turned to see Major Featherstone on the other side of the bars. The door was unlocked again. As he shook Skoyles's hand, Caffrey gave him a sly wink, then he went off with one of the guards. The other man locked the door.

"Leave us alone," said Featherstone.

"My orders are to remain here, sir," said the guard.

"Don't you recognize a command when you hear one?"

Reluctant to desert his post, the man wilted under Featherstone's glare and crept away. The major smiled as he beheld the prisoner.

"You're in the right place at last, Captain," he observed. "I feel like a hunter who has finally caught a dangerous mountain lion."

"The animal is on the other side of the bars," said Skoyles.

Featherstone laughed. "Let's see how ready you are with insults when you face that court-martial tomorrow. Did you know that my uncle, Brigadier General Malloby, will be among those on the tribunal? I felt obliged to tell him the truth about Captain Jamie Skoyles, friend of the Continental Army and its ridiculous objectives."

"There's nothing ridiculous about a desire for independence."

"Are you trying to convert *me* to their cause?"

"I know you better than that, Major. Rational argument was never something that appealed to you. And you never learned the wisdom of respecting an enemy."

"You're my enemy," Featherstone taunted him, "and I certainly respect you. I'll be sure to doff my hat when they bury you."

"The court-martial has not reached its verdict yet."

"Yes, it has. I made sure of that." He grinned at Skoyles. "I wonder what will happen to Elizabeth when you're gone?"

"Keep away from her!" warned Skoyles.

"Oh, I will—for a time. I'll allow a decent interval for her to mourn. I'll wait until the memory of an executed traitor starts to fade away in her mind. Then I'll be able to court her without interference."

"Elizabeth will not let you near her!"

"At the moment, perhaps. But time can do extraordinary things." He put his face close to the bars. "She came to see me, you know. She begged for my help because she knew that I was in a position to save your undeserving neck. In exchange, Elizabeth was ready to do *anything,* except the one thing that I wanted." He smirked in triumph. "That's how much you mean to her, Skoyles. Elizabeth would rather preserve the sanctity of her body than save your miserable life."

Skoyles's left hand darted out and took him by the neck, so that he could pull Featherstone forward and bang his head against the bars. His retaliation was only momentary. The major used both hands to detach himself, then stood back out of reach. Blood was trickling from a gash in his forehead. His eyes were blazing.

"I'll make you sorry you did that!" he threatened.

When she walked past the room, Lucy Tillman heard the sound of sobbing from inside. She tapped on the door and went straight in without waiting for an invitation. Elizabeth Rainham was lying on the bed, crying into the pillow. When she became aware of her visitor, she sat up at once and began to dab at her eyes with a lace handkerchief.

"Oh, you poor thing," said Lucy, coming to put an arm around her shoulders. "This must be agony for you."

"It is, Lucy."

"You should never have gone to see him."

"I had to," said Elizabeth. "I couldn't leave Jamie there on his own, wondering where I was and what I was doing. I had to show that I care."

"I know, Elizabeth, but you've been in a terrible state ever since you got back. I could see it in your face. Were you so upset by what you saw at the jail? Or did Jamie say something to distress you?" Elizabeth shook her head. "Try to be brave, for his sake. He'd not want you to suffer like this. And if he's innocent of the charges," she added with a hopeful smile, "then his name will be cleared at the court-martial."

"If only that were true!"

"Surely, you do not doubt him."

"No," said Elizabeth. "I know that Jamie is wrongly accused, and I know why. He has no chance of exoneration at the court-martial, Lucy. The judgment is a foregone conclusion."

"But it can't be until all the evidence is given."

"Yes, it can."

Elizabeth wiped the last tear from her cheek with the handkerchief and looked into her friend's eyes. Fond as she was of Lucy, she was not ready to confide in her completely. Feeling too embarrassed to raise the subject, Elizabeth decided to say nothing. Lucy Tillman, however, was not going to be shaken off. Sensing that something else had happened to plunge her friend into despair, she was determined to find out what it was.

"Come on," she coaxed. "You can tell me."

"No, Lucy. I can't burden you with my troubles."

"What else are friends for?"

"It's a . . . private matter."

"If it's causing you such unhappiness, I want to hear about it. I may be able to help." Elizabeth turned away. "I may, Elizabeth. At least, give me the opportunity to do so. I'd never forgive myself if I didn't do all I could for you."

"That's very kind of you."

Elizabeth still hesitated. Lucy tried to prompt her.

"I think that this has something to do with Major Featherstone." There was a lengthy pause. "It does, doesn't it? Tell me the truth."

Elizabeth bit her lip. "Yes, it does."

"In what way?"

"I went to see him," she said, forcing the words out. "I knew that Harry—the major—would be giving evidence at the court-martial and I also knew that it would be false. He simply wants to get his revenge and he admitted as much. His uncle is Brigadier General Malloby."

"But he'll be there tomorrow, according to Roderick."

"Yes, Lucy—primed by his nephew. Harry has told him all kinds of dreadful lies about Jamie."

"That's shameful!"

"Harry Featherstone is capable of far worse than that," said Elizabeth. "Well, you know what happened in my tent at Saratoga. He did something equally bad today."

Lucy gasped. "He tried to force himself upon you again?"

"No, he tried to trick his way into my bed this time. He told me that there was only one means by which Jamie would escape execution and that was if Harry spoke up for him at the court-martial. In order to do that, of course," Elizabeth continued, bitterly, "he would need a reward. You can guess what it was."

Lucy was disgusted. "That's abominable!"

"When I refused, he accused me of not loving Jamie enough."

"The man is a monster."

"It was my fault, Lucy. I should never have gone to him."

"But you did, and he revealed himself in his true colors. That may yet be his downfall, Elizabeth." She thought hard, pursing her lips and wrinkling her brow. At length, she gave a nod. "He must not be allowed to get away with this," she insisted. "Write to General Howe. Tell him the truth about Major Harry Featherstone."

"I'm not sure that he'd take any notice."

"He must. Otherwise, Jamie will not get a fair hearing."

"I know."

"Get pen and paper this instant," urged Lucy.

"I'm not certain what to say."

"Tell him the truth." Elizabeth was still reluctant. "It's got to be done. It's your one hope of saving Jamie. Why dither?"

"Because the army does not usually pay much attention to women."

"General Howe does. Look at Mrs. Loring."

"You know what I mean, Lucy."

"Yes, I do," said the other, "but that would not put me off. I promise you this, Elizabeth. If you won't write that letter, then I certainly will."

Pretending to sleep that night, Jamie Skoyles missed nothing of what happened outside his cell. When the two guards were relieved, the man who was on night duty replaced them. All that he had to do was sit on his chair and watch a lone prisoner on his bed. It was felt that only one guard was necessary during nighttime. The problem was that the new man, a young private, soon grew bored with sitting there alone. At one point, he even thought of rousing Skoyles so that he could have some conversation, but the prisoner appeared to be slumbering quietly. The guard therefore sat in the half-dark and waited. After an hour, he was yawning; after two, he was trying to fight off fatigue. It was well past midnight when he finally dozed off.

Once he was certain that the guard was asleep, Skoyles went swiftly into action. He got up silently and, from under his blanket, he brought out the little coil of rope that Tom Caffrey had passed to him during his visit. Using it to make a ligature, he slipped it around his neck. Then he began to make gurgling sounds. The guard was jerked out of his dreams. He looked up to see that the prisoner was trying to hang himself from the bars. His first impulse was to call for help but that would expose the fact that he had fallen asleep long enough for Skoyles to make an attempt at cheating execution by taking his own life.

The guard therefore rushed across the room and clutched at the rope. Skoyles was ready for him. Grabbing him through the bars, he turned him round and slipped the rope deftly around his neck, pulling it tight and applying steady pressure. The guard was trapped. His arms flailed and his legs kicked out but he could not escape or even cry out. When he tried to take hold of the rope and pull it away from his neck, he found that his strength was seeping away from him. Skoyles was careful not to strangle him. He tightened his hold until he had rendered the man unconscious, then he let the body slowly down to the ground. Reaching for the man's key, he unlocked his cell door and came quickly out.

The first thing he did was to drag the guard into the cell and strip him of his coat and hat. Then he used the rope to tie the man's hands behind him. After tearing a strip from his blanket, Skoyles gagged him so that he could not raise the alarm. The coat was rather tight on Skoyles, but he did not mind that. When he put on the hat, he knew that he could pass for the guard in the gloom. Leaving the cell, he locked it and put the key in his pocket. He picked up the prisoner's musket, then took a last look at him. The man was starting to revive. Skoyles gave him a farewell wave and left the room.

He went down a long passageway. To get to the main door, he had to go past another holding cell. Because it contained ten prisoners, two guards were on duty. Skoyles opened the door and went into the room. One of the guards was asleep but the other looked up in surprise.

"Where are you going, Martin?" he asked.

Skoyles pointed to the other guard. When the first man turned to look at his companion, Skoyles used the butt of his musket to knock him senseless. He slumped to the ground with a thud, waking up the other guard as he did so. Before the man could even open his mouth, Skoyles hit him with the butt and sent him sprawling to the floor. Some of the prisoners were still awake. They came to the bars to see what was going on. They could hardly believe their good fortune when Skoyles—another guard in their eyes—found the key that unlocked their cell. He crooked a finger to beckon them out. The rest of the prisoners were woken up, and they poured out of their cell.

Skoyles led the way to the main door and inched it open. A finger to his lips to signal that they remain silent, he opened the door, scanned the yard outside, then let them all go out before him. Once they were clear of the building, he yelled at the top of his voice.

"Help! Prisoners have escaped! Help!"

Guards came running from all directions and started to chase the main body of fugitives. Skoyles, meanwhile, took advantage of the disturbance to cross the yard, unbolt a side door, and slip out. Clear of the prison, he ran off in the direction he had warned others that he would go. Skoyles had managed the most difficult part of the operation. It remained to be seen if his friends were standing by to help. Running fast through the dark streets, he dived into a doorway until a night patrol had marched past. Then he continued on his way.

Still carrying the musket, he made for Front Street. That was the place he had suggested in one of the two letters he had given to Elizabeth to deliver. The other message, addressed to Tom Caffrey, had obviously been handed over because his friend had brought the rope that Skoyles had requested. He could rely totally on Caffrey. The same did not go for the recipient of the second letter. Skoyles had been compelled to take a risk, and when he reached Front Street, he began to fear that the risk had been a mistake. The street was cold and deserted. Though he waited at the designated corner, nobody appeared. A quarter of an hour sped by. His escape would have been discovered by now, and patrols would soon be scouring the streets. Skoyles could not stay there indefinitely.

Eventually, someone did appear, a stooping figure with a large pack on his back. Musket at the ready, Skoyles watched him carefully as he approached. He was about to challenge the man when he felt a pistol thrust against the back of his skull. Skoyles had been hoist with his own petard. Having used other prisoners as his decoy, he was now the victim of a similar ruse. While someone held his attention, an accomplice had crept up behind him. The man who had been shuffling toward him straightened up and broke into a trot. He snatched off Skoyles's hat and looked him full in the face.

"Put the gun away, Pearsall," said Major Clark. "It's him."

Wearing his dress uniform in readiness for the court-martial, General Howe sat behind his desk and perused the letter that had arrived that morning. It had been sent by Elizabeth Rainham and contained an impassioned plea for leniency toward Captain Skoyles. She had included enough details of his military career for Howe to be reminded what an outstanding officer Skoyles had

301

been, but that was not the part of the letter that made the general sit up in consternation. It was the allegation of improper behavior by Major Featherstone that troubled him, coupled as it was with an explanation of the long-standing hatred that the major nursed against Skoyles.

Howe was forced to reconsider. If the allegations were true, and the major really had offered to help the prisoner in return for the Elizabeth's favors, then Featherstone's role in the court-martial was suddenly called into question. So was that of his uncle, Brigadier General Malloby. The major had tried to take cruel advantage of a woman in a vulnerable position. While her charges might turn out to be groundless, they somehow had the ring of truth about them. Howe resolved to confront Featherstone, and if he denied the claims made in the letter, the general would speak to the lady herself. At all events, the court-martial would be delayed until the matter was sorted out.

Hearing a tap on the door, he glanced up from his desk.

"Come in," he said.

Lieutenant Hugh Orde opened the door and entered the room. He looked apprehensive. Howe rose to his feet immediately.

"Your arrival is timely, Lieutenant," he said. "The court-martial will have to be postponed. Pass that information on please."

Orde cleared his throat. "It may have to be postponed indefinitely, sir," he said nervously. "Captain Skoyles escaped during the night."

"Escaped!"

"I fear so."

"But he was under constant guard."

"It seems that he somehow acquired a rope, general. He tricked the guard into thinking that he was trying to commit suicide, then overpowered the man. Captain Skoyles got away in the guard's uniform."

"This is unpardonable!" Howe roared. "Organize a search."

"Patrols have been out all night."

"Use every available man. Skoyles must be caught."

"Yes, General."

"And find Major Featherstone for me."

"He's waiting for the court-martial to begin."

"He may well face one of his own," Howe muttered.

"What was that, sir?"

The general exploded. "Are you still here, Lieutenant?" he yelled. "Do something useful for once, man. Get out and bring the major back with you before I lose my temper."

Orde was gone in a flash.

Harry Featherstone took charge of the men who guarded the road that led out of the city in the direction of Valley Forge. He was still smarting from the harsh rebuke administered by General Howe, and still reeling from the news of the escape of Jamie Skoyles. Those guarding the roads out of the city had insisted that nobody had left Philadelphia. It meant that Skoyles was still there. While search parties combed street after street, Featherstone chose to wait at the most likely exit that the fugitive would take. The major was anxious to be the person to recapture Skoyles. It was the only way he could redeem himself.

When he had been shown Elizabeth's letter, Featherstone had been caught off guard and retreated into bluster. It was clear that Howe had not believed his protestations, and there would be further questioning to face when the general had spoken to Elizabeth herself. Lucy Tillman had been mentioned in the letter as the person in whom Elizabeth had confided the indecent proposal that had been put to her at Featherstone's lodging. General Howe intended to speak to Lucy as well, to listen to her testimony. The major was in deep trouble. Having an uncle on the tribunal was no use to him now.

People had been coming into Philadelphia since dawn to visit the market. Redcoats checked each one of them before allowing them to proceed. But it was those wanting to leave the city who were questioned most closely. They had to show their passes and explain exactly where they were going. Though it was a slow and tedious process, Featherstone believed that it would prevent Skoyles from escaping in disguise. He encouraged his men to be direct and uncompromising.

It was the middle of the morning when the cortege appeared. Drawn by black horses, with their black plumes tossed by the wind, the funeral cart trundled into view with a small group of mourners walking behind it. Featherstone raised a hand to stop the procession.

"Where are you going?" he demanded.

"To the Church of St. Mary," replied the driver of the cart, a tall, cadaverous Quaker. "It's a mile out of the city."

"I thought that you worshipped in meetinghouses."

"This is not a Quaker funeral, sir. St. Mary's is a Protestant church. The deceased was brought up in the village nearby."

"Show me your pass," Featherstone ordered.

"Of course." The man handed it over. "The deceased is an old woman whose last wish was that she should be buried in the churchyard where her own parents lie." The major was taking a long time to study the pass he had been given. "Is everything in order, sir?"

"I hope so, for your sake."

"May we drive on?"

"Yes," said Featherstone. "We'll follow."

Something about the cortege had aroused his suspicion though he could not tell exactly what it was. Thrusting the pass back at the driver, he detached five men from the post. Featherstone rode at the rear of the procession and the redcoats marched behind him. The funeral cart rattled over the road, its iron-rimmed wheels leaving tracks in the light fall of snow. Heads down, lost in their collective grief, the mourners followed at the same unhurried pace.

When they finally reached the little church, Featherstone gave them time to unload the coffin and carry it into the building. He then placed his men in a circle around the churchyard, noting that a fresh grave had been dug. Tethering his horse, he went to the church itself and opened the door a few inches so that he could watch. The service was short but moving, and some of those present wept as they paid their last respects. Featherstone stood back so that the vicar could open the door wide and lead the way to the churchyard.

Clustered around the grave, the mourners listened in silence as the burial service came to its conclusion. The coffin was then lowered into the open grave with the help of ropes. Holding a handkerchief to his face, as if trying to stem tears, the first person to toss some earth onto the coffin was Pearsall Hughes.

Jamie Skoyles, meanwhile, was lying in the vestry in the coffin that had been brought out of the city in the funeral cart. He had no idea of time or place. All that he had been aware of was a bumpy journey to their destination. He had then been lifted and carried somewhere. Unbeknown to him, a second coffin was already waiting inside the church and it was that which had been duly buried. There was a prolonged silence. It was very uncomfortable in the narrow confines of the rough wooden coffin, and he began to worry that they had forgotten he was there. Even though holes had been drilled so that he had enough air to breathe, he was finding it very oppressive.

He tried to divert himself by recalling the elements of his escape. It had only been possible because he had been allowed to write a letter in his own defense to General Howe. Having duly penned it, he also wrote two notes that he concealed inside his shirt before he surrendered the letter, and the writing materials, to the guard. The two messages had been slipped surreptitiously into Elizabeth's hand during her visit. She had duly delivered them and, without realizing it, had aided his escape. Thanks to her, Skoyles had spent the night at the Quaker funeral home where she had delivered the second letter.

It was difficult to hear much through the timber, but he felt every tremor as the coffin was suddenly moved from its hiding place in the vestry and brought into the nave of the church. Chisels began to work away at the coffin lid. A surge of relief washed through Skoyles. Ever since he had been hammered into the coffin, he had felt trapped and helpless. It had been a gruesome experience. Someone was at last coming to rescue him. It was like being pulled out of the grave itself.

The timber splintered and the nails groaned in protest as they were levered out. When one side of the coffin lid had been worked free, several hands took hold of it and pulled hard. It creaked open. Light spilled in for the first time, and Skoyles had to screw up his eyes until he got used to it. Able to see properly, the first person he recognized in the ring of faces peering down at him was Ezekiel Proudfoot.

"You've been reborn, Jamie," said his friend, offering a hand to pull him upright. "You're one of us now,"

"Where am I?" asked Skoyles, sitting up.

"On your way to Valley Forge."

Major Harry Featherstone was too good a soldier to be easily fooled. Though everything about the funeral had appeared to be in order, he had a nagging feeling that something was amiss. For that reason, he only pretended to withdraw with his men, hiding, instead, in some bushes not far from the churchyard. It was the coffin that had triggered his curiosity. He had been led to believe that an old lady had died, yet the coffin was so long and heavy that it had taken six men to carry it. When it later emerged from the church, it seemed to have shrunk in size. Only four bearers were now required.

A long vigil ensued. A portly man, who had been one of the mourners, then came out of the church and looked around to make sure that the soldiers had gone. He ambled around the perimeter of the churchyard. Satisfied that nobody else was about, he waved to the group of people who were hiding in the porch. They came out in a group. Two of them went back to the funeral cart but most went over to the fresh grave.

Featherstone's interest was in the tallest of the men. He wore nondescript clothing and a wide-brimmed hat but there was a familiarity in his gait that alerted the major. He peered through the bushes. The party stood quietly around the mound of earth. When the tall man took off his hat as a mark of respect, Featherstone felt a thrill of excitement.

"Skoyles!" he said.

Jamie Skoyles was deeply grateful to her. Buried beneath six feet of earth was Mary Anne Coveney, an old woman from Philadelphia, who had led a blameless life and whose body had been smuggled out of the city at night so that Skoyles could occupy the funeral cart in her stead. While her burial certificate had allowed him to reach St. Mary's, she had been waiting patiently in the vestry to be exchanged with his coffin. The least that Skoyles could do, he believed, was to offer up a prayer for the salvation of her soul. Within a matter of seconds, however, it was Skoyles's own salvation that was at issue.

"Stay where you are!" Harry Featherstone ordered.

Mounted on his horse, and with his sword in his hand, he came out of the bushes. The five soldiers formed a line behind him with their muskets trained on the group. Skoyles made an instant decision.

"Scatter and run!"

They obeyed at once. Having no weapon, Skoyles seized the spade that had been used to dig and fill the grave, then he, too, took to his heels. Shots rang out, but he knew that none of the soldiers had aimed at him. Featherstone would want to take him alive so that he could enjoy his humiliation at the court-martial and his death at the end of a rope. The fact and nature of

Skoyles's escape from the jail would be further damning evidence against him. Whatever happened, he could not allow himself to be taken. Most of the shots had gone astray, but one had grazed the forearm of Pearsall Hughes. As the bookseller staggered forward, Ezekiel Proudfoot helped him back inside the church and the door was locked behind them. Temporarily, at least, they were safe.

Skoyles was the main target. His recapture was paramount. Directing three of his men to round up the others, Featherstone sent the remaining two after Skoyles while he himself rode in a circle around the church to cut off any escape in that direction. The one thing in the fugitive's favor was that the two soldiers had not had time to reload. Their orders were to overhaul him. If he resisted, bayonets would be used to disable him. Skoyles was in a quandary. Determined to get away, he did not wish to kill a British soldier in order to do so. That made his predicament even worse.

Major John Clark had no scruples about killing redcoats. He used a pistol to shoot one of the pursuing soldiers dead, then reloaded his weapon behind the cover of a gravestone. Skoyles now had only one man at his heels. Stopping abruptly to face him, he used the spade to parry a bayonet thrust, then hit the man hard across the side of the head with the flat of the implement. The soldier went down in an undignified heap with blood streaming down his face. Seizing his musket, Skoyles also took his powder and ammunition. Before he could reload, however, he had another problem with which to contend.

Seeing what had happened to his two fellows, one of the other soldiers was so enraged that he turned his attention to Skoyles. He ran straight at him, musket fully extended, so that he could stab him with his bayonet. Skoyles was governed by instinct. During his years as a sergeant, he had conducted endless sessions of bayonet practice, and he did what he had always taught his soldiers to do. Deflecting the thrust with his own bayonet, he brought the butt of his musket sharply upward to hit the oncoming man on the chin. The moment he touched the ground, the soldier was expertly stabbed through the heart.

When he pulled out his bayonet, Skoyles was momentarily shocked. He had just thrust naked steel through a uniform that he had always revered. There was no turning back now. He had killed a British soldier. A pistol shot rang out, and he swung round to see another redcoat falling to the ground. Major Clark had claimed a second victim. The major had no time to reload.

307

The remaining soldier came running in his direction, determined to impale him on his bayonet. Clark turned and fled. Skoyles finished loading his musket. When he looked up, he saw that Clark had tripped and fallen to the ground. As the soldier bore down on his intended target, Skoyles took aim and fired, hitting the man in the middle of the back. The redcoat stiffened, stumbled forward, then lunged drunkenly with his weapon. Clark had the presence of mind to roll out of the way and the bayonet sank deep into the earth.

The casualties were not all on one side. Harry Featherstone had hacked one man to death with his sword and wounded another in the thigh. Seeing that he had been deprived of his men, he rode up to a woman who was cowering beneath a tree and pointed a pistol at her head She screamed in terror. Clark and Skoyles looked up.

"Throw down your weapons," Featherstone ordered, "or I blow out her brains." They hesitated. "Hurry up! Do as I say!"

"It's Miranda Hughes," said Clark.

"I won't ask again," Featherstone warned.

Skoyles felt desperately sorry for the woman. In trying to help him, she had put her own life in danger. There was one sure way to rescue her. Featherstone would not waste a shot on a woman if he thought that his quarry was escaping. Skoyles spun on his heel. Musket in hand, he sprinted across the churchyard and off into the bushes beyond, keeping low and zigzagging to make pursuit more difficult. Harry Featherstone was seething. Forgetting all about his hostage, he rode off in pursuit between the gravestones, fired with determination to capture or kill Skoyles.

Footprints in the snow guided him to the place where Skoyles had dived into the bushes. Beyond that point, Featherstone had to be more circumspect. There were no more footprints to follow and no sign of anyone running headlong through the undergrowth. Skoyles had gone to ground somewhere. He was armed and he was waiting. Featherstone was not deterred. He had all the advantages. In his hand was a loaded pistol, and from his position in the saddle, he could look over most of the bushes. He nudged his horse slowly forward with his knees.

"The game is up, Skoyles," he called. "Come on out."

Skoyles did not reply. That would only have given away his position. Kneeling behind a bush, he was reloading his musket with the speed and precision he had built up over the years. Featherstone was a dangerous adversary. Skoyles could take no chances. Crouching low, he listened for the sound of the horse, pushing a way through the bushes. One shot was all that it would take, but that would be a merciful end for his hated enemy. Featherstone deserved a slower death. As he waited, a stream of painful memories flashed through Skoyles's mind. Major Harry Featherstone had once paid men to beat him up. During one of the battles at Saratoga, he had tried to kill Skoyles even though the latter had actually saved his life in an earlier encounter.

But it was Featherstone's treatment of Elizabeth that really ignited Skoyles. It was unforgivable. Spurned by her in Saratoga, the man who had once been engaged to her had tried to rape her with brutal force. Only the timely arrival of Skoyles had rescued her. Since he had met up with them again in Philadelphia, Featherstone had sought his revenge. He was instrumental in getting Skoyles arrested and, with Elizabeth at her most vulnerable, he had tried to lure her into bed. Skoyles's temples began to pulse with indignation. He was ready.

"Where are you?" demanded Featherstone, looking around in vain. "Damn you, man! Have the courage to show yourself."

Skoyles took him at his word. Leaping from his hiding pace only two yards ahead of him, he aimed the musket at the horse's head then deliberately fired above it. He achieved the desired result. The horse reared so high and so suddenly that Featherstone was thrown backward from the saddle. As he hit the ground, the pistol went off and the second shot caused the horse to bolt through the bushes. Slightly dazed by the fall, Featherstone took time to collect himself. Skoyles could easily have jumped forward and thrust his bayonet into the man, but he wanted the fight on more equal terms. He therefore waited until his enemy had got up, shaken himself, and drawn his sword. Featherstone showed no gratitude for the quarter he had been given.

"You're a fool, Skoyles," he said as he advanced. "Always strike a man when he's down. That's what I'd have done."

"Yes," said Skoyles with contempt, "and you'd do the same with a woman. You'd seek to take advantage of her weakness, as you did with Elizabeth. That's despicable."

"All's fair in love and war."

Without warning, Featherstone tried a first thrust with his sword but Skoyles parried it with ease. Featherstone circled him before making another attack. This time, he flicked his wrist from one side to the other so that Skoyles had to dodge or parry a series of vicious slashes. As he backed away, Skoyles came up against the trunk of a tree. Featherstone saw his opportunity. After putting Skoyles on the defensive with another fierce attack, he tried to skewer him to the tree with a powerful thrust. Skoyles eluded it just in time, and the point of the sword went into the wood. Before Featherstone could pull it out again, Skoyles smashed the butt of his rifle down hard on the blade and knocked the weapon from his enemy's grasp.

"What are you going to do now?" Featherstone taunted him, backing away. "You don't have the nerve to finish me off, do you? Captain Skoyles would never kill an unarmed man from his own regiment."

"Watch me," said Skoyles.

Tossing the musket away, he flung himself at Featherstone and they grappled hard for a while before trading punches. Skoyles was lighter on his feet and able to evade some of the blows, but he was conscious of the fact that he was still carrying a wound in his shoulder. Within seconds, it had reopened and started to bleed. Skoyles needed to bring the fight to an end. The longer it went on, the more the advantage would swing in favor of Featherstone. The other man seemed to realize that. Though blood was gushing from his nose, Featherstone gave a wolfish grin and closed with him again, grabbing him by the arms and trying to throw him to the ground.

Skoyles could see what his adversary was doing. As they swayed to and fro, Featherstone was keeping one eye on his discarded sword, waiting for the chance to retrieve it. There would be no thought of mercy then. Skoyles would be cut to shreds. To avoid that fate, he did his best to stay between Featherstone and his weapon, but it was not easy. The pain in his shoulder was intense and his strength was fading. With a supreme effort, Featherstone hurled him to the ground and ran back to the tree to pick up his sword. Skoyles rolled over several times and grabbed his musket but he was too late to defend himself. Featherstone's weapon was already raised for execution.

Then a shot was fired nearby. It made Featherstone pause and look up for one, fleeting, lifesaving second. It was all the time that Skoyles needed. With a decisive upward thrust, he pierced the other man's heart with the bayonet and held it there, watching the expression on Featherstone's face change from triumph to horror and then to a glassy-eyed despair. His victim shuddered uncontrollably. It was all over. Dropping his sword, Harry Featherstone collapsed sideways to the ground in a pool of blood. Skoyles withdrew his bayonet and tossed his musket aside.

As Skoyles struggled to his feet, Major Clark came through the bushes with Ezekiel Proudfoot behind him. They looked at the disheveled victor and saw the blood staining his shirt.

"Are you hurt, Jamie?" asked Proudfoot with concern.

"Not anymore."

"What happened?"

Skoyles looked down at the body. "We settled an old argument."

"He was the last of them," said Clark.

"Who fired that shot?"

"I did. I killed the man you knocked out with that spade."

"You also killed Major Featherstone," said Skoyles. "But for that shot, I might not still be alive." He put a hand to his wounded shoulder. "What happens now?"

"We get out of here fast."

"The horses are waiting," said Proudfoot.

"What about the dead bodies?" said Skoyles.

Clark was practical. "No better place to hide those than in a churchyard," he said. "We can't leave them aboveground as evidence."

"This one does not deserve a Christian burial."

"He'll have to go into the grave with the others. After we've taken off his boots, that is."

"His boots?"

"Yes, Jamie," Proudfoot explained. "Boots are much needed in Valley Forge. We've six pairs to take with us."

"As well as all the weapons we've just acquired," said Clark. He shrugged an apology. "I'm sorry that this had to happen. We hoped to give you a quiet funeral."

Skoyles gazed down at Harry Featherstone. "I would not have had it any other way," he said. "This man was my nemesis. Not anymore."

He continued to stare at the corpse as the full implications of what he had done slowly dawned on him. In killing Featherstone, he had exacted revenge for past crimes and liberated Elizabeth from the man's unwanted attentions. But he had done much more than that. Skoyles had, in effect, changed one life for another. He had severed his links with a British army that he had served devotedly since he was a callow youth. What lay ahead for him, he did not know but he was keenly aware of the friendships and camaraderie and the unquestioning loyalty to the Crown that now lay behind him. Standing over the dead body of Major Harry Featherstone, he was renouncing his birthright and becoming an American. The impact on him was profound.

"We must go," said Clark, crisply. "I've organized a burial detail to take care of things here."

"Did you hear that, Jamie?" asked Proudfoot, touching his arm to bring him out of his reverie. "Are you ready to come to Valley Forge?"

"Yes," replied Skoyles with conviction. "I am."